To Shona,
I'm so glad
on Facebook. I
person with a g
Hope you enjoy
and thanks for being my best
customer!
Best Wishes,
Rachael Allen
xx

Velvet Hellion

Velvet Hellion

by
Rachael Allen

First published in 2014 in Great Britain by
i.Line Design - www.ilinedesign.com

This edition was published October 1st 2014.

Cover Designed by Mark Barnes.

ISBN: 978-0-9929336-2-3

www.velvethellion.com

iLine

For my late mother, father and brother David: Mom, I finally made it. May God hold you in His loving arms.

For all those who suffer with Fibromyalgia and Myalgic Encephalomyelitis, you are in my heart and prayers. One day there will be a cure for us.

For my husband, who never complains, but I think he personally believes I'm the real Hellion... I love you, darling!!

CHAPTER ONE

Nicole screamed.

Blood was everywhere... splattered across the sofa and coffee table, speckling the wall, dark crimson stains eating through her rug... Nicole caught her breath in huge gulps and convulsively swallowed. It took a moment for her mind to recall it was only a memory; yet, the realism of the nightmare still made her shudder. Glancing at the bales of straw beneath her, she winced. "Hope Cristoff didn't hear me scream," she said, aloud. "He'll be disappointed I'm not over the tragedy." The truth was, she would never be over it—not until the murderer was found.

The horror of that fateful day, one year ago, still terrified Nicole. She had just returned from visiting her parents in Maryland, when an ominous feeling swept over her. Confiding in her ranch hand, Cristoff, she expressed her concern; but he merely shrugged, then parked his car and pulled out her luggage. As the two of them neared Nicole's house, her apprehension increased until she felt compelled to run up the few steps and quickly throw open the front door. There, just a few feet inside, laid her husband's dead body in a crumpled heap.

Through two years of marital abuse she had suffered, and not once had she wished Philip dead. Maybe it was because she had seen the softer side of him, the generous heart and whispered fears. He confused the hell out of her. But she'd never have hurt him. Yet, she had become the prime suspect. Nicole still remembered the countless hours of questioning after the murder, despite the fact that there was ample proof she had been in Maryland with her parents. The sheriff went so far as to imply she had hired an assassin to do the job for her. To this day, there were still some townspeople who glared at her, accusingly.

"Nicole!" shouted a male voice, breaking the silence of her thoughts. As the sound of running footsteps neared, the young woman slowly got to her feet and picked out several pieces of straw from her long, dark hair.

"I'm in here," she yawned, still making no move towards the stall door. Cristoff skidded to a halt in the aisleway of the barn and sighed with relief.

"You scared me to death!" he scolded. "I heard you scream. Are you okay?" But he already knew the answer to that question. It was obvious Nicole had fallen asleep amidst the extra bales of straw in the empty stall and had experienced another one of her nightmares. The raven-haired beauty casually nodded as if nothing out of the ordinary had happened, but she hadn't fooled Cristoff. Sliding open the wooden door, he quickly stepped inside. One calloused hand gently lifted her chin until she was forced to meet his gaze. "It was bad, wasn't it?" he whispered. "Why don't you take the advice I gave you the other day?" She heard the concern in his tone, yet shook her head, saying, "I'll never go to a psychiatrist. I've told you that before, Cristoff. It's a dead issue."

"But, Nicole, not all doctors are like the ones you met in that mental ward."

"I don't care," she retorted in anger. "When Philip put me in the nuthouse, I thought there was no chance the psychiatrists would believe his word over mine. It was all so absurd."

"He probably paid them off," Cristoff added. "At least you were only there for two weeks."

Nicole's tone turned bitter. "It felt like two years! I'll never forget it, nor will I ever trust a psychiatrist again. Besides," her dark brown eyes captured his, "I don't need a doctor. I have you to help me through this."

Her rose-colored lips curved into a warm, friendly smile; and in that moment, Cristoff knew he had to find an excuse to leave—if not, his brotherly affection for Nicole would surely be tested. With a lingering look, he quickly muttered, "I'd better get back to mucking stalls." Then he grabbed a pitchfork and resumed his task, trying to occupy his mind with other thoughts. This proved useless, however, mainly because his boss was not like any ordinary female.

He had never met a woman like Nicole. Sure, she was ultra-conservative in her values, but she also exhibited a fierce loyalty which hinted at an inner passion so intense, it had to be forcibly suppressed. This was clearly evident in her loyalty to Philip during the early days of her marriage. No matter how often Philip's brother had accused him of shady dealings, Nicole always jumped to his defense, even threatening her brother-in-law. She suddenly transformed into a furious feline, the panther variety, as she mentally sharpened her claws. Cristoff could almost visualize her tearing flesh from bone. A woman with this much passion, remaining loyal to a man who ended up mistreating her, was beyond his comprehension.

"Something on your mind?" called Nicole, breaking his concentration. He hadn't seen her sneak up on him.

"Nothing important," Cristoff answered, then increased his shoveling speed until manure was flying half out of the wheelbarrow, half into the wheelbarrow.

Nicole grinned. "Must be girl trouble."

"Don't you have work to do?" He scowled.

"Maybe." She was in a teasing mood now and needed someone to be her victim. But one look at the serious expression on Cristoff's face changed everything. Something was bothering him—something secretive. She eyed him suspiciously, then gradually lost her train of thought as she caught sight of his powerful biceps flexing with each lift of the pitchfork. He really was quite nice looking, she admitted, with his tawny-colored hair and hazel eyes. Even though he was four years older than her, he never acted superior. Together, he and Nicole had kept the small Arabian ranch operating after Philip's death.

But it hadn't been easy. For a long time, Nicole had kept herself quite distant from Cristoff, never offering more than a few words of conversation, and only speaking when it was absolutely necessary. There were plenty of awkward moments, too, when Cristoff would glance in her direction, only to find she had chosen that exact same moment to look over at him. They would pretend not to notice each other, yet somehow it only heightened their awareness.

It had taken some time before Nicole realized she was unconsciously punishing Cristoff for having been Philip's friend. It never occurred to her that he might not have agreed with everything Philip had done, until Cristoff finally told her, several months after her husband's death. Cristoff had been quite drunk that day, thus easily rambled on about it all. She was even more surprised when she learned Cristoff had had many bitter arguments in regards to the matter. It touched her to think someone had come to her defense, even if it was to no avail.

Since that time, she and Cristoff had become quite fond of each other. He recognized her fear of men and kept their relationship purely platonic. She overlooked his habitual drinking, kept him on the payroll, and allowed him to remain in the tenant house on her property. The house was only a stone's throw from her own, providing her with a sense of security. Plus, she could go to him whenever she needed someone to confide in. He never tired of listening to her, no matter what the problem.

"Did I ever tell you how much I appreciate all you do for me?" Nicole suddenly asked as she went towards the handsome

25 year-old.

"No. How much?" he teased, tossing a fork load of manure and wet straw high into the air.

"This much," came the quick reply. Before he realized it, Nicole had planted a soft kiss on his cheek, turned, then dashed out of the barn. Cristoff stared at the fleeing figure, bewildered and slightly amused. If it was one thing he had learned over the year, it was that Nicole was quite unpredictable. Today, it had been to his advantage.

Meanwhile, Nicole scooted up the front steps to her house and found the nearest mirror so she could pick out the remaining straw from her hair. Then she returned to the barn, exercised a few horses, cleaned some stalls, ate lunch, and viewed the ranch's finance books in the barn office. She was still engrossed in her work, when a light tapping sound drew her attention towards the door. "Come in," she called, assuming it was Cristoff. A tall, well-dressed man stepped inside, his cheerful voice filling the room.

"Hello, Nicole."

"Hi, Daniel," she replied, admiring his nice clothes. "What brings you here, today? I haven't violated any federal laws, have I?"

Having no quick retort, Philip's brother simply smiled. Ever since Nicole found out he worked for the federal government, she took great pleasure in teasing him, probably because she could never find out exactly what he did for a living. He had only told her it was Top Secret. Glancing at the book on her desk, he remarked, "Just a social call, my dear. How are the profits?"

"Holding," she answered, watching the 26 year-old slide onto a nearby chair, lean backwards, and casually lace his fingers together behind his neck. A lock of dark brown hair fell across his forehead, which he ignored.

"This is the second time you've stopped by this week," Nicole remarked with a suspicious smile. "Has your job become that boring?" Daniel forced a small chuckle, his brown eyes penetrating her own. Unlacing his fingers, he suddenly leaned forward and rested his chin on his hand.

"You certainly are inquisitive, aren't you?" he grinned. "I merely came by to remind you of your financial resources."

Nicole's expression soured. "I've told you before, Daniel, I don't want your money. I'm doing just fine on my own."

"Oh?" he differed. "I bet I could count on my fingers how many mares were bred this past year. It isn't enough, Nicole—not to keep this ranch in business."

"You've been talking to Cristoff again!" she stormed, jumping up from her seat. "It's none of your concern, Daniel. I won't have you checking up on me, do you understand?"

"Hold on a minute!" he exclaimed, standing now to confront the angry woman before him. "I care about you, Nicole. I want to see this ranch prosper just as much as you do, that's why I want to help. I've never felt right about keeping all that money Philip left me. It should have gone to you. Only a madman would have willed all his wealth to his brother instead of his wife! It was bad enough he gave me the mansion..." Daniel's voice trailed off hopelessly as he threw his hands up in the air. The distraught look he gave Nicole assured her of his sincerity.

"Daniel," she began in a lowered voice, "the ranch was all I ever needed. I was thankful Philip left it to me. And you," she placed her hand on his arm, "you were kind enough to offer financial assistance. But remember, I still have plenty of money in my bank account to hold me over until the ranch becomes more profitable. If I get in a bind, you're the first one I'll run to. I promise."

He gazed at the young woman for what seemed like an eternity, before turning away. Walking towards the door, he had a change of mind and pivoted back around.

"I still feel responsible for you," he said softly. "After all, it was my fault Philip married you. If I hadn't dared him to do it—"

"Yes, yes, things would be different," she interjected, the pain of knowing it had all been on a dare, stabbed at her. "And if I hadn't been so naive, I would have seen the warning signs. I actually thought he loved me."

"Oh, Nicole," Daniel soothed, "he did love you. Why else would he have stayed married for two years?"

At that, the dark-haired beauty burst out laughing. "You don't know? You really don't know? Come, come, Daniel. I thought you were so close to your brother. Surely you understood the way his evil mind operated? Philip simply couldn't stand the thought of another man having what was once his. He'd lend me out, oh, yes—like a minnow tossed before sharks, something to tease and wet their appetites. Then he'd carefully reel me back in, knowing his little game had provided enough excitement to guarantee his friends' return!" She clenched her fists with frustration. "But he'd never legally divorce me. Once I was his pitiful victim, I was always his victim, his possession." She walked to the window and gazed out over the landscape, mentally distancing herself from her brother-in-law. "And I'm still his victim... in some ways..." she softly murmured, unable to stop the tears from building.

Daniel drew near, a protective arm encircling her waist. "Nonsense, Nicole. You're nobody's victim—least of all, Philip's. He's dead now. He has no hold over you."

"If he has no hold over me," she slowly replied with a slight pause, "... then why am I still tortured by what you told me about those... disgusting parties?" Contempt filled her eyes as she glared at Daniel, daring him to answer; and as he struggled for what to say, she suddenly yanked his arm from around her waist, as if somehow it had tainted her.

"Nicole," he pleaded, startled by her action. Before she could respond, he took hold of her elbow, swinging her around to face him. To her surprise, there were angry creases in his brow, and his cheeks were tinged red. He seemed to be experiencing some difficulty controlling his emotions, so the next few words came out rather harsher than he had intended. "Don't assume I was in favor of those parties just because I was in attendance."

"And just for the record," a muscle along his jaw twitched, "I never laid a hand on you. I swear it."

She studied him for an agonizing minute or two before replying in an icy tone, "I wouldn't know if you did, Daniel, now would I?"

She let the words sink in, their meaning all too clear. Daniel's gaze fell to the floor as he gently released her from his grip. In the back of his mind he could hear Philip's sinister laugh, even picture the devilish gleam in his eyes as Philip joked about Nicole's lack of memory after the wild parties. It had all been so cleverly planned—the pills, the alcohol—and each had to be carefully administered to attain the desired effect, that delicate balance which made Nicole not only completely submissive, but also a happy exhibitionist. Philip was lucky she always had an after dinner drink. Daniel recalled how Philip laughed when he told him Nicole had gone to the doctor's, wondering why she had lapses of memory, and the doctor said it was probably due to fatigue and stress. Daniel wanted to slug Philip right then and there, knowing he had taken things too far. But he was wrestling with his own tortured thoughts and regret.

"Nicole, don't forget," Daniel reminded, "it was Cristoff and myself who told you what really went on at those gatherings. You would have never known, otherwise. Doesn't that prove we care about you?"

"Perhaps. Or perhaps it proves you have a guilty conscience?" Nicole retreated a safe distance behind her desk before confronting him further. "Why did you attend those parties, Daniel? After all, Cristoff didn't. He had the guts to refuse Philip."

She had that accusing look in her eyes again, causing the young man to shift nervously from one foot to the other. He wasn't sure if she was able to accept the real reason, but felt he owed her some kind of an answer. "Okay," he relented. "I'll tell you." He hesitated. "I attended the first party, expecting to find a normal poker game in progress. The game was normal, all right, but it was apparent you definitely were not." He raked his fingers through his thick, brown hair before continuing. "I knew that Philip's pals were rowdy drunks who didn't take kindly to his repeated winnings, but I was stunned to hear Philip offering you as a consolation prize to the losers. When I informed Cristoff, he suggested I continue attending the gatherings in order to keep tabs on the shenanigans, so to speak. We were concerned that violence might erupt and you would get hurt. If I was in attendance, I could get you out of there." He deliberately neglected to mention another reason he had remained at the parties. He hoped she'd be satisfied with this explanation, alone.

He was right. Her expression softened. Her voice became a quiet whisper as she asked, "Couldn't you have stopped him, Daniel?"

"I tried. I truly tried, my dear. I reasoned with him, I begged him. I even bribed him, to no avail. However, I had to remain on good terms with my brother so I could still attend the parties. I left the bitter arguments to Cristoff. You know, Philip almost fired him?"

"Yes, he told me," she replied before bowing her head. "I'm sorry for asking so many questions, Daniel. But you and I never really talked much—about Philip, I mean. I had to know where you stood."

"It's quite all right," he smiled. "If you want to make me feel better, why don't you accept a check to help with the bills?" Nicole stubbornly shook her head, just as Cristoff entered the office.

"Sorry to interrupt, Nicole," Cristoff began. "Oh, hello, Dan." He nodded in his direction. "I have to go into town for some errands and thought I'd see if you needed anything."

"No," Nicole replied, "but I was wondering if you could ask the postmaster about our new neighbors on the adjoining property. Since I take my walks along the beach in that area, I don't want to be surprised by some stranger sneaking up behind me."

Cristoff gave her a stern look. "You shouldn't be walking alone, Nicole. I've warned you about that. This is the 1970's, you know?"

"I couldn't agree more," chimed in Daniel. "You have

woods nearby, too. Any lunatic could be hiding there, watching and waiting."

Nicole rolled her eyes. "Oh, please. I'm not going to sacrifice my private strolls along the waterfront just because you two have vivid imaginations. I simply would like to know how many people moved in across the way, and whether they are male or female. They've been there a full month, already. Yet, I haven't seen hide nor hair of them."

Cristoff scratched his head. "Then how do you know they've been there a month?"

"They have a beautiful palomino corralled outside," she grinned.

"Perhaps we should be good neighbors and make a surprise visit to welcome them to the community," Cristoff offered, knowing full well Nicole was too shy to knock on a stranger's door.

She quickly changed the subject. "It was nice of you to stop by, Daniel. If you'll excuse me, I think I'll head inside the house to do some laundry."

Leaving the two men to chat by themselves, the young woman exited the stable and walked across the plush lawn to the first fenced pasture. A shrill whinny pierced the air as a gorgeous white stallion bounded towards her. "General!" called Nicole, laughing like a pleased little girl. "Come here, you rascal."

The General was her favorite, and he knew it. Tail held high like a flag blowing in the breeze, the glamorous Arabian strutted and pranced before his owner, his head bowed to display the brilliant arch of his muscular neck. Nicole swore there wasn't a horse on earth like him, and the fact that he was wild and spirited made him a handful for even an experienced rider. But she liked him that way. There was a bond between the two of them since the day Philip gave him to her. The stallion had been an unexpected present, one of the best things to come out of her marriage. Nicole had spent many a night in The General's stall, when Philip and she had argued. Sometimes it was the only place she could feel at peace. Even

Philip noticed the change in his wife when she was with her equine companion. She was more relaxed and happy. Realizing such, he decided to never use the horse as the object of a threat. No matter how angry he became with Nicole, he controlled his impulse to sell the animal. The General was actually Philip's saving grace. As long as he kept the horse at the ranch, Nicole was reluctant to leave him. If she ever entertained the notion of taking the horse with her, it was quickly dismissed at the thought of how difficult it would be to hide such a stallion. After all, even an untrained eye could see that this was no ordinary piece of horseflesh.

Nicole gave her pet a sugar cube and rubbed the itchy spots on his coat before finally departing for her house. Once inside, the stereo was turned on while she sorted the laundry, and Nicole soon found herself singing along with her favorite tunes. She had just finished putting the clothes in the washer when a hauntingly familiar song reached her ears. It piqued her curiosity. Venturing into the living room, she poured herself a glass of brandy, slowly sipping the sweet liquid while her mind searched for the missing link. What was so special about this song?

She sat on the sofa, listening carefully to each word. It was common enough. Nothing in particular made it stand out from any other melody. What, then, caused it to trigger such an odd feeling? She gulped down the remaining brandy and poured another one. This drink, too, disappeared quickly. Too late, Nicole realized she had consumed the alcohol on an empty stomach. A wave of dizziness swept over her when she rose from the sofa, forcing her to swiftly descend back to her original position. "I never could drink much," she muttered with annoyance. Leaning back against the fabric, she closed her eyes and waited for her stomach to settle.

The song was nearly over, now, the familiar words still haunting her. She was about to drift off to sleep when a mental picture suddenly flashed in her mind. It came and went so quickly, she didn't even have time to discern its meaning. Her body jerked in response when another vivid display soon followed. This one, too, vanished before she could comprehend its contents. Then, without warning, she was bombarded with a whole barrage of pictures flashing in rapid succession before her eyes—pictures of hands, clothing, sheets, objects in her bedroom…

The assault on her senses was disturbing, yet fascinating. Her interest ended, however, when the hallucination struck a nerve deep inside. What had started as unusual entertainment had now transformed into something ugly. The pieces of the puzzle were beginning to fit together and, little by little, Nicole realized she was seeing things she would rather forget. With horror, she acknowledged the hands as belonging to Daniel. The eyes, too, were Daniel's. Detailed pictures of Daniel with her in bed filled Nicole's mind. The song… The song on the stereo was the same one playing back then in her bedroom. Perspiration beaded her brow as the young woman desperately tried to stop the torrent of mental flashbacks assaulting her brain. But it took several minutes before they finally departed.

Nicole threw her head back against the sofa and gasped. Her heart was racing, hammering against her ribs so hard she thought it would eventually burst through. She lifted one shaky hand to wipe the sweat from her forehead, then suddenly felt the full impact of what had just happened.

Daniel. Everything he had said had been a lie—a rotten, filthy lie! He had taken advantage of her at those parties. The realization of this fact, alone, caused her to redden with rage and humiliation. What a fool she had been to believe him. "You pig!" she screamed, hurling her empty glass across the room. The sound of tinkling crystal smacking the wall had no effect on the inner turmoil building inside. She succumbed to the overwhelming urge to destroy everything in sight, venting her anger with loud wails of anguish as she yanked every book from her bookcase and threw it to the floor. Tables were knocked over, cushions pitched through the air, as the mental wound was re-opened anew. It didn't take long to create a mess in the room, yet Nicole found no satisfaction in the brief tantrum and finally collapsed in a corner, sobbing wretchedly.

It was there that Cristoff found her. When he had returned from town he had phoned her several times, without any result, and eventually walked over to the house. Nicole heard him knocking, but refused to answer, thus prompting Cristoff to try the door. It was unlocked. The sight he beheld upon entering was alarming enough, but to see Nicole huddled in the corner, crying her eyes out, made him want to kill the perpetrator. "Tell me everything," he quietly commanded, stroking the long, dark hair. At the touch of his hands, Nicole shuddered, unable to mask the sudden repulsion she felt. Cristoff took notice at once and drew back, then patiently waited for her to explain. He felt relieved when he discovered Nicole had been the one who destroyed the place, not some intruder. Yet, as she described the events leading up to her temper tantrum, Cristoff grew apprehensive.

"You're sure the vision was of Daniel?" he quizzed.

"Yes. Of course, I'm sure! I saw him, clear as day."

"Well, the nightmare is over with for now."

Nicole blinked with surprise. "Nightmare? You think this was just a nightmare?"

"Of course it was, Nicole. You had one earlier this morning, remember?"

Nicole jumped to her feet, wiped her eyes with a tissue, then stated, "This was no nightmare, Cristoff. This was real."

"What makes you think so?" he challenged. "You even said you drifted off to sleep."

"Not completely. What I mean is… it was different. I was partially awake. And the song... the song created a feeling of déjà vu. I think the song triggered the memory. Is that possible?" The frustration in her tone matched his own. Cristoff was beginning to believe her.

"Let's say it is possible," he agreed, "but highly unlikely. I wouldn't go throwing stones just yet."

"Well, don't expect me to allow Daniel admittance onto this property, again. I can't trust him. Surely you understand that?"

Cristoff emitted a long, drawn out sigh. Everything boiled

down to whether Nicole had been dreaming or if it truly was a flashback. He had seen her have flashbacks before, when the two of them drank a bit too much alcohol. But after she hallucinated, Nicole never remembered doing so. In fact, she denied it. Although Cristoff repeated every word she uttered during those episodes, he still could not convince her.

Today, however, was different. Nicole actually remembered a vision. It seemed logical to assume that if she remembered it, it had to be a nightmare, not a flashback—and nightmares were often twisted works of the subconscious mind.

"Cristoff? Aren't you listening? What are we going to do about Daniel?"

A frown creasing his brow, the ranch hand took a firm stand. "We aren't going to do anything," he said.

"What?" piped Nicole. "Are you crazy? Daniel lied to both of us. Maybe he has a hidden motive for visiting us so frequently. Maybe—"

"That's pure conjecture, and you know it," came the quick reply.

Nicole stared blankly at her friend. Something was wrong here. She had never seen Cristoff so serious, so worried, so... Her jaw dropped open in amazement. "You're afraid," she blurted.

"Am not," he snorted, beginning to straighten up the room so she wouldn't see his expression. Nicole followed his actions with her eyes, studying the man she had come to know so well.

"Cristoff Colvert," she announced in a very authoritative tone, "you are afraid of Daniel, and I want to know why?"

Cristoff didn't answer. Nicole changed her tactics. She went to the liquor cabinet, poured some scotch in a glass, and handed it to him. "Ah," he grinned. "Truth serum, eh?" Nicole's soft lips formed a simpering smile. Cristoff downed the drink, then took her by the shoulders. This time, there was no resistance. He looked deep into her eyes as he mentally prepared the words he needed to say. "You must trust me, Nicole. I know that's asking a lot, but what I am going to tell you is for your own good." He paused a moment, then warned,

“Do not anger Daniel. No matter how justified you think you are, do not confront him with these premature accusations.” She started to object but he silenced her by placing his finger against her lips. “Hear me out. I’m well aware of what I’m saying. You’re very emotional right now and not thinking too clearly. Daniel knows every last detail about you.”

It finally dawned on her what he was hinting at. “You think he’ll ruin my reputation,” she guessed.

“Or worse,” he revealed. “He could also put this breeding farm out of business.”

Nicole was skeptical. “How, Cristoff?”

“This is where trusting me plays a role, my girl. Daniel is a dangerous man. I’ve known it for quite some time. He has friends in very high places. The only reason I’ve remained sociable with him is because I definitely don’t want him as a foe. Besides, he’s always looked out for you. No, don’t laugh. You know it’s true. He defended you when the sheriff thought you murdered Philip.”

“Well,” she conceded, “he did take my side.”

“And he’s constantly asking me how you are,” Cristoff pointed out. “Really, if you think about it, if Daniel took advantage of you in the past, why hasn’t he attempted to do so, now—or, at least ask you out on a date? He hasn’t, has he?”

“No. He’s been a gentleman.” Nicole was beginning to feel confused. “Then, why did I have that awful vision?”

“I’m not saying it wasn’t real. But, perhaps it was a little distorted. For instance, maybe the event was real, but you substituted Daniel’s features in place of someone else’s. After all, you did just meet with Daniel prior to going inside the house.”

“Yes, you’re probably right,” Nicole agreed, wishing she hadn’t been so quick to judge her brother-in-law. With a sigh, she glanced around the room at the disarray. “I’d better start cleaning up.”

“Here. Let me help,” offered Cristoff as he picked up two sofa cushions.

“Oh, no. That’s not necessary. It’s all my fault, anyway. I’ll take care of it. You go on home and get some dinner. Thank you, Cristoff, for everything."

He smiled in response, walked to the door, then stopped. "Oh, I almost forgot," he said. "I asked the postmaster about our new neighbors. He wouldn't give out the name, but he said a blond-haired fellow moved in, a real nice guy, he said. He's spoken to him several times."

"Don't trust first impressions," came the quick reply. Cristoff merely shook his head, unable to comprehend her suspicious nature.

CHAPTER TWO

Justin MacFierson could not erase the woman from his mind. It was her eyes that plagued him—so mysterious, so disturbingly bright, with the promise of a hundred secrets hidden in their depths. Sometimes those eyes danced and flickered with amusement; her mouth would then follow their lead with a smirk. Other times, they became dangerously magnetic, a fixed gaze of icy fire. Justin shuddered at the memory. Ah, yes... her eyes... an eternal brown abyss of emotion... dark chocolate icing. Bewitching indeed, they emitted a power all their own, a life force so strong that even the animals responded to it.

He would not have believed this, had he not seen it for himself one Saturday afternoon. He had been casually strolling through the woods when he caught sight of her, quite by accident. The raven-haired woman was completely engrossed in her artwork, busily sketching away on her drawing pad. To his amazement, squirrels and rabbits were scurrying about her feet, devoid of all fear. He watched, in awe, as the enchanting female paused to give one of the bunnies an affectionate pat on the head. Such a sight was rare, and it prompted Justin to advance several more steps for a better view.

Instantly, he regretted it. A blue jay squawked its warning, sending a large number of birds into flight which had previously been singing contentedly, perched on the branches overhead. The noise alerted Nicole of the intrusion. She promptly closed her sketch pad and swiftly departed, leaving Justin darting amidst the trees and shrubbery in search of her. Like a deer, she had blended into the scenery without so much as a single footprint in the dirt. "It's unnatural, that's what it is," the handsome man muttered, angrily. "Next time, she won't be so lucky!"

Cursing, he trudged slowly back to his house before conjuring up the vision he beheld moments earlier. The alluring image was no dream; this woman was real, yet unlike any other female. She was almost magical—a fantasy. She took his breath away. If only he could find some manner of introducing himself without looking like a complete idiot. Oh, well. At least he saw her often, his room holding full view of the shoreline where she often walked.

Watching for the mystical lady soon became part of Justin's morning ritual. This new day was no exception. Feeling brave, he decided it was time to meet her. After checking his appearance in the mirror, he waited near the window until she came into sight, then dashed outside. His heart pounding wildly in anticipation, Justin jogged quietly across the sand. His muscles tensed, his side developed a cramp, and his adrenalin went into overdrive. Just my luck, he thought. I'll suffer a heart attack right here on the beach, in front of her. He fancied the idea of her administering CPR to his lifeless body. A slow grin spread across his face.

Suddenly, as if on cue, the mystical lady's eyes captured his, and Nicole froze. Justin continued advancing until he was a few yards away. Then he, too, stopped. To him, she was a sculpture to be admired, standing so boldly without any sign of fear. She was tall, almost six feet tall, with shiny, thick, ink-black hair cascading down her back like an exotic waterfall. She also had the largest, darkest brown eyes he had ever seen; they were almost black. What he couldn't notice at this distance was how they were speckled with flecks of amber, more typical of a tigress. Prominent cheekbones added to her beauty, as did the rose petal lips and tan complexion. What man in his right mind wouldn't desire a woman such as this? Never having experienced infatuation before, Justin could not fathom what course of action to take; so he stood there like an idiot, paralyzed, speechless, and staring.

Like an idiot, Nicole stared back. She should have run the minute she saw him bounding towards her, but curiosity kept her feet firmly anchored in the sand, and now her vocal cords refused to utter a single sound. Get a hold of yourself! she silently scolded. This is no Prince Charming. Men are never how they first appear to be and this one was smart enough to catch me alone on the beach. Nicole searched his eyes for some sign of evil intent, yet saw none. What she did sense, however, proved quite unnerving; it was a stubborn streak accompanied by a strong will. This, alone, could give him the power of a giant. As if that wasn't enough, every muscle in his being boasted of strength. As she assessed his fighting potential, her dark eyes feasted upon the hard, lean body. Was this the new neighbor? Heaven help her!

She couldn't deny the obvious; the man was built like an ancient warrior. She memorized every last detail, taking notice of the thick, blond hair falling about his face like a lion's unruly mane, the crystal blue eyes which reminded her of a December sky, the strong jaw line so firmly set, and those shoulders! They were so broad she could picture a child sitting upon each one. Place a sword in his hand and he was a Viking stepped off of a painting. Nicole's heart slammed against her ribs.

Excitement, like an electric current of magnetic energy, raced between them, devouring any rational thought in Justin's brain. At first, he had only wanted to meet the bewitching beauty. Now, he wanted to touch her, kiss her, unravel the mystery hidden in the depths of her eyes. Daringly, he moved forward.

Nicole retreated, backwards. Inwardly, she cursed these quiet adventures she took by herself. Hadn't Cristoff warned her not to travel without a companion? But there was no companion, except Cristoff, and he was currently busy mucking stalls.

Suddenly, a seagull flew between the two of them, startling Nicole. Justin took advantage of the minor distraction and increased his speed to a brisk walk, frowning with annoyance when he noticed the temptress quickening her backwards gait, also. Did she want him to chase her? Surely, if she had wanted to escape she could have done so several minutes ago. What was this little game she was playing? He had no intention of trapping her like a wild animal; yet, if he did not pursue her, he felt certain she'd never return to this part of the beach. The thought was enough to prompt Justin to find his voice.

"Please stay. I won't hurt you."

His words sounded sincere, even though Nicole picked up on the uncertainty in his tone. The rigid muscles down her back finally relaxed with this new understanding of the man's predicament: He was afraid of losing her. It was that simple. A faint smile touched her lips.

For a moment, Justin prematurely assumed the victory was his. After all, she was smiling, wasn't she? But the victorious feeling quickly vanished when, to his alarm, the lovely woman spun around and darted across the sand with lightning speed. Panic seized him. "Wait!" he shouted. "I just want to..." The words died in his throat as the elusive beauty faded into the distance. Shoulders slumping forward in defeat, Justin uttered a long, agonized groan.

She was gone. She was truly gone, and he had been so close to her only a minute before. Damn! What was wrong with the woman? Didn't she know he was just being friendly? Who was she, anyway? He assumed she lived close by, since she always walked the distance. Justin frowned. The closest neighbor lived a half mile away. Widow Tyler, they called her. The Black Widow. Although there was no hard evidence to support the claim, the townspeople swore she murdered her rich husband, Philip. Justin remembered his friend, Shane, telling him the story. His mind scrambled for the details. It was a bizarre killing; it kept the town buzzing for months—a rich man brutally murdered, shot through the head at close range, barely married two years… no eyewitnesses, no clues, not one shred of evidence to lead the authorities to the killer. According to local reporters, Mrs. Tyler was the first to have discovered the body and showed little emotion when being questioned.

Justin shuddered. He normally ignored gossip, but now that he suspected this woman on the beach to be the former Mrs. Tyler, he gave the rumors some serious consideration. After all, this lady could be dangerous. Still, he tried convincing himself otherwise. He reasoned that Widow Tyler was probably in a mental institution somewhere since witnessing such a gruesome tragedy. Maybe she had even sold her property and was residing in some exclusive mansion hundreds of miles away. He sincerely doubted she would be drawing happy pictures in the woods, nor would she dress so commonly after inheriting all that wealth. No. The more he reflected on the issue, the more positive he was this young lady on the beach was not the Black Widow.

Yet, with that realization, his anger returned, full force. Then, who was the mysterious female? And why was she so damn unsociable? "Women!" he spat. It was just his luck. Every boring beauty at the brothel clamoring for his attention, and he had to be drawn to an arrogant little tease! Temper rising, Justin raced to the ocean to dive into its healing coolness, his mighty roar of rage splitting the heavens like a loud clap of thunder. "Next time, woman, I'll have the upper hand!" It was a promise he intended to keep, although no sooner had the words been uttered, his face met the slap of a breaking wave.

While Justin lingered in the ocean to soothe his bruised ego, Nicole coped with her anxiety by running all the way home. She was gasping, clutching her side, as she stumbled into the barn office to check for phone messages. Cristoff glanced at the young beauty from where he sat at her desk, his hair all mussed up, his shirt half unbuttoned. It only took one look at his glazed eyes for Nicole to see he had been drinking, and pretty heavily at that. The last time she had seen him this drunk was just after Philip's murder. Fear clutched her heart.

"What's wrong?" she blurted, going to him. "What is it, Cristoff?"

He ignored the question and, instead, peered curiously at her rosy red cheeks and tangled hair. "What've you beennn up to?" he slurred.

"I, I ran home from the beach," she stuttered. "I needed the exercise. Your turn now. Why have you been drinking? Has something happened?"

Cristoff slowly rose from the chair, drawing himself up until they were eye to eye, both being exactly the same height. "No, nothing's happened," he replied, still studying her. Nicole was amazed he wasn't even swaying. He held his liquor well, she had to admit. "I called Daniel. He's coming over."

Nicole waited for him to continue, but he offered no further explanation, prompting her to ask, "Well? Why did you call him? Is something wrong?" It was like pulling teeth, trying to get him to talk.

Cristoff suddenly realized he had already said too much. He frowned, then brushed past Nicole and headed through the doorway. "If you see 'im, tell 'im to come to my house."

"Cristoff!" called Nicole as she caught hold of his arm. "You're not going anywhere until you tell me what is going on?"

In a flash he whipped his arm out of her grasp, turned, and gave her a look that clearly told her she had overstepped her boundaries with him. The silent warning only lasted a few seconds, though. He now forced a smile. "You needn't worry, my dear," he said in a sugar-coated voice, patting the top of her head like he would a puppy. "I'm not going to ask Daniel for any money. Oh, no. No need to worry. You have enough on your mind, now, don't ya, girl? Yes, yes. Cristoff will take care of everything. You can always count on me, can't ya?" Without waiting for a reply, he turned and ambled down the aisleway, leaving Nicole totally exasperated. She threw up her hands in defeat, knowing there was no point in pursuing him when he was in such poor condition.

To get her mind off him, she straightened her desk,

checked her phone messages, then took The General out for a ride. Although she longed to venture onto the trails, she rode in one of the pastures near the house so she could keep an eye out for Daniel. The General, however, proved almost too much for her to handle. He sensed Nicole's nervousness from the day's events and pranced in reckless haste, throwing in a few good bucks to protest her rigid hands. Just as she decided to call it quits, Daniel pulled up and motioned to her. "Anything wrong?" he asked. "Cristoff sounded a bit under the weather, so to speak."

"Your guess is as good as mine," she answered. "Do me a favor and let me in on the big secret, okay? He's in his house. I'm going to put The General away and check over the rest of the horses out in the field."

Daniel nodded, watching Nicole's lithe body swing down from the saddle before she led her prized stallion away; and as he continued staring after the alluring female, he felt the odd sensation of someone's eyes upon him, someone who had a wee bit too much alcohol today. Strolling across the grounds to the tenant house, Daniel decided it was high time to confront Cristoff about his addiction. He had second thoughts, however, when the ranch hand jerked open the door in a fit of temper and nearly yanked him inside.

"What the...?" Daniel stumbled over the living room runner, almost sprawling onto the floor.

Suddenly realizing what he had done, Cristoff quickly apologized. "So sorry, Danny, boy. The front door got stuck and I had a devil of a time opening it. No offense, eh? Here. 'ave a drink." He hurried to the liquor cabinet to fetch some bourbon.

"Never mind the drink," frowned Daniel. "And that wasn't any accident, either. You pulled me through the doorway, Cristoff. What the devil's got into you?" He folded his arms across his chest as he waited for an answer.

"I needed to speak with you about Philip's parties," the ranch hand admitted. Since there was no delicate way to ask, Cristoff came right out and popped the question, "Did you sleep with Nicole?"

"We've been over this before," Daniel reminded him. "I told you I didn't."

"Yeah, that's what you said," came the measured reply. Cristoff scratched his head and took a step closer, hoping to catch some indication of dishonesty in his eyes. "I have reason to believe otherwise, and I'd like to know the truth. It matters to me. It matters to Nicole."

"I don't understand why you're rehashing this," protested Daniel. He was getting hot under the collar, and Cristoff took notice. "Did Nicole say something?"

At that very moment Cristoff wanted to grab Daniel by the scruff of his neck and throw him against the wall. He despised being played a fool. "Funny you should ask that," he said, dryly. "If you've been honest, it doesn't matter what Nicole has said, does it?"

"I told you, Cristoff. I never touched her. And while we're on the subject of Nicole, what kind of protection do you offer her if you can't even stay sober?"

"Defensive, aren't ya?"

"Oh, grow up, Cristoff! Nicole doesn't need a worthless drunk stumbling around her ranch. Maybe I should fetch her right now and show her your ugly side, huh? What do you think she'd say then? Perhaps I'll even mention the reason you brought me over here? She wanted to know. She asked me. Shall I tell her, Cristoff? Shall I drudge up all the bad memories again for poor Nicole?" Angry eyes clashed as Cristoff considered the proposition.

"I'll call your bluff," the ranch hand retorted. "Yeah, Danny. Let's get Nicole. She would be very interested in this conversation. You see," he paused before delivering the final blow, "... she was the one who told me you had slept with her."

A myriad of expressions crossed Daniel's face. "So, she did say something. I can't fathom why she'd invent such a story. It makes no sense."

"Well, let's ask her," smiled Cristoff, reaching for the door. The truth was, he was banking on Daniel stopping him. Cristoff had no intention of bringing Nicole in on the discussion. He never wanted her to confront Daniel. It would be much safer if Cristoff handled him. That way, if the man lost his temper, any retaliation would be aimed at Cristoff, not Nicole. Cristoff turned the doorknob.

"You pig-headed moron!" snarled Daniel.

In three strides he was upon the young ranch hand, a fistful of shirt in his hand as he jerked him away from the door. Cristoff barely had time to catch his breath before being slammed against the wall, his attacker's hand holding him motionless as it pressed into his throat. "What kind of game are you playing here?" Daniel hissed through clenched teeth. Cristoff managed a few guttural noises to convince him to ease up on his hold so he could answer; then, in two swift moves, broke free. He resisted the urge to retaliate, knowing such action would just make matters worse. Instead, he retreated a safe distance away, allowing Daniel time to cool off.

"You're the one playing games," Cristoff remarked. "I only asked for the truth. Seems I have the real facts now, don't I, Danny? Why else would you feel the need to stop me at the door?" He was sobering up fast.

Daniel Tyler stared coldly at the man who knew too much. A hundred thoughts played havoc with his brain while he contemplated his options. Finally, he said, "No one believes a drunk, Cristoff."

"Who would I tell? Nicole already knows."

"You're lying."

"I'm telling you, she knows."

"How?"

"A flashback. She was drinking and had a flashback. The alcohol must've triggered it."

Daniel glanced from Cristoff to across the room, then back to Cristoff. He was weighing this new information, carefully. "I think I will have that drink, after all," he mumbled, helping himself to the bourbon. Cristoff watched him swallow a couple mouthfuls before calmly asking, "Why'd ya do it, Dan? I trusted you. I thought you were lookin' out for her."

"I was," came the quiet reply. After gulping down another drink, the 26 year-old slowly turned to face him, a pained expression on his face. "I never planned it, Cristoff. It just happened."

"Just happened?"

"I had too much to drink one evening. It was the night my wife asked me for a divorce." His eyes narrowed at the recollection. He remembered the lack of emotion in his wife's voice as she announced her intentions, her green eyes cold and empty. "Anyway," he continued, "I took the news pretty hard; didn't tell anyone until days later. But that night... that night I needed something, someone to ease my pain. Nicole was only too willing. Sure, I knew she wasn't herself, but it didn't matter. She was just carefree and eager to please. So, yes, I took advantage of her. If you think I don't regret my actions, you're mistaken. I've felt nothing but guilt ever since." Putting his glass down on the table, Daniel stepped up to Cristoff. "Well? I'm sure there's something you want to say to me, so, go ahead. I can take it."

Cristoff paused a moment, considering the request. Then he drew back his arm and punched Daniel squarely in the face, knocking the startled man to the floor. It had been a powerful hit, and Daniel landed with a thud, nearly upsetting the coffee table in the process. With no regard as to the consequences, Cristoff spoke freely, now. "Nicole was right when she said there was an underlying reason you were hanging around. You were waiting for a chance with her again, weren't ya?"

"No, I wasn't," Daniel replied, getting to his feet. He should have been furious at the ranch hand; but, instead, was relieved Cristoff had defended Nicole's honor. Touching his swollen nose to check for broken bones, he said, "I have no intention of taking advantage of her. Be logical, Cristoff. If I wanted Nicole for myself, do you think I'd wait a whole year before making my move?"

"Then, why are you still coming 'round here? Why won't you leave her alone?"

Daniel looked at him as if he had two heads. "Because I feel guilty, that's why! Can't you piece it together? I've been trying to ease my conscience by offering her money. I want to help her out."

Cristoff studied him for a minute, finally sensing some sincerity; at least he had come clean. Then the rugged 25 year-old walked to the living room window and caught sight of a young woman in the pasture, playing happily with a chestnut stallion, not a care in the world. The portrait of such innocent pleasure suddenly became dirtied by visions of Daniel with Nicole, Daniel kissing her, touching her… Cristoff had to close his eyes tightly to force out the image, while fresh anger burned in his veins. He wheeled around to face Daniel, his voice cold as sleet. "If you want to help Nicole, stay the hell away from her. She's trying to erase the past. You'll only be a reminder. Do us both a favor, Daniel. Break off all ties. I'll be here to look after Nicole. She doesn't need you. She never needed you."

A cocky grin spread across Daniel's face. "Said like a true drunk, Cristoff, my boy. Who the hell are you to decide what Nicole needs? Do you really think the two of you can make something of this tiny ranch?"

Cristoff saw the challenge in his eyes and instantly regretted his loose tongue. "The ranch has nothing to do with this," he quickly said.

"Sure it does," Daniel pointed out. "That's the real reason you're sticking around, isn't it? You'd like to see Desert Wind Arabians become famous, see your name up on the sign beside Nicole's? You always wanted to be a partner in the breeding industry. I know, because Philip told me." Strolling over to the liquor cabinet, Daniel held a bottle of scotch high in the air, taunting, "Isn't that why you drink, Cristoff? Because, deep down, you know you'll never amount to anything but a—"

"That's enough, Daniel!" shouted Nicole. Both men turned, in surprise. They hadn't even seen her push open the front door. "You've worn out your welcome."

"So I have," he agreed, smiling to conceal his fury. Putting down the bottle of scotch, he brushed past Cristoff and headed for the door, stopping briefly to address Nicole. Motioning towards the intoxicated ranch hand, he remarked, "You know, my dear, you really should choose your friends more wisely." Then he simply walked out, got in his car, and left.

"What was that all about?" quizzed Nicole.

"Nothing," mumbled Cristoff, avoiding her gaze.

"Oh, it was something, all right," she insisted, going to him.

"Me and my big mouth." Cristoff could have kicked himself. "I did the one thing I swore I'd never do."

"Which is?"

"I made Daniel my enemy—our enemy."

"How?"

He took one look into Nicole's innocent eyes and felt his stomach drop. He couldn't tell her. He just couldn't.

"I... I said I could manage the ranch better than he could," Cristoff lied. "I'm afraid I've destroyed the friendship."

"So," Nicole shrugged, "say you're sorry."

"What?"

"Apologize to him. He seems like a forgiving person."

Her suggestion caused him to give a little chuckle. Then, cupping her chin in his hand, he whispered, "Oh, Nicole. Sometimes you are so naive." He breathed the last words with a sigh as he stared at her luscious lips. And as he drew closer, the full realization of what he was about to do struck Nicole like a lightning bolt. She parted her mouth to protest, and instead, found herself on the receiving end of a deep, penetrating kiss. It went on and on and on, until Nicole could no longer breathe. She pushed frantically against Cristoff's shoulders, but his arms had encircled her, giving her no means of escape. Twisting so she could turn her face to the side, she finally gasped for air.

"Relax," soothed the ranch hand. "It's a harmless kiss, Nicole—nothing more. Enjoy it." Without waiting for a response, his mouth found hers again, the taste of her sugary lips filling him with erotic ideas. He would sell his soul for a kiss like this, and not think twice.

Nicole, on the other hand, wasn't sure what she was feeling. Her emotions were a jumbled mess, falling somewhere between excitement and fear. She reminded herself that Cristoff would never hurt her, that this was just the result of too much alcohol. Couldn't she just enjoy it, like he said? After all, she hadn't been kissed since… Nicole refused to think about it. Instead, she allowed her body to go limp in his arms, her lack of resistance encouraging him to explore the sweet interior of her mouth. This wasn't so bad. No harm done.

Pausing to come up for air, Cristoff caught a fleeting glimpse of passion in Nicole's eyes; and, in that second, felt a twinge of guilt. Was he no better than Daniel? His heart pounding against his ribs, Cristoff finally understood Daniel's weakness. It was easy to get carried away with Nicole. She enclosed him in a cocoon of desire so thick it smothered every other emotion. If he kissed her one more time, there would be no turning back. He had to stop himself while he still had the willpower.

"Well," he suddenly said, breaking away. "We shan't do that again, hmm?" Acting nonchalant, he thrust his hands in his pockets, rocked back on his heels, and stared at some remote spot on the wall.

Nicole was baffled. What was wrong with the man? He appeared so uneasy, it made her feel lacking, as if he had found something undesirable about her. She was sorry she had even kissed him. Like a six year old child, she quickly wiped her mouth with the back of her hand to erase the memory. Cristoff couldn't help but notice. "It wasn't that bad, was it?"

Nicole blushed beet red. Cristoff nervously cleared his throat. Silence filled the room. A minute ticked slowly by.

"Well, now," he finally spoke, "that's two things I've done which I swore I'd never do: the first, was making Daniel our enemy; the second, was kissing my boss." He forced a small chuckle and glanced at Nicole. She remained sullen, however.

"There's no need to apologize," she said in a curt tone. "I allowed it. If it's anyone's fault, it's mine. As for Daniel, you never did tell me why you called him over here?"

"I had to speak with him, man to man," he lied. "It doesn't concern you. It was about... you know... girl trouble."

Nicole raised an eyebrow. "Girl trouble? You haven't got someone pregnant, have you?"

"No. Nothing like that."

"Then what? You were pretty upset when I saw you in the barn."

Cristoff was reluctant to continue the conversation. He despised lying, even little white lies. She couldn't force him to reply, although she might, instead, seek out Daniel for the answer. "It was just some friendly rivalry between Danny and myself," he finally said.

"Ohhh," she nodded. "That was some friendly rivalry, all right. He was going for your jugular! Who's the lucky girl?"

Cristoff grit his teeth. "Don't you have something to do, Nicole?"

She cracked a smile. "I get the message. Okay. I'll leave you be. By the way, I met our new neighbor." Pausing as she recalled his handsome face, she added, "We have nothing to worry about. He's as harmless as a pussycat."

CHAPTER THREE

Justin, the pussycat, roared like a lion.

"She's a damn wild mustang," he cursed to his friend. "I was this far from her," he demonstrated the distance with his hands, "and she gave me this cute, little smile and hightailed down the beach!" He kicked the dirt hard with the edge of his boot. Even though several days had passed since the incident, fresh anger quickly resurfaced. "I can't understand that woman."

Shane chuckled, quietly. "What did you expect? She knew she had you around her little finger." He slapped the blond on his back before chuckling again, unaware Justin was in no joking mood. "So," Justin said, "you think she was merely playing with me, do you? I'll show her! Just wait until next time. I won't give her a chance to mesmerize me with those hypnotic brown eyes." With a scowl, he pitched a stick high into the trees.

Shane threw him a curious glance. "Is she that beautiful?"

"It's sort of an interior beauty," came the reply, "a magnetic personality. I can't explain it. She's just not like any ordinary woman."

His words brought another smile to Shane's lips. "You make her sound magical. Maybe I ought to have a look at her?" Shrugging his shoulders in response, Justin continued walking through the woods. They both knew the path by heart and stared at the open land that lay just beyond the old trees. A little farther out it changed to sand, enticing them with the promise of cool, ocean water. Both men were glad they had taken the day off from work. Justin nudged his buddy. "Feel like a swim?"

Shane suddenly stopped. "Looks like somebody beat us to it."

There, along the bleached sand, paced a magnificent Arabian stallion; neck arched, tail held high with excitement. The two young men were so entranced by the beautiful creature, they barely noticed the woman now emerging from the water. The sound of her voice snapped them back to reality as she laughingly called to the powerful beast, "Come now, General. You mustn't be impatient. If you can't wait for me there, then you must come in the water, too!" The soft, melodic voice sent shivers up Justin's spine. He stared with disbelief, faintly mumbling, "It's her..."

"Her?" echoed Shane, eyes glued to the captivating vision. They grew silent as they watched Nicole walk towards the frantic pet, who was now tossing his snow-white head with defiance.

It was then she saw them. Instantly, her smile disappeared. She studied them briefly, dark eyes searching for details. Yes, the blond she already knew and could spot him a mile away. His power was definite; his body carved from rock, itself. She shuddered, realizing the threat he posed to her safety. Then her eyes rested upon Shane, her senses tingling with caution. He was taller than Justin, his hair black as sin, with dazzling thick waves. Although Justin resembled a rock, Shane resembled a Thoroughbred—he was built for action, swift action, and probably agile as a cat. The two men proved a dangerous pair. Nicole felt a lump form in her throat at the thought of having no weapon for defense—none at all. She turned her attention to her pet.

Preoccupied with his owner, the snow-white stallion hadn't even noticed the intruders until he caught sight of Shane's hand moving to shield his eyes from the sun. The General jerked his head around to face the pair, and, with a loud snort to demonstrate his displeasure at being surprised, reared high into the sky. “Down, General!” commanded the enchantress, to no avail. With a neigh of alarm, the great white stallion pivoted, darting away from the fearful woman, taking with him her only means of escape.

Now, Shane could see her more clearly. “Lord, she’s nice!” he breathed, green eyes devouring the slender curves, and the thick, dark hair glistening black from her recent swim. Scanning her long, tapered legs and muscular thighs, he assumed her strength in those areas was due to horseback riding.

“Come on,” motioned the blond, walking onto the sand. Shane hesitated before following his friend, unsure of Justin’s motive. “What are you up to?” he whispered, not really expecting an answer. None was given. Like a pack of wolves, they stalked her.

Nicole watched them approach, cold shivers passing over her slim body from the wet blouse and shorts. Her first instinct was to run, but her pride would not allow it. Besides, she seriously doubted she could outrun Shane. Thus, she quickly devised a new plan, pretending to ignore them as she turned and walked in the opposite direction. Granted, she wasn’t crazy about turning her back on them, but she hoped they would lose interest. Her plan backfired.

“Let’s go after her,” Shane prompted. “We have her outnumbered.” Without a reply, Justin stared straight ahead, continuing to advance towards the retreating young lady. He wanted to be close to her again, to feel the excitement pass between them, to catch a fleeting glimpse of acknowledgment in her eyes. He was determined not to give up—not this time, he swore.

Sensing the danger, Nicole’s hope vanished like quicksilver. She’d have to decide another course of action, swiftly. There was no telling what type of characters these men were. Obviously, the blond would prove the more powerful of the two. Yet, as odd as it seemed, she felt tempted to challenge him, to do something completely unexpected. Stand her ground? Maybe. It was risky, but so was trying to outrun them. Her jugular veins throbbed in her throat, a slight tremor rippling beneath the cool, aloof appearance. Would they sense her fear? She prayed not.

Nicole listened patiently to the approaching footsteps. She had deliberately slowed her own gait so they could catch up, and now, with them almost upon her, it was time to put her plan into motion. Wearing a mask of pure defiance, Nicole turned abruptly on her followers, staring straight into their confused faces as she donned the meanest, fiercest look she could muster. Startled, Justin stepped backwards into Shane, sending them both stumbling to regain their balance. Shane's mouth opened in astonishment as he gaped at the young woman's beauty, while Justin tried like the dickens to collect his thoughts.

"Can I help you?" quipped the enchantress, raising a brow. Only for a second did her fiery eyes weave their magic around Justin's heart. He fought it off, admiring her tactics, but refusing to be the pawn in her little game. She may have caught him off guard, but it was time for him to take the reins, now. He'd play "the protector" and win her respect. It was his favorite charade.

"Good day, madam. My friend and I," he motioned towards Shane as he continued, "could not help noticing you alone on the beach, which could prove quite dangerous for a young woman so lovely. Please permit us to escort you to your destination?" A Cheshire Cat smile slid easily across his face as he folded his massive arms across his chest to further impress her.

Nicole, however, was immune to the cunning flattery. In fact, she grew colder with each passing second. Yes, Justin could definitely feel the wall emerge between them when her eyes began to glare menacingly into his. "I am quite touched by your concern, sir," she mocked, furious that the men's eyes were riveted to her wet, clinging blouse. "But, since I'm not appropriately dressed for company, you shall have to excuse me. Perhaps you could escort me another day—say, twenty years from now?" Pleased with herself, Nicole spun around to briskly walk away.

"Well, you little spitfire!" hissed Justin. Roughly, he grabbed her arm. "Oh, no you don't! Not this time." He swung the astonished woman around to face him, increasing the pressure on her soft flesh. If she was frightened, she was an expert at concealing it, for she offered no resistance, nor did she cry out in pain. "Just who do you think you are, Miss High and Mighty?" he demanded with anger, his eyes hardening to steel blue. Nicole was speechless, shocked by the sudden outburst. "You think you can just dismiss me with a wave of your hand, do you? Well, you listen to me! All I wanted to do was get to know you, but that lofty attitude of yours is enough to freeze boiling water!" He shook her hard, hoping to scare the daylights out of her.

He was mistaken. The electric current between them turned to static. Shane watched the beautiful woman transform into a panther. Her claws had sprung, her brown eyes glittering with specks of orange flames. It was apparent Justin was playing with fire. His fury dominated his reasoning, and apologies were out of the question. It no longer mattered that he had just insulted an absolute stranger; he wanted to put this woman in her proper place. The very sight of her made his blood boil, although he wasn't quite sure if it was due to her rude behavior, or the fact that he was finding it difficult to keep his hands off her. Whatever the reason, he needed this confrontation.

Then it happened. In the blink of an eye, Nicole smacked her free hand against his jaw. The loud crack made Shane wince. Justin merely froze, unable to believe he had just been slapped by a woman. Before he could regain his senses, Nicole struck him again, delivering the second malicious blow with incredible force. It hurt like hell, and now Justin's thoughts took a twisted turn. With a loud roar of rage, he threw the vixen to the ground.

Shane was horrified. This was his mild-mannered buddy? "Let her go, Justin!" he yelled. "She's not worth the trouble." Holding his breath, he waited for the fighting to stop. It didn't. In fact, it escalated. The two wrestlers had created a minor sand storm on the beach within the first three minutes. "This is ridiculous," muttered Shane, now afraid one of them would become seriously injured. Finally stepping forward to intervene, he heard a pitiful howl. Nicole had taken advantage of an unguarded moment to solidly ram her knee into Justin's groin. She scurried out from under the giant and fled, with Justin making a futile attempt to follow. Shane grabbed his arm. "Let her go, pal. She's not your type, anyway."

The blond yanked his arm free, then spat into the sand. "Little wench!" he growled. "She'll get hers... I promise."

"Why bother, Justin?"

"She needs to be taught some manners, that's why!" He picked up a handful of sand and flung it through the air. A slow, wicked smile formed on his lips. "And I'm just the one to teach her."

Shane allowed that remark to slide by, knowing the less said, the better. This was not the time to lecture his friend on the perils of vengeance. Following Justin back into the woods, he mentally replayed the reckless fight for his own enjoyment while he searched for some way to soothe the man's bruised ego. But, Justin's ego was not what needed soothing; his groin was throbbing painfully—so much so, he winced with every step. Whenever Shane thought he had something to say to lighten the mood, he took one look at the blond's dark scowl and quickly changed his mind. Thus, no more words passed between the two men until they finally reached Justin's house. Only then did the blond open his mouth. "Know what I need?"

"What?" answered Shane.

"A good, stiff drink. How about the two of us going into town after I get cleaned up?"

Shane knew it was safer to drink inside the house, but wasn't about to cause an argument. "All right," he agreed. "Mind if I grab something to eat first?"

"Help yourself," called the blond as he headed for the bathroom. "You know where the kitchen is."

Shane entered the brightly colored room and fixed a quick sandwich. Unexpectedly, an image flashed across his mind. Dazzling... truly dazzling. He pictured Nicole's sparkling brown eyes daring them to defy her, so bold, so confident. Her shimmering blue blouse had been clinging provocatively to her tan skin, the bright material providing a sharp contrast to those flaming red cheeks; long, dark hair caressing her body with each gentle wave of the breeze. No wonder Justin was upset. The woman incited certain desires which were better left suppressed in a man. Yes, this was no ordinary female. She was unique—a bewitching enchantress, an untamed wildcat when provoked...

"Ready?" called Justin, appearing from around the corner. Shane's mind suddenly went blank. He stuffed the remainder of his sandwich in his mouth, tossed his paper plate in the trash and swiftly joined Justin at the door. When the blond gave him a curious look, Shane felt the muscles in his stomach begin to tense. At first, he assumed the food hadn't agreed with him. But after a few more minutes, he realized the origin of his problem was not physical at all; it was emotional. His conscience was playing tug o' war and he dreaded acknowledging the truth. He wanted the woman, too.

Little did he know, Nicole was thinking of him at that very same moment. It had just occurred to her that she had left The General's bridle back at the edge of the woods, not far from where she had met the two men. When she had headed for the beach earlier, she had ridden her horse bareback, carrying his halter for when she'd dismount. After sliding off him, she'd removed his bridle and placed the halter on his head. The General usually remained wherever Nicole was, today being an exception. She now had to return to the scene to fetch the leather bridle before someone else picked it up—that someone else being Justin or Shane. Perhaps they hadn't even noticed it. Nevertheless, Nicole was not looking forward to going back there. Justin would be temporarily disabled, posing no threat, but Shane… She could only hope he had left the vicinity.

To her good fortune, neither man was in sight when she reached her destination. Reclaiming her riding equipment, she slowly jogged back through the woods and headed home. The General nickered his greeting from beside the broodmare paddock, where he was presently entertaining a lovely dapple-gray mare. "You rascal," smiled Nicole as she grabbed hold of his halter and returned him to his rightful pasture. She then put the bridle away and took a quick shower to wash the sand from her skin. It reminded her of her narrow escape earlier, causing her to frown with anger.

"The nerve of that guy!" she fumed. She was still irritable when Daniel found her in the barn office. He could tell she was in a foul mood by her reluctance to acknowledge him, which piqued his curiosity.

"Is Cristoff around?" he casually asked.

"He's in town. I'll tell him you stopped by."

"Ah, that won't be necessary," he replied. "I came to see you, Nicole. We need to talk."

He had her attention, now. Nicole emitted a frustrated sigh, leaned back in her chair, and motioned for him to sit down. "I suppose you didn't come here to apologize for the way you treated my ranch hand," she remarked.

Daniel looked her straight in the eye. "No, I didn't. But I want you to pay close attention to what I have to say about him."

"Oh, please," she protested, rolling her eyes. "Can't the two of you work this out like nice little boys?"

"Look, Nicole, I have your best interest at heart. I want to see this ranch succeed, with or without Cristoff. It's obvious he is not the ideal ranch hand—"

"I don't want to hear it," she broke in.

"Well, you are going to, because I know a few things about Cristoff that you don't."

"Not interested," she said, dismissing him with a wave of her hand.

Outside the office, Cristoff had just stopped from walking

in on the heated conversation. Fortunately, no one had heard his approach, so he simply remained near the doorway, hidden from view. He wasn't surprised to hear Daniel blackballing him, but he was surprised when Nicole vehemently defended him.

"I don't understand why you get so wrapped up in my business?" Nicole fussed.

"And I don't understand why you keep defending a drunk!" Daniel retorted. "Is there something here that I am missing? Are the two of you more than just friends?"

Nicole's mouth flew open in astonishment. "How dare you question me about any of my relationships!"

Standing up, Daniel placed both palms down on her desk, leaning forward as his eyes narrowed to two, tiny slits. "Well, are you more than friends, Nicole?" he slowly repeated. "Is Cristoff your lover?"

She smacked him with all of her strength—a huge wallop which spun his head sideways, causing Cristoff to almost burst out laughing. There was no mistaking the sound of that slap. Nicole was becoming quite good at it. This one was much, much better than the blow she had dealt Justin.

Unlike Justin, Daniel took it like a man, never losing his cool, never raising a hand, although he wanted to. Like a true gentleman, he merely held his breath as he decided the next course of action. Nicole, however, was no fool. She saw the malicious gleam in his eyes, the hurt, the surprise. She had risen from her chair, and stood balanced on the balls of her feet, ready to flee, her chest heaving from the rush of adrenalin. In that moment, Daniel thought he had never seen her look so alluring. It frustrated him to no end.

Acting as if nothing unordinary had happened, he quietly retrieved a piece of paper from his pocket and placed it on top the desk, saying, "I did some research. Here are the names of three excellent prospects to help you with the ranch. I'll pay their wages. I don't care if you choose all three or just one. What is important is that you get rid of Cristoff. I told you Philip said Cristoff wanted a partnership in the business. You have to watch your back. He's not to be trusted."

"And you are?" came the mocking reply. "I thought you were his friend?"

"Not any longer. Things have changed. Be a smart girl, Nicole, and take my advice."

"You know what you can do with your advice," she quipped, tearing the list of names into tiny shreds which floated slowly into the wastebasket. "If I have to watch my back, Daniel, it's because of people like you, not Cristoff. Seems to me, you are a little too anxious in becoming involved in this ranch's affairs. The question is... why? You never showed any interest in the horse industry before. Why the sudden turnaround?"

"I'm only looking out for you," he replied.

"Why go to all the trouble?" Afraid no longer, Nicole folded her arms. "Gee, Daniel, with all the personal questions you bombarded me with, I'd be inclined to think you have more than just a passing interest in my daily transactions—or, perhaps I'm completely off the mark. It's not my daily affairs you're really concerned about, is it? It's my nightly affairs."

Daniel gave a twisted, little smile. "Don't flatter yourself, my dear. You're not my type. I know firsthand you'll do whatever you damn well please. I couldn't control you any more than I could lasso the wind." He glanced at his watch. "I see this has been a waste of time." Heading for the door, his fingertips traced the outline of his jaw. "You should seriously consider boxing, Nicole." He hesitated, taking one last look at her before exiting.

Outside the office, Cristoff had taken his cue from the tail end of the conversation, scurried down the aisle, pivoted around, and casually strolled back towards the office as if he had just arrived. Daniel barely took notice, until Cristoff said with an ironic smile, "Let's do lunch sometime, Danny boy!"

"Like hell," came the reply, as Daniel kept walking.

Cristoff shook his head. "Sheesh! Ya just can't please some people." He broke out in a grin, striding into the barn office with a light spring to his step. Nicole had been standing near the window and now turned to greet him.

"I'm glad you're here," she said in a quiet voice. "I need to speak with you about Daniel."

Cristoff plopped himself down in a chair and propped his feet up on another, still smiling. "Yes, he looked rather perturbed when we passed in the aisle."

"I'm worried about him, Cristoff. He came here to rat on you, plus he asked some rather personal questions."

The young ranch hand twirled a stem of hay between two fingers. "Oh? What kind of questions?" He didn't dare look at her, for fear he'd start to chuckle. He was just so doggone happy and she had no idea she was the cause of it. He still found it difficult to believe she had taken his side against Daniel, especially since Cristoff knew Nicole didn't approve of his drinking. But, like a trooper, she had defended him. "You say he asked personal questions?" he repeated.

"Never mind," she quickly replied, wringing her hands. "I did something awful."

Letting his feet slide off the chair so he was sitting upright, Cristoff mouthed a huge "No! What could you have possibly done, Nicole?" and grasped the back of the chair in front of him, pretending to brace himself for the shock of his life.

Nicole's eyes narrowed suspiciously. Placing her hands on her hips, the young woman chided, "Cristoff Colvert, were you eavesdropping on my conversation with Daniel?"

Cristoff leaped to his feet, holding the chair as his defense weapon. "Don't hit me, Nicole!" he begged. "Please don't hit me. I heard you pack a powerful punch." Then he broke out in a series of laughs that even made his employer crack a smile.

"Oh, Cristoff, I'm so embarrassed. Did you really hear me slap him?"

"The whole stable vibrated," he grinned, then added, "Don't worry about it, Nicole. Daniel was angry long before the slap."

"Then you heard the terrible things he said about you? I'm so sorry, Cristoff."

"He sure has it in for me," he agreed.

"I don't think I'm on the top of his Christmas list, either. I just can't figure out why he keeps pestering me?"

"My only explanation was assuming he was sweet on you, but he put my mind to rest on that issue, today."

"That's right. He said I'm not his type."

"Yeah, but some men like a challenge. I wouldn't trust him. In fact, I've decided I don't want him anywhere near this property. If we have to get a restraining order, we will."

"But, Cristoff," she protested, "this will all blow over in a few days. Don't you think we should stay on the good side of him? I mean, if he's dangerous—"

"You don't understand," he interjected. Knowing he now had to reveal the truth, Cristoff frantically searched for a polite way to tell her. "I... I withheld some information from you, hoping to spare you the pain, but, um..."

"Spit it out," she calmly said.

Cristoff hung his head. "You were right about Daniel, back when you had hallucinated inside your house."

Nicole was stunned. "Wh-What? Are you saying that the vision I had of Daniel and me..." She couldn't finish the sentence.

Cristoff was slowly nodding, sadness in his eyes. "That's what we were fighting about when you entered my house. I had confronted him and called his bluff."

"He actually admitted this?"

"He claimed it was the night his wife asked for a divorce. He said he was really down and, well, you get the picture." Cristoff reached out for her hand. "I'm very sorry, Nicole. I didn't want to bring back the bad memories, but I felt you should know before you start making amends with him. He's not worth it. He lied, to both of us. I don't care what type of problems he might cause, I've come to the conclusion we're better off severing all ties with him. You agree, don't you?"

Nicole let out a long, weary exhale, then softly said, "Yes and no. I sure would like to know why he keeps coming around? If we ban him from the ranch, we'll never find out."

"He claims it's because he feels guilty for taking advantage of you. He says that's the reason he offers you money."

"He's a bit too persistent for me to buy that excuse. I was even wondering if Philip had buried something of value on the property—something Daniel might want?"

Cristoff shook his head. "Naa. Good grief, Nicole, Daniel inherited enough wealth to keep him comfortable the rest of his life! Why would he need more?"

"True. I propose we wait him out. He's bound to slip up and give us a clue."

"Curiosity killed the cat." Cristoff studied her expression. "Can you handle seeing him again?"

Nicole shifted her gaze to the floor, fresh anger burning her cheeks red. "I'll handle it. Let's just hope he hasn't any need to return."

"In the meantime," Cristoff suggested, "you had better exercise that trigger finger. I've got some work to do. Call me if you need anything. Oh, and Nicole?" He smiled. "Why don't you go into town once in a while to lift your spirits?"

"Are you kidding?" she replied. "The local people still call me the Black Widow. The men avoid me, the women fear me."

"You have to interact, that's all. Speak to the women. As far as the men go, why don't you play a little poker with them? You've certainly seen enough winning hands in the past. You'd be great at it. Soon, you'd earn their respect."

Nicole gave a light, little laugh. "Maybe you're right, Cristoff. I just may do that one evening." He turned to go and she heard her stomach growl, prompting a sudden thought. "Cristoff?" she called. "Have you eaten yet?"

"No. Why?"

"Would you like to come inside the house and I'll fix us lunch?"

"Sure," he grinned, unaccustomed to such an invitation. He followed her lead back to the house where they spent the next hour discussing horses while they ate. Then afterwards, Cristoff thanked her and departed. Nicole ventured upstairs, opened a bureau drawer and rummaged under some clothes to retrieve her gun. "Yep," she said out loud, "I had better start practicing again." She took the small frame, semi-automatic weapon outside behind the stable to the edge of the woods and set up her targets, smiling to herself as she recalled the shocked look on the gunsmith's face when she had purchased the piece. It had only been two weeks after Philip's death. Cristoff had insisted she learn to protect herself, and he was right. He had even picked out the gun, a Walther PPK .380 caliber, costing just under four hundred dollars. It wasn't as large as a policeman's piece, but Nicole felt more comfortable with the smaller size. Cristoff had shown her how to use it, since he had several guns, himself, but he was not prepared for the expert display of marksmanship she exhibited at the very start. It was uncanny. She had a keen eye and steady hand, almost as if she had had previous experience. "Beginner's luck" she had called it. If Cristoff hadn't known her better, he'd have thought otherwise.

Nicole concentrated, then began firing. She liked the feel of the gun, liked the cool metal against her palm, the sense of security it gave her. All the troubles of the day melted away as she focused on the targets, and when the shooting was finished, she no longer felt anxious or afraid. More relaxed now, she put the gun away, played back her phone messages off the answering machine, and returned a few business calls. By the time she was able to exercise some of the horses, Cristoff had finished his chores and joined her.

CHAPTER FOUR

Justin was in a terrific mood this beautiful September evening. One week had passed since he had last seen Nicole, allowing him plenty of time to cool off. She had not returned to the beach since their little skirmish in the sand, which suited him fine.

Glancing at his watch, he stepped on the gas pedal. He had called Shane the minute he was off work to arrange for them to meet for a few drinks, and he wanted to be on time. Pulling into the parking area at the boarding house where Shane lived, he greeted his friend, who was patiently waiting outside.

"Why don't we walk?" Shane suggested. "The sun won't be setting for a while. Besides, we can flirt with the pretty women in the street." Justin smiled his approval.

The town of Coltsville, Virginia, had a good selection of pretty women; the problem was, they were far outnumbered by the amount of men, due to the fact that the lush countryside was a horseman's paradise. There were equine breeding farms everywhere, mostly Thoroughbred. Competitors constantly updated facilities to include the latest advancements, in hope they could remain one step ahead of neighboring farms.

Yet, despite such interest in modernization, the town remained an odd mixture of old and new. The streets were still cobblestone, with a dirt shoulder on each side for those who preferred traveling by horseback. Every time the state ordered the area to be paved, the townspeople banded together to protest until, eventually, the authorities just gave up. It wasn't a well-known town, anyway.

As for the variety of buildings, most of them still had hitching posts out front. Some of the shops and boarding houses were updated, but other property owners refused to cooperate; thus, visitors could find newly constructed buildings as well as historic ones. Remodeled boarding houses now contained small apartments instead of just rooms. There was even a livery stable for those who desired apartment living, but wanted to keep their horse nearby. A few old-time saloons, complete with piano player and poker games, dotted the street. Farther down, however, a modern bar took in its share of customers. Stranger still, was the local church—it was next door to the bar. Needless to say, many of the townspeople chose to travel to another place of worship. Other miscellaneous buildings included a pool hall, recreation center and gun shop.

Then, of course, there was Carla's—where a man could get good food, good lodging and whatever else he needed for the night. That "whatever else" prompted many local women to loudly complain to the sheriff in hopes of having the place shut down. It was the type of dispute that often pitted sister against brother, neighbor against neighbor. The sheriff and his deputy recorded the ladies' complaints until they added up to a certain count, then the two law officers raided the brothel. As usual, someone would tip off Miss Carla, and all illegal activity would temporarily stop. The sheriff would then apologize for any inconvenience before quickly departing the scene. Such was life in Coltsville. It suited Justin and Shane just fine.

"This is my kind of town," beamed the handsome blond, watching with mild amusement as a drunk was booted out of a nearby saloon. Laughter spilled onto the street as the unfortunate man fell face first into a large puddle of mud. Shane's eyes widened with excitement, but not because of the nearby spectacle. He elbowed Justin in the side, exclaiming, "Look! It's her horse... in front of the saloon."

Blue eyes zeroing in on the spot, Justin's muscles tensed beneath the cotton skyblue shirt. It was her horse, all right. He'd recognize that white Arabian anywhere. "Well, well, well..." He let the words trail off absently, his cold December eyes narrowing.

Shane flashed him a wary smile. "Now, just remember, ol' buddy, this is a public place. No point in settling your feud here. Just stay calm. Sooner or later, she has to come out of there."

Justin's step purposely quickened. "Do you really think I'm going to wait?" came the dry reply. Never mind the fact that he had no immediate strategy. He'd simply let her have the first word; he'd have the last, even if it meant embarrassing the little vixen in public. Justin's long-legged stride carried him swiftly through the saloon doors as he scanned the surroundings for Nicole. Very few people were at the bar, even fewer at the tables. A large crowd was gathered in the middle of the room, their backs facing the newcomers.

"Must be a big poker game," remarked Shane. Justin nodded in agreement, a bit peeved the elusive female was nowhere in sight. Secretly, he wondered if she was upstairs with another man. His expression turned hard. He motioned for Shane to follow his lead, and together they mingled into the crowd. He needed a distraction right now to give him time to calm down. Already, Justin's adrenalin was racing in his veins like wild fire. Perhaps if he watched the card game for a few minutes, he'd feel better. Squeezing between several people, the two friends were finally able to obtain full view of the players. Three distinguished men in their thirties were cursing aloud at another loss while a dark-haired princess pulled in her winnings.

"I don't believe it..." muttered Shane, emitting a soft groan.

That very instant, Nicole glanced up from the table and gasped. Velvet brown eyes widened with alarm as she met the icy blue stare of Justin, who was now taking great pleasure in watching the color drain from her face. It had happened so quickly, Nicole was unable to compose herself before the bystanders took notice. Their curious glances bounced between the two enemies as they pondered the reason behind Nicole's stunned expression.

She wanted to crawl under the table. Instead, she forced herself to look away from the newcomers and concentrate on the cards being dealt to her. This was only achieved with great difficulty, though; and now that her mind was focused on playing poker, it left no time to plan a proper defense.

Justin knew he had an advantage and smiled. It was all so very simple. He waited patiently until the current game was completed, when the defeated men announced their reluctance to engage in another round. Devilish eyes flashing, he nudged Shane. "The little lady's winning streak has just come to an end. What a perfect way to even the score."

"You can't be serious," Shane blurted, watching the flustered female. She had already guessed their intentions and now jumped to her feet for a hasty departure. In one huge stride, Justin's towering frame blocked her path, his large hand firmly clasping Nicole's upper arm.

"Leaving so soon?" he sneered in a gruff voice.

Nicole's mouth went dry. It was bad enough the man almost ruined her concentration during the poker game, but to have him this close, with all these people looking on...

"Take your hand off me, sir!"

She delivered the command like an old war admiral, bringing another smile to Justin's lips. The woman had guts, no doubt. She returned his penetrating stare, held it even after he had freed her, silently daring him to provoke her again. Loud whispers filled the room. Making light of the ordeal, Justin leaned closer to his victim, his face only inches from her own as he taunted, "Afraid your luck has run out, little lady? Is that why you are in such a hurry?"

Nicole stubbornly raised her chin. "Luck has nothing to do with it. Winning is an acquired skill, so is knowing when to quit. It would do you well to remember that, sir, considering the last time you challenged me... ah... I left you quite disabled." She calmly added, "I see you've recovered."

His reaction was immediate, his hand once again finding its mark on the soft flesh. "Oh, I've recovered, all right," he leered. "Come join me in the back room and I'll show you just how well I've recovered!" His promise was delivered so convincingly, several men lined up to bravely defend the young beauty.

Nicole merely smiled. "Why don't you show me, right here?"

Justin could have thrashed her. "Don't tempt me, you little wildcat!" With a menacing growl, he yanked her up to his face. Before another word left his lips, four men jumped him from behind, easily restraining the blond giant and simultaneously freeing Nicole. Shane stared at the floor to keep from laughing. Everyone else held their breath, quite shocked by Justin's behavior. He had always been such a polite fellow; yet, to see him now they would swear he was demonically possessed. All eyes locked upon the feuding couple.

Nicole suddenly smiled. The bickering had provided her with enough time to form a battle plan. "Well?" she purred. "Are we going to play poker or aren't we?"

Justin cocked his head in disbelief. Was she serious? Shaking off the hands which held him, the blond straightened his clothes, then threw Shane a curious glance. Shane simply nodded, watching as Nicole seated herself at the table. Neither of the men could fathom why she had changed her mind, unless, of course, she had planned on cheating. Nicole, however, was no cheat. She was quite capable of winning, as she had proven earlier. If the suckers wanted to lose their money, she'd gladly be the one to do the honor.

"All or nothing!" Justin snapped, jerking a chair out from under the table before promptly plopping down. The crowd closed in as Shane seated himself on the other side of Nicole. Like a brilliant beacon of light, the full realization of what was just said suddenly flashed across his mind. "All or n-nothing?" stammered Shane. "What do we have to bet with?"

"I have an antique diamond ring." Justin placed the piece of jewelry on the table while the crowd pushed and shoved to see. Shane recognized the ring; it had belonged to Justin's mother. Ever since her death, he carried it with him religiously, claiming it brought good luck. It was impossible to believe he would part with the sentimental object, and, spotting the smug look on the blond's face, Shane now understood he had no intention of parting with it. Justin was assuming he'd win. Why not? He'd won almost every game Shane had seen him play. He was an expert, one of the best. He was also calling Nicole's bluff by wagering such a valuable piece. This was his way of giving her an excuse to back out of the game. All she had to do was admit she couldn't match his offer. Of course, she'd have to suffer the embarrassment, which was what Justin truly wanted.

"And you, sir?" Nicole's gaze settled on Shane.

"Me?" he squeaked. "Uh, um, just a minute." Giving Justin a long, hard stare, he reluctantly pulled out an antique gold watch to set beside the ring. It had been his great grandfather's, passed down through the family. People "oohed" and "aahed" with excitement.

Nicole thought they were crazy. She uttered a nervous, little laugh before lowering her voice to a whisper. "Gentlemen, as you can see, I have only played for a short while tonight."

Just what I wanted to hear, thought Justin. Come on, honey. Back out. Revenge is so sweet!

Nicole continued. "I haven't enough winnings to wager against your possessions, especially when I'm sure they hold some sort of sentimental value." She paused, batting her long lashes to distract their attention while she studied each one's expression. The cocky grin on Justin's face brought new color to her cheeks. "Nevertheless, let it be noted that I am a woman who meets a challenge. I wager my earlier winnings plus my Arabian stallion, whom, if you have noticed, is worth a great deal of money." The crowd buzzed noisily. Shane cast Justin a look of utter disgust. The woman was actually sacrificing a purebred Arab—all because of some silly battle of pride! She hadn't the slightest inkling that Justin was an experienced cardsharp. Worse yet, no one in the audience clued her in. They all knew it, though—every last one of them. Shane and Justin played poker here, often. Fickle people, thought Shane, so quick to defend her earlier, yet so quick to let her lose now. He leaned across the table, vibrant green eyes throwing daggers at his friend while he growled, "May I have a word with you, in private?"

"No," came the quick reply. "Shuffle the cards, Shane." It was an order, a very curt order. Blue eyes pierced green.

Nicole's gaze shifted between the two. "Is there a problem, gentlemen?"

"You could say that," Shane muttered, ignoring a pointed jab from Justin's boot. "Are you positive you want to wager that stallion, Miss? He's a mighty fine piece of horseflesh."

Nicole looked coolly at Justin, noticing the flicker of amusement in his eyes. "I'm sure," she stubbornly replied. In a gesture of complete disapproval, Shane shook his head from side to side, then finally shuffled the cards. His long, frustrated exhale could be heard clear across the room as he slowly dealt the hand. Justin rocked back in his chair, smug as usual.

It felt like the longest game the three had ever played. Studying his cards, Justin tried not to let his itching for revenge preoccupy his mind. He honestly hadn't expected the woman to foolishly risk losing her stallion. Surely, the Arab was worth far more than their own wagers. Was she that positive she'd be the victor? He threw a look in her direction. If he could just read her expression, he might be able to guess her hand…

Nicole intercepted his thoughts in the nick of time. Like a pro, she mirrored the blond's stoic face. It was then Justin began to feel uneasy, scratching his chin and arms as the tension mounted. The crowd grew impatient, too, fidgeting and whispering while each player took their turn. Meanwhile, the minutes dragged on and on...

As the game finally drew to a close, Nicole was the first to give evidence of good fortune, a tiny smile tugging at the corners of her mouth as she took her last card. The time of reckoning had come. All eyes focused on the dark-haired princess. Very gingerly she placed a Straight upon the table, her soft brown eyes glancing sweetly at Justin's, in search of some indication of loss. To her dismay, she saw none. In fact, a distinct twinkling surfaced in the crystal blue eyes. A subtle grin played upon his lips. With great pleasure, he set his Full House down.

The crowd murmured excitedly. All eyes flew to the last player, who, up until now, had not even concentrated on his hand. Instead, Shane had been silently rehearsing the apology he'd give Nicole when Justin stole the prized stallion out from under her nose.

"Well?" prompted a man, his elbow gently nudging Shane's arm. Instantly, lucid green eyes darted to Justin. An awkward silence followed. No one moved. No one spoke. Nicole neatly folded her hands in her lap, fighting back tears. This wasn't supposed to happen. She wasn't supposed to lose. It was all a mistake, a terrible mistake.

"Well?" echoed Justin, his smug grin irritating his longtime friend. Shane took a deep breath, then slowly, very slowly, placed four kings next to the Full House. A loud cheer rang out in the room. Justin's eyes narrowed with disbelief. Shane innocently shrugged, then scooped up his winnings.

"That's my ring," snarled the blond, full of resentment. Surely, Shane would return it.

"I know ol' buddy," grinned Shane. "Don't tell me you're a sore loser?" He promptly dropped the piece of jewelry in his own pocket and pushed back his chair. It was all Justin could do to keep from wringing his neck, but he swiftly dismissed the notion as his mind turned to more pressing matters; a very depressed female needed consoling—or, at least he thought so.

"Excuse me," mumbled Nicole, unable to bear the embarrassment any longer. Never in her life had she made such a risky wager and now she was paying dearly for it. The General was much, much more than just a horse—he was the only living creature she could trust, the only source of comfort during troubled times. Even Cristoff could not understand her bond with the horse. Cristoff! What would he say when he found out? The thought brought new humiliation to Nicole as she hastened towards the door. Both men dashed after her.

"Wait!" Shane called, catching her arm as she prepared to unfasten the saddle on her once-prized stallion. "Let me take you home, Miss. You didn't expect me to win. It isn't right for you to walk the distance." A fresh wave of fury burned Nicole's cheeks, setting her eyes ablaze. She was about to retort a smart reply, when she caught sight of Justin's arrogant smile. The beast! He was actually enjoying this. Nicole turned back to the handsome, dark-haired man beside her and fluttered her long, sable lashes.

"I'd be honored if you'd escort me home, sir. After all, I do have to give you The General's pedigree papers." The sweet voice and cheerful smile boosted Shane's ego. He responded with all the joy a little boy feels when he's given a brand new toy, promising, "You won't regret your decision."

Justin, on the other hand, had grown hot under the collar at this turn of events. His lips parted to say something, then firmly drew together again. Why was he so mad? It shouldn't bother him that Shane was the one escorting her home. Hell, he didn't even like the woman anymore! Let Shane be the scratching post for the furious feline.

"See you later, Justin," Shane called as he stood near The General. Tossing the diamond ring towards the blond, he smirked. "Don't bother thanking me. After all, what are friends for, eh?"

Angry blue eyes ricocheted from the ring, to Nicole, now seated upon her horse, then to Shane. Still smarting from his recent loss, Justin was determined to find some way to ruin Shane's evening.

Suddenly, a shrill voice pierced the air. "Shane! Shane Anderson, you rascal!" Twisting around in the saddle, Nicole spotted a young girl dashing across the street, waving frantically. "I knew that was you!" she squealed.

"Uh, hi, Judy." There was an obvious lack of enthusiasm in Shane's voice while the girl scurried around The General, her voluptuous figure straining against her sharply cut dress. Heavy make-up covered her face, hiding whatever natural beauty she had been blessed with. It only took one look to discern her reputation, much to the dismay of Nicole.

"I know you're busy," the girl continued to address Shane while staring at Nicole, "but Miss Carla wants to know when you're coming back to..." She paused, eyeing the pretty woman on the white stallion. "back to... her house. She says things just aren't exciting without you, honey, and the girls are worried sick. Why have you stayed away so long, darlin'?" She squeezed his arm, her baby blue eyes pleading.

Justin couldn't resist jumping in, mimicking the female's sultry tone. "Yes. Why have you stayed away so long, darrrrlin'?" Shane flashed him a silent warning, but Justin ignored it. This was payback time. He pressed his luck and moved closer to The General, gently tugging on Nicole's sleeve before whispering, "He's polite with his manners, but quick with his hands. Better watch it!" His words had the desired effect. Nicole's eyes widened in alarm. To add the final touch, the blond gave her a knowing wink. The seed of suspicion was planted so easily, Justin almost felt guilty.

"Listen, Judy," Shane began, containing his frustration. "Why don't you run back to where you came from and tell Miss Carla I have other business to tend to." He gave her an irritated smile before removing her hand from his sleeve. Judy pouted, then glared at Nicole. "So. I see!" she said in a snippy tone. With a huff, she promptly whisked herself away, amidst beckoning whistles from other male admirers.

Shane uttered a nervous laugh as he turned back to the dark-haired princess. No sooner had he mounted behind Nicole, he sensed a change of mood; it was as if someone had placed a solid brick wall between them. Immediately, his eyes searched for Justin, but the blond had miraculously vanished. When he was about to mention this uncanny disappearance, Nicole swiftly dug her heels into The General's sides, forcing the steed to leap into a rolling canter. She was hoping he'd fall off. The fact that he didn't, told Nicole he was accustomed to riding. Too bad.

"Disappointed?" Shane shouted over drumming hooves.

Then he let go a boisterous laugh, interpreting her silence as quiet admiration for his skill. So, the little vixen wanted to unseat him, did she? He extended his arms to encircle her waist, clasping his hands together at her stomach. "A little extra security," he explained in her ear. He was daringly close now, his face in her hair, his chest firmly pressing against her back. A hot warmth spread up his thighs, surprising him, for he had never been so easily aroused by a stranger before. He pondered this new experience while The General was finally slowed to a brisk walk. Then he loosened his hold and asked, "You already know my name, sweetheart. Do you mind telling me yours?"

"I am not your sweetheart, Mr. Anderson," she said through clenched teeth. "My name is Nicole Tyler, and I am definitely not looking forward to handing over my stallion to you." The icy tone quickly shattered any hopes for the evening. Shane frowned. He wondered if she was the famous Black Widow, but quickly dismissed that thought; the widow was wealthy and wouldn't be in town playing poker, for sure!

"Perhaps we could make a deal?" he suggested, trying to appease her anger.

"A deal, Mr. Anderson? What type of deal do you have in mind?" She was already suspicious.

"For instance..." He hesitated. "You can keep The General at your place and, in return..."

"Yes, Mr. Anderson?"

He carefully chose his words. "And in return, I'll visit to ride him."

"Visit!" she retorted hotly. "You can't just come and visit me whenever you happen to feel like it!" At the sound of Nicole's outburst, The General jumped sideways, forcing Shane to increase the pressure of his hold on the young woman's waist. When his grip tightened, Nicole exploded with anger. "I do need to breathe, Mr. Anderson! Take your filthy hands off me!"

Shane was insulted. "Stop the horse!" he commanded, reaching around to pull back the reins. Nicole shrieked. He ignored her, swiftly dismounted, then jerked the young woman out of the saddle to stand her on the ground directly in front of him. Even with dusk settling in, she could plainly see his expression darkening to mirror his hostile mood. He stared at her in a fit of temper, a mysterious gleam in his cat-green eyes as his gaze boldly traveled over the slender figure.

For a moment, Nicole was truly afraid. She was completely alone with this audacious young man who was now struggling with some sort of inner conflict. She was struck by his sinister appearance, and wondered why she had never noticed it before; the jet-black hair, thick and wild, the emerald eyes glittering with devilish ardor so intense it brought goosebumps to her flesh.

"You know, Nicole..." he began in a deep, raspy voice.

"Miss Tyler," she corrected; then, changing her mind, "Mrs. Tyler."

"Pardon me," he mocked, "but which is it? Miss or Mrs.?"

"It's Mrs."

"Well, then... Mrs. Tyler," he continued, still unsure of her true marital status, "as I was saying... since you insist on complaining about the way I ride, I have decided we will finish our journey on foot. I'd hate to be labeled a 'pervert' or be accused of sexually assaulting you just because my hand happened to slip while your horse shied at his own shadow."

"If you remember correctly, Mr. Anderson," she pointed out, "this is no longer my horse. And he does not shy at his own shadow. As for your tainted reputation, sir, it seems to me you earned that long before I came into the picture!" Satisfied with her accusation, Nicole folded her arms in front of her chest, her fears suddenly forgotten. Shane folded his arms, also, and coolly studied the angry wildcat glaring back at him. All the cards were in his favor. If she wanted to argue, he could stay here all night. Nothing would please him more than spending an evening alone with such a passionate female.

This thought hadn't yet occurred to Nicole. She shifted her weight to the opposite leg, glanced nervously about and waited for the silence to be broken. The sky overhead grew darker and darker. Five more minutes passed.

Finally, it dawned on her that Shane was biding his time. The discovery of his clever scheme pushed her patience to the limit. "I suggest we complete our journey, Mr. Anderson," she flatly announced, noticing an impish grin flickering at the corners of his mouth.

"On horseback?" he quipped.

"No. On foot."

"Well then, I hope we don't have far to travel. It's going to be pitch black soon and I still have to make it back to my place."

"If worse comes to worse, I'll drive you," she replied.

He gave her a genuine smile. "I had a feeling you'd say that." Although Nicole was not thrilled with walking the rest of the way home, at least she didn't have to worry about Shane's wandering hands. Hadn't Shane's friend warned her about this? Her curiosity got the better of her, prompting her to ask, "What was your friend's name, Mr. Anderson—the fellow with the blond hair?"

"Justin. Justin MacFierson. The two of us grew up together. He's like a brother to me, though recently I've begun to wonder if I really know him as well as I thought I did."

"Why do you say that?" she queried.

"It just wasn't like him to wrestle with you on the beach. Usually he's a real gentleman. I've never seen him so riled up over a female." He grew silent, allowing Nicole the option of pursuing the topic. She chose not to, and took a firmer hold on The General's reins as he pranced eagerly with anticipation at the familiar sight of Nicole's home. She absently glanced at the spot where her Desert Wind Arabians sign usually stood; it was in the barn now, getting repainted.

Shane scanned the surroundings as they continued, noticing how small the modestly built house looked amidst all the acreage. The large, empty pastures seemed lush and well kept; yet, try as he might, Shane could not picture Nicole maneuvering farm equipment around the premises. That was a man's job, which, to his dismay, probably meant she was married. He dwelled on the thought until they reached her home, where Nicole tied The General to a hitching post.

"It will only take a minute to get his papers."

"If it's not too much trouble," he said, "could I have a glass of water?"

Nicole hesitated, then forced a tiny smile. "Sure. I'll be back in a flash." She had no intention of inviting him in. Realizing such, Shane quickly added, "These mosquitoes are awful, aren't they?" and started slapping his arms for emphasis.

"Yes, they are," she agreed, her smile widening as she continued inside the house, leaving one frustrated male admirer standing outside. She had a change of heart, however, when she noticed he was still slapping his arms and neck after she had left. Albeit reluctantly, she walked over and held the screen door open, asking him in. "Here you are," she said, handing him his drink. "I have to go upstairs to retrieve The General's papers. I won't be long."

He watched her disappear up the steps, then slowly took in his surroundings. Her feminine touch was everywhere, from the soft pastel blue walls to the vase of bright yellow roses on the dining room table. Setting his glass down on the coffee table, he walked around the room, studying ornamental arrangements and several interesting paintings. Beautiful pictures of Arabian stallions came alive on her walls, some prancing, some fighting, but all in motion; not one standing peacefully. He found that a bit odd. Still engrossed in the artwork, he never heard the young woman approach from behind.

"Here you are," she said in a lively tone, scaring the daylights out of him. He jumped, uttering a curse which rather amused Nicole. In her outstretched hand were The General's papers.

"Mrs. Tyler," he began, "I'm quite concerned about this whole ordeal. Your husband will probably get very upset when he finds out I have your horse." He held his breath, waiting for her reply. This would settle once and for all the question of her marital status.

"Oh, you needn't worry about my husband," she answered coolly. "There isn't very much he can say about it." Her eyes nervously swept the room.

"Still," persisted Shane, "I wouldn't want him to take out his anger on you." He watched as she went deathly still, the color leaving her face.

His words had brought to mind her horrible past, those certain memories which she now tried desperately to forget. A faraway look emanated from her eyes as she gazed hypnotically past him. "My husband is dead, Mr. Anderson," she stated coldly. "He was murdered last year."

Shocked, Shane quickly apologized. He felt the urge to reach out and comfort her in some way, but refrained when he saw the lack of emotion in her eyes. It was very strange—very strange, indeed. It piqued his curiosity but he dared not inquire. He had more manners than that. Nicole, however, decided to enlighten him.

"No need to apologize, Mr. Anderson. I don't grieve for him because our marriage was a living hell."

He had no response to that sudden statement. In fact, he was feeling very uncomfortable at the moment. Change the subject, he told himself before uttering, "Do you run this ranch by yourself?"

"No. Cristoff lives on the premises. He's my ranch hand. He was also my husband's drinking buddy and close friend. After Philip's death, I kept him on the payroll. It's a small Arabian ranch and only needs a few people to take care of it."

At the mention of Cristoff's name, a look of recognition flashed in Shane's eyes, but he didn't inquire further about the man. He was more interested in her husband. "You said your spouse's name was Philip?" he pursued.

"Yes."

"William Philip Tyler, the Third?"

"That's correct."

Shane felt his throat constrict; his skin broke out in goosebumps. This was the Black Widow! This was the lady who instilled fear into the hearts of men. To think, Justin had thrown her to the ground! He gaped at the young beauty, his palms clammy with sweat. Although he had read the story of Philip's murder in the newspaper, all funeral pictures of the widow had shown her with a black veil over her face; thus, he never truly knew what she looked like. Now that he realized who he was dealing with, he had no intention of owning the white stallion. Who knows what path of revenge she might take? He began hunting for some excuse to give the horse back, and while he did so, reality suddenly set in. Wait a minute, he thought. If Philip was this woman's husband, why didn't she reside in a mansion? After all, Philip Tyler had been enormously rich. Where was all the wealth? Perhaps she had made up this story to scare him.

"I know what you're thinking," Nicole perceived. "Where's all the money, right?" A smile lit her face, as if somehow Shane had magically flipped a switch. "Mr. Anderson, if I was so terribly rich, do you honestly think I'd have brought it to your attention by disclosing the name of my husband? The truth is, Philip was extremely wealthy, but he also was a compulsive gambler. He squandered much of his money and willed the rest of his estate to his brother, except for this ranch. So you see, I am not wealthy at all." She spoke as if a weight had been lifted from her shoulders, yet she couldn't fathom why she had felt compelled to have even told him. It wasn't like her to blab personal information. She nervously glanced towards the window. "You had better be going. It's getting dark outside."

"I can't take your stallion, Mrs. Tyler," he confessed. "I would feel just awful."

"You won him fair and square," she argued, an odd twinkle in her eye. "You had better hurry. The General gets quite impatient sometimes."

"But your saddle and bridle—"

"You can return them to me when it's convenient for you." She motioned him towards the door, but Shane was reluctant. The knife of guilt was wedged tightly between his ribs. Nicole wasn't the spoiled ball of fire Justin had painted her to be. She was an honestly kind woman—a little spirited, yes, but that could be worked on, sort of like tarnished silver. She wasn't to be feared, either. The townspeople were a bunch of idiots, and he had been an idiot to have believed them.

"I'll bring your equipment by tomorrow, then," he promised, knowing in his heart he'd also give back the stallion; he no longer desired the animal. All he wanted now was to become better acquainted with the dark-haired beauty.

Nicole simply nodded, then closed the door behind the young man and let go a small chuckle. A sadistic smile turned the corners of her mouth as she listened for the first thud from outside. She was not disappointed. Slinking to the window, she carefully peeked out at the astonished man who lay sprawled, flat on his back, in the dirt. Like an undaunted hero, he bravely climbed aboard the white steed for a second battle of wits. "You fool," laughed Nicole, shaking her head. Intelligence can master most animals, but The General knew every trick in the book. There was simply no way he'd tolerate a stranger on his back, unless Nicole was also astride. Of course, Shane was just finding this out. He sailed through the air a second time, landing quite hard on his side. Nicole winced, unable to allow the spectacle to continue.

She threw open the front door and casually leaned against the frame. "Problem, Mr. Anderson?" she quipped in a dry tone.

Emerald eyes glared back from the ground. It wasn't until he detected the sarcasm in her voice, it dawned on Shane why she had insisted he take the horse. "You damn well know there's a problem!" he spat, getting to his feet and brushing the dirt from his clothes.

Nicole played coy. "Whatever do you mean?"

Stifling the urge to give her a good spanking, Shane marched up to the raven-haired beauty and accused, "You knew all along that your horse wouldn't let me ride him."

"Actually, I wasn't sure," she admitted. "However, since you have excellent horsemanship abilities, I truly thought you could handle him. I hope you weren't hurt?"

"I'll be okay," he replied. "I've been pitched before. You'd think I'd have learned how to land by now." His comment caused her to chuckle, and he finally joined in. "I sailed through the air like a human cannonball, didn't I?"

"Yes," she laughed. "Yes, you did." She picked up her purse. "I'll drive you home after I put The General in his stall."

He handed her the folded pedigree papers. "I guess I won't be needing these, but I will hold you to your end of the bargain. You're going to have to make this up to me, you know."

"I can just imagine," she said under her breath as they walked her horse back to the stable. Once inside, Shane gave a low whistle. "This is some barn," he said, eyeing the numerous immaculate stalls.

"It is lovely, isn't it?" she said proudly. "Cristoff and I work hard to keep it looking this way. The breeding barn is attached at the far end, then a corridor leads from it back to my house. So, I don't even have to walk outside to get here, if I don't want to. The corridor comes in handy during heavy snows."

"Is business good these days?" he asked.

"This is the off season. We're the busiest from April to July. Everyone wants a Spring foal, you know. Some don't mind a Summer foal; then there are a few clients who don't care what time of year the babies are born." She finished with The General and beckoned for Shane to follow her to her car, where he assisted in removing the car cover from the shiny blue automobile. Shane emitted another low whistle upon seeing the vehicle.

"Wow," he breathed, staring at the 1968 Shelby GT350 Mustang. He ran his hand lightly over the exterior, letting it skim the hood until it finally came to rest on the two low scoops near the front edge. He turned to Nicole. "You and I have a lot in common."

"Well, don't just stand there, silly," she smiled. "Get in." She unlocked his door and settled herself in the driver's seat.

"How come I've never seen this car in town?" he questioned.

"I usually ride my horse to town or take my farm truck.

Cristoff borrowed the truck tonight, that's why we're taking the Shelby."

"How fast have you pushed it?"

"The max—125." She glanced over at him. "It scared me half to death."

He laughed, shaking his head. This girl liked to live dangerously. "Next thing you'll be telling me is that you can shoot a gun." No sooner had the words left his mouth, he wanted to kick himself. Nicole grew silent, unsure of his intended meaning. Was he insinuating she had killed Philip? "Uh," stammered Shane. "What I meant was, you seem to be skilled at things women aren't too knowledgeable about."

She relaxed, sinking deep into her seat. "I have many interests," she explained, before changing the subject. They spent the rest of the journey discussing a safer topic—horses. She discovered Shane's father operated a Thoroughbred farm, which was how he acquired his riding ability. Knowing how Thoroughbred owners usually thumb their noses at the Arabian horse, Nicole was surprised by Shane's interest in her ranch. She was even more surprised by his admiration for the breed, and finally decided he was faking interest to score points with her. Then he said a curious thing. "I miss the Arabian business."

Nicole was puzzled. "What did you say?" she asked.

"Oh, um... I, uh, miss the Arabian horse shows. I always attended them when they were local, just to watch those beautiful creatures prance around with their tails held high." He pointed towards the left. "Turn here. This is the boarding house where I live. Want to come in?"

Nicole pulled up near the front door. "No thanks. Perhaps another time."

"We haven't discussed how you'll compensate for keeping your horse," he reminded her. "I was thinking maybe we could have a picnic together, tomorrow?"

A picture of Judy, Miss Carla's employee, flashed across her mind. Nicole suddenly remembered what type of man Shane Anderson really was. When he had been with Justin on the beach, he had stalked her, hadn't he? "Mr. Anderson," she began, "excuse me for speaking my mind, but how do you think it would look for me to be seen on a picnic with a man of your character? Especially after only one year since my husband's death?"

Shane's jaw dropped. "Which are you more concerned with, Mrs. Tyler—your reputation, or mine?" Upon hearing her utter a nervous little laugh, he suggested, "All right. If it would make you feel better, we'll have a chaperone, then." He stepped out of the car, closed the door, and leaned inside the open window. "You can ask Cristoff to accompany you."

"But he can't," she exclaimed. "I'm sending him to an auction tomorrow to purchase more Arabians."

"Well, then it's settled," he smiled, straightening up again. He turned to leave. "I'll have Justin come along with me to pick you up at noon. Dress comfortably. I'd like to go to the beach. Oh, and... fried chicken will do just fine. Until tomorrow!"

"But, but..." Nicole tried in vain to get his attention to continue the discussion, but he had already thrown open the door to his building and disappeared, and she had no intention of following him. "Oo! Men!" she screamed, pounding the steering wheel with the palm of her hand. She zoomed out of the parking lot, unaware how lucky she had been to have refused Shane's invitation to join him inside.

For, the moment Shane's hand touched the doorknob to his apartment, he discovered it had been unlocked. A light burned brightly in the kitchen, although he distinctly recalled turning it off prior to leaving.

"Good evenin' ol' friend," slurred a familiar voice. Shane ventured into the lit room to confront Justin, who sat tall in his chair, arms folded across his chest, eyes narrowing. On the table stood a bottle of tequila, three quarters empty.

"What are you doing here, drunk as a skunk?" Shane demanded.

"I can hold my liquor," answered Justin as he slowly got to his feet and advanced towards his friend. "That was a great game of poker you played tonight." Irritation laced his comment.

"Oh, so that's what this is about," retorted Shane. "You've come to punch me out for spoiling your plans for revenge. Well, I had no idea I was going to win the game. You usually beat me!" He reached for the tequila, gulping down some artificial courage. The last thing he wanted was to tangle with the blond, especially over a woman. It was simply ridiculous.

Running his fingers absently through his hair, Justin muttered, "I guess you're right. I don' know what's wrong with me. I'm jus' edgy as all hell. That woman practically laughed in my face when she rode off with you."

"Nicole?"

"Is that her name?"

Shane nodded, taking a seat before urging Justin to do the same. "You won't believe this, Justin. Nicole is Nicole Tyler, the Black Widow." The blond's eyes lit up as his friend continued. "But she's not like any of those stories we've heard."

"Do go on. I'm all ears." Elbows on the table, his chin resting on the heels of his hands, Justin listened intently while Shane relayed the evening's events. It was obvious from his friend's tone of voice, he was in awe of the young beauty—which was no simple feat, considering Shane had so many notches in his bedpost it was difficult for him to remain interested in a woman longer than a few hours. "So you like her, eh?" Justin challenged.

Shane hesitated before his reply. "She's okay... for now. We're taking her on a picnic tomorrow."

Justin raised a brow. "We?"

"Sure. She owes me for giving me a bum deal. I told you I couldn't ride her horse, so, instead, I asked to go on a picnic."

"But you said 'we'."

"Well... um, she insisted on a chaperone." He half mumbled the sentence, a little embarrassed. Justin roared with laughter, clutching his stomach as he did so. When he had finally settled down, he queried, "What about her ranch hand? Why couldn't he go with you? What was his name?"

"I never mentioned his name," remarked Shane. "I

forgot what it was." He deliberately lied, but Justin wouldn't remember, not after drinking most of the tequila. "So, tell me... will you go with us?"

"A chaperone, huh?" the blond grinned. She'd definitely need one with Shane. Although Justin was still a bit miffed at the girl, he suddenly felt protective of her virtue. The idea of his buddy bedding her disturbed him deeply. "Sure," he answered. "I'll go."

"Even with a hangover?" persisted Shane.

"I might be mean as hell," he warned.

"I don't care. Just don't open your mouth, then. I don't want anything to spoil this outing."

Justin eyed him carefully. "If I didn't know you better, Mr. Anderson, I'd say you're smitten with this young lady."

"Not a chance," came the denial. "She's like any other woman, and all women are like sports cars—the minute you see one, you can't wait to jump into the driver's seat and take 'em for that first ride." A wicked smile on his lips, Shane held up the bottle of liquor in a toasting gesture, then swallowed a few gulps while his friend coolly looked on.

CHAPTER FIVE

The morning of the picnic found Nicole up at dawn; she hadn't slept very well and was growing more nervous by the hour. To pass time, she exercised a few Arabians, but even they sensed her anxiety.

"Daggonit!" she yelled as the dapple-gray stallion beneath her grabbed the bit between his back teeth. Frantically, she tried to seesaw it out of its position, which proved useless. The powerful horse galloped out of control across the grass, throwing in a couple of dangerous bucks amidst his thundering strides. Sheer determination kept her on board. With one last effort, she gathered the reins, sat deep in the saddle and pulled his nose in towards his enormous chest to cut off his wind. A sigh of relief passed her lips when the long strides began to shorten. Within minutes she had brought him to a halt. "Can't trust the opposite sex, whether it's man or beast," she breathed angrily.

"Oh, tut-tut," Cristoff reprimanded, coming to her side. "King Arthur merely took advantage of your carelessness."

"Carelessness?" fussed Nicole. "I wasn't aware of any carelessness, and I would appreciate you using his real name instead of King Arthur."

"My girl," Cristoff explained, "how can I call him by his Arabian name when I can barely get all those syllables out of my mouth?"

His wish was granted and Nicole smiled. She quietly apologized, then dismounted. Together, they walked the horse in large circles to cool him off. Cristoff gave her a curious look. "What's bothering you, Nicole? It's not like you to be this nervous."

"I've got a date with two fellows today," she complained. "We're supposed to go on a picnic."

"How'd you get yourself into that one?" he grinned.

"Trust me. You don't want to know." Sheepishly, she looked down at the ground, unable to tell him how she had foolishly wagered The General in a poker game.

"So you have a date." He studied her for a minute, deep in thought. Of course, he wanted her to date again; she had been alone for a whole year. Yet, he had grown close to her during that time and now felt like a protective brother watching over her shoulder. "Who are these guys?" he blurted, knowing it was none of his business.

Nicole didn't mind. She was glad he cared. "One of them is our new neighbor, Justin MacFierson. The other is Shane Anderson." At the mention of their names, Cristoff slapped his knee and whooped and hollered so loud Nicole winced. Then he laughed and laughed and laughed, until she insisted he explain his crazy antics.

"Oh, my girl," he chuckled. "You don't know what you're in for! I've known those two since school days."

"Tell me you're kidding," she said with a stone face.

"It's the truth. I can't believe it, myself! Justin? Our new neighbor?" Suddenly, Nicole remembered the flash of recognition in Shane's eyes when she had mentioned Cristoff's name. Why hadn't he told her he knew the ranch hand? She questioned Cristoff about Shane's odd behavior.

"Well, that's a long story," he replied. "To sum it up, Shane is very possessive about Justin. You see, Shane is an only child; he looks to Justin as a brother. Justin and I used to ride the horses at Shane's father's farm. We went after school on a regular basis to exercise them. When Justin started spending more time with me, Shane became jealous and convinced his father to dismiss me. Justin and I eventually drifted apart. There were no hard feelings; we just went our separate ways. It's a shame I have to go to the auction today. I'd really like to see Justin, again."

"Perhaps I can keep them here a while," she offered. "Can I trust them, Cristoff?"

"Justin, yes. Shane... he's a horse of another color. He's unpredictable. I've spoken to him in town, even invited him over to my house, but he always has some excuse why he can't come. Maybe he feels awkward around me because of the past. He's a likeable guy, though. I don't hold any grudge against him. Heck, we were all so young then, 14 or 15 years old. My family moved to Florida soon after, but I decided to come back here to live."

"He seems pretty nice," she stated. "Actually, I thought Justin was the unpredictable one."

Cristoff gave her an odd look. "How so?"

"I'd rather not go into the details right now."

"Okay, but do me a favor, Nicole? Don't mention my name to Justin. I'd like to surprise him."

"I understand." She glanced at her watch. "Oh, dear. I'd better grab a shower and cook the chicken. Are you fixed okay for the auction?"

He nodded. "I'll get the best deal I can. You go ahead and run inside. I'll take care of King Arthur, here." She thanked him before running back to the house. Cristoff watched her leave, his mind working overtime. If he could get Justin interested in Nicole, there was a good chance she'd conquer her fear of intimacy. He couldn't have picked a better man for the job. Justin was the complete opposite of Philip. He was mild-mannered, polite, and never raised his voice—at least that's how he behaved back when Cristoff knew him. Hopefully, he hadn't changed.

Nicole thought differently, but didn't want to be the one to destroy Cristoff's image of his longtime friend. She had been wise to keep her mouth shut about her recent confrontations with the blond. Hearing Cristoff speak so highly of the guy, she did feel less apprehensive in regards to today. She even hummed a song while she cooked the chicken. Afterwards, she hurried through her shower, then dawdled over her wardrobe, eventually deciding on a beautiful lavender top with a scoop neckline and a drawstring that crisscrossed up the middle. When she tried it on, however, she groaned with dismay. It was too tight. "Too bad," she muttered, yanking on the string to force the material to meet. It would have to do since she had forgotten to do the laundry. She pulled on a pair of dungaree shorts, then glanced at the full length mirror.

When was the last time she had really looked at herself? Was this the same person who, up until a few minutes ago, had been covered in dirt and smothered with the scent of horses and leather? Color flooded her cheeks as she stared at the provocative reflection. A tinge of excitement rushed over her as she recalled the admiring look Shane had given her yesterday. Not having had much experience with dating during her teenage years, she truly was unaccustomed to such attention. Philip had been her first and only love. His name brought tears to her eyes, not tears of remorse, but tears of anger. He had wasted two years of her life; and in those two short years he had managed to undermine her self confidence, make her feel undesirable and completely strip her of her dignity. "I hope you're rotting in hell, Philip," she mumbled.

A knock on the door sounded, snapping her out of the trance. Grabbing a hairbrush, she took a few last strokes at the long, thick hair. Then she charged down the staircase, snatched the cooler of food and blanket, and raced to the door, throwing it open with such haste she nearly collided with her guest. Breathless, she gaped at the towering figure of Justin. He seemed just as surprised as she, especially to be received in such a reckless manner. Actually, if he didn't have such a nasty hangover, he would have found the ordeal quite amusing.

"Where's Shane?" Nicole spouted, now feeling awkward.

"He's coming," drawled Justin. "He's parking his car around the side." Eyes glued to the feminine temptress, he watched the rapid rise of her chest as it strained against the confining material. Noticing the path his gaze had taken, Nicole remarked wryly, "Didn't your mother ever tell you it's impolite to stare?"

Two blue eyes captured hers. "My mother never met a girl like you," he said slowly, steadily, embarrassing Nicole to the roots of her hair. To her horror, her mind went completely blank. Had it not been for Shane's sudden appearance, she would have stood there like an idiot, absolutely speechless.

"Afternoon, Nicole," smiled Shane. "You don't mind if I call you Nicole, do you?" Catching sight of her, he drew in his breath and exhaled a soft whistle. "You sure do look pretty today." His green eyes scanned the skimpy attire, lapping up every last detail. Then he remembered his manners and reached for the cooler. "Here, let me carry that. Which way are we heading?"

"Over there," Nicole pointed. "Beyond those trees. We can walk the distance." She had closed the front door and started down the steps when she saw Justin's hand reach out for the blanket.

"I'll take that," he offered, politely.

"I don't mind carrying it," Nicole answered, stepping onto the ground.

Justin kept pace with her, his fingers still wrapped around the soft fabric. He gave a small tug. "I insist."

Nicole tugged back. "I said I don't mind."

"But, I'd like to help."

"I appreciate the offer," she snapped. "Would you mind letting go?"

"You don't have to get all fired up over it. I was only being a gentleman."

At that, Nicole had a good laugh.

Shane grew uneasy, positive now another fight was brewing, so he tried to change the subject. "How many horses do you own, Nicole?" The couple, however, paid no attention to him, and to Shane's dismay, Justin still kept a firm grip on the cursed blanket.

“What’s so funny?” the blond demanded, stopping in midstride. Since Nicole’s hand was also on the item, she, too, was forced to stop.

She began to pull against him. “You! You big ape,” she scoffed. “I can’t believe you’d call yourself a gentleman. You don’t know the meaning of the word.”

“Oh, I don’t?” he growled, giving a good yank.

She yanked back. “No. You don’t!”

His head throbbing now, Justin jerked the blanket forward, and Nicole with it. She reciprocated the action with such strength, he discovered he had underestimated her. In a matter of seconds a tug o’ war ensued, with both parties hurling accusations at one another. Shane would have stepped between them, but the blanket held that unfortunate position. All he could do was shout above them, his own temper rising. “For Pete’s sake!” he yelled. “Give her the blanket, Justin.”

“Gladly!” came the sudden reply, with Justin releasing his grip at the exact moment Nicole made a furious yank. A tiny gasp caught in her throat as the surprised woman toppled backwards, her arms now flailing wildly as she attempted to regain her balance. Unable to do so, her bottom smacked the ground, hard, sending tiny splinters of pain up her back. Shane grimaced in sympathy.

Justin merely picked up the blanket, extended his hand to help her rise, and stated, “If you had just given me the damn thing, you wouldn’t have been hurt.”

With that, Nicole flew at him, fingers curled to scratch out his eyes. She would have reached him, too, had it not been for Shane’s strong arm snaking forward to wrap around her waist. The force of impact nearly knocked the breath from her, but she still made a valiant effort to continue, her arms and legs pumping furiously to free herself, causing Shane to drop the cooler. Swinging her around to face him, Shane had no option but to pin her arms behind her back and press the young lady against him to hinder the use of her knees as weapons. “Stop it, Nicole,” he gently said. “This is supposed to be a picnic, not a midday brawl.”

"It's his fault!" she accused, flinging her head in Justin's direction. "I'm not going anywhere with that macho pig."

"Fine with me!" boomed the blond, throwing down the blanket with haste. "I can think of a hundred better things I'd rather be doing! Why don't you drive me home, Shane? Then you can return for your little rendezvous with the Ice Princess."

"Oo!" fumed Nicole, squirming with renewed strength, forcing Shane to tighten his hold in order to subdue her. She could now feel the heat from his body penetrating his clothes and silently glanced up, startled to find excitement flickering in his eyes. She suddenly had a change of heart. "Wait, Justin!" she called, almost frantic. "Don't go. I'm sorry. I didn't have much sleep last night and I'm... I'm low on patience, that's all. I shouldn't have taken it out on you." She held her breath and waited, counting the seconds. Slowly, Shane eased his hold, his disappointment clearly visible. Justin turned and approached the young woman, not at all puzzled by the change of events. Nicole's voice had betrayed her. He knew she was deathly afraid of being alone with Shane, although he wasn't quite sure why she had reacted so strongly.

"All right," he said with hesitation. "I'm sorry, too. I have a killer headache. Truce?" He held out his hand.

"Truce," she agreed, simply nodding to avoid any further physical contact. She then walked to where the blanket laid, picked it up and handed it to him, smiling as she did so. She decided to be nice, even if it killed her. After all, didn't Cristoff say Justin was the safer choice?

"You two are going to drive me nuts," muttered Shane as he picked up the cooler. He threw Justin a look of utter exasperation before they started on their journey once again.

Walking between the two men, Nicole grew apprehensive. Gone was the feeling of adventure and the thrill of the unexpected. Now she experienced a dire need to be back home, safe within the walls of her own fortress. Why, oh, why had she agreed to this stupid picnic? She wanted to kick herself.

"Hey, look!" Shane exclaimed, veering off towards a tree.

"A frisbee. Good. We can use it on the beach." He picked up the flat white disk and rejoined them. Nicole recognized the object as belonging to Cristoff. She had seen him tossing it around with one of his girlfriends recently.

"I think that belongs to my ranch hand," she stated. "He won't mind if we borrow it, although, truth be told, I haven't thrown one of those things in years."

"Nothing to it," Shane smiled. "I can teach you. I used to spend hours throwing these, didn't I, Justin?"

"Yeah," the blond grunted. "And I used to spend hours getting them back down from the trees." They all chuckled at his comment, easing the long period of tension between them. At the pleasant sound of Nicole's laughter, both men tried to entertain her with more humorous stories of their youth, succeeding to the point where it caused a stitch in her side and she had to beg them to stop making her laugh.

"You could be a comedy team, you know," she grinned, placing the blanket on the sand and beginning to unload the cooler. Much to the men's delight, she pulled out two bottles of wine. Actually, Justin was a bit surprised. Drinking with two strangers did not fit Nicole's image. Perhaps she needed it to help her relax. Whatever the reason, she was already pouring the sweet liquid into several plastic cups and handing it to them.

"A toast," Shane announced, raising his cup high in the air. "To our new friendship."

"Friendship," repeated Justin while he watched Nicole. She silently smiled, raised her beverage, then took several large swallows of wine. Justin sipped his, the headache prompting a decision to remain quite sober.

"I hope you're both hungry," she said. "We have plenty of food."

"Don't say it too loud," warned Shane. "We'll have swarms of insects here in no time." He had no sooner finished the sentence when a large dragonfly appeared from out of the blue, buzzed noisily above them, then darted near Nicole's hair. When Justin's hand protectively shot forward to shoo it away,

Nicole visibly flinched, crossing her arms in front of her face in self-defense. "You scared me," was all she said, quickly handing out several pieces of chicken. But Justin was not so easily fooled. He glanced at Shane, who had also noticed her odd behavior, and the two of them exchanged knowing looks. They watched Nicole down the rest of her wine and refill the cup to the brim, nearly spilling it in her haste. To say she was nervous was an understatement. Feeling sorry for her, Justin came to the young woman's rescue by starting a lively conversation centering on the pros and cons of the Thoroughbred industry. From that point on, talk flowed freely amongst the trio.

"I understand Shane's father has a wonderful breeding business," Nicole said to the blond. "Shane's an excellent rider. Do you ride, Justin?" She was baiting him, wondering if he'd be honest. She already knew he rode. Cristoff had told her that much.

"Sure," came the reply. "I used to ride for Shane's father."

Nicole smiled. "How interesting. Did you ride often?"

"When I was a teenager I rode after school."

"That doesn't leave much time for a social life, does it? Most boys are more concerned with hanging around with their friends; unless, of course, your friends also rode for Shane's father?" She finished her piece of chicken and casually glanced at Shane, who shifted uneasily on the blanket.

"A lot of our friends rode for my dad," Shane interjected before Justin had a chance to answer. "Justin was the best, though. He could ride English or Western."

"Oh, really?" Nicole was impressed.

"I gave up Western riding," Justin added, finishing his food. "I wanted to get into jumping, you see."

"And did you?"

"To some extent."

Shane quickly cut in. "Tell her why you stopped."

As Nicole refilled their cups she noticed an annoyed look cross Justin's face.

"I, uh, needed to spend more time on my school work," he replied.

"School work, hell!" Shane laughed, spitting a mouthful of wine into the sand. "You were too busy chasing girls."

Justin scowled at the untimely remark and sipped his drink. Nicole let a few giggles escape, her eyes darting from one man to the other. Obviously, teasing was part of the bond between them. She didn't believe Justin was truly angry with his friend. To play it safe, though, she politely changed the subject to a more impersonal level, amazed to discover she was actually enjoying their chitchat. The alcohol had relaxed her so completely she was rambling on as if she had known them all her life.

Shane didn't mind. He stared at the bewitching beauty while she spoke, still unable to comprehend why he was so attracted to her. After all, he had seen many beautiful women in his time. Yet, when those fiery brown eyes captured his own… Shane shifted his gaze towards the ocean to ease his carnal thoughts. The wine was rapidly diminishing whatever control he had over basic urges, making him wish he'd never suggested Justin accompany him on this outing. If he could just find some way to get rid of his friend for an hour… This would take some thought, and Shane could not think properly while being talked to, so he politely excused himself to attend to some necessary bodily function up in the woods.

The minute he left, Justin took advantage of the situation to confront Nicole about a more personal matter. "Your husband," he began, knowing this was a touchy subject. "You must miss him terribly."

Nicole froze, the alcohol dulling her senses. Had she heard him correctly? "Pardon?" she asked.

"Your husband," he repeated. "I suppose you're still grieving over him?"

She blinked in surprise. "Why ever would you bring that up?"

Justin stared off in the distance, then calmly stated, "You didn't answer my question, Nicole. Do you still grieve for him?"

"That's very personal, Justin. I don't believe I owe you an

answer." She spoke in a clipped tone, but he expected such. Not one to beat around the bush, he finally cupped her chin in his hand, forcing her to look him in the eye as he slowly commented, "I know he beat you, Nicole."

It would have been easier if he had just shot her through the heart. The blow was staggering. Her face turned blood red, tears filling her eyes, and all this in a matter of seconds. Jerking away from his grasp, she quickly jumped to her feet, opened her mouth for a smart reply, and promptly lost her balance, nearly toppling onto the various items of food. Apparently, she had misjudged her consumption of wine. Had it not been for Justin's swift reflex, she would have most likely have injured herself. As it was, the blond caught her during the first sign of wobbling and now held her against him, his hand softly stroking the long, dark hair. "I'm sorry," he whispered in her ear. "I'm so sorry to bring it up, Nicole. But when you flinched, earlier..." He drew in a deep breath to hold his own emotions in check. "You covered up for it, Nicole. You said I had scared you and you laughed it off."

The young woman in his arms could not believe what she was hearing. How on earth could a stranger be so forward as to discuss her personal life so openly? The nerve of him! Embarrassed to her toes, Nicole shoved the blond backwards, startling him. "Don't you ever touch me again!" she warned, eyes ablaze. Justin wanted to take the discussion a step further, but noticed Shane jogging towards them.

"Did I miss something?" Shane shouted, halting at the blanket to study the expression on Nicole's face. He could see she was furious. Neither Justin, nor the elusive woman honored him with a reply. Instead, Nicole wordlessly put the remaining food away. "Don't tell me you're leaving?" Shane persisted.

"No," she finally said, picking up the frisbee and handing it to him. She gave him a generous smile, a smile that clearly told him whatever had taken place between his friend and Nicole had definitely been to his advantage. "Teach me to throw, will you, Shane?" she purred, in the sexiest voice he had ever heard. "My pleasure," he beamed, taking her hand to lead her onto the sand.

Justin stood and watched, amazed by the sudden miracle taking place before his very eyes. Nicole had magically transformed into a cheerful, happy-go-lucky girl without a care in the world. Her smile danced easily and often. She was witty; she was charming; her interchange of expressions mesmerized him. She was a walking kaleidoscope. Her magnetism drew him, as it was now drawing Shane. And, although Justin knew it was all an act on her part, he could not deny the joy he had felt when he held her in his arms; it was like nothing he had ever experienced before. Even though she had been angry, he had felt a bond between them... something mystical... something intangible.

"Come on, Justin!" Shane yelled. "Let's play Keep Away. You can be in the middle." With a groan, Justin walked out to where the couple stood. He could tell Shane was feeling no pain—he had a silly grin on his face which was usually his first sign of intoxication. Gazing towards Nicole, the blond noticed she seemed a bit unsteady on her feet, apparently feeling no pain, either. "This shouldn't be too hard," he mumbled to himself, trying to intercept the flying disk. It sailed over his head towards Nicole, who had to spring into the air to end its flight. She pitched it back with ease.

"Good throw!" Shane yelled, suddenly noticing the rushing form of Justin heading straight for him. Afraid of losing his position, Shane tried to shove him out of the way, but it was useless. Justin grabbed hold of the frisbee, a triumphant smile on his face. "Who's in the middle?" the blond asked. "The person who last touched the disk or the person I'm closest to?"

"I'll be in the middle," offered Nicole as she trotted towards the two men. Shane whistled loudly at the enticing sight. "Animal!" she shouted in anger.

"That's right," Justin pointed out. "Shane, you know women don't want to be thought of as a piece of meat."

"They just want to be treated like one," laughed Shane. "Isn't that right, honey? Why else would you wear seductive clothing? To preserve your chastity?" He snickered again, unaware his remark had cut her deeply.

"Everyone wears shorts," she protested hotly.

"I'm not talking about the shorts, sweetheart," he continued. "I'm talking about that tight little top which laces up the middle. I've seen more threads in a handkerchief."

Hands on her hips, the young beauty glared at him with fiery eyes. She would teach him a lesson, show him how much she resented his rude behavior. "The picnic's over," she announced flatly, turning her back and walking away.

"Oh, come on, Nicole!" he whined. "I was only teasing."

"I find that hard to believe," she retorted. "Actually, Mr. Anderson, I didn't think you knew what chastity was? Who made you the expert on women? Just because you lay the local whores doesn't mean you understand how a decent woman thinks or feels!"

"Really?" he sneered. "And are you a decent woman, Mrs. Tyler?"

"Shane!" barked Justin. "Knock it off! You're getting yourself all worked up over something insignificant."

Shane turned on his friend. "Are you insinuating I'm irrational just because I had a few good swigs of wine?"

"Precisely! And it was more than just a few swigs."

"I agree," Nicole added, rearranging items in the cooler.

"Now, just a minute!" bellowed Shane as he pointed at Nicole. "You had more than just a few swigs yourself, Miss Goody Two Shoes. And you're the one who started this dispute anyhow by wearing that, that… that thing you call a top!"

"I suppose you'd rather have me take it off," she leered.

"I have a good mind to take it off for you!" he threatened.

Nicole's eyes widened. "Well, I never!"

"Oh, I bet you have!"

"Stop it, you two!" warned Justin, too late.

Nicole snatched the blanket, grabbed the cooler and headed towards the forest in silence.

"That woman's got a devil in her!" hissed Shane.

"You weren't much of a gentleman," Justin reprimanded before starting towards the forest to pursue the fleeing woman.

"I guess she'll never want to see us again."

The thought struck panic in Shane. Suddenly he felt the urge to set things right between them. "Nicole!" he called, bounding after her, his stomach protesting with every leap.

The elusive beauty glanced over her shoulder at the two men as she made a mad dash for home. She was glad she had a head start, for the weight of the cooler slowed her considerably. Tiny branches and stickers stung her flesh as she ran, but the liquor had intoxicated her far beyond the point of feeling them. Her house loomed up ahead, yet seemed so far away. It felt like she had run a marathon to get there.

Justin was horrified. "She'll kill herself running like that with the cooler. Maybe we should just leave her alone."

"No," breathed Shane. "I've got to catch her and apologize before she reaches her house and locks the door on me." He groaned in despair when he saw her climbing the few porch steps and setting down the cooler to find her key.

And that was the last thing Nicole remembered before a wave of dizziness overcame her. Clutching the doorframe, she leaned against the wood and frantically gasped for air while her surroundings began to spin in slow motion. "Oh, no," she groaned, sweat lining her brow. "Not now..." She clung to the framework in desperation, floating in and out of consciousness, fighting against her body's inclination towards the black void before her. She never felt the two pairs of hands peeling her fingers from the painted wood, never realized she had been carried through the doorway and over to the couch. Images and lights flashed in her mind, familiar sounds filled her ears, shadows flickered amidst some forgotten room where music played, memories slipped past a hidden door and slithered silently across the recesses of her brain. Dreams became reality, current events forgotten. Wild hallucinations surfaced, making her tremble uncontrollably. The minutes ticked slowly by.

"We'd better call a doctor," Shane blurted. "Something's terribly wrong! It looks like she's having a seizure."

"If that's what it is," answered the blond, "there's nothing we can do to help. She'll need to be taken to the hospital." Both men watched with astonishment as the young woman suddenly lurched forward, her eyes opening wide while she screamed, "No! Philip! Stop!" She then began to thrash about wildly, making it impossible for Justin to restrain her. "You have to help, Shane," he ordered. "Hold down her ankles while I hold her arms, otherwise, she'll hurt herself. Let's move her to the floor, where it's safer." Justin never felt so helpless in all of his life. It was agonizing to witness such terror in another human being. What was worse, neither he nor Shane could leave the scene to use the telephone. The minute they tried, Nicole attempted to get to her feet, her eyes still glazed, but open.

"This is no seizure," spoke Shane. "She's hallucinating. She must have taken a drug before she started drinking." Justin made no reply, hating to admit he had been thinking the same thing. All his attention was now focused on the young woman before him, who had finally ceased struggling for the moment. He noticed her lips moving nonstop as she murmured a quiet prayer, repeating it over and over until the words gradually increased in volume. And then, suddenly, he was able to decipher the whispered litany, and it made him want to vomit.

"Please don't hit me... Please don't hit me... Please don't hit me..." She curled her fingers into fists, holding them rigid by her side like a frightened child. And in that moment, Justin knew he would never forget the way she looked, the utter terror on her face. He was sickened by it, but controlled the bile in his throat, saying, "It's okay, Nicole. No one's going to hurt you. You're safe. Shane and I are here with you. You're safe, Nicole." Sensing the worst was over, he gently rocked her in his arms.

"Still think I should call for an ambulance?" asked Shane.

"No," Justin replied. "I think she's coming out of it. She's much quieter now. She despises us enough already; can you imagine how angry she'd be if she woke up in the hospital? She'd never forgive us."

"True," Shane agreed. "But what the devil are we going to do with her? We can't just leave her here, alone."

"Why don't you go on home? I'll stay with Nicole until she's all right."

Shane bit his lower lip. This wasn't how the day was supposed to end. He was the one who deserved to be with the woman, not Justin. "If you're staying, so am I. I'll put away the stuff in the cooler." He went into the kitchen while Justin continued cradling Nicole. She began to moan softly, rapidly blinking her eyes.

"O-o-h..." She peered up at the familiar face with confusion.

"It's okay, Nicole. You passed out," he said, smiling with relief. When he entwined his fingers in her hair, she catapulted out of his lap, accusing, "Why is it you always have your hands on me?!"

Upon hearing her voice, Shane hurried into the room. "Nicole! I'm so glad you're all right. We were so worried about you—" He stopped in midsentence when he noticed Justin motioning for him to keep quiet.

"Worried? What on earth for? People who drink too much always pass out," she reasoned, stunning both men by her return to complete normalcy. She was acting as if nothing out of the ordinary had happened. She was even walking and gesturing with total coordination, as if she were sober. This prompted Shane to throw Justin a quizzical look, but the blond shook his head to signal they should act as if everything was fine.

"Nicole," Shane began, going to her side, "I was an idiot today."

"As usual," mumbled Justin.

"And I apologize for upsetting you. I had no right talking to you the way I did on the beach. Please forgive me. I'd do anything for your forgiveness."

Standing behind Nicole, Justin made a puking gesture to let Shane know he was sounding sickeningly sweet.

"I forgive you," she replied. "It takes a lot of guts for a man to say he's sorry." While she turned to look at Justin, Shane stuck his tongue out at the blond.

"Hear that?" she suddenly squealed with delight, running

to the front door. The distinct sound of a trailer could be heard outside. "It's Cristoff! He's back from the auction. Come and see the new horses." Without waiting for either man, she bounded down the steps to greet her ranch hand, who had just pulled the trailer up to an empty corral and shut off the motor.

Before Justin could reach the door, Shane grabbed his arm. "Hey, wait a minute. When are we going to confront the damsel in distress about what occurred here a few minutes ago?"

"We're not," the blond simply stated. "She's been traumatized by the abuse, Shane. Reminding her of it would cause unnecessary pain. Do you want to be the one responsible for dredging up those bad memories?"

Shane shook his head, then said, "I feel sorry for her. Isn't there some way we can help her?"

"She needs professional help, but I'm not going to be the person to suggest it. I'm in enough hot water with the little wildcat." He opened the screen door to go outside, with Shane close on his heels. "Nicole," he called. "Your house key is inside, on the coffee table."

"Thanks," she yelled back, motioning for them to join her. "There's someone here who's been waiting to meet you." Both men ventured over to the trailer, although Shane already knew who that "someone" was.

"Oh, yeah!" Shane lied. "I forgot to tell you, Justin. Cristoff Colvert works for Nicole."

"What? You're kidding!"

"Well, bless my hide!" bellowed the object of their discussion, emerging from the side of the trailer. "If it isn't Justin MacFierson!"

"Cristoff!" shouted the blond, grabbing his hand in greeting. "So you're Nicole's ranch hand. Long time, no see. How have you been?"

"Great. And yourself?"

"Just moved in a short while ago. We're neighbors."

"You don't say," Cristoff grinned, slapping him on the back. "I couldn't believe it when Nicole told me she was going on a picnic with you." He glanced at Shane, who was standing a few yards behind his friend. "Hello, Shane. Good to see you." He almost said "again" but refrained, sensing Justin would be mad if he found out Shane had known for some time that Cristoff was living in the area.

"I hate to break up the happy reunion," Nicole interjected, "but Cristoff and I have to get these horses into the corral before they kick down the walls."

"You'll stick around, won't you?" Cristoff asked his longtime friend. Justin nodded, then watched as the two of them unloaded each new arrival down the trailer ramp and released them into the corral. Snorts and whinnies filled the air, all sweet music to his ears.

"They're some fine looking animals," Shane commented, eyeing a brilliant bay. "Hey, Cristoff? What type of bloodlines do they have?"

"A few are Crabbet stock, which is what Nicole wanted. One or two are pure Polish."

"But we won't mix them," she added. "I want each line to remain pure." Closing the corral gate, the three men and Nicole leaned on the fence to watch the spirited bunch. "I really like the black one, Cristoff."

"Ah, better leave that one to me," he warned. "He's not fully broken. I had a devil of a time getting him into the trailer. It was difficult walking him with a lead rope, too."

"Then I'll just have to break him," she announced, a spark of challenge in her eyes.

"Oh, no you don't," he argued. "Leave him to me, Nicole."

She yawned. "My mind's made up and you can't change it. As soon as I decide it's time, I'm going to break him." Dismissing the matter as resolved, she turned to her two guests. "You're welcome to stay as long as you wish. I have some business to tend to, though, so if you'll excuse me?" She tried to sound as polite as possible, but she really wanted them to leave. She had no intention of seeing either of them again, not if she could help it. They locked horns far too much for her liking. Justin turned to watch the gentle sway of her hips as she walked back towards the stable, barely hearing the concerned voice near him.

"How much did she drink?"

Cristoff's question took the blond by surprise. He looked at the ranch hand whose gaze remained fixed upon the horses in the corral. "How much, Justin?" he asked again.

"I don't know," he shrugged. "A couple glasses, maybe."

"Cups," corrected Shane. "And they were larger than wine glasses. Why, Cristoff?"

"Just curious," the ranch hand replied. "I can usually tell when she's been drinking." He looked steadily at Justin. "She didn't pass out, did she?"

"Funny you should mention that—"

"Aw, she's always passing out," Cristoff quickly added, chuckling to prevent any further discussion of the matter. "How about these horses, huh?"

"You know, I wanted to ask you about Nicole," Justin continued, trying to return to their topic. Cristoff, however, refused to cooperate, interrupting him in midsentence by suggesting, "Why don't you help me clean out the trailer, Justin? I really shouldn't let fresh manure sit in there for too long. Now, where did I put those shovels?"

"I have to be going," blurted Shane. "I have a dinner date tonight. Do you want to ride back with me, Justin?"

Seizing the opportunity, Cristoff offered, "I can drive him home later, if he wants to stay."

"Okay," smiled the blond. "I'll catch up with you sometime tomorrow, Shane."

Shane nodded. "Nice seeing you, Cristoff."

"Take care," called the ranch hand as he watched him walk towards his car. Cristoff chuckled. "I knew if I mentioned any kind of work, Shane would hightail out of here. Listen, Justin, I didn't want to discuss Nicole while he was with us."

"I see," said the blond. "Looks like we have a lot of talking to do, wouldn't you say? I haven't even asked you how your family is doing in Florida?"

"Oh, they're fine. In fact, my sisters..." His voice trailed off as he recognized a car pulling onto the property. "Well, I'll be... This day is just one surprise after another."

CHAPTER SIX

Justin studied the well dressed man exiting the vehicle, flowers in hand. He carried a rectangular shaped box under one arm as he called to Cristoff to inquire where Nicole was. "In the barn," Cristoff replied, before commenting to Justin, "I don't believe my eyes."

"Who is he?" the blond asked. "Nicole's boyfriend?"

"Nicole's brother-in-law, Daniel. We both had a fight with him, recently. After Nicole walloped him right across the face I didn't think he'd come around anymore."

"Walloped him, huh?" the blond repeated, clearly recalling a similar incident. Absently, his fingers traced the outline of his own jaw. She could wallop, all right. "So you think this Daniel character is up to no good?"

"Positive. He's been checking up on Nicole for a year now. We can't figure out what he wants."

"Obviously, he wants her."

"I don't think so. He's never asked her out on a date. Come on. Let's get some shovels and the pitchfork from the barn so we can clean out the trailer. It'll give us a good excuse to be in the stable while Daniel's there." Cristoff led the way at a brisk walk, hoping they'd be able to pick up bits of conversation from inside, but the hope was dashed when he saw the office door closed—no doubt, Daniel's doing. Cristoff couldn't hear a thing.

"This stable is fabulous," Justin praised. "What I wouldn't give to work with horses again."

"Why don't you get a job with Shane's father?" quizzed Cristoff, handing him a shovel.

"I don't like what he's doing to stay competitive."

"What do you mean?"

"For one thing, he's training the young horses before their bones are fully developed. Several good horses have already been injured, all fractures of the leg."

Just then, the office door opened. Cristoff and Justin headed up the aisle, pretending to leave, while Daniel approached from behind. "Hello, Cristoff." The ranch hand stopped and turned. "Hey, Danny, boy. What's up?" He was truly stunned that Daniel had even addressed him, but now Philip's brother acted as if they were still buddies, placing a hand on Cristoff's shoulder.

"I want to apologize for any hard feelings," he said, looking sincere. "We'll get together, soon."

Cristoff ignored the remark and introduced Justin, watching as the two men greeted with a handshake—dueling hands, to be exact. Each tried to outsqueeze the other in as briefest time as possible. Eventually, Daniel simply released his hold, then bid them farewell and exited. Cristoff turned to his friend. "Well? Who won?"

"Of course, I did," smiled the blond. "Shouldn't you check on Nicole?"

"Oh, yeah. Are you coming?"

"No, thanks. I'll stay out of this one. If you need me, I'll be working in the trailer."

"Afterwards, we'll have dinner at my place," spoke Cristoff, leaving his friend to go to the office. Since Nicole was on the phone, he walked over to the bright arrangement of flowers on her desk and inhaled their sweet fragrance. "Not bad," he commented, brushing the tip of his finger across one of the rose petals. Catching sight of an oriental vase filled with silk flowers, he gingerly picked it up to study the design.

"What do you think?" asked Nicole, hanging up the receiver.

Cristoff frowned. "I smell a rat."

"Yeah. Me, too. Of course, he apologized like a blithering idiot; he really should practice that routine a bit more. He even invited me to a party he's throwing tonight. Of course, I declined."

"The nerve of him," pretended Cristoff. "And he didn't even invite me!"

Nicole laughed, then grew serious, rising from her chair to approach him. "I think I've figured him out, Cristoff." She bit her lower lip, worried. "I truly believe he thinks I killed Philip."

"And he invites you to a party?"

"The party is only a means to an end. He wants to keep tabs on me. Don't you see? He thinks I'll slip up and say something to incriminate myself."

"But he's defended you in the past," Cristoff pointed out.

"Yes, but perhaps he has now changed his mind. I'm assuming since no leads have turned up in the murder case, he's becoming frustrated, needing to blame someone."

Cristoff exhaled, slow and deep, tossing the idea around in his head. "You could be right," he finally said. "It would make sense. He was extremely interested in what you had to say when I told him you had hallucinated, uh, I mean, had a vision. Maybe he thought you were going to reveal some deep, dark secret?"

"Maybe," she replied, repositioning the silk flowers in the vase. "He bought me these while he was on a business trip."

"It's odd, don't you think?"

"Yes. I never expected Daniel to buy me a present."

"No. I mean, it's odd he'd get real flowers plus silk flowers."

"The silk flowers are for the new vase, silly."

"Why didn't he just put the real flowers in the new vase? I think it'd look prettier." To prove his point, he removed the artificial arrangement and put the other in its place.

"I like it the way it was," she insisted, switching it back.

"Oh, drat. A fresh petal fell inside the vase. If I don't get it out, it'll smell in a few days."

"Are you sure it went inside?" Cristoff picked up the vase, turned it upside down and peered into the bottom. Then he placed his index finger on his lips to silence Nicole, walked out of the office to a nearby trashcan and gently set the object inside, sealing the container with its lid.

"Cristoff! What the devil are you doing?"

"I don't think you want that vase," he casually replied, steering her back inside the office. "It's bugged."

"It has bugs?"

"No," he said slowly, shaking his head. "The other kind of bug, girlie."

Nicole's mouth flew open. "You're joking, right?"

"Nope. That's why Daniel didn't want real flowers in the vase. He didn't want you to fill it with water. Son of a gun." He scratched his head. "Come on." He took her hand, pulled her out the door and down the aisle before she could say another word. "Justin!" he shouted, gesturing for the blond to join them. "I have a special project for you. I'll take care of the trailer tomorrow."

Nicole moaned. "Oh, no. He's still here?"

"We're going to need him," Cristoff replied. He turned to his friend, briefly explaining the situation. "So, it's my guess he's bugged Nicole's house, as well. We have to search the rooms."

"Even if we did," explained Justin, "we may not find all the mikes. I have a good friend who's a detective. Why don't you let me call him?"

"I, I don't know," Nicole spoke up, unsure if she wanted Justin involved in her personal matters. She truly wished Cristoff had never included him in the ordeal.

"What are you afraid of, Nicole?" Cristoff quizzed.

"Yeah. This isn't the time to be stubborn," Justin reprimanded, sounding like her father.

"Oh, don't you start with me!" she warned, shaking a finger at him.

"Be reasonable, Nicole," Cristoff whispered. "Do you want to know if the house is bugged?" They were inside now, and he was unscrewing part of the telephone. Not finding an object similar to the one in the vase, he pieced the contraption back together, then motioned for them to walk back outside, where it was safer to talk.

"All right," she relented, looking at Justin. "Better have Cristoff's house checked, too. I suppose I'll owe you, big time, for this."

He half grinned. "Why? You're the one paying for it." Then he blessed her with a genuine Cheshire Cat smile. "I'll make the call at my house tonight. Afterwards, I'll contact you and just mention the day and time when the detective will show. We have to be careful when talking. By the way, what's your phone number?"

Nicole's lips drew a tight line. She didn't want him to have her private number. "You can just call Cristoff. He'll let me know." Justin feigned indifference with a shrug.

Cristoff put his arm around the blond's shoulder. "Hey, buddy? How about eating out this evening? I'd rather not spend time talking inside my house until it's checked out."

"Fine with me," came the reply.

"Nicole and I have to put the new horses in their stalls and get them fed, first. Work before pleasure." They walked to the stable.

"I can help," Justin offered; then, upon seeing Nicole's agitated expression, added, "that is, if you don't mind, Mrs. Tyler?" She threw him a sideways glance at the mention of her formal name.

"Mind? No, I don't mind. Why should I mind? Here." She tossed him several lead ropes; well, actually, she threw them at him. "Sure! Bring in the horses. Feed them, if you like. Heck, clean their stalls while you're at it. When you finish that, you can scrub the floors of the breeding barn!" Satisfied with her tantrum, the young woman stormed out of the barn, tripping over her own lead rope in the process. Cristoff snickered, while Justin nudged him in the side. The blond winked. "I think she likes me, Cristoff."

"She did kind of glare at you with a spark of affection in her eyes, didn't she?" laughed the ranch hand. "It gets you, right here," he pointed to his heart before chuckling again. After exchanging a few more jokes at her expense, they went out to the corral to resume the task at hand. Justin forgot how skittish horses became when placed in a new environment and was almost trampled by an excitable stallion. If it hadn't been for Nicole grabbing the lead rope from him the instant she sensed a change in the horse's attitude, he would have been badly injured.

"If you walk beside the stallion, at his shoulder, and not in front of him, you'll be safer," she suggested.

"I already know that," he mumbled. "I just forgot." He looked down at his boots, angry with himself.

Nicole patted his arm. "Don't take it too hard. Cristoff says we're all allowed 30 seconds of stupidity per day." A smirk on her face, the dark-haired princess suddenly perked up, whistling a happy tune as she continued on her merry way. His ego knocked down a peg or two, Justin steered clear of her while he resumed assisting his friend.

"I really appreciate your help," Cristoff said when they were finally finished. "We can go inside my house and get cleaned up." The two men walked towards the tenant house.

"Why don't we buy some carry out food and go over to my place?" Justin suggested. "You haven't seen the house yet, and it'd be more private." Cristoff readily agreed to the offer. They washed up in the kitchen sink before Cristoff went upstairs to change his dirty clothes. They then headed into town, finally deciding on chinese food for dinner. As they drove back to Justin's residence, Cristoff questioned him about his current job as a carpenter and discovered that his friend was looking elsewhere for employment. "I thought about subcontracting," the blond said, "but I'd have to pay my own insurance and you know how expensive that can be."

Cristoff agreed, closing the car door as they stepped out onto Justin's driveway. The individual home was freshly painted and, upon entering, decorated with new furniture. "There's nothing like a new home," commented the ranch hand.

"I had a little help with the painting," Justin said, dishing out the food. "Aaron pitched in. He and Jan moved in last week."

"Both of them? I figured your twin brother would live with you—you two were inseparable, but… your sister? She was always so independent."

"I wanted her to," Justin replied. "Jan needs someone to take care of her. She's been sick for some time. She even had to quit her job because of her illness."

"I hope it isn't anything serious?"

"The doctors don't think so. She has migraine headaches. They say it's quite common. I wish she were here right now. She'd love to see you, again." He opened a beer for his friend. "Jan's spending the night over our cousin's house."

"How are your parents?" Cristoff asked. "Does your dad still play golf?"

Justin took a deep breath. "They passed away two years ago, Cristoff, in a car accident."

"I'm so sorry," he replied. "I truly am. I really liked your parents."

"Everyone liked my parents," the blond smiled. "They were great. I still miss them." His gaze dropped to his food while he composed himself. "It was Shane's idea I move out of the old house and find some place close to him. Funny thing, though… he sure tried his best to persuade me out of this deal. He never did mention why I shouldn't buy this particular place."

Cristoff wisely kept his mouth shut. He knew exactly why Shane didn't want Justin living here—it was too close to the ranch. He had noticed the old spark of jealousy in Shane's eye the moment Justin had decided to remain with him this afternoon. Cristoff decided to change the subject and asked, "How's Aaron?"

"Now, that's a loaded question. Let's just say he isn't the boy you remembered him to be." Upon seeing the puzzled look on Cristoff's face, he added, "Aaron has become the complete opposite of me. I don't know when the change happened or why. He's the black sheep of the family. He's into some bad stuff."

"Drugs?"

"Yeah. I didn't really want him living with me but I'm hoping to be a good influence on him. He's not even here most of the time. How's your family, Cristoff?"

"Pretty boring," he laughed. "They're still residing in Florida. Nothing exciting ever happens to them." The two men finished eating and moved into the living room, where Justin politely told him to help himself to the liquor cabinet. Watching his friend pour a glass of scotch, he remarked, "So, that's what you're drinking now, ay? Remember when we were teenagers and we would fill our milkshake containers with beer so the cops never suspected we were drinking?"

"Yeah," Cristoff chuckled. "I couldn't wait until I was of legal age. The first thing I did was go to a bar and get stinking drunk. I puked my guts out. You'd think I'd have learned my lesson."

"I know what you mean. I usually drink tequila. The first time I did, though, I was sick as a dog." He swallowed a mouthful of beer, then suddenly quizzed, "Hey. Why haven't you run into Shane in town? You've lived here a while, haven't you?"

"Four years," Cristoff replied, searching for some white lie to use as an explanation. He definitely did not want Justin mad at Shane, which he would be if he discovered that Shane had seen Cristoff quite a few times in town, but never told him. "To tell you the truth, I have so much on my mind when I go into town, I've probably seen Shane and haven't even recognized him." Justin nodded as if he understood.

Cristoff quickly changed the topic again, this time to a subject that had been on his mind since earlier that day. "How did the two of you manage to convince Nicole to go on a picnic?"

"She didn't tell you?"

"No."

"She wagered The General in a poker game which Shane won. When he found out the horse couldn't be ridden by anyone except Nicole, he decided to give the horse back and take Nicole on a picnic, instead. She insisted on a chaperone—that's where I came into the picture."

"You don't say," remarked the astonished ranch hand. He could hardly believe his ears. Had Nicole lost her mind? She'd never part with that stallion. Then Cristoff smiled. Of course, she had no intention of parting with him. She knew very well Shane couldn't ride the animal. How very clever of her—and stupid. What would she have done if Shane took the horse and handwalked him home, anyway?

While Cristoff was busy thinking, Justin grew uneasy, afraid he had made a mistake in mentioning it. His blue eyes coolly studied his friend, suddenly seeing him for the first time, taking in the deeply tanned skin, the sun-streaked hair—thick, but well styled in fashionably flowing layers, the boyish face almost too cute to be masculine. Cristoff had always had a flock of girls around him, and Justin knew it was no different now. The ranch hand's hard labor had paid off; he had enormous muscles and broad shoulders. If his boyish looks camouflaged his masculinity, the body sure didn't.

Justin felt his stomach begin to churn. What if Cristoff was Nicole's lover? Surprised at the path his thoughts were taking, he swiftly walked to the liquor cabinet and poured some tequila. Cristoff had begun to babble on about the ranch and its future, completely unaware of the change in Justin's mood, until finally, the blond simply blurted out what was on his mind.

"How close are you to Nicole?" The question had popped out of his mouth before he could stop it, and now Justin stood still as a statue, feeling quite the fool for having asked it. After all, it wasn't any of his business.

Cristoff showed mild surprise, but there was a definite twinkle in his eye as he returned the steady stare. "What's it to you?" he calmly replied, unsure of Justin's motive.

The blond feigned indifference with a shrug. "Just wondering."

"Do you like her?"

"You didn't answer my question."

"Do you like her?" Cristoff persisted.

"I guess that means you're going to modify your answer, depending on what I say," the blond stated. "Why can't you just tell me the truth?"

"All right," he relented. "I've known Nicole for three years. I'd have to be blind not to see how beautiful she is. However, the woman's my employer. I'm not about to become involved with her." Justin relaxed, expelling a rush of air from his lips. Cristoff couldn't help but notice the relief on his face, and smiled. "You like her," the ranch hand teased. "A lot."

"Not really," came the protest. "She's not my type at all. I prefer passive women."

"Uh, huh."

"Really."

"I hear you," Cristoff grinned, swallowing the rest of his scotch. "When will you ask her out?"

"I'm not."

"You will."

An agitated look crossed Justin's face. "She has problems," he simply said.

"Oh?"

"You know it. You have to know it."

Cristoff's smile vanished as he studied his friend. "Yes," he finally agreed. "Nicole has her problems; which brings me to my next question: Did anything odd happen to her today?" He watched the expression change on Justin's face, and in that instant knew he had been correct in assuming the worst.

"Let's not beat around the bush, Cristoff. I'll tell you the truth as long as you do the same. Deal?" The ranch hand nodded while he poured another drink. "I know Philip abused Nicole. She cried out while having some kind of hallucination today."

"After drinking?"

"Yeah. Shane made her angry, so she took off running towards her house. When we reached her, she was losing consciousness, or so we thought." The blond went on to describe what followed, carefully monitoring Cristoff's reaction to his every word. When he had finished, the ranch hand remarked, "I need to know how interested you are in her, Justin, because I don't think it's right to discuss her problems with just anyone. Nicole is very sensitive. I don't want word of this getting back to her. I especially don't want Shane to be privy to any details of her private life."

"Then you know what's wrong with her?" Justin insisted. "Is she on drugs?"

"No." Cristoff finished his scotch, feeling quite relaxed now. If Justin thought he'd simply offer information on Nicole without any guarantee, he was mistaken. The ranch hand grew quiet and patiently waited.

After swallowing another mouthful of tequila, the blond wiped his moist lips with the back of his hand. "All right, Cristoff. Out with it."

"Do you promise this goes no further than this room?"

"Yes."

"First, tell me why you want to know? You said she wasn't your type, so… why the interest?"

Justin frowned, clearly agitated. "Why the devil are you being so protective?"

"Why would that bother you?" countered Cristoff, forcing a stalemate.

Justin made a rapid circular motion with his hand until the sweet liquor swirled inside its glass. All this pussyfooting around was giving him second thoughts about Cristoff's true relationship with the woman. If she was nothing more to him than an employer, why the third degree?

Looking again at his old friend, he decided to admit the truth. "Okay. I like her. Satisfied?"

Cristoff remained serious. "How much?"

"Oh, come on!" scowled the blond. "Give me a break."

Leaning forward with new interest, Cristoff explained. "I

was hoping you'd like her. Nicole needs someone—someone strong enough to handle her. She's spirited, you know."

"Oh, I know, all right," Justin muttered.

"But she also needs a man who is patient and gentle. Her former husband put her through hell, even shut her away in a mental institution for two weeks."

"How did she ever meet this creep?" Justin asked.

"At a horse show. Nicole and her parents are originally from Maryland. They came here on vacation some years ago and Nicole insisted on going to the local Arabian horse show. Philip and Daniel had taken a few of the Desert Wind stallions to compete. Nicole voiced her objection to how Philip's rider was handling one of the horses; so, after that particular class was over, Philip sarcastically challenged her to ride the animal. She took the dare."

"Somehow that doesn't surprise me," Justin remarked.

"Well, it surprised Philip. It surprised him even more when she put the stallion flawlessly through its paces. He was very impressed and invited her and her parents back to the ranch for a tour of the facility. It became a private joke between the two brothers. The joke turned into a dare. You see, Daniel and Philip had a habit of daring each other to do outrageous things. Daniel dared Philip to date Nicole. Then he dared him to get engaged."

"You're putting me on," Justin objected. "You expect me to believe that Philip became engaged on a mere whim?"

"It's the truth," Cristoff insisted. "Daniel and Philip turned dares into a macho pride duel. This one went too far."

"Why didn't Philip back out?"

"He actually liked Nicole. Plus, he had never met a girl who could ride so well. She could make his horses perform better than I could. She had taken riding lessons in Maryland but has some kind of natural affinity with horses. So, eventually, he convinced himself that marrying her would prove a wise business decision."

"And she never knew he had been stringing her along?"

"Not a clue. Philip was a real charmer. Nicole was swept off her feet."

"Then when did the abuse start?"

Cristoff dropped his gaze to the floor. "On their honeymoon. I remember the expression on Nicole's face when they returned from their trip. Philip owned a mansion, but Nicole talked him into living at the ranch, instead. When they pulled up here, I noticed that the girl he had married was not the same girl getting out of the car. She had a vague look in her eyes, as if she wasn't focusing on anything in particular, and her actions were almost robotic. It was as if she was just going through the motions of walking and talking, without any purpose. I suspected something had occurred, yet couldn't get Philip to discuss it. Then I saw bruises on her wrists.

Justin stared into the bottom of his glass. "I guess the abuse continued?"

"Unfortunately. She tried to leave him once, on The General. I'll never forget that day. He yanked her off the horse and cracked the dressage whip across her back—tore right through her blouse. I ran outside and restrained him until he had cooled off. Then the two of us got into a heated argument over the way he was treating her. He told me that if I didn't like it, I could leave. After thinking it over, I decided to remain at the ranch so I could help protect Nicole."

"Why didn't she just go back to her parents?"

"Philip had threatened her. He caught her making plans to escape and had her committed to the local mental ward, just to give her a taste of what power he held; remember how wealthy he was. Money is power. Plus, Philip always carried through on a threat. He never bluffed. She learned the hard way, poor thing. She was definitely trapped into remaining his wife. He kept close tabs on her, too. He knew every person she spoke to, and he dictated where she was allowed to go and when."

Justin poured another drink and refilled Cristoff's glass, asking, "What about the hallucinations? Are they from the abuse? What triggers them?"

"It's a long story, Justin. Are you sure you have the time to listen?"

"I want to know," he stated. "Besides… the story can't get any worse."

"Oh, yes it can," came the resounding reply. "Abuse wasn't Philip's only problem. He also loved to gamble, big time. He began having friends over for poker games, usually once a week. One evening, I brought a girl home who was crazy about a certain rock group. I went over to Philip's, knowing he had some of the group's albums, and knocked on the door to ask if I could borrow them. Lo and behold, I witness Nicole dancing on top of the table, performing a slow striptease."

Justin froze. "You're kidding."

"Nope. Daniel pulled me off to the side and told me how she had been offered as a consolation prize to the losers. He assumed she was drunk. Later, much later, Philip confided to him that he had spiked her drink—he had a psychiatrist friend who was supplying him with special pills which he used to make Nicole lose her inhibitions."

"I don't understand," Justin interrupted. "Didn't she realize what he had done?"

Cristoff shook his head. "Philip told Daniel that she never remembered anything the next morning. Sometimes she did get a headache, though. It seems Philip had to precisely balance the mixture of alcohol and narcotics to achieve the desired effect, making Nicole willing to cooperate with any suggestion given her. It sounds absurd, I know, but it truly happened."

"Did you see it happen?"

"No, but Daniel did. He said Philip showed him how it was done. Daniel and I decided he should continue attending the parties, in case violence erupted. He could remove her from the scene without angering Philip. Philip trusted Daniel."

"Then why didn't Daniel make him stop the abuse?"

"He tried. We both tried. Philip was stubborn."

Justin thought this new information over, a hundred questions springing forth. "I can't believe she never suspected anything. How often did this go on?"

"About a year before his death."

"Why didn't you tell Nicole?"

"I wanted to, but if she failed to believe me she could have me fired, and then who would look out for her? I lived on the premises. I could intervene if I had to—like the time Philip whipped her. I did try to convince Daniel to tell her, but he refused. He said he wasn't about to go behind his brother's back."

"How loyal," scoffed the blond. "He probably enjoyed every minute of her performance."

"He did take advantage of her one night, but that was because his wife had asked him for a divorce earlier that day. He claims he still feels guilty about the incident and wants to offer financial assistance to Nicole. He even tried to give her the mansion which Philip willed to him."

"Philip chose to give the house to Daniel?"

"You don't realize how close those two brothers were. Why, Philip left the mansion and most of his money to Daniel! Can you imagine that? The only thing Nicole inherited was the ranch and a small bank account."

"If Daniel inherited so much wealth, how do we know he didn't murder Philip?"

"He claimed he was with a girl that night. His alibi checked out."

"The girl could have lied."

"True. But after the death, he even hired a detective to help search for clues."

Justin ran his fingers through his hair, pondering everything Cristoff had said. It was almost too much to believe. "Let's return to the topic of Nicole," he finally said. "Tell me exactly how Philip drugged her."

"According to Daniel, Philip put the pills in their brandy decanter the day of the poker game. Nicole always had brandy after dinner; however, none of the guests drank it. If she didn't want brandy, he simply plopped the dope into whatever she was having, always offering to fix her drink for her."

"You said the guests didn't drink brandy. Don't you find that odd?"

"I wouldn't know. I wasn't familiar with the men."

"But I thought you knew Philip's friends?"

"Some of them. However, during those poker games, I never recognized the men going into the house. It wasn't that unusual, because Philip knew lots of people. He always had visitors."

"Have any of those men made contact with Nicole since her husband's death?"

Cristoff shook his head. "Daniel told me he'd 'take care of them,' so to speak. He was very adamant about protecting Nicole. No word leaked out about the parties."

"But wouldn't they be questioned during the investigation? The interrogation should have blown the lid off of Nicole's party entertainment. I find it odd that those men kept their mouths shut about what went on."

"Not really," spoke Cristoff. "I think they were a little afraid of Nicole. After all, most people did suspect she was the one who killed Philip."

"What about the psychiatrist who supplied Philip? Have you spoken with him?"

"No one can locate him."

"And you don't think that sounds fishy?"

"Of course I do, but what can be done about it? Daniel already had his detective try and find him. The man has disappeared without a trace. I even hired someone to search for the guy. Nothing turned up."

"What was his name?"

"Dr. Bohman."

"Maybe he never existed. Maybe Philip stole the drugs, himself."

"Maybe," agreed Cristoff.

Justin put down his glass and leaned back on the sofa, the liquor obstructing his ability to think clearly. He groaned, remembering he had just survived a hangover earlier today. He had been a fool to have these last few drinks. "So, Nicole doesn't know?"

"Know what?"

"About her performance at the parties."

"Danny and I told her after Philip's death."

"I bet that went over real well," he remarked, dryly.

"She's tougher than you think. She took the news better than we expected, although it did take some time to convince her."

"The hallucinations. Why was she experiencing them?"

"I have noticed on occasion, after drinking, she sometimes slips into a trance-like state. During this period, she has flashbacks. They can be good, or bad. Regardless, she never remembers what she has said or done when she comes out of it, with the exception of one episode in which she accurately described Daniel's affair with her."

"How interesting," Justin slowly commented. "I suppose whatever drug Philip gave her still has an effect on her system with the intake of alcohol. Is she also open to suggestions during these flashbacks?"

"I've never made an attempt to suggest anything except for her to come out of the trance, and that hasn't proven very successful."

A moment of silence passed between the two men. Justin stood up, stretched and yawned, then offered Cristoff another drink, which he declined. "Let me call that detective before I forget," he mentioned, going to the phone. He placed the call, made the appointment, then relayed the information to Cristoff. A picture of Nicole flashed through his mind. "We have to find out what type of pills Philip used," he said. "It's our only hope for correcting the problem. Once we know the medicine, we can find something to counteract it."

Cristoff looked surprised. "Then, you do want to help?"

"Why not?" shrugged the blond. "I know that when I close my eyes tonight to sleep, I'm going to see the tortured look on Nicole's face when I had held her in my arms today. I'll never forget it. If we don't help her, no one else will. Has she spoken to any doctors?"

"You can forget that idea," Cristoff frowned. "She won't go near a psychiatrist since her stay in the mental hospital."

Justin tried another strategy. "What if we get a more

detailed description of those pills from Daniel?"

"He said they were tiny, round, and white; and I've already spoken to several pharmacists and doctors, inquiring as to what medicine has such an effect. They claim they aren't familiar with any drug which makes you susceptible to suggestions."

"Just great," moped the blond. "So much for that idea." He tried to focus on another plan, but his thoughts kept returning to Daniel. Curious, he asked, "How does Daniel find time to check up on Nicole?" Cristoff shrugged. "What does he do for a living?"

"Works for the government."

"Which branch?"

"I don't know. He's never told me."

"That figures," came the wry reply. "No wonder he has so much time on his hands; he's a government employee. I took an instant dislike to the man."

"Danny used to be my friend, but I'm not so sure anymore. I can't think of any good reason he'd bug Nicole's office. None of this makes sense. He's always protected her. I just can't believe he suddenly decided she killed his brother; it's just not like Daniel."

"Unless," Justin snapped his fingers. "he knows Nicole still has flashbacks."

"He does. I told him. In fact, I confronted him with the information that Nicole remembered him sleeping with her."

"That's it!" Justin exclaimed excitedly. "He thinks she may recall some pieces of conversation from the past, during one of these flashbacks, which might reveal a clue as to who killed Philip. Daniel probably suspects one of the poker players—not Nicole."

"You could be right," Cristoff nodded. "But why doesn't he just induce one of the trances by getting her drunk?" Then a sudden thought occurred to the ranch hand. "Hey, wait a minute. He did invite her to a party. Maybe this is why?"

A negative look crossed Justin's face. "Something doesn't add up here. Why wouldn't he simply approach Nicole with the idea? I'm sure she'd readily agree to go into a trance, or under hypnosis, if it would yield a clue to the murder."

"Yeah," sulked Cristoff. "Back to the drawing board." Depressed, he rested his chin on his hands, his elbows on his knees, and attempted to rethink the whole situation. Eventually, neither one of them could come up with another suggestion, so they changed the conversation to an unrelated topic and spent the rest of the evening catching up on important events in each other's lives.

After a brief business discussion with Justin, Cristoff finally mentioned he should be leaving. "Remember," he said, shaking his friend's hand in a farewell gesture, "not a word about Nicole's problems to anyone."

"You've always been able to trust me, Cristoff," the blond reaffirmed as he stood at the door. They parted company, and Cristoff drove slowly home, his conscience nagging him. Had he been wise to reveal so many intimate details about Nicole's life? He was counting on Justin to use the information to better understand Nicole's actions. The compassion in his friend's eyes proved him correct—Justin's feelings for her were deeper than he let on. Cristoff smiled. The two of them would make a good match. He entered his quiet home, switched on the lights and grabbed a quick shower before collapsing in bed.

CHAPTER SEVEN

Several hours later, Cristoff was awakened by the sweet, melodic voice of an angel calling his name. "Cristoff," it whispered. "Wake up." Still intoxicated, he slowly raised one eyelid to peer up at the vision before him. "I'm dreaming," he murmured, entranced by the lovely woman who stood by the side of his bed. He opened his mouth again, this time to comment on her rapturous beauty, when suddenly he was drowned in an ocean of ice cold water. He sputtered, coughed, nearly choked to death, and bolted upright in bed.

"I thought that would get your attention," snapped Nicole. She ignored the curses spewing from his lips and returned the large, empty glass back to the bathroom.

"What are you doing here?" he demanded.

"Well, now," she drawled, tapping her index finger against her cheek, "what possible reason could I have to enter my employee's house?"

"I'm not in the mood for games, Nicole. What's going on?"

"You!" she exclaimed, pointing at his naked chest. "You forgot to tell me the detective was coming this morning. He banged on my door at six o'clock. Who told him to arrive that early? Was it that pigheaded friend of yours? Did he think it would be a good joke to play on me? The nerve of that man! I opened my door, clad only in a bathrobe, and turned three shades of red! So help me, Cristoff, if this was your idea—"

"Justin made the appointment," he quickly interjected. "I must have forgotten to warn you."

"I'll say!" she fumed. "You also forgot to feed the horses this morning, which, by the way, I've already taken care of."

"I'm sorry. I got in late last night. As for the detective, well, Justin told him it was urgent. The man explained to Justin he was going out of town today, but he'd make a quick stop to your house first. That's why it's such an inconvenient time. He didn't have to do this, you know; after all, it is Sunday." Cristoff held his aching head between his hands. "I've got to get some coffee. Do you mind?"

Nicole remained standing, not comprehending his implication. Then her gaze fell to the thin summer sheet that had slipped just below his hips, and she suddenly realized he was completely naked underneath. "Oh," she faltered. "Uh, yeah, I'll meet you downstairs." Quickly exiting the room, she flew down the steps with amazing speed. Cristoff eased himself out of bed and got dressed. Joining her in the kitchen, he said, "So, did the detective leave?"

"No. He's still at my house. I felt funny watching him, so I decided to come over here and pry you out from under the covers. He'll be heading over to your house, next." She finished making coffee and opened the refrigerator door.

"What are you doing?" he quizzed.

"Looking for eggs. Where are they?"

"On the right. Why?"

"I'm fixing us breakfast. Scrambled or fried?"

"Scrambled, but you don't have to do that."

"I know," was all she said, grabbing a pan.

"I'll toast some bread."

"No. You sit down and rest your sore head. I'll take care of everything."

Cristoff's eyes narrowed suspiciously. "You're being awfully nice this morning."

"I'm always nice."

He laughed, loud and clear. Then it dawned on him. "I

know why you're doing this." She didn't dare look at him. "To answer the question you're afraid to ask: Yes, I know all about the poker game with Shane and Justin."

Nicole slammed the frying pan down on the stove with a bang, causing Cristoff to grimace with pain. "I knew it!" she fussed. "He told you. I knew he would. Wait until I see that mule-faced backstabber!"

"How could you wager The General?" he accused. "Of all the stupid, idiotic—"

"Okay, okay. So, I did one dumb thing. It was all your fault."

"My fault!" he shrieked, holding his head.

"Yes, your fault. Don't you remember suggesting that I go into town and play poker?"

"Sure. But I was taking for granted you had common sense."

Angry, Nicole hurled a raw egg at him, hitting him square in the chest. A look of pure satisfaction crossed her face as she watched the runny yolk ooze down his shirt. Cristoff leaped from the chair, cursing. She laughed, then held up her hands in protest as Cristoff reached for the opened carton. "Don't you dare," she warned, backing up against the wall. A sinister grin slid easily up the corners of his mouth. "Cristoff!" She tried to shield herself, but it wasn't in time. The attack of eggs was swift and unrelenting, until every last one had pelted her body. She was a walking mess. Now, it was his turn to laugh, and he did—very boisterously.

Just then, a knock sounded at the door. "Oh, great," Nicole moaned. "The detective. I can't let him see me like this." Ignoring her, Cristoff stripped off his ruined shirt and went to the door. Still in the kitchen, the young woman could hear the detective's voice, but it was too quiet for her to decipher the words. Thus, she took a step closer. Unfortunately, her foot landed in egg and promptly slid forward, causing her to fall backwards with a loud thump. She groaned, feeling the seat of her pants slowly dampening with crushed egg white. Then, as if things couldn't get any worse, Cristoff and the detective hurried to the kitchen to make sure she was all right. Nicole wanted to die. "Don't mind me," she simply said. "I was just cleaning up a small mess Cristoff made in here." She saw the detective glance around the room, no emotion on his face at all, and she swallowed a laugh.

"I was just telling your employee," the man began, as if nothing out of the ordinary had happened, "that I found a microphone in each room of your house. Shall I get started here, or would you prefer I wait?"

"If you'll give me five minutes, I'll have this area cleaned up for you." Nicole made a feeble attempt to brush the egg off her clothes.

"I'll wait," came the stoic response as Cristoff ushered the detective into the living room.

Nicole went to work in the kitchen, managing the best she could with paper towels and rags. While she cleaned, anger raced through her veins at the realization of what she had just been told. How could Daniel do such a thing? It was so out of character. When did he do it? There was nothing worse than the feeling of having your privacy invaded. The thought of someone entering her home without her permission was unnerving. She was becoming madder by the minute, bent on forming a plan of action. Finishing her task, she briskly walked into the living room to speak with the detective.

"I want to see one of the mics." He obliged her request and Nicole committed the object to memory. "I have to leave for an appointment, so I'll get my checkbook and pay you now."

"There's no need," he announced. "I owe Justin a favor. I'm doing this free of charge."

"Oh," Nicole said, surprised. "Well, thank you very much. I truly appreciate it. Now, if you'll excuse me—"

"What about breakfast?" piped Cristoff.

"Looks like you're fresh out of eggs," she jeered, heading for the door.

Cristoff raced after her, taunting, "What about your house? Do you have eggs?"

Nicole turned, stuck her tongue out at him, then continued

on her way until she cautiously entered her house. As fast as she could, she changed her clothes, washed up, then bounded down the stairs and out the door. The distinct roar of the Shelby engine filled the air when she raced off the property. Too late, Cristoff guessed where she was headed. There was nothing he could do. If he showed up at Daniel's house, she'd be furious he followed her. His only choice was to wait for her return; although, if too much time passed, he'd have to risk her wrath and check up on her. To take up time, he watched the detective do his job, slowly moving from room to room.

While Cristoff counted the minutes, Nicole zoomed up Daniel's driveway, screeching to a halt in front of the large iron security gate. She punched in a special code, waited for the gate to open, then continued towards the huge stone mansion. When the butler finally opened the door, he was still tying the sash to his robe.

"Good morning, William. Is Mr. Tyler at home?"

"Are you aware what time it is, Mrs. Tyler?"

"7:30 a.m., to be exact," she announced. "I need to speak to Daniel."

"I'm sorry, madam. He's still in bed. He usually sleeps in on Sunday."

"I'm sure he does," she said flatly, waltzing past the astonished man. "Will you wake him, please?"

William became flustered. "I certainly will not! You will simply have to come back later."

"This can't wait. Which bedroom is his?"

"Mrs. Tyler!"

Nicole bounded up the spiral staircase, two steps at a time, calling, "Never mind, William. I'll find him, myself," leaving the butler no choice but to run after her, shouting, "Wait! Mrs. Tyler! You can't go up there! It's improper." But she was already up there, popping in and out of various rooms until she found the object of her wrath, peacefully snoring in his king sized bed.

"Daniel, dear," she called in a gentle voice, hiding her anger. "Wake up."

"You simply must leave!" William ordered, finally reaching the young woman. "If you don't, I shall have to call the police."

"Call them," she replied, turning her attention once again to the man in bed. She shook his arm. "Daniel. Wake up."

"Madam, please!" whined the butler.

Finally roused, Daniel opened his eyes. "Leave us, William," he commanded, motioning with his hand.

"B-B-But, sir—"

"Now!" he barked, causing Nicole to jump. She wasn't accustomed to him raising his voice; Daniel had always been a quiet man. After a quick bow, the butler backed out of the room, and the minute he did so, Nicole shut the door.

"Well," smiled the 26 year-old, "to what do I owe this honor?" Hoisting himself into a sitting position, he calmly rearranged his pillow, then patted a spot on the mattress beside him, saying, "Have a seat."

Nicole glared at him. "No, thank you."

"Oh, dear. You look terribly upset."

"This definitely isn't a social call, Daniel. Why did you bug my house?"

"Um..." His eyes scanned the room as if the answer were hidden inside one of the walls. "I apologize. I know it's an invasion of your privacy."

"Then, you don't deny it?"

"Of course not," he said, matter of factly. "It was my sincere hope you wouldn't discover it."

"I bet! Well, let me tell you something, you, you—"

He silenced her with his hand. "Save your breath, Nicole. I did it for your own good. I wanted to spare you the worry, but now since you've found the microphones..." His voice trailed off as his tone turned serious. "There was a death threat against you. No, don't laugh. I'm telling the truth. One of the men who played poker with Philip has voiced his intent to have you killed."

"You're lying," she accused. "Why would he want me dead?"

"You had no knowledge of this, but Philip won the man's

Quarterhorse business during a game. He promptly sold it. Shortly afterwards, this man went bankrupt. He blames Philip and wants revenge. Since my brother's no longer living, he thinks he can satisfy his vengeance by substituting your life, instead."

"How would you even know about his plan?"

"One of my friends overheard him talking in a bar. He was trying to find someone to do the dirty deed for him."

Nicole scoffed. "If he was bankrupt, he couldn't pay an assassin."

Daniel shrugged. "I'm just telling you what I heard. Why do you think I've been checking up on you? Cristoff is no protection. I thought that if I could hear what was going on in the barn and house, I could find out if any strangers suddenly showed up. That's the reason I offered to employ three men at the ranch. They were going to be your bodyguards."

Nicole slowly sank onto the bed, completely speechless, the remnants of her anger dispelled with each tiny breath. Daniel had to be saying the truth; no one could think up such a detailed lie on such short notice. Still, she was overwhelmed by it all. "Which of Philip's friends was it?"

"George Craiger. Do you remember him?"

"Yes," came the quiet reply. "If he's in such financial trouble, perhaps I should offer some help. I truly didn't know the stakes were so high at the poker game. I feel terrible about this. Do you have his phone number?"

"I do, but you should rethink this, Nicole. You can't be dishing out money to every sore loser. Besides, what are you going to say when he answers the phone—'Hi, George. I heard you want to kill me?'" Daniel was right, of course. But Nicole wanted to test his story, wanted to speak with George Craiger to verify what Daniel told her. After all, if his facts were correct, it'd explain everything Cristoff and she had been questioning about her brother-in-law's visits. It was the answer to their riddle.

"I want his phone number," she repeated.

"All right," he concurred. "I'll give it to you. But I suggest you wait an hour or two before phoning. It is rather early." His eyes gazed steadily into hers, and Nicole suddenly felt two inches tall. She had come bursting into his bedroom like a madwoman, without even allowing him time to dress. Where were her manners? Why had she become so impetuous? Daniel saw her face redden, and smiled. "Don't feel bad, Nicole. You had every right to be furious with me. I was in the wrong, not you. I should have just told you about George. It seems I waste a lot of time going out of my way to look after you." His eyes darted away. "I wish I could simply let you live your life. But I can't. I'm obsessed with keeping you safe from all the rotten things in this world, including anyone who could hurt you." His hand slowly reached out for hers, bringing it to his lips for an affectionate kiss. Nicole was moved.

"I'm very sorry, Daniel," she said. "You understand why I thought the worst, don't you?"

"Of course," he smiled. "Who wouldn't? Perhaps when you talk to George you'll win him over. He can't very well shoot someone who expresses sympathy for his plight, now can he?"

"And I'll offer him some type of compensation."

"I've already offered him money." Daniel admitted. "He wouldn't take it." Downhearted, Nicole lowered her head, only to have Daniel place a finger under her chin to lift it again. "Don't worry, my dear. I'm sure you'll come up with something."

She forced a tiny smile. "I had better let you get back to sleep."

"Unfortunately, I'm very much awake, so why don't you stay a while? Have you eaten?"

She thought of the egg throwing escapade back at Cristoff's house. "Actually... no."

"Good. Will you have breakfast with me?"

Nicole felt her stomach growl. "Well... okay, only if I can help."

Daniel smiled. "You go ahead downstairs and I'll meet you in a few minutes." After watching the young woman exit the room, he expelled a long, drawn out exhale. Several minutes later, he joined her in the kitchen and placed several eggs in a frying pan.

"Daniel?" Nicole asked as she put bread in the toaster. "Did you also bug Cristoff's house?"

"No," he answered.

"I'm curious. How did you manage to get inside mine?"

"Getting inside wasn't the problem," he explained, pouring orange juice. "The difficult part was not being seen. I had to be dropped off quite a distance away because I couldn't just drive my car onto your property and risk it being noticed. After I was dropped off I made my way through the woods along the bordering edge until I was directly across from the side of your house. Then I made a run for it."

"But how did you get in?"

He smiled. "You don't lock your windows. All I had to do was find a time when you and Cristoff were both off the property. You really should take better precautions, Nicole."

"I will," she assured him.

"By the way," he said. "Who was the blond-haired fellow at the ranch yesterday?"

"Justin. He's my new neighbor. He's also an old friend of Cristoff's."

"Really... Who was the other guy driving off when I pulled up? He had dark hair."

"Shane. He's Justin's friend."

Daniel sat down to eat, motioning for her to do the same. "So they were visiting Cristoff?"

"No. We went on a picnic. It's a long story and would probably bore you."

"You never bore me," he said in a suave tone. "Please continue."

So, Nicole quickly ran through the circumstances leading to her date with Shane and Justin, then briefly described the outing. When she finished, she changed the subject to ask him if he had spoken to his ex-wife, Maureen.

"No," he replied, hearing his telephone ring. "She won't have anything to do with me. In fact, she has a new boyfriend.

I forget his name." He watched William enter the kitchen.

"Excuse me, sir," the butler began, "but I have a phone call for Mrs. Tyler from Mr. Colvert."

"Thank you, William," Daniel replied before throwing a curious glance in Nicole's direction. "I hope it isn't anything serious?"

"Probably not," she said, pushing back her chair. "Will you excuse me, Daniel?"

"Of course."

She went into the other room and picked up the receiver. While waiting for her to finish, Daniel placed the dishes in the sink and put on a pot of coffee. "Trouble?" he asked, upon her return.

"No. Cristoff was worried, that's all. I left the ranch without telling him where I was going. I don't usually go anywhere this early in the morning." She began looking for dish detergent, causing Daniel to grin.

"What are you doing?" he quizzed.

"Where's the detergent? I'm going to wash the dishes."

"Silly girl," he chuckled, guiding her away from the kitchen area. "That's what a maid is for. When will you ever learn? Now sit down and relax while the coffee brews."

"I wish I could, Daniel, but I really must be leaving. I have to change for church."

"Oh, that's right," he remarked, dryly. "I forgot your need for religion."

"It wouldn't hurt you to attend once in a while," she suggested.

"Religion is your crutch, not mine," came the cool reply. Nicole held her tongue, walked to the door, then thanked him for breakfast.

"Aren't you forgetting something?" he asked.

"Oh, yes. George's number." She waited while he jotted it down on a piece of paper and handed it to her. "Thanks, again."

"Don't mention it." As he watched her walk to her car, he called, "Say a prayer for me, will you?" She turned and grinned. It was when she drove off, a sad smile slowly snaked across his lips. "Yes, my sweet Nicole. Say many, many prayers… "

Nicole hurried on her way, spending the remainder of the morning at church and then relaying Daniel's story to Cristoff. He listened in while she called George Craiger, and, just like Daniel had said, the man seemed to be holding a grudge. After offering him money, which he flatly refused, she offered him a job at the ranch, despite Cristoff's protest. To Cristoff's relief, he refused that, too. But by the time the conversation ended, Nicole sensed that George's attitude had remarkably improved. "See?" she said to Cristoff, after hanging up the phone. "He definitely sounds better now."

"Uh, huh," was all the ranch hand replied, deep in thought. "If Daniel's right about this guy, we shouldn't take any chances. Maybe it's time we surrounded this place with a security type fence."

"That costs a lot of money."

"What about an alarm system for the house and barn? Or a guard dog?"

"I don't want a dog and I'd probably set off the alarm system by mistake. I don't know why you're so worried, Cristoff. For goodness sakes, I'm certainly not. George Craiger isn't going to bother me, especially not now that he knows Daniel was the person who informed me of his business loss. I'm sure he's afraid of Daniel, just like the other men. Daniel told me he's threatened them before and there's nothing worse than thinking someone from the government is after you." Considering the argument finished, Nicole quickly called Daniel to tell him he need not worry about Mr. Craiger anymore. Afterwards, she motioned for Cristoff to accompany her outside.

"What?" he asked as she led him to the barn.

Nicole glanced shyly into his large hazel eyes. "Come down to the beach with me?" she softly said, her voice like a frightened child. The ranch hand nervously cleared his throat, astonished by the request. She had never asked him to accompany her before. He felt awkward.

"I have some things to do," he explained. "Maybe another time."

"Please?" Her hand rested upon his arm, then just as quickly fell to her side. He could tell it had been difficult for her to muster enough courage to make the offer.

"I suppose I could join you, for a little while." Her eyes met his and she graced him with a smile. Then she grabbed The General's bridle and a blanket. "What are you doing, Nicole?"

"It'll be faster if we ride there," she called over her shoulder, heading out to the pasture where her stallion grazed.

"Bareback?" he mumbled, following. The General pricked his ears forward with curiosity while he was bridled. Throwing the blanket onto his back, the young woman hoisted herself up on the horse, then waited for Cristoff to do the same. "If he tosses me," he said warily, "you're going to be my servant for a day."

"Deal," she giggled, assisting him up. He settled in behind her, but refrained from grasping her waist when they started off, not wanting to be plagued by desire. The General was urged into a slow jog while they chatted about their goals for the new horses. "I looked over their papers," Nicole said. "I see a lot of potential in those stallions."

"I agree," he said. "However, it's going to take a great deal of work." He dismounted, having reached their destination, and assisted Nicole as she swung down. Removing the blanket from The General, she spread it upon the sand and unbuckled the bridle, setting the Arabian free to play in the cool water. Cristoff unbuttoned his short-sleeve shirt before proceeding to stretch out on his back to enjoy the sun's rays. He looked dead, his hands clasped atop his stomach as if he were inside a coffin. "Nicole," he quietly said, a soft breeze rippling through his hair. "We need to talk."

"Oh? This sounds serious." She laid on her side, facing him, one elbow propping her up. She was so close he could smell the perfume of her lipstick. She was so close it would take less than a second to kiss her. "Well, Cristoff?"

"Huh?" He had completely forgotten his request.

"You said we needed to talk. What about?"

"You wear too much lipstick." He had said it without thinking, knowing darn well that wasn't the subject he needed to discuss.

"I barely have any on," she protested, hurt by his remark. "Does it offend you?"

"No, not really. Actually, it smells quite nice."

She scrunched up her face in a look of utter confusion. He glanced up at her, realized how ridiculous he had sounded, and quickly got to the issue. "Didn't I ask you once before to be careful drinking alcohol?"

"Yes, but I never take anything you say seriously."

"Gee, thanks," he muttered. "Anyhow, I'm reminding you again to watch your alcohol consumption."

"Why, Cristoff? You have no right telling me what to do, especially when you're just as guilty of taking a nip."

"It's for your own good."

"Why? What have I done? Does this have something to do with yesterday? It's Justin, isn't it?! What did he say?"

"Nothing. Forget it."

"Men! Loyal to the end, aren't you?" she fumed.

"I didn't come here to fight," he said hotly.

"What did you come here for, then? To discuss my makeup? The way I fix my hair? Or how about my future plans for marriage?"

"Stop it!" he commanded, sitting up. "Why are you so edgy lately? I thought you asked me out here to enjoy a peaceful afternoon. Instead, I get a—"

"Don't say it," she warned. "And don't skirt the issue. I don't understand why you're concerned about my drinking. I wasn't drunk yesterday. You saw me."

"Oh, yes," he admitted in a stern voice. "I saw you, all right. You were in a skimpy little top and hot pants. Damn near thought I had pulled in to the wrong ranch!" Nicole bit her tongue to keep from arguing. "Thank goodness it was Justin you were with and not some lecher."

"Justin," she spat. "There's that curse word again. I wish I'd never met him, the creep. I suppose while the two of you were discussing my shortcomings, he didn't happen to mention our little tug of war with the blanket, did he?"

"No."

"Nor did he mention the day we first met, how he threw me down on the sand like some common trollop and tried to subdue me?"

"Uh, oh," mumbled the ranch hand, a guilty look on his face.

"Uh, oh?" she repeated. "Uh, oh, what? What do you mean, 'uh, oh'?"

"I suppose you'll find out, anyway," he frowned, barely speaking loud enough for her to hear. "I, uh, sort of did something without your permission, Nicole."

"Like what?"

Unable to meet her gaze, he sheepishly hung his head. "I knew we needed an extra hand with the new horses, so I hired someone."

"So? I trust your judgment. I was thinking of adding another employee, too. You did the job for me." Cristoff suddenly got to his feet and put a little distance between himself and Nicole. The young woman eyed him suspiciously. "Cristoff? Why do I get the feeling I'm not going to like what you'll say next?"

"Because..." He backed up a few steps, then mumbled something inaudible.

"What? I can't hear you, Cristoff."

"I said I hired Justin."

It took a few seconds for the name to register. Nicole's heart skipped a beat. She jumped to her feet, screeching, "You what?!" and slowly advanced towards the retreating man.

Cristoff held his hands out in front of him as if he were stopping an oncoming locomotive. "Now, Nicole, just wait a minute. Let's sit down and talk this over like two civilized human beings."

"You wish!" she exclaimed, breaking into a jog. Cristoff

turned and hightailed it to the woods without a backwards glance. "Come here, you coward!" she screamed, returning to snatch the blanket and bridle before darting off again. The General galloped serenely past the flying woman, clearly enjoying this new excitement. "Come here, General!" she now called, hoping to board the winged Pegasus. But her stallion, true to his nature, sided with his male companion and promptly increased his speed until he had left Nicole running in his dust. She coughed and sputtered, then slowed her gait. It was no use. Cristoff had too much of a head start. She'd catch up with him at the ranch. Then, what? She'd make him call Justin on the phone and fire him. Yes. That sounded good.

Brushing the light dusting of dirt from her clothes, she finally arrived home and headed over to Cristoff's house. When no one answered the door, she let herself in, thinking he was playing games. But Cristoff was nowhere to be found. "Okay, you rascal," she said. "Where are you?" Leaving the tenant house, she walked to the stable. The General was safely in his stall. "Ah, a clue," she smiled, glancing about the barn. A board creaked overhead, prompting her to gaze up towards the hayloft. Without a sound, she sneaked up the ladder and began her search, moving from bale to bale, looking around each stack of hay and straw. A quiet clinking noise sounded on the floor behind her, causing her to turn in its direction. The minute she did so, a powerful arm firmly closed around her neck, making her gasp, startled. Mustering up the deepest pirate voice he could manage, Cristoff laughed wickedly in her ear.

"You beast," she grinned. "Let go." The muscular arm was causing some discomfort now as Nicole tried to pry it loose. She had no idea Cristoff was this strong. "I give up. You win."

"Not so fast, lassie," he snarled in his best pirate voice, faking anger. "I'm not through with ya yet." His fingers curled tightly around her wrists while the villain produced a long strand of baling twine.

"Please!" begged Nicole, playing along. "Not that!"

"Har, har, har," he laughed, binding both wrists together.

"That'll hold ya." He pulled her towards the back of the loft, finding a suitable hook on the wall to string her to, tying her with both her arms stretched high in the air.

"Hey, that hurts," she remarked, yanking against the rope. "Game's over. I quit. Cristoff?" Her back was to him, forcing her to strain her neck as she looked over her shoulder. The ranch hand had disappeared. "Cristoff?" she squeaked, emitting a nervous chuckle. "I'm ready to be untied now." No answer. Nicole was not stupid. She knew he had to still be up here because he hadn't had enough time to shimmy down the ladder. "Cristoff Colvert!" she shouted, clearly angry. "I am not fooling. Untie me, this minute!" She glanced over her shoulder again. "Gosh darn you! I'll kill you when I find you!" She squirmed and wiggled, tugged and pulled, all to no avail.

Unbeknownst to the young woman, her favorite ranch hand was perched quite happily above her, to the right, stretched out on his side across a bale of hay, watching the whole episode. Since he was rather close to the ceiling, it would be difficult for her to notice him. He lazily chewed on a long stem of hay, twirling it between his fingers while looking on with amusement. The girl was actually bracing her feet against the wall, attempting to climb up it. He shook his head with amazement. Did she ever give up?

After ten minutes went by, Nicole had finally loosened the rope enough to slip one hand through. "Wait until I get hold of you, Cristoff!" she swore, easily breaking free. He continued to watch her search amidst the bales for him, almost tempted to give her a hint when she eventually stopped. "You have to come out of here sometime." Hands on hips, she glanced around once more, this time allowing her intuition to choose the next sight. And it did—straight up. Cristoff applauded.

"You!" she shrieked, bounding up the stacked hay.

"Nicole, watch out for the third row. There's a loose bale—" His words died as he saw her falter. She would have tumbled backwards had it not been for his grabbing hold of her arm, one large hand yanking her upwards. Nicole thought her arm was coming out of its socket. She took hold of him with her other hand before he could warn her against it, the full weight of her now jerking him downward. Too late, Cristoff felt the bale of hay he had been perched on slowly begin to tilt, then roll towards the young woman, taking him with it. "Get out of the way!" he called, hoping to save her from injury.

She released her hold and darted to the side, but not quick enough, finding herself trapped amidst the falling body and bale of hay. All three toppled to the floor, finally ending with Cristoff and Nicole intertwined as they crashed onto an opened fresh bale beneath them. It provided a soft landing and prevented any injury. Nicole glanced to the side where Cristoff's perch now lay. "I could have been crushed," she gasped, not moving a muscle to detangle herself.

"Are you okay?" Cristoff inquired, laying very still. His leg was caught under hers and he longed to free it.

"Yeah," she breathed. "I think so."

"No. Don't move. You might have broken a bone. I'll get up first." He slowly inched his leg out from beneath Nicole, but before he could separate completely, she blurted, "Don't you move, either. You could have a broken bone, too." He looked at her like she was daft, knowing very well that one of them was going to have to eventually move or they'd starve to death. He honored her wish, however, and lay there for a few moments, enjoying the warmth of her body against him. And after those few moments, he was surprised to hear her breathing deepen, indicating she had somehow managed to fall asleep. Cristoff had two choices, now. He could wake the sleeping beauty, or remain a little while longer. He chose the latter, gradually drifting off to sleep.

Next time he awoke, it was pitch black outside. "Nicole," he whispered, nudging the tired woman.

"Mm?"

"Wake up. It's nighttime."

Using the beam of moonlight streaming through the large doorway in the wall straight ahead, he saw her eyelids flutter once, twice, then slowly open. "We left the horses out," he reminded her. Still groggy, Nicole murmured, "They'll be okay. What about The General? He's in his stall and is probably hungry."

"I fed him when I put him in," Cristoff replied, shifting his aching body. Nicole's head still rested on his chest. "Look at the sky," he whispered. "Have you ever seen so many stars?"

She glanced out the wide opening that was used when they brought up bales of hay and straw. "It's beautiful," she breathed. "I've never noticed how pretty it looks from up here. This is a great location."

"Yeah," he said in a quiet voice, inhaling the sweet scent of her hair. Very slowly, he raised one hand to softly stroke the long strands, fully expecting Nicole to leap up at any minute. Instead, she nuzzled closer, uttered a weary little sigh and closed her eyes. Cristoff swallowed. He could not believe she had allowed it. Perhaps the fall had rattled her brain?

"Cristoff?" she whispered.

"Mm?"

"That feels wonderful."

He kissed the top of her head. "Good," he replied.

"Cristoff?"

"Mm?"

"Let's not ever leave here." Her words caused him to smile.

And then Nicole did something completely unexpected. She tilted her face to gaze into his eyes, then slowly, ever so slowly, raised her soft, sensuous mouth to his. It wasn't a passionate kiss, but a precisely executed one, delivered with sincerity and purpose. Cristoff was so startled he simply froze, waiting for it to end. But it didn't; and the longer he waited, the more intense it became. It suddenly occurred to him, Nicole wasn't coming up for air. This was not the Nicole he knew. She was supposed to be afraid of men, unapproachable. However, this woman was completely in control, seductively inviting, and clearly determined. Determined to do what? He tore his mouth away for a brief second. "What do you want from me, Nicole?"

"Want?" she breathed, her voice husky. "I don't want anything. Last time we kissed, though, you broke away and said it would never happen again." She traced his bottom lip with the tip of her finger. "You were wrong, dear friend, and I don't see you tossing me to the side in your haste to get up."

He rolled his eyes towards the ceiling and swallowed. Was this only a game? "So you did this, just to prove a point?"

"No."

"Then why did you kiss me?"

The young woman silently rolled off to the side, then assumed a sitting position with her knees drawn up under her chin. Cristoff rose to a sitting position, too, still intent on extracting an explanation. "Answer me, Nicole."

She refused to meet his gaze. "I got caught up in the moment, that's all—the peaceful atmosphere, the romantic night air, the stars brightly shining like a thousand polished diamonds."

"I can't do this," he said with regret. "I can't get emotionally involved with you. You're my employer. Sooner or later we'd have a huge dispute and I'd be out of a job. You understand, don't you?"

Without a word, she stood up, searched for the light switch, found it, and illuminated the loft so she could see the ladder. Cristoff made a feeble attempt to go after her, his hand catching hold of her arm just before her foot met with the top rung of the ladder. "Wait," he begged. "You can't leave like this. Please don't be angry."

"Why should I be angry?" she said, a little too quickly. "I should be commending you, Cristoff. You've behaved like a true gentleman. I'm the one who stepped over the boundary line. I deeply apologize. I assure you, it won't happen again. You'll never need to worry if I'll be lurking around some corner, just waiting to catch you unaware so I can passionately smother you with kisses."

Jerking her arm free, Nicole quickly descended the ladder to the aisleway below, with Cristoff close on her heels.

"I swear I didn't mean to hurt your feelings," he called after the retreating figure. But Nicole was through discussing the matter. Wordlessly, she left the barn to head to her house.

She had only traveled several yards across the grass, however, when a loud noise sounded from the stable. Curious, she backtracked to the entrance and swiftly glanced inside. The large wheelbarrow which had previously been filled with manure was now laying upside down in the middle of the aisle, its contents carelessly scattered across the floor. Brown eyes widening with surprise, Nicole's gaze shifted to the ranch hand. He was making his way towards the opposite end of the building, kicking several buckets that lined the aisle. Every few steps he would stop, turn, and ram his fist into the wooden door of a stall. The pattern continued until he disappeared inside the tack room. Nicole had never seen Cristoff in such a fit of temper. Her instinct warned her to leave him alone. So, she did.

But as she resumed her walk to her house, her thoughts centered on what she had just witnessed. Cristoff had practically thrown a heavy wheelbarrow across the barn. It would have taken tremendous strength to accomplish that feat, and, frankly, even though Cristoff was muscular, Nicole had always thought his physique was too compact for that type of a challenge. Now she realized she had been wrong—about a lot of things, including his self-control.

Cristoff's tantrum brought new questions to mind. How bad was his temper? Was his rage directed at her, or at himself? Why did the kisses so easily provoke him? If he was so quick to anger, who was to say he couldn't have flown off the handle the day Philip was murdered? After all, he admitted having had many heated arguments with the man and he had a weak alibi as to his whereabouts at the time of the murder. Cristoff had simply said he had been in town. Yet, those who were questioned couldn't recollect seeing him, except for one of the local whores. "I'm being silly," Nicole chided herself. "Everyone knows Cristoff wouldn't harm a flea. Besides, the police searched his house thoroughly. There was no weapon which matched the bullets the killer had used." Satisfied, she promptly dismissed all further suspicions and washed up for bed.

CHAPTER EIGHT

"Oh, no!" cried Nicole, staring in horror. She had just awakened and reached for her clothes when she saw the ghastly purple bruises around both wrists. Glancing over the rest of her aching body, Nicole groaned at the sight of several more colorful markings, mostly on her arms and hips. She knew they were the result of her fall in the hayloft, with the exception of her wrists—those bruises came from pulling against the baling twine when she was tied in the barn. "Ouch!" Even her butt was sore. It was a miracle she had slept at all. "I'm going to hate having to ride today," she muttered, slowly easing herself into her jeans. Although the day would be warm, she donned a long-sleeved shirt to hide the discolorations.

By the time she finished breakfast and headed inside the barn, Cristoff had already put all the horses in their stalls and fed them. "Aren't you going to be a bit warm today?" he quizzed, upon seeing her attire.

"Oh, I don't know," she casually replied, pulling up both sleeves to show him her colorful display. "What do you think?"

"I've got a few of those, myself," he replied, "but I won't mention where." Stepping closer, he lifted one of her arms and examined her wrist, frowning as he did so. "I didn't realize I had tied it that tight. I'm really sorry, Nicole."

"It's not your fault. It's from pulling against the rope. Don't look so concerned." Her eyes met his and they both suddenly felt awkward, especially when Cristoff dropped her wrist like a hot potato. Nicole changed the topic. "I want you to get in touch with Justin and tell him he's terminated." She raised her hand. "No. Don't say it. I don't want any argument from you. I won't have him working here; my decision is final. When did you tell him to start?"

"Tomorrow. He's notifying his boss today."

"Oh, dear! Do you have his work number? Maybe you can get hold of him before he quits."

"I don't even have his home phone number, Nicole. But his sister and brother live with him and I imagine they could get in touch with him."

"Then you'd better get over to his house." She looked at her watch. "Wait a minute. He probably hasn't even gone in to work yet. It's too early. Good. If you leave now, you can catch him."

"We really need the help, Nicole. You're making a big mistake."

"No. You were the one who made the mistake. Goodbye, Cristoff." She turned around and headed to the office, leaving the ranch hand with no other choice but to do her bidding. Cristoff, however, had other ideas. He got in his car, zoomed off the property, then returned in five minutes.

"Well?" smiled Nicole. "How'd he take it?"

"He didn't," Cristoff replied.

"What's that supposed to mean?"

"I knocked on the door, but no one answered."

"Did you really?"

"Scout's honor. I knocked and knocked, but nobody came to the door." He failed to mention how lightly he had knocked—the best ears in the world couldn't have heard him, but he wasn't about to tell her that. Hopefully, by the time he checks back at his friend's house, Justin will have already have left for work and given notice. Even Nicole was not spiteful enough to refuse the man a job if he was left unemployed.

"Was his car there?" she quipped.

"I don't know which car is his."

"Well, how many cars were there?"

"Three."

"Well, one of them had to be his!" she insisted, raising her voice. "Go back and try again."

"I already went once. Why don't you go over there?"

"I wasn't the one who offered him a job."

She glared at him until he was left with no other choice but to get back in his car and drive over to Justin's. Yet, when he returned to the ranch, Nicole could tell in one glance that he had had no success in meeting with his friend. "Try in another hour," she suggested, resuming her chores.

Cristoff reluctantly obeyed. To his relief, Justin had already left for work. Neither sibling was able to contact him by phone. "He must be out on a job site," Cristoff explained to Nicole. "I have no idea when he'll return."

"Perhaps he hasn't given notice yet, Cristoff. I'll take a chance and visit him later today."

She dreaded the thought, but someone had to do this dirty deed. The young woman nervously wiped her hands on her jeans. Why, oh, why had Cristoff put her in such a predicament? She wanted to scream. Instead, she snatched a broom and roughly swept the aisle. The remainder of the day was spent mucking stalls and cleaning tack.

Since The General had not been given his daily exercise, she saddled the stallion during the end of the afternoon and rode across the wide expanse of beach to her neighbor's place. Two vehicles were parked beside the house; she hoped one of them belonged to Justin. Dismounting, she commanded, "Stay," to The General, then stepped up to the front door and gave several hard raps.

"Well, what gives me the pleasure of finding such a lovely young lady on my doorstep?" beamed the blond in a cheery voice. "Come in. I can't tell you how grateful I am that you wanted to hire me. You should have seen the look on my boss's face when I told him I quit. It was indescribable. He was such a nasty guy—the kind you'd like to punch in the nose, know what I mean? Oh, excuse me for rattling on. You must have had some reason to see me, eh?"

Nicole felt the anger drain from her body. The man was obviously on top of the world right now, and she had to be the bearer of bad news. This wasn't going to be easy. Blast, that Cristoff! If he had just kept his mouth shut.

"Would you like something to drink?"

"Uh, no," she faltered. "This won't take long."

"That's too bad," he smiled wistfully as he poured himself some brandy.

"I'm afraid there's been a mistake."

"Oh?"

"Yes," she restated, advancing several steps towards him before straightening her posture. Justin's warm blue eyes began to slowly freeze over as he read her intentions.

"Do go on, Mrs. Tyler," he offered politely, casually fingering his glass.

"I must be candid with you, Justin. I came here to tell you I have no need of your services. It seems Cristoff took the liberty of hiring you without my consent—"

"I was under the impression that you needed the help," he interrupted, coolly.

"True," she admitted. "But I am the one who does the hiring—"

"And the firing? Oh, I understand you very well, Mrs. Tyler. Such impeccable timing, I must say! Did it ever occur to you to call me last night, before I was to give notice?" His voice was cold as sleet—his eyes, tiny blue slivers of steel. He set down the brandy glass, afraid of crushing it in his bare hand.

"Well, uh, no, I didn't. We don't have your phone number, which, of course, is Cristoff's fault. He should have asked you for it. I'm sorry for the inconvenience—"

Justin cut her off. "Inconvenience? You call losing my job an inconvenience?" His voice was raised to a howl, sending Nicole into a minor panic. She bit her lower lip, her face red with embarrassment.

Just then, a weak voice called from upstairs. "Justin? Could you get me a glass of water, please?" Simultaneously, the phone rang.

"In a minute, Jan," Justin replied as he strode over to the phone. Nicole wanted to use the opportunity to depart, but hesitated when Jan called out a second time. Her voice sounded so frail, Nicole knew she must be ill. By the tone of Justin's conversation on the telephone, he was going to be a while, so, Nicole took it upon herself to fetch a glass of water from the kitchen and take it upstairs to the sick girl.

"You must be Justin's sister," smiled Nicole, handing her the beverage. "I'm Nicole Tyler."

"Oh, yes. My brother's new boss. I'm Jan," she replied with a tiny smile. "I'm sorry you have to see me like this." The girl looked to be a year or two younger than Nicole, with dark blonde hair and brown eyes. Her complexion, although flawless, was terribly pale. Unlike Justin, there was nothing striking about her appearance; in fact, she was rather plain-looking.

"Do you have the flu?" Nicole inquired, curious.

"Nothing contagious. I have a migraine. I get them all the time. I'm doing better, though. This is my second day of pain. It doesn't hurt to talk like it did yesterday."

"What if I get you some aspirin?" Nicole suggested, to which Jan simply smiled.

"It won't help. You see, that's the difference between a regular headache and a migraine. Over the counter medicine can't deaden the pain of a migraine, and it's usually located on one side of the head."

"I'm so sorry. Can't a doctor help?"

"That's a problem, too. The common medicine prescribed is called a beta blocker, but I have low blood pressure and shouldn't be on it." Jan grimaced as she attempted to resituate the pillows propping her up, so Nicole quickly went to her side to assist her. "Have you ever experienced a migraine, Mrs. Tyler?"

"Please call me Nicole. No, I haven't."

"You're lucky. Sometimes the throbbing is so severe you

just want to die. Sometimes it even hurts to blink an eye, let alone breathe, and you can forget about walking. I try to slow down my heart rate, but it usually takes two days before the pain subsides. That's why I can't work." She hung her head, her eyes filling with tears. "If it wasn't for Justin taking care of me, I don't know where I'd be." The sight of the poor girl's tears drew sympathy from Nicole, who compassionately reached out to touch her hand. Jan gradually lifted her eyes to meet Nicole's. "You seem very kind," she said. "I'm so glad my brother is going to work for you. He hated his other boss. I hope you'll take good care of him. He's such a special guy. I love him, dearly."

The knife of guilt was firmly wedged in Nicole's chest; she took a deep breath to free it. She couldn't have felt any worse than this very minute, looking at the pathetic face of Justin's sister, listening to the poor girl's saga of repetitious misery, then discovering what a compassionate hero the blond-haired madman had become—at least in his sister's eyes. Nicole didn't have the heart to tell her the truth. In fact, she was now beginning to think she had misjudged Justin. Not many brothers would take on a sick sibling.

"I know this will sound odd coming from a stranger," confided Jan, "but I liked you the minute I saw you. You just seem so... warm-hearted." Nicole's gaze shifted to the floor as Jan continued. "I so much wish I could find a job where the employer understood my illness. You don't know what it's like to feel you're a burden to another family member." She was unable to stop the tears from spilling down her cheeks while she spoke. Nicole calmly looked about the room for a box of tissues, found one, and handed it to the crying girl, just as Justin walked into the room.

"Sorry, sis. It was an important phone call." He glanced at Nicole. "Is everything all right?" Jan nodded her head and sniveled.

Nicole, who had been sitting on the bed, now rose and addressed the concerned man. "Jan was explaining the extent of her disability and it gave me an idea." She nodded towards

Justin. "Since you'll be starting work for me tomorrow morning, I was wondering if your sister would like to join our team, when she feels up to it, of course? Since I've acquired more horses, business will undoubtedly pick up and I'll need someone to work in the office, answering phones, filing, and doing odd jobs. She could take off when she's ill, without any fear of termination. What do you think?"

"Oh, yes!" cried Jan, beaming from ear to ear. "Wouldn't that be great, Justin? We'd see each other every day—every day that I'm well, that is. I feel better already!"

Nicole and Justin exchanged uncertain smiles. It was obvious to Nicole, he was still in shock. He hadn't even blinked during the length of her speech. What's more, he almost seemed reluctant to respond.

"If you'll excuse us, Jan," he stated, "Mrs. Tyler and I have some unfinished business to discuss." He took hold of Nicole's arm and steered her out of the room.

"Thank you, Nicole," Jan called. "Goodbye."

"I hope to see you soon," came the reply as Nicole removed her arm from the blond's grasp. The minute they had descended the stairs, Justin wheeled around to face the young beauty.

"What kind of cruel joke are you playing on my sister?"

"It's no joke. I meant every word. Is this how you show your gratitude?"

"I thought I was fired!"

"You were. I had a change of heart."

Justin paced the length of the room like a caged lion. "You're truly sincere?"

"Yes. I wouldn't hurt that poor girl's feelings for anything in the world. How dare you insinuate such a thing!"

He paced some more, then stopped, put his hands in his pockets and relaxed the tense muscles in his back. "Thank you, Nicole," he finally said. "This means a lot to Jan."

"But not to you?"

"Of course it does! I'd be unemployed, otherwise. I just hadn't expected you to change your mind."

"Neither had I, especially when I was so angry at you."

"For what?"

"Several things. First of all, for telling Cristoff about me wagering The General in the poker game. Did anyone ever tell you you have a big mouth?"

"I thought you had already told him. Sorry."

"Secondly, your detective showed up at six o'clock in the morning! I could have killed you."

"Didn't Cristoff warn you?"

"No."

An irritable growl escaped him.

"I do thank you for the detective's services. My house was bugged."

"I know. The detective called me after he was finished."

"Oh," mumbled Nicole, suddenly feeling uneasy. "He didn't happen to mention anything... unusual... did he?"

"Like what, pray tell? Voodoo in the basement? Bats in the attic? Eggs all over the kitchen floor?"

Nicole frowned, unsure if he was pulling her leg. Then she saw him crack a smile, and she, too, grinned.

"What were you and Cristoff doing, anyhow?" he finally asked.

"We... sort of had a disagreement."

"I'll say." He was about to comment, when a loud whinny sounded outside. Alarmed, Nicole rushed to the window to see her stallion darting off down the beach, reins flapping against his neck.

"He'll kill himself if his legs get tangled in those reins!" she cried, running to the door. She was too late to stop him. The Arab was quickly fading into the distance.

"No use chasing him now," added Justin.

Nicole pointed an accusing finger at his chest. "Why don't you stick a hitching post in front of your house?"

"Why don't you learn how to take care of your horse?" he shot back. "Every good equestrian knows you shouldn't leave a horse standing without being tied."

"He's different. I taught him to stand without being tied."

"So, I see," came the dry reply.

"Oo!" Nicole seethed. "I don't know how we're going to get through one day without strangling each other!"

"Hide the rope," he muttered, turning from the door. "I'll get my keys and drive you home." As he searched for the item, Nicole nervously glanced about the room, taking in the beautiful furniture and several paintings. Her eye caught sight of a family picture, so she ventured over for a closer look. "How lovely," she breathed when she saw Justin's mother, snow-blonde hair piled high on her head. Justin was the spitting image of her, he had been blessed with the same vivid blue eyes, high cheekbones and thick hair. Nicole studied his father: Irish red hair, wild and curly; dark brown eyes, scattered freckles, strong bone structure. It would be easy to picture the man chopping firewood or wrestling a calf to the ground.

"Sorry I took so long," broke in Justin as he re-entered the room.

"That's okay," she replied. "I was just looking at the picture of your family. You have a twin?"

He nodded. "Aaron."

"How does Shane tell the two of you apart? You look so similar."

"Shane knows the difference. He and Aaron don't get along."

"Really. I can't imagine Shane being enemies with anyone."

"Don't kid yourself. Have you ever known two Casanovas to be friends?"

"Are you serious?"

"Indeed, I am," he replied, studying her for a moment. "My brother is very... shall we say 'hot-blooded', Nicole. It would be in your best interest to stay away from him, if possible." His steady stare remained fixed upon her until she uttered a reassuring reply. "Shall we go?"

She followed him outside to his jeep, climbed into the passenger seat and asked, "Where do your parents live?"

"They were killed in a car accident. If you don't mind, I'd rather not discuss it."

"I'm sorry," she apologized, quickly changing the subject. "What did you and Cristoff talk about the other night?"

"I'd rather not discuss that, either."

Nicole threw him an agitated look. "What exactly would you like to discuss, then?"

"What time I have to be at work. What my benefits are and, most importantly, whether Cristoff talked to you about my salary."

"Be at the ranch at seven. We can discuss the other topics when you arrive." Nicole fiddled with the seatbelt, trying to decide how she could bring up Cristoff's name again. Finally, she resorted to blunt honesty. "I know you don't want to discuss it, but I have to know if you said anything to Cristoff about our picnic together."

"Why?"

"Because he gave me a lecture on the perils of alcohol, that's why, which is rather odd coming from Cristoff."

"I don't understand."

Nicole stared at him. "You do know he drinks, don't you?"

"So? I do, too."

"Then, you truly don't know."

"I'd appreciate it if you'd get to the point."

"Cristoff is an alcoholic." She gave him a minute to digest the information. "Even I drink. But Cristoff... goes overboard quite often. I thought you knew. I assumed he was always an alcoholic."

"Not when we were teenagers," Justin replied, feeling disappointed in his friend.

"So, you see, that's why I found it odd he'd lecture me about drinking. I gathered that you must have said something to him."

Justin grew quiet.

"Well, did you?" Nicole looked out the window. "Hey, what are you doing? Where are you taking me?" Justin had turned the jeep around and began heading in the opposite direction. Despite Nicole's protests, he traveled a small distance from the ranch, then shut off the motor. "What's the idea?" she fumed, unbuckling her seatbelt.

Justin took hold of her arm to make sure she didn't leap out of the vehicle. "Calm down. I'll take you back home in a minute. I just didn't want to be sitting out in front of your house when I tell you what Cristoff and I discussed. You're going to get mad and it would be too easy for you to hop out of the jeep and run away from me. You'd lock the front door and I'd never be able to finish explaining."

"Explaining what?" she demanded.

"First, promise you'll stay right here until I'm through talking."

Nicole eyed him, warily. "Okay. Is it that bad?"

Justin took a deep breath. He then revealed what had happened to Nicole the day of the picnic and what she had said when she was inside her house. He also told her how Cristoff had assured him Nicole had not taken any drugs. "I know about your past," he quietly said, watching the color drain from her face. "Don't blame Cristoff. I asked all the right questions. He chose not to lie. He also made me swear that no one else would ever know."

"Yeah, right," Nicole scoffed, wringing her hands in her lap. The color returned to her ashened face while tears of humiliation sprang to her eyes.

"I want to help you, Nicole."

His voice sounded so far away to her, or was it that she was silently shutting him out? In her mind, she was no longer inside the jeep. She was enclosed in a deep, dark dungeon. Nicole began to build invisible walls around herself, building them higher and higher, forcing the truth to remain a safe distance away, at the outside of the fortress walls. Only she could control what entered... who entered... Alone in her fortress, she was safe. Or was it the dungeon? She could no longer tell.

"Nicole?" Justin angled his body so he could touch both her hands, which he did, gently rubbing his thumbs back and forth over the cold skin. He had seen the dull look in her eyes and knew she had mentally blocked him out. He silently cursed his impulsiveness. He should have never told her this soon. They barely knew each other, for crying out loud. Why did he expect her to readily accept his help?

"Nicole," he called again, cupping her chin, forcing her to turn and face him. "I was a fool to tell you. I should have waited."

That snapped her back to reality. "Waited?" she mocked. "Waited 'til when? 'Til a local horse show was in progress and you could get the full attention of the crowd with my amazing story? Why wait, Justin? Perhaps there is some other little tidbit of information you have on me which you'd like to get off your chest? Apparently, you know me so well. So, tell me, what other deep, dark secrets have you discovered? Did Cristoff reveal every personal detail of my married life?"

"Nicole, don't."

Salted droplets coursed their way down her cheeks, yet still she continued. "Did he tell you how I danced upon tables? How I gladly serviced Philip's friends? Did he tell you about my wonderful honeymoon?" She buried her tear-streaked face in her hands, unable to stop the sobs that racked her slender body. Justin reached across to enfold her in his arms, but she pushed him away, crying, "Haven't you done enough?"

"I didn't expect such a strong reaction," he confessed. "I haven't said anything you don't already know. Besides, you demanded the information. Against my better judgment, I met the demand. I want to help you, Nicole. I think Cristoff and I might be able to find out what drug Philip used, and if that's so, we can find something to counteract it."

"What?" she questioned, her expression changing to one of confusion. "What the devil are you talking about?"

Justin stared at her in silence. Hadn't Cristoff told her? Yes, he remembered now. Cristoff did try to tell Nicole she was having flashbacks. He said she hadn't believed him. Nicole wiped the rest of the tears away with the back of her hand, took a tissue from her pants pocket and blew her nose. "Why do you need to counteract the drug?" she asked, intent on getting an answer. "Is there something I haven't been told?"

“No,” came the slow reply. “Cristoff has enlightened you about your flashbacks.” He carefully watched her reaction.

“Flashbacks. It isn’t possible. It just isn’t.”

“It is, Nicole. When you passed out from drinking on the day of the picnic, you relived those past events with your husband. Cristoff thinks the alcohol triggers flashbacks. We have to find out what drug Philip used on you. It’s the only chance you have of putting an end to the flashbacks.”

“I drink all the time at home and never have a flashback. Well, almost never.” She gazed out the window again. “I’ll have to think about this. Take me home, Justin.”

“Will you be okay?” he asked with concern.

She gave a slight nod, then shivered as a cold chill ran up her spine. Justin started the jeep.

“What if I stay with you for a little while, Nicole, until you’re feeling better?”

In a robotic manner, her head turned in slow motion to face him while she glared. “I don’t think so.”

An uneasy silence filled the vehicle the remainder of the journey until the young woman finally departed in haste and Justin reluctantly left. But instead of entering her house, Nicole briskly walked behind the building to the stable area, where Cristoff was dishing out the evening meal to the horses. He had his back to the oncoming hurricane, never even heard the silent footsteps approaching.

And then the storm hit. Nicole belted him square in the jaw. Cristoff dropped the bucket of oats to defend himself, the identity of his attacker still not registering yet. One arm shielded his face as he blindly struck back, hitting Nicole hard in the stomach. She went down on her knees, clutching her abdomen, her face ghastly white as she struggled to breathe.

Swearing filled the air when Cristoff realized whom he had just hit. He was at her side in an instant, talking her through the disabling incident, reassuring the young woman her health would improve in a few minutes. Of course, he didn’t expect a response since the wind had been knocked out of her. He simply assumed she was heeding his advice for a quick recovery. He'd wait until she felt better before demanding an explanation for her actions.

But, much to his astonishment, the moment Nicole resumed normal breathing, she turned on the ranch hand and threw another punch, yelling and screaming like a wildcat. Fortunately Cristoff saw this one coming, easily dodging the attack. He suddenly realized he had no other choice but to subdue her, which he eventually did, although it was no easy chore this time. He had to press her against the outside of a stall wall, face first, and twist one of her arms up behind her back.

"How could you?!" she ranted and raved. "How could you tell Justin about the parties?" She was almost in tears now, with only her ferocious rage keeping her from crying. "I hate you, Cristoff! I don't want to see you on this ranch ever again! Do you hear me? You're fired. You have one week to get out of here." She felt the energy drain from his body as he suddenly released his hold.

"He was asking questions," Cristoff countered. "What did you want me to tell him, Nicole?" His eyes were cold and accusing.

"Anything but the truth!" she shouted.

"He can be trusted. I need his help."

"It's been years since you've seen him! How do you know he can be trusted? Why would you need his help? Oh, yes," she scoffed, "I do remember him mentioning some heroic effort to find an antidote. Why even bother? I can just stop drinking—that'll cure it."

"What if another triggering factor turns up? What if it isn't only the alcohol, Nicole? What if emotional stress sets you off?"

"Then I'd be hallucinating right now, wouldn't I?" she said through clenched teeth. "One week, Cristoff. I won't have anyone disloyal working for me."

"I'm not disloyal!" he yelled to her departing figure as she walked up the aisle. Cursing like a madman, he kicked the bucket of oats clear across the barn, prompting the horses into a series of snorts and whinnies. He couldn't believe this was happening to him! He ran up the aisle and across the lawn until he was within shouting distance of his employer. "I'll be gone in two days!" he promised. "How does that suit you, Your Highness?"

Nicole ignored him, rubbing her tender abdomen with the palm of her hand while she scanned the surrounding scenery for some sign of The General. She finally caught a glimpse of his white rump behind several trees and called to him. Since it was feeding time, the horse readily obeyed, allowing his owner to catch him with relative ease and walk him back to the stable. After untacking the stallion, Nicole fed him, cleaned up the spilled oats and completed the barn chores for the evening. She then flopped into bed and cried herself to sleep.

The next morning, Nicole was barely able to rise from bed, her stomach cramping with pain. She felt as if a horse had kicked her in the abdomen and silently wondered if men experienced this much discomfort after a common fistfight. She grunted, dragged herself out from between the sheets and sought the relief of a hot water bottle. It took almost a half hour before the cramping ceased, but she was finally able to fix some breakfast before venturing out to the stable. Knowing Cristoff would be absent, she put up with the aches and pains which still remained from yesterday, and began the morning chores until Justin arrived. They greeted each other, Nicole masking her discomfort with a forced smile.

"Where's Cristoff?" the blond asked. It was the one question Nicole had been dreading to answer.

"I had to fire him," she plainly said. "He betrayed me when he disclosed the details of my private life to you."

Justin was stunned. "He did it in your best interest, Nicole! Can't you see that? I pumped him for answers."

"Yes, I know. It doesn't matter. I don't take kindly to having my past paraded around before strangers."

"We're not strangers."

"I don't care to discuss this, Justin. I have a million things to do and now I'm shorthanded. Let's go over your benefits and salary so we can get started on the real work."

The blond shook his head. "No," he said quietly. "I can't, in good conscience, work for you when I know I am the reason Cristoff was fired. If I had kept my mouth shut, none of this would have happened. You can find yourself another man to do the job. I quit."

"But..." Nicole's fingers closed around his upper arm, causing him to hesitate. "You can't just leave me here like this! I can't handle the work by myself. You know darn well it will take several days or more to find someone I can trust to replace you. It'll take even longer than that to hire a new manager. Please," she implored, "I'll make it worth your while to stay."

Justin arched one blond brow. This new promise piqued his curiosity. He had no intention of remaining, but he was definitely interested in hearing what the little hellcat had to say. "What could you possibly offer to change my mind?" he said with amusement.

Nicole blinked, already regretting her reply. "Liberal benefits, a higher wage, a longer lunch hour, a share of the profits, whatever it takes."

"Oh?" He coolly glanced at the hand which still held him hostage, felt it tremble slightly before she swiftly released her grip. "Whatever it takes?" he repeated slowly, purposely leering at the young beauty to emphasize his meaning. He wanted to scare her good before bowing out. She did not disappoint him, her expression a mixture of fear and loathing.

"That depends on what you have in mind," she quietly replied, managing to contain her anger.

"Eh." Justin shrugged his shoulders. "You don't have anything I'm interested in." With that, he turned and strolled out of the barn, leaving his stunned employer standing with her mouth open. Nicole then knew she had been taken for a fool.

"Fine!" she yelled to no one. "I'll do everything myself. I don't need you. I don't need Cristoff, either!" In a tizzy, she grabbed some grooming supplies and started taking care of the horses before their morning turnout. The newspaper ad for hired help would just have to wait until tomorrow, she decided. There was too much work to be done today.

Exercising so many horses nearly exhausted her, not to mention the fact that she had somehow skipped lunch and it was well into late afternoon. Thankfully, no customers had called. She doubted she would have had time to return the calls, especially when she still had all the stalls to clean. That chore was left until dinnertime. Nicole, however, had underestimated the amount of time involved in the task. Her back sore and stiff after only several hours of mucking, she had to work straight past midnight to accomplish the feat, only then to decide she might as well let the horses stay out in the pasture for the remainder of the evening. "This is hopeless," she cried, sinking down to collapse on the floor of the aisle. The cold stall wall felt good against her aching back, yet she only enjoyed the sensation for a moment before succumbing to the beckoning call of dreamland.

Cristoff had seen the light on inside the stable all evening, but wasn't concerned until the wee hours of the morning. It was then he casually strode into the barn and discovered Nicole fast asleep, her forehead resting against bent knees. He touched her with the toe of his boot, with no response. "Nicole," he called softly, tilting her head back to its normal position. She looked pathetic, dirt smudges dotting her tan skin. She also reeked of soiled straw and manure, making Cristoff realize she had spent all night cleaning the stalls. "Stupid girl," he sighed, finally picking her up in his arms. The motion didn't even wake her, not until after the ranch hand had gently kicked her front door shut and carried her upstairs to the bedroom where he laid her on top of the spread.

"What happened?" she mumbled, eyes fluttering open. She suddenly grew fearful. "Oh, no! I was trampled, wasn't I? Is it bad? Anything broken? Are the horses okay?"

"You're all right," Cristoff comforted her. "You just feel like you were trampled, Nicole. What the devil did you hope to accomplish by working around the clock? You nearly killed yourself."

"What other choice did I have after Justin quit?" She tried to sit up, but gave an anguished cry, instead. Her stomach had a million knives in it. She looked helplessly at the man before her.

"It's that bad, huh?" he frowned. "Did you eat supper?"

"A piece of bread. Didn't have time."

"I'm going down to the kitchen and fix some soup. I want you to eat, even if you don't feel like it. You have to keep your strength up. Then I'm going to run the bath water for you and I want you to soak for a good half hour." Nicole simply nodded, unable to argue. She felt too miserable. But while she waited for his return, she recalled the day's events and suddenly realized how unfair she had been to Cristoff. To think that she had even socked him in the jaw without ever asking if he was okay! Somehow her previous anger no longer justified the action and the young woman found herself feeling the first pangs of guilt. Here he was, taking care of her, when she had already dismissed him from the ranch. Justin was correct when he claimed that Cristoff cared about her. He truly did. Perhaps he had confided in Justin only as a last resort for finding help for her. "I can't think about it," she said out loud, shifting onto her side. "I'm in too much pain. Maybe later..." Her voice dropped off as she fell back asleep, only to be awakened by Cristoff, again. He had set a tray near the bed, complete with chicken noodle soup and toast. Reaching over, he slowly helped her sit up.

Before she took a spoon of food, however, she gazed up at the silent man, tears in her eyes. "I'm so sorry, Cristoff," she whispered, unable to convey the true depth of her feelings. "I don't want you to leave."

Upon hearing her words, he dropped his gaze to the floor. "Of course, you don't. You just realized how difficult it is to manage the place by yourself."

"No!" she emphatically stated, reaching out to take hold of his hand. "If I had to, I could find someone to replace you. But I don't want to, Cristoff. I just now understood everything you said today, the reasons why you talked to Justin. Sure, I heard them earlier, but I was too angry to believe you." She pleaded with her eyes. "I've never been able to trust men, not after Philip. I know I can be stubborn sometimes."

"All of the time," he corrected.

"Won't you please stay here at the ranch? I'll even give you a raise."

"I don't know," he drawled, rubbing his fingers along his sore jaw line. "This job is hazardous to my health."

"Oh, Cristoff, I am so sorry I hit you. Does it hurt very much?" He could tell she was overly concerned.

"I think you fractured it, Nicole. See right here?" He pointed to an imaginary spot.

"No," she frowned, squinting her eyes to find the indentation.

"Right here," he insisted, leaning towards her. "You'd have to be blind to miss it. It's as big as a nickel."

Nicole stretched out her neck until she was inches from the wound. "Where? Move your finger. Maybe you're covering it."

"The pain is just awful," he complained. "Perhaps I should have a doctor look at it." No sooner had the words left his lips, he closed the distance between them and stole a quick kiss from the unsuspecting female. Nicole stared dumbly at the 25 year-old, then broke into a smile.

"You're going to stay, aren't you?" she beamed.

"Only if you make up for busting me in the chops."

"Deal," she agreed. "Name your price."

"Let me have your Shelby Mustang for one night."

"Hot date, huh?" she teased.

"Yeah."

"Okay, but don't mess up the interior and absolutely no racing. When do you want it?"

"Tomorrow night." He looked at his watch. "Oops, that would be tonight."

"The keys are in my purse. I won't be needing them yet. I have a feeling I'm not going to be able to move a muscle tomorrow." She took a few spoonfuls of soup. "Will you ask Justin to come back to work for me?"

"Sure. He called me earlier this evening to tell me he had quit. I have his phone number now, so I'll write it in your telephone book downstairs." Nicole waited until he had left the room before she resumed eating. She was glad there were no hard feelings between them, but then Cristoff always was easy to get along with. She wondered why he hadn't touched any liquor after their dispute. Usually, he would have drowned his sorrows within an hour. Lucky for her he had chosen to remain sober, otherwise she wouldn't be up here in bed, finishing a good meal. She was taking a last bite of toast when the ranch hand returned.

"Okay if I start the bath water now?"

"I can do it, Cristoff. Go home and get some sleep." He ignored her, which was becoming normal behavior for him, and headed into the bathroom anyway. After adjusting the water temperature, he reappeared to fetch her tray. "Thank you, Cristoff," Nicole said. "I really appreciate what you did for me tonight."

"You're welcome. I'll be taking this down to the kitchen and then leaving, unless you need help undressing?" He gave her a big wink, to which she lightly laughed. Then he was gone, and the sudden silence in the room became deafening. She was beginning to enjoy Cristoff's company, even when they weren't working—especially when they weren't working. Her thoughts turned to his request for her car. Whoever his date was, she had to be special for him to ask for the Shelby. Perhaps he and Justin were double dating?

Nicole fancied what it would be like to begin dating again, then quickly dismissed the idea as ridiculous. She didn't have time for dating, nor did she believe she could find a man who didn't lie. As far as she was concerned, dishonesty seemed to be second nature to the opposite sex. Besides, men were too fickle. They only paid attention to you until a cuter girl entered the picture. Of course, this was what she had been told by teenage girlfriends when she was younger. She imagined the dilemma worsened with age. Even Cristoff dated so many women, Nicole lost count several months ago. She wondered if he had ever fallen in love or had his heart broken. Perhaps that was the reason he drank? She'd have to ask him sometime, when they were having a heart to heart talk. "I really should quit thinking about him so much," she scolded herself as she got undressed. Slipping into the hot tub of water, she tried to focus her mind on something else. But as she allowed the warmth of the water to envelop her sore, weary body, Nicole was reminded of another time, not so distant, when she experienced a similar feeling. It was when she had slept peacefully in Cristoff's arms, up in the hayloft. She could still feel the heat from his body radiating through his shirt.

Then she recalled another incident, when she had awakened in her living room to find herself cradled in Justin's lap, his vivid blue eyes full of compassion and concern. It had been the day of the picnic… Nicole closed her eyes, trying to recapture that secure feeling. It had been wonderful, but she wasn't about to tell Justin that. It was her tiny secret. As much as she hated to admit it, Nicole was developing a real yearning for a man's embrace. She never experienced such tenderness with Philip. He always had a detached air about him, as if he were mentally and emotionally distant. She merely assumed that was normal behavior for a husband. No one had told her differently.

But now, now Nicole knew otherwise. Granted, she had only been given a small piece of the pie to savor. Yet Nicole hungered for the rest. She wanted to feel loved, cherished, desired. But, by whom? Nicole frowned. "I don't like this feeling," she whispered. "I'd better stop daydreaming." So she turned her thoughts to cleansing the soil from her soft skin, hoping her passionate nature would wash away with the rest of the dirt. She nearly scrubbed herself raw, causing her to yowl in pain at the touch of a towel. Glad when the task was finished, she changed the bedspread before climbing back under the sheets. In three hours she'd have to get up again to face a new day's worth of chores. If she could just erase the thoughts of Justin and Cristoff from her mind... if only... if only...

CHAPTER NINE

Yet, three hours came and went. Nicole still lay in bed. When she finally did awaken, it was eleven o'clock. "Oh, no!" she cried, making a feeble attempt to rise. Her body would not allow it. She grimaced in agony as every muscle disobeyed her command. Yesterday's pains were trivial compared to the torture she experienced now. It was as if each limb was being torn from her body.

A pair of footsteps could be heard approaching before a familiar voice called out from the hallway. "Nicole? I heard you cry out. Are you okay?" The sleeping beauty blinked in surprise, then asked, "What are you doing here, Jan?"

Justin's sister entered the room, her expression cheerful and apologetic. "I didn't mean to startle you," she explained. "Cristoff suggested I wait downstairs until I heard you wake up. He thought you might need someone to take care of you today."

"He did, did he?" came the dry reply. Nicole didn't like feeling helpless, and to be stuck in bed, unable to move about without wincing made her feel like a big baby.

"He meant well," Jan continued. "He and Justin are splitting the chores so you can rest. Everything's under control, Nicole. Really. We all know what you did yesterday and we want to take some of the burden off you. I was going to start work today, anyhow. It makes no difference to me whether I stay here and assist you, or go to the stable office to answer the phone."

"That's very sweet of you, Jan. Thank you, but I doubt the phone would be ringing much. Business won't pick up until word gets out about our new stallions." She studied the young girl. "You look well. How are you feeling?"

"Fine. My strength has returned. I couldn't wait to come here. Cristoff showed me around and gave me the information on my benefits."

"Did he discuss your wages?"

"No. He said you would do that."

Nicole sank back against her pillow and gave the topic some thought. "How does seven dollars an hour sound?"

Jan's jaw dropped. "That much?" she asked, amazed. "Just for office work?"

"For starters," Nicole smiled. "I'm known to give raises."

"Thanks!" chirped Jan, full of enthusiasm. The happy expression vanished, however, when Nicole pulled her arm out from under the covers to scratch an itch on the opposite shoulder.

"What?" Nicole asked, upon seeing a look of utter horror cross the blonde's face.

"Y-Your arm! Your wrist! Oh, Nicole!" She jumped up to get a better view of the assorted bruises while Nicole frowned.

"You weren't supposed to see those, but now that you have, don't be concerned. Cristoff and I had a spill up in the hayloft the other day."

"Whatever you say," remarked Jan, eyeing her with suspicion.

"I'm serious," Nicole insisted. "Ask Cristoff. He'll tell you. Oh. You're studying my wrist. Well... I didn't get those marks from the fall."

"You don't have to explain. It's none of my business, Nicole."

But Nicole could see the girl did want her to explain, so she gave it a shot. "All right. If I tell you what happened to my wrists, promise you won't say anything to your brother?"

"Promise." Jan crossed her heart.

"Cristoff and I were playing a game." A bit embarrassed, she looked away. "He was pretending to be a Pirate and I let him tie me up. No. Don't laugh. It's the truth."

Jan's lighthearted giggles filled the room, causing Nicole to turn three shades of red. "I can't believe you were suckered!" Jan confessed. "He used to try that trick with me when I was younger, but I wouldn't let him." Her giggles became a series of good-natured laughs, until she finally covered her mouth with her hand to stifle the noise. "I'm sorry, Nicole. How rude of me."

"I suppose I'd laugh, too, if it didn't hurt so much. Are there any other tricks from the past I should know about?" Jan smiled and shook her head. "Good. Then, would you do me a favor? Find your brother and tell him I want to see him. I need to discuss his wages, also."

"Sure," she replied, quickly departing. The way she ran down the stairs reminded Nicole of an ecstatic little girl. It was several minutes later before she returned with Justin. Jan, however, remained downstairs while her brother visited.

"You wanted me?" Justin quizzed, his deep, masculine voice causing her heart to pound. Just the sound of him prompted the temptress to draw the covers up to her neck, carefully keeping both arms hidden beneath the fabric.

"Yes," she answered, trying to be authoritative. "Close the door, please. We need to discuss your salary."

"First, how do you feel?" His ocean-blue eyes pierced through the blanket as if it was transparent, making her blush.

"I'm all right. Now, back to what I was saying—"

"How do you really feel?" he interjected, folding his massive arms.

Nicole frowned, clearly agitated at his insistence on a more detailed answer. "I'm in so much pain I could fire the first person who annoys me. Is that explicit enough?"

He yawned, not intimidated at all. "Think you need a doctor? You could have sprained something, you know."

"I doubt it. Can we return to the original topic of this conversation?"

"Oh, yeah. My salary."

"I think three hundred and sixty dollars a week is a fair amount to start. After I see how well you do with the horses, I'll consider increasing your salary."

"Fair enough," he agreed. "Are we finished?"

"In a hurry, huh?"

"No. But I do have something on my mind which I had hoped to discuss with you."

"Be my guest." He chose to sit in the chair across from her.

"I've decided to engage the services of my detective friend, Charles King, to search for Dr. Bohman. I have to wait, of course, until Charlie returns from his business trip. Any objections?"

Nicole looked perplexed. "You'd waste your money to chase an elusive doctor? Didn't Cristoff tell you we've already tried?"

"I trust my friend," he persisted. "He's very thorough."

"But, Justin, it could cost a fortune."

"Let me worry about the cost. It's important we find this doctor, if he exists. I'm still not sure. I have a lot of questions, including why no evidence of the drug was found during a routine search of your house. The investigative team did search your house, didn't they?"

"Of course. The sheriff brought in a special team from the next district."

"And no one questioned you about any narcotic they may have discovered?"

"No."

"It doesn't make sense, Nicole. If Philip used these pills on you, why wasn't there a stash of them anywhere in the house? Can you think of a special hiding place he may have used?" Nicole shook her head. "What about the barn? Could he have hidden it in the barn?"

"They searched that area, too. They combed the grounds. They even tried pulling some of the wooden boards loose in the stable to see if a weapon could have been stashed there."

"But if Philip didn't have his own bottle of pills, that would mean he had to have had someone supply him with the exact dosage for each episode—which would prove very inconvenient, unless... one of the poker players brought the dope with him. Could Dr. Bohman have been one of the players?"

"None of the men went by that name."

"Maybe he used an alias." Justin pondered the idea. "I could have the detective check into each man's background."

"Now you're talking big bucks," Nicole reminded him. "Tell you what. I'll pay for the investigation for each of Philip's friends. I think there were only five of them."

"If that's how you want to do this?" he replied. "In the meantime, Cristoff is going to ask Daniel out for a few drinks and pump him for more details. I just thought you should know."

"Thanks." She sincerely meant it. At least the guy was honest. "If Daniel bursts in here, raving like a madman, I'll know why." She graced him with a smile, watching as the tall blond stood up.

"I guess I'll be getting back to work, then."

"Tell Cristoff I'm grateful for what the two of you are doing for me, especially taking care of things today while I recuperate." He nodded, smiled, then opened the bedroom door before heading downstairs. Nicole listened for the soft thump of the front door closing, then relaxed her hold on the blanket. No sooner had she done so, Jan entered the room with a tray filled with various breakfast items. "You're a dear," Nicole commented, her mouth watering at the sight of so much food. "Sit down and talk with me, Jan; that is, unless you have other plans?"

"Oh, no," she quickly replied, occupying the same chair her brother had used. "I'd love to sit and talk. Actually, I was hoping you could answer some questions I have about the ranch?"

"Shoot."

"Why aren't there any foals here?"

Nicole took a bite of food. "Perhaps in the future I'll try my hand at raising one. Currently, I'm not informed enough about their upbringing. They need special diets, you know. Plus, I'm not familiar with helping a mare give birth. That's why I stick to strictly breeding stallions. It's what my late husband, Philip, taught me."

"Do you show the horses?"

"No. Philip did. I just haven't felt ready to take on that challenge after his death. I prefer remaining at the ranch. But I know I'll have to have someone show the horses or we won't acquire new customers. Ribbons and trophies mean money in the breeding business. Everyone wants to breed to a champion."

"Maybe Justin could show the horses for you?"

"I haven't even seen him ride, yet. Whoever shows them has to be an expert rider." Just then, both women heard the front door open.

"Nicole? Are you decent?" called Cristoff.

"Come on up," she yelled back, finishing her orange juice.

As he entered the room, he nodded towards Jan. "Would you excuse us for a few minutes?"

"Sure."

He waited until she had disappeared down the steps, then promptly shut the bedroom door. Turning to Nicole, he quietly mouthed, "Are you crazy? We can't hire Justin and his sister at that rate of pay!"

"Yes, we can," Nicole argued.

"No, we can't. You have to hire a trainer for the new horses. We need someone to take them to shows, too. Have you given that any thought?"

"The trainer can also show them, which means hiring one more person, not two. So?"

"You don't realize how expensive trainers can be."

"We'll manage. We may have to settle for second best, that's all."

"You're not going to pull in much money until those stallions have earned a nice reputation, and that could take months. The profits are dwindling, Nicole. Now Justin tells me you're planning to use his detective to check up on Philip's old friends. How do you expect to pay for it?"

"I have another bank account, Cristoff. Relax. Even if I didn't have the money, all I have to do is ask Daniel for a loan. He's been so anxious to help me, remember?"

Cristoff waved his index finger at her. "Mark my words: If you borrow from Daniel, you'll regret it. I still don't trust him."

"Well, he does lie." She shrugged. "My money will hold out until the ranch becomes more profitable."

"I sure hope so," Cristoff stated, then asked, "How do you feel today?"

"I'll live. Remind me never to clean more than four stalls a day. Ouch!" She shifted in bed and sucked in her breath at the fresh stab of pain. "Would you mind getting me some aspirin out of the medicine cabinet?"

"Sure." He retrieved the pills and handed them to her. "I'd better get back to the barn. You rest and take it easy. Yell, if you need anything. I told Jan to keep an eye on you."

Nicole smiled. "Thanks, Cristoff." She watched him depart, wishing she was going to the stable with him. After a few minutes, Jan reappeared, eager to continue their conversation.

Once the two women began talking, they discovered they had a lot in common: both had been shy, introverted children with wild imaginations. Jan had an interest in creative endeavors, also, including art. She was fascinated by Nicole's paintings and expressed the desire to be able to accomplish such an achievement. When the topic turned to men, Nicole realized Jan was as inexperienced in dealing with the opposite sex as she had been before her own marriage. In fact, the more they talked, the more Nicole was drawn to Justin's sister; it reminded her what it was like to have a best girlfriend—something Nicole hadn't had in years. They chatted through lunch and soon found themselves becoming hoarse, thus the two women decided to play cards until dinner. Nicole was feeling much better now, the aspirin eliminating most of the pain. She got dressed and ventured into the kitchen to begin the evening meal, inviting Jan to stay.

It was a few hours after supper when Nicole heard the familiar sound of her car's engine start. "That must be Cristoff," she told Jan. "He wanted to borrow my car tonight."

"I know," the blonde replied. "Justin is going with him." Jan's expression brightened. "Hey! Why don't we go out, too? I haven't had anyone to pal around with for quite some time. Would you like to go to a club?"

"Oh, I don't know," Nicole answered, until she saw the look of disappointment cross her friend's face. "Well, okay. Do you mind riding in a truck?"

"We could take my car," she offered. "But I'm not too familiar with these surroundings at night. I haven't lived here very long."

"I'll take the truck. Let me change clothes. Then we'll drive to your place and you can freshen up."

"Great." Jan calmly walked the perimeter of the living room, studying various equine pictures until Nicole returned from upstairs. "You look like a million bucks," she complimented, eyeing the slinky leopard print dress clinging to her friend.

"It's one of my few outfits having long sleeves," Nicole remarked, demonstrating how the fabric conveniently hid her bruised wrists. "Have you decided what you're wearing?"

"Uh, no." Actually, Jan had. But after seeing Nicole's stunning dress, she realized none of her clothes could compete. Intuitively intercepting her thoughts, Nicole suggested, "I have an idea. Since you have been such a dear to sit with me today, I'd like to repay the kindness by purchasing a new outfit for you. Let's head into town. I know a great little shop that has the most gorgeous clothes." Jan opened her mouth to protest, but the dark-haired beauty had already taken her by the elbow and guided her out the front door.

A half hour later, Nicole's new friend was beaming from ear to ear as they drove to Justin's house. "I can't wait to wear my new dress!" she exclaimed excitedly. "Thank you so much, Nicole. But shouldn't we have bought something less expensive?"

"Only the best for my friends," Nicole smiled, pulling up the driveway. They hurried inside the house, and went upstairs. Within minutes, Jan had slipped into her new dress and stood proudly before a full-length mirror. "I love it!" she cried, twirling about while staring at the black velvet material. It was strapless, gathering at the waist with a wide sash that tied into a big bow in the back. From the hips down, the fabric softly billowed out in gentle waves.

"The dark color accents your blonde hair," Nicole added, nodding with approval. "What type of makeup are you going to put on?"

"I have some blue eye shadow and pink blush."

"Oh, perhaps another color would suit you," Nicole said. "If you don't mind my opinion?"

"Sure."

Nicole fished through her purse to pull out a small object. "I have a smoke color eyeshadow which would really bring out your eyes. If you want, I could do them for you?"

"Would you?" Jan begged, plopping down at her vanity. She watched with fascination as Nicole applied the makeup, her true artistic talent apparent when the finished product was viewed.

"Do you have any rose blush?" Nicole asked; then, upon seeing her friend shake her head no, reached inside her purse one more time to retrieve the desired object. After shading and contouring Jan's cheekbones, she studied the girl's mouth.

"I know," Jan guessed. "Do I have any red lipstick, right?"

"You're not the type to wear red, if you don't mind me saying so. Red is too bold."

"Pink?"

"Not with rose blush. Hmm. Let me think." She tapped her chin with her finger. "Burgundy. Yes, that's it. Burgundy. Do you have any?"

"The closest color I have is wine."

"Great." After outlining her lips with a lip pencil, the

lipstick was carefully applied. Eyeliner and mascara were added as a final touch before Jan stood up to view herself again in the full length mirror. Both women grinned with approval. This was not the same girl at Nicole's house earlier today.

"Oh!" cried Jan, unable to believe her reflection. "I'm actually pretty."

"Pretty? You're beautiful!" Nicole commented, unable to stop smiling. The transformation was truly remarkable, and the air of confidence Jan now exuded was even more alluring. "Keep these," Nicole said, placing the smoke eyeshadow and rose blush on Jan's vanity. "I can buy more."

"But, but..." The blonde's protest was cut short as Nicole grabbed her hand and pulled her back down the stairs.

"We have to run if we're going to find an open table at this hour of the night." Jan snatched her purse on the way out, then the two of them jumped in the truck and sped off for a hopefully fun evening. "Which club would you like to go to?" Nicole politely asked.

"I heard that the Midnight Lounge was pretty good," Jan replied.

"It's one of my favorites. I'll have us there in no time." And she meant it. Nicole raced through town as if her life depended on it, making her friend a nervous wreck by the time they reached their destination. Nicole took one look at Jan's frightened face and instantly apologized, ashamed of her actions.

"Once I have a glass of wine, I'll be okay," the blonde said, seating herself at a table. Nicole ordered an iced tea for herself, deciding to refrain from alcohol tonight. She watched the couples dancing while loud rock music blared from several large speakers, leaned back in her chair and sipped her beverage.

"Aren't you going to drink?" asked Jan, practically yelling to be heard over the music.

"No point in it, since I'm driving," she explained. The words were no sooner out of her mouth when a handsome young man appeared, inviting her to dance. Nicole politely declined, smiling as the fellow then asked Jan. She quickly agreed and the two of them walked out onto the dance floor. "Good," Nicole said to herself, hoping this would be the first in a long line of invitations for the blonde. She wanted this evening to be special for the young girl. It was evident from the glowing smile brightening Jan's face, she was eager for the attention.

"Well! Look who's here!"

Nicole's head shot around to place the deep voice with a face, and inwardly groaned. "Hello, Justin. Cristoff." She forced a tiny smile, realizing the chance meeting was probably not by chance at all.

"You must be feeling pretty good, ay?" Cristoff shouted, pulling up a chair. Justin did the same, his eyes never leaving his boss's tightly wrapped body.

"How'd you get into that thing?" he quizzed, motioning towards the dress. Nicole could have coshed him on the head, but chose to be civil, saying, "If the two of you sit here, you'll never have any luck with the young women. Shouldn't you be off to yourselves?"

"Oh, we will," assured Cristoff. "Just as soon as Shane shows up with our dates."

Nicole now relaxed. So... Jan hadn't planned this little meeting after all. Nicole had thought the girl was trying to fix her up with her brother. Thank heavens she had been wrong! The dark-haired princess reached for her iced tea and took a long sip.

"What happened to your wrist?"

Justin's question caught her off guard. How stupid of her! She should have known that the minute she raised the glass, her sleeve would slide back, revealing the bruises. In her haste to set the glass back down she nearly spilled it all over the table.

"I said..." yelled Justin, assuming she hadn't heard him over the noise, "what happened to your wrist? It looks awful." He noticed Cristoff and Nicole exchanging looks, making him even more suspicious now.

"I fell, in the hayloft," she replied.

"You don't get a bruise like that from a fall," Justin insisted, his tone growing serious. He was about to make another remark, when he stopped in midsentence. The song had ended and everyone returned to their tables, including his little sister, who, much to his dismay, did not look like his sister at all. "What in the blazes..." He stared at his sibling as if she had two heads, his eyes wide with disbelief. This was Jan? This was his innocent Jan?

"Hi, Justin," she beamed, flicking her soft blonde hair back over her shoulder. "Like my new dress?" Nicole cringed at the sound of admiration in her voice, unable to fathom why she'd want his opinion. She could already tell Justin was not impressed, but he held his tongue and lied through his teeth.

"Marvelous," he said, nearly choking on the word. Before the conversation could continue, he got up from his chair, approached Nicole from behind, and leaned close to her ear, saying, "Please join me outside for a moment, Nicole. I need to discuss something with you, in private."

"I don't think so," she coolly replied, sipping her drink. "I can't think of anything we need to discuss." She then proceeded to talk to Jan, completely unaware of the seething giant still standing behind her. Jan took one look at her brother, saw the frustration and anger in his eyes, and gulped down the rest of her drink. It was then she noticed Justin crooking his finger at her, ordering her to come to him.

"Sit," commanded Nicole, upon seeing the girl rise. She had guessed Justin's beckoning gesture and chose, instead, to face the monster, herself. The last thing Nicole wanted was for Jan to be the recipient of a moral lecture from her long-winded brother. It would devastate the girl. So, Nicole did the proper thing. She walked outside with Justin and allowed him to blow off his steam.

She almost regretted it.

"Are you the one responsible for the way she looks?" he barked, clearly disgusted.

"Yes," Nicole simply agreed, yawning in the process.

"How could you let her wear something like that? She looks

like a tart!"

"She looks stunning and everyone knows it. Now be a good boy and let her enjoy the evening. Have you ever seen her so happy?"

"Happy isn't the word I'd use to describe her. Brazen, perhaps. Good grief! Did you see the way she guzzled her drink?!"

"No thanks to you," muttered the temptress, studying her nails.

"What's that supposed to mean?" he boomed.

"Look, Justin. Your opinion means the world to your sister. Why—I don't know. But it does. You can make or break her spirit tonight. If you go in there with this type of attitude, I'll guarantee you she'll be in tears within ten minutes. Is that what you want?"

"Of course not!"

"Then tell her she's beautiful and leave her alone. She's almost 21, for goodness sakes! She has to grow up sometime."

"Not until I'm ready," he fumed, folding his arms. Nicole swallowed a laugh. The man was being absolutely ridiculous, although she did envy his protective concern for his sister. "I don't want her lounging around at clubs. Men will think she's easy."

A simpering smile slid up the corners of Nicole's mouth. "Isn't that why you visit nightclubs? To pick up those types of women?"

"And are you that type of woman, Nicole? After all, you are at a club, aren't you? How often do you come here?"

Nicole bristled. "This discussion is not about me, if you'll remember."

"Now it is."

She gave him one final glare, then turned on her heel, with every intention of going back inside the building. Justin, however, had other ideas, and took hold of her arm. She grimaced in pain. He instantly let go, but demanded, "Where did you get the bruise, Nicole? And don't tell me it was from a fall. I'm not that stupid."

"If you're so smart," she said in a clipped tone, "then you figure it out." Marching inside the building, she lengthened her distance from the blond male and sat back down at her table, pleased when she saw Justin enter the room wearing a smile for his sister. At least he had taken her advice. Shane came in not long after, accompanied by three gorgeous blondes. Nicole rolled her eyes with exasperation at the first utterance from one of the dates, who constantly cracked her chewing gum while asking dumb questions. Jan held a napkin over her mouth to keep from outwardly snickering as the entertainment continued. Apparently Cristoff and Justin's dates were misinformed as to who was dating whom. This mild disagreement led to loud bickering as the two females fought to over shout each other.

"Girls!" Cristoff called, moving to stand between the two bleached blondes. "I'm not picky. I'll date either one of you." This seemed to satisfy them for a few minutes, but Nicole could still hear them sniping at one another as they walked with their escorts to a different table. Luckily, it was far across the room, leaving Nicole and Jan once again to themselves.

"You knew your brother was coming here, didn't you?" Nicole quizzed. "That's why you suggested this place."

"Well, yes." Jan gave a sheepish grin. "I didn't know they would have dates. Are you disappointed?"

Nicole nearly spit out her drink. "No. I'm not disappointed. But I can see you are. Who were you hoping to dance with, Cristoff or Shane?"

"Cristoff. I've always liked him. Shane isn't my type. He goes out with too many women."

Nicole didn't have the heart to tell her that Cristoff was never at a lack for companionship, either. She'd let her find that out on her own. "Let's enjoy the rest of the evening, shall we, Jan?" They clinked glasses in a toast and ordered a new round of drinks. As the night wore on, Shane Anderson sauntered over and invited Nicole to dance, which she declined. It was then she discovered he did not take a refusal very lightly. In fact, he remained at their table for what seemed like an eternity. "Shane," spoke Nicole, "it isn't polite to ignore your date. Just look at her over there, pouting like a poor, neglected child."

"Let her pout," he said in a suave tone. "If I had known you were going to be here, I wouldn't have brought a date. Now, won't you join me for just one very short dance? I won't keep you long."

"Go ahead, Nicole," prompted Jan.

"Actually, I thought we were getting ready to leave, Jan?"

"Oh, we have time for one more dance."

Nicole threw her a tortured look. "But then, again, we do have to get up early in the morning. Maybe we should go." Both women withdrew some money from their purses and placed it on the table. Shane sighed, wished them a safe trip home, then returned to his own table. The minute the two women stepped outside, Jan confronted her new friend. "Why didn't you want to dance with him?"

"He wanted to slow dance. He'd be holding my one hand and my sleeve would slip. He'd see the bruises."

"Oh. You could have danced with your arms around his neck."

"Please!" Nicole frowned. "I don't want to get that close."

"Why not?"

"I just don't," she said softly, starting up the truck. Jan let the subject drop, saying instead, "I had a wonderful time tonight."

Nicole smiled. "The night isn't over, yet." She drove down the main highway and pulled into the parking lot of another club, much to Jan's delight. "And this one is my treat."

Despite her friend's protest, Nicole insisted on buying all the drinks, and the two of them enjoyed two more hours of fun before finally calling it quits and heading home. "Five different guys asked me for my phone number," laughed Jan. "Can you believe it?"

"Yes, I believe it." Nicole had just pulled onto a dark country road off the highway. "Hey!" she yelled, shaking her fist out the window as a car flew past, nearly sideswiping them in the process. “Did you see that guy?” she fussed. “He could have hit us!”

“There’s all kinds of crazy people on the road late at night. What was he driving, anyway? Must have been a race car.”

“I think it was,” Nicole agreed, still shaken by the near accident. “I’d like to give that creep a piece of my mind. Hold on, Jan.” The blonde quickly obeyed, sinking her nails into the dashboard as the truck jerked forward. “Don’t get us killed, Nicole!” Her words were lost in the roar of the truck’s engine as they whizzed down the road to catch the perpetrator. It was all Jan could do to keep from vomiting as the vehicle bounced along at such a high rate of speed, and now she deeply regretted consuming so many glasses of wine. “I think I’m going to be sick,” she called to Nicole.

“Can you wait a few more minutes? I see their taillights.” Jan clutched her stomach, praying for a miracle. Glancing over at the sick girl, Nicole pulled off the side of the road.

“Sorry, Jan. Want to step out, or are you okay?”

Her face looked pale. “I’ll be all right, I think. I didn’t mean to make you give up the chase.”

“I haven’t,” Nicole replied. “I know exactly where they’re going. Philip took me there, once.”

“Where?”

The dark-haired beauty smirked. “They’re heading for a country road that’s used for racing.”

“How can you be sure?”

“Oh, I’m sure,” she said, dryly. “That was my car.”

Jan was horrified. “Oh, no.”

“Oh, yes. And I gave strict orders to Cristoff not to race it.”

“Can you stop him?”

“I certainly intend to. If you’re feeling better, we’ll proceed to the drag strip.”

“Drive on,” Jan announced, her health suddenly restored.

Now knowing her destination, Nicole traveled at a more civilized speed, pulling off the road a few moments later to park amongst other vehicles gathered for the competition. The minute Cristoff saw the truck, he swore softly under his breath and alerted Justin. Together, they decided to tell Nicole they were only here as observers, but the chance never came. Nicole assumed they had told their dates that this was Cristoff's car, not hers, and she fully intended to let the story ride—no need to embarrass them... yet. There would be plenty of time to make them look like fools later.

So, playing dumb, the dark-haired beauty donned a sexy smile and sauntered up to the two flustered men, directing her attention to Cristoff, who now looked completely baffled as she slung her arm affectionately across his shoulders. "Daaarling!" she purred. "You didn't tell me you were such a daredevil. I do hate to bother you, Cris dear, but I believe I left a pair of earrings in the glove box of your car last time we were out." She seductively ran her fingers up and down the back of his neck, which had suddenly become a tense mass of knotted muscles. Inside the truck, Jan watched with amusement at the scene her friend was causing. Already, Cristoff's date was complaining to the other bleached blonde. "If you don't mind," Nicole continued, "I'll just reach inside to retrieve them."

"N-No. I..." His voice cracked. "don't mind." He couldn't fathom why she hadn't screamed and yelled, knowing full well she was aware of his intentions to race. Perhaps she had decided to allow it? He frowned. Highly unlikely. She was up to something and he was going to find out what that something was. He tried to watch as she opened the driver side door and slid across the seat to reach the glove compartment, but his date suddenly obstructed his view, bent on stealing the show away from Nicole. She planted a generous kiss on his mouth, out of desperation, then proceeded to hold him hostage with her voluptuous body. "Not now," Cristoff protested, angling himself so he could continue to check on Nicole. However, the effort was too late. She was already emerging from the vehicle, an innocent giggle on her lips as she said, "My mistake, darling. I guess I misplaced those earrings in someone else's car."

"Hey, baby!" called a male admirer. "Why don't you come over here and check out my car?"

"Mine, too!" yelled another, amidst beckoning whistles. Nicole turned, smiled, and casually waved a dainty farewell, oblivious to Justin's angry stare as she sashayed back to her truck. It would be understood if he forbade Jan to ever go out with her again.

"You're going to have a lot of explaining to do," she warned Jan once they departed. "Justin thinks I'm very promiscuous. You'll have to tell him this was all planned, although I think it will dawn on him in a few minutes."

"What did you do?" Jan quizzed, excitedly.

Nicole grinned. "I had a special switch installed in my car, unknown to Cristoff, called a 'cut off' switch. It's camouflaged on the dashboard as another item. I simply flipped it when I slid across the seat. It won't allow the car to start."

"You didn't!" cried Jan, bursting into laughter.

The raven-haired beauty chuckled. "Even if they realize I tampered with the car, they'll assume it had something to do with the glove box. I wish I could be there to see their faces! Can you imagine how embarrassed they'll be? Their dates will probably go off with some other guys." They were both in stitches now, tears filling their eyes as they pictured the scene.

"You are so bad," Jan giggled.

"Serves them right. I have to go back there though, to pick up my car. Luckily, I keep an extra key in my purse. I figured I'd wait about a half hour—that should be enough time for the girls to ditch them."

"You don't think Justin and Cristoff would abandon your car, do you?"

"No way. One of them will stay. Cristoff knows I'd kill him if anything happened to my Shelby."

And she was right. Both men were still with the vehicle when the women returned, Cristoff with his head under the hood, and Justin keeping an eye out for Nicole. Upon seeing her, the car hood was swiftly closed and both men assumed a casual position of leaning against the side of the Shelby, as if nothing out of the ordinary had happened. To Nicole's delight, neither guy was quite sure if the engine failure was truly due to her, thus the look of intense guilt on their faces proved her trick had worked. Jan accompanied Nicole this time, slowly walking up to Justin and Cristoff, an innocent look on her face. "Where are your dates?"

"Oh, they had to be home early, so we told them to hitch a ride with one of the other fellows," Cristoff said.

"But isn't that them, over there?" Nicole pointed out, clearly enjoying the awkward position she had put him in.

"Son of a gun," exclaimed Justin. "She's right, Cristoff. The nerve of those women!"

"By the way, Nicole," spoke Cristoff, "thanks for letting our dates think this was my car."

"Oh, I wouldn't want to embarrass you, Cristoff," she artfully smiled before changing the subject. "Jan wanted to take a spin in my car, so I thought we could switch vehicles." She took a step towards the driver's side, not surprised to find Cristoff blocking her path.

"But you said I could use the Shelby tonight," he said.

"You can, Cristoff. Just let me give Justin's sister a quick spin."

"But, but..." He stammered like an idiot, panic in his voice as she climbed into the driver's seat. Jan got in on the passenger side, gently pulling the door shut.

"Yuck," Nicole frowned, brushing her hand across the top of the dash. "So much dust. Remind me to run a cloth over the interior." As she brought her hand back down from the top, she flipped the "cut off" switch, then turned the key in the ignition. Cristoff nearly had a heart attack. The engine instantly cranked over.

"Tah tah," Nicole waved, zooming past the astonished men who stood like zombies amidst the dirtcloud as they watched her quickly fade into the distance.

"I think I heard her laughing," Cristoff commented, putting his hands on his hips.

"I think you're right," mumbled Justin. "Know what else I think?"

"What?"

"I think they're not coming back."

CHAPTER TEN

The next day, Cristoff wordlessly returned the key to the Shelby to Nicole. He was still unsure what had caused the vehicle's engine to quit and decided it was best not to mention the incident. As for Nicole taking the car away from him last night, there wasn't much he could say about that either—he knew he shouldn't have been at the local drag strip. "Are you mad at me?" he asked before returning to his chores.

"No. Disappointed, maybe. It's forgotten." Nicole studied him a moment. "Jan looked pretty, didn't she?"

"Smashing, is more like it. If she wasn't Justin's sister..." Cristoff never finished the sentence, a bit embarrassed.

Nicole smirked. "Do go on. You were saying? Oh, for goodness sakes, Cristoff! What difference does it make if she's Justin's sister? She likes you. She told me so. Don't tell her I said it, though."

The ranch hand's face brightened. "She likes me, huh? Ain't that a kick in the pants." His smile slowly faded. "Doesn't matter. We wouldn't get along."

"How can you say that? Why don't you at least give it a try? Take her out."

He suddenly turned on Nicole, startling her by his harsh reply. "Don't tell me who I should take out. It's none of your business."

"I'm sorry, Cristoff. I was simply making a suggestion." She truly meant what she said, but he had already walked away from her and joined Justin out in the field, leaving Nicole to wonder as to the sudden change of mood. Just a few seconds ago, he had been thrilled to learn of Jan's fondness for him. So, why was he so sure the relationship wouldn't work?

Nicole could hazard a guess. It was just an assumption, but a good one, all the same. Cristoff was ashamed of his drinking problem. Yes. That was it. He was afraid to ask Jan out—afraid she'd eventually reject him because of the alcohol abuse, afraid he might become too attached to her, especially since he saw her at the ranch during the day. That also explained why he only participated in one night stands. Come to think of it, Nicole hadn't seen him date the same girl more than twice. "Oh, well," Nicole sighed. "If it's meant to be, it'll happen, whether I push it or not."

She watched Cristoff rest his foot on one of the boards to the corral fence while he talked with Justin, the two men studying the nervous stallion pacing its interior. They didn't notice the graceful form gliding across the grass towards them, bridle held in one hand, dark eyes flecked with the spark of adventure. It wasn't until she unlatched the corral gate, Cristoff realized the inevitable.

"Nicole!" he called. "Don't you dare get on that horse. I told you he isn't fully broken, yet." The bewitching beauty gave him a lazy smile, the kind which said, "Thank you very much for the unwanted advice, but I'll do as I darn well please", and she continued on her way, stepping gingerly to the side as the huge stallion darted past, his ears pinned back, menacingly.

A fluid string of curses filled the air as Cristoff angrily banged his fist on top of the fence. "I can't teach that woman anything! Confound it, Nicole! Why don't you listen to me?" He swung open the gate to go after her, then swiftly shut it when the vicious beast decided to charge him, nearly ripping Cristoff's shirt from his back while the ranch hand quickly exited. "Mercy!" he exclaimed in fear. "Get out of there, Nicole! That horse is crazy."

"You bought him," she yelled.

"I didn't know then he had such a temper."

"He's just grouchy, that's all. Probably left his lover back at his old ranch. Didn't you, boy? Poor baby." She cooed and wooed him, did everything but wipe the dribble off his chin. Cristoff rolled his eyes with disgust. She sounded like an idiot, talking to a fully grown stallion like that. What was even crazier, the stupid beast was actually listening to her! The animal's ears pricked forward, although his eyes were still rolling in their sockets, peering over at the mesmerizing beauty intermittently as he pranced about with true arrogance. He paraded around the corral a few times, a gorgeous display of rippling muscle.

Nicole soothed him with her melodic voice, whispering words of praise and reassurance. Justin, himself, was captivated by the tone she used, noting how pleasant it sounded to the ear—like the gentle strum of a harp. The longer he listened, the less surprised he was at the effect it had on the stallion, who now began to settle down. Within minutes, the Arabian was dancing towards Nicole, a bit sideways for caution, but nevertheless towards her. After concentrating on the horse's change of mood, she relaxed, knowing the worst was over. A mystic bond formed between the pair, and to seal it, she encircled his huge neck with her arms and laid her head against the black cheek.

"See why Philip married her and fired his former rider?" Cristoff pointed out. "Nicole has a gift with animals."

Justin nodded. "She certainly quieted the big bay."

"Bay? He's black."

Justin shook his head. "You missed the spot of brown near his flank. A black horse is black all over."

"Wonder why I didn't notice the brown area before?"

"Wonder why you didn't notice his temper?" Justin said, under his breath.

Cristoff scratched his head. "He was quiet as a mouse when I bought him."

"They may have dosed him with a tranquilizer for the

auction." Justin saw an uneasiness in Cristoff's eyes and glanced back at Nicole, who had just bridled the horse.

"I'll bring you a saddle, Nicole," Cristoff called.

"Don't bother," she replied. "He'll be much calmer if I ride bareback."

"You're daft!" Cristoff hollered, shaking his head and then turning to Justin. "I'd give anything to have her under me one day. Just one day! I'd teach her a thing or two!"

"Sure, Cristoff. I hear you," laughed Justin, while Nicole sat perched on her black charger, galloping around the corral. She interrupted their conversation, warning them, "Better step away from there. He has jumping in his blood; I can feel it. He wants to sail right over the fence!" Heeding her words, both men took a safer position, several yards away, just as the huge animal cleared the top rail. The landing was hard, nearly jolting Nicole off the stallion's back, but she had been prepared for it and used her knees to absorb most of the impact. Allowing the young horse to canter across the grass a few strides, she finally reined him in and dismounted.

"Nice jumping," Justin commented, walking beside Nicole while she cooled off the bay. He saw Cristoff scowl before heading towards the barn. Nicole had noticed the ranch hand's expression, too, and said, "He's such a grouch sometimes."

"He's only looking out for you, Nicole."

"Oh?" She suddenly stopped in her tracks and faced him. "And do you think I need looking after, Mr. MacFierson?" Dark brown eyes held him hostage, daring him to agree. Instead, he responded, "It was rather stupid for you to get on an inexperienced horse without wearing a riding helmet. I don't blame Cristoff for being upset. You could have been killed."

"My! I didn't know you cared?"

"I probably shouldn't—not after that little stunt you pulled last night."

Nicole started walking again, conveniently placing the horse between herself and the blond. "What little stunt?"

"You know exactly what I am talking about," he gently

chided. "If I didn't know you better, I'd swear you were trying to ruin our dates."

"My car was my only interest, thank you." Her jaw dropped as Justin suddenly took the reins from her and halted.

"Are you sure, Mrs. Tyler?" he slowly drawled. Upon seeing a vehicle pull up in the driveway, Nicole used the handy excuse to avoid an answer. She hurried over to her visitor, then slowed the pace when she saw the familiar form of Shane step out of the car, a crisp breeze tousling his shiny, black hair. "Afternoon, Nicole!" he grinned.

"Hello, Shane." Nicole admired his handsome outfit—a forest green suit to match his eyes. "What can I do for you?"

"I decided to stop by to ask you over for dinner tonight, say about seven o'clock?"

"Oh..." She faltered, caught off guard. "I don't know..."

"I understand," he politely said, glancing down at his newly polished shoes. She could hear the dejection in his voice. "It's just that... coming home to an empty apartment every day gets a bit lonely sometimes." He paused, allowing plenty of time for her to succumb to the urge of pitying him. Nearby, Justin was observing the little charade Shane had conjured up, but now he advanced towards the two, aware of Nicole's discomfort.

"Oh, I sincerely doubt you go home to an empty apartment," the blond coolly stated. "It's no secret you have every female in this town at your beck and call."

"And hello to you, too, Justin," Shane smiled, not missing a beat. "Playing 'stableboy' today? Oh, that's right! You did tell me you were working for Nicole, now. What were your duties?" He pretended to think. "Ah, yes. Mucking stalls, I think." His cynical tone made Justin's lips tighten in anger, although Justin had expected the verbal attack. Nicole looked on, slightly amused.

"I prefer physical labor," the blond retorted. "It builds muscle, which comes in very handy when some snobby, silver spooned brat steps on my toes. What are you doing off work, anyway? Get fired?"

"Hardly," Shane said. "They owed me a few hours." He

turned back to Nicole. "When I saw you last night, well..." He sucked in his breath. "You just knocked the wind right out of me. You have class, Nicole, real class. I couldn't stop thinking about you today. I want to make up for the day of the picnic, when I had offended you. I want to show you how it feels to be treated like a true lady. Will you let me do that for you? Will you let me pamper you this evening?"

Nicole was flabbergasted. He was good. Oh, he was very good! But before she could open her mouth to respond, Justin opened his instead, blurting, "She already knows what it's like to be treated like a lady."

"I do?" Nicole chirped, blinking at the blond, to which he emphatically announced, "Yes, you do! Cristoff and I have the utmost respect for you."

She swallowed a laugh. "The utmost, huh?" Shane began to chuckle. Nicole glimpsed the silent challenge in Justin's eyes and couldn't believe it. He was jealous. She thought it rather odd, considering they had never even dated. In fact, it was more than odd; it was downright absurd. She glanced back at Shane, a twinge of excitement stimulating her curiosity about this Casanova. "You're very persuasive, Shane," she smiled. "I'd be delighted to have dinner with you. What time shall I arrive?"

"I'll pick you up at six-thirty. Is that all right?"

"I'll be waiting."

"Fine. I'll see you then. And, uh, nice talking to you, Justin. Keep in touch." Aware of the cold, blue eyes staring after him, Shane quickly jumped into his car and departed. Nicole's vision focused on the blond. "If I didn't know you better, Justin, I'd swear you were trying to ruin my date."

"Ruin your date?" he grunted. "Not at all. Shane's a good friend. I was simply trying to prevent a disaster. I wouldn't want his heart stomped on." Turning his back to the astonished female, he broke into a huge grin. That would teach her! He continued to walk the new horse towards the stable, pretending not to hear Nicole's angry muttering. Once inside, he met Cristoff in the tack room and told him of Nicole's acceptance of Shane's invitation. Little did he realize, Nicole had followed, mainly to give him a piece of her mind; however, upon hearing the current discussion under way, she chose not to enter the tack room, remaining outside and within earshot.

"I tried to tell her about Shane," Cristoff explained. "I told her not to trust him."

Justin snorted. "A lot of good that did! Why would she go out with him, anyway? I thought you said she's afraid of men?"

Cristoff looked uneasy, his mind recalling how eager Nicole had seemed up in the hayloft. "I could have been wrong. Maybe she's finally ready to date again. Why don't you just ask her out?"

"She doesn't want to be with me. I've insulted her too many times. Heck, I insulted her only a minute ago. No. There's no way she'd go on a date with me."

"Why don't you ask me?" Nicole quizzed, stepping through the entrance. The sound of her voice caused Justin to drop the bridle he had been fidgeting with. He leaned over, picked it up, and promptly banged his head on a saddle rack, emitting several choice words in the process. Cristoff turned away to keep from laughing. "What?" Justin blurted, staring at Nicole.

"I said, why don't you ask me?"

He appeared dumbfounded, but quickly recovered. "W-would you like to go out sometime? There's a nice restaurant on the other side of town. Or, we could have dinner at my place, if that's what you'd like? Or, we could see a movie, go to the theater, visit the museum..." He was rambling on like a nervous schoolboy, and Nicole let him, reveling in the power of this one, single moment in which his alter ego was at her mercy. The very fact that he was describing every possible form of entertainment to entice her proved that he had lied when he had claimed he was only interested in Shane's welfare when they were outside. Come to think of it, she remembered the day Justin had quit, how she had tried to tempt him with various offers. What was it he had said? Oh, yes. He said she did not have anything he was interested in.

"Well?" the blond's masculine voice echoed. "When do you

want to go out with me?"

Nicole paused, drumming her nails against her folded arm. She gave a sweet smile. "Never," she calmly replied, delighting in the lovely vision of red creeping up Justin's neck.

He masked his hurt pride, grinning instead. "You will, eventually."

"Not a chance," she firmly stated.

"You will."

"I won't!"

He suddenly advanced towards her, easily closing the distance, his towering form forcing her to retreat backwards. Looking into his eyes, she noticed he was gloating as he confidently repeated, "You will."

She became flustered. "I won't!" Since he took another step towards her, she quickly inched backwards once more, all the while staring into his deep blue eyes, all the while forgetting the depression in the floor behind her, then remembering it as her foot collapsed beneath her, sending her sprawling like a clumsy oaf into the corridor.

Justin shook his head. "Perhaps you're right. We probably shouldn't date. I can see you now in some fancy restaurant, rising from your elegant chair to go to the ladies room... the edge of the tablecloth mistakenly tucked in your belt..." The soft rumble of laughter coming from his throat made her frown with disdain. Why, he wasn't even making a move to help her to her feet! What gall!

"'Xcuse me," murmured Cristoff, quickly exiting the tack room. He offered his hand to Nicole, but couldn't refrain from grinning. She refused the gesture and picked herself up off the floor, saying through clenched teeth, "I'm still your boss!"

"Where are my manners?" mocked Justin. "I'm very sorry you didn't see the hole in the floor, Nicole. I'll look into having it fixed, tomorrow."

"Yes. Do that," she wryly replied. "And while you're at it, the floor of my office could use a good cleaning and waxing." She watched Justin's smile slowly vanish. "Better bring knee pads. Some of those scuff marks won't come up without solid scrubbing with a stiff brush." Now it was her turn to smile, and in so doing, she left him one last instruction: "Do come in extra early so the floor is dry by the time I arrive." With that, she turned on her heel and headed into the office to speak with Jan. Justin started after her, but was stopped by Cristoff's hand on his shoulder. "Easy, now," the ranch hand soothed. "You'll only make matters worse. She's right, you know. She's still the boss." Justin mumbled something inaudible before resuming his chores.

The rest of the day flew by. After quitting time, Nicole stole a luxurious bath to relax her frazzled nerves, then studied her wardrobe, eventually selecting a lacy, highnecked blouse with ruffles and gold trimming. A burgundy velvet skirt with gold etching completed the picture. Now her hair. To attain an old-fashioned look, Nicole swept the long strands upwards, securing them in place with small, gold-colored combs. A faint curve touched her lips when she admired the end result. She looked like an innocent schoolteacher, definitely not the promiscuous type. "That should deter any amorous actions," she smugly smiled, hearing a firm knock on the front door. She glided down the stairs to join her dinner companion.

Strangely, Shane appeared quite nervous. Driving to his apartment, he rambled on about all sorts of insignificant things, leaving little time for Nicole to respond. She eventually gave up and resigned herself to merely sit and listen to the idle chatter, while her own mind wandered off on another tangent. It was when they pulled up to the boarding house that he finally stopped talking. When he escorted her inside the building and up the stairs, he remained silent, although his green eyes did sparkle with delight at the admiring glances being thrown their way.

"Don't they look like they belong together?" commented one woman to another as the two passed by.

"You know him," the other replied with a look of pure condemnation. "Every time he escorts a woman up there," she motioned with her eyes, "she doesn't come down until the next morning. Then we never see her again." The two females clucked disapprovingly.

Meanwhile, Nicole had just entered Shane's living quarters. "Very lovely," she remarked appreciatively, studying the room. Gold velvet drapes flowed softly to the carpeted floor, adding a warm touch to the rich shades of gold, fawn and auburn interspersed throughout the apartment. Antique ornaments decorated various pieces of furniture.

"Without sounding impolite, may I ask what your line of work is?" she inquired.

"I'm a bank supervisor. However, if you're wondering about the extravagance of my apartment... everything was a gift from a friend."

Nicole smirked. "I see."

"Actually, the owner of this building." He awaited her reaction and was disappointed; she didn't even bat an eyelash. He motioned towards the dining room, where the table was already set for two, complete with red roses and candles.

"It's beautiful, Shane. You really shouldn't have gone to this much trouble."

"It was no trouble at all. Come. Sit down." Like a true gentleman, he held her chair for her. Nicole was impressed. Then the dashing young man disappeared into the kitchen and returned with shrimp cocktail for an appetizer. Picking up the bottle of champagne from the table, he popped the cork, all the while staring at his lovely guest. At first, Nicole was flattered. But then she caught a glimpse of something in those emerald eyes that made her very uneasy. She couldn't quite put her finger on it, but her keen sixth sense went on red alert. Several seconds later, the feeling passed, leaving the young woman restless and spooked. She eagerly took a sip of champagne.

"Is it to your liking?" Shane asked, his voice lowered to a deeper tone. She noticed the change in pitch at once. "It's fine," she replied, staring at the pale liquid in her crystal glass.

He struck a match, lit the candles and dimmed the lights. Then he joined her for the appetizer, bestowing a wide, generous smile upon her from the opposite side of the table. Somewhere between uncorking the champagne and adjusting the lights, a major transformation had taken place. She observed Shane had become extremely serene. It was then she noticed his attire; he was dressed in black, completely. When he got up from his chair to fetch the main course, Nicole felt her lower spine tingle. Even his shoes and socks were black. That's not uncommon, she told herself, trying to be rational. But her imagination, like a wild horse, was galloping out of control. By the time he reappeared with the lobster soufflé, she was convinced he resembled Dracula, almost expected to see fangs when he opened his mouth to eat. No matter how hard she tried, she could not shake the sensation of impending doom that had settled in the pit of her stomach. She was beginning to feel like Little Red Riding Hood dining with the big, bad wolf. When he spoke again, his voice was even deeper than before.

"Aren't you hungry, Nicole?"

Her mouth went dry, her throat felt scratchy, and she had the dire need to use the bathroom. She refused to meet his gaze, afraid he might steal her soul if she did so. Swallowing a mouthful of champagne, she finally spoke. "I'm sorry, Shane. My mind was preoccupied. The food looks delicious. If you'll excuse me for a moment, may I please use your bathroom?"

"Certainly. It's the second door on the right." He jumped up to ease her chair out from under the table.

Once inside the restroom, the jittery woman took some time to compose herself, mumbling, "I'm going to enjoy myself this evening, even if it kills me." She forced all previous terrible thoughts from her mind and rejoined her handsome host, who was now giving her a curious look.

"Is something bothering you, Nicole?"

"No."

"You just seem so... apprehensive."

"I haven't really dated anyone, Shane, since..." She couldn't finish the sentence. He reached across the table to cover her hand with his own. "I understand," he murmured, allowing his touch to linger.

Nicole slowly raised her eyes to meet his. Jagged shadows

from the candlelight sliced the masculine face into several pieces, grotesquely distorting his features. "Nicole," he suddenly spoke with concern. "You're trembling. What's wrong?" She eased her hand out from under his and placed it in her lap.

"Nothing's wrong," she quickly replied. To prove her point, she began eating her meal and smiled. He did the same, but at a much slower pace, continuing to watch the young woman, carefully.

"You don't have to feel nervous, Nicole. I'm not going to bite you. Perhaps some soft music might relax you." He rose from the table to put on a classical record. She didn't have the heart to tell him that classical music did nothing for her; she simply smiled and endured it. Then she began to inquire about his banking experience, and the conversation finally flowed between the two of them.

When the main meal was finished, Shane brought out dessert: Baked Fruit Flambé, which Nicole thoroughly enjoyed, feeling very at ease after two glasses of champagne. She did remember, however, to decline a third glass of alcohol, much to Shane's disappointment. He had hoped she was a heavy drinker. In fact, he had wanted to question her about the day of the picnic, when she had passed out after drinking wine, but he knew it would be impolite to bring up the bad experience. Justin had said it might stir up horrible memories, and Shane certainly didn't want a teary-eyed date crying on his shoulder. No, that wouldn't be conducive at all to this evening's plans.

"You really outdid yourself," Nicole commented, beginning to clear off the table. "Everything was wonderful. Thank you so much, Shane."

"Leave the dishes," he said. "I'll take care of them in the morning."

Nicole protested. "The food will stick to the plates if you wait. I don't mind washing them. Really."

No sooner had the words left her mouth when he came to her side, removing the dinnerware from her hands. "I said I'll take care of them in the morning." His tone was commanding, but soft as he gently pulled her away from the dining room and into the living room. "I believe you owe me a dance, Mrs. Tyler." Opening her mouth to argue, she found herself swept up in his arms and gently guided about the plush carpet. It was too late to refuse without appearing rude, so she made the best of it, allowing her host to have this one, insignificant dance before she'd politely ask to be driven home.

Shane, however, had other intentions. He gradually drew closer to the alluring female, whispering, "Your blouse is gorgeous, Nicole. How did you know that I have a passion for lace?"

"Actually, I had no idea," she murmured, wanting to kick herself for choosing that article of clothing.

"And your skirt..." His hand slowly traveled down the soft material to her thigh. "Velvet is such a rich fabric, don't you agree?" She patiently waited for his hand to return to its normal position, but, as luck would have it, he made no motion to do so, leaving it attached to her thigh like an extra body part.

Nicole forced a tiny smile. "As far as fabric goes," she replied, sliding her own hand up his shirt until it reached the collar. "I prefer cotton." She then positioned her long fingers so that the front of his neck was nestled between her thumb and forefinger. Then she gently squeezed, uttering a quaint, playful laugh. It only took a small increase of pressure for Shane to realize the subtle choking threat. He promptly removed his hand from the velvet skirt, forcing a small chuckle in return. "You're witty," he grinned. "I like that."

"Oh, really?" she smiled, plainly seeing the spark of anger in his eyes. The room was dark, true, but she was close enough to notice. There was a wolfish gleam in those eyes, as if he'd devour her at any minute. It was scary, yet, oddly stimulating, too. She felt his fingers trace an imaginary line up the middle of her back, then reach under her thick hair, coming to rest near the nape of her neck. Too late, she realized why. His mouth covered hers at the same instant his hand slid up to cradle the back of her head. In this manner, he held her captive, assaulting her with his sensuous mouth for as long as he pleased. Or, at least, that was what he thought. Nicole had other ideas. She delivered a blow to his right cheek with the heel of her left hand, momentarily stunning the handsome man.

"I should have known you'd try something with me!" she hissed, promptly stepping away.

"Good grief, Nicole!" he yowled. "It was only a kiss."

"A forced kiss!" she spat. "I don't appreciate being held hostage on a first date. Kissing is a mutual expression of affection, the key word being 'mutual', Shane."

"If I waited for you to join in, I'd have cobwebs in my hair. I thought you needed a little push."

Just then a knock sounded on the door, startling both of them. Nicole stood and glared at her host until he finally moved to greet his visitor, a glamorous brunette.

"I brought you something, tiger," the girl giggled, strutting right past him, into the living room.

"Jenny. What a surprise," Shane pretended. "I'd ask you in, but I know how busy your schedule is."

"Oh, a cake!" exclaimed Nicole, going to the girl. "Isn't that thoughtful? You will stay a while, won't you? Shane, introduce me to your friend."

The dashing young man flashed a frigid smile. "Jenny, this is Nicole Tyler. Nicole, this is Jenny Duvall."

"Hi, there," the girl chirped, trying to hide her jealousy.

"Pleased to meet you," Nicole answered. "I'm just a distant friend of Shane's—very distant." She ignored the host's angry stare. "In fact, he was just about to drive me home. Say, why don't you come along, Jenny? It's not very far from here. Then you and Shane can spend the rest of the evening together."

"Sure!" came the cheerful response, prompting Shane to intervene.

"I thought you had to take care of your sick mother tonight, Jen?" he lied.

"Mom isn't sick."

"I could have sworn you said she was. Besides, Nicole and

I were in the middle of a very important discussion when you came to the door."

"No, we weren't," Nicole piped up. "I really am tired, Shane. Could you please take me home now?" Put in an awkward position, she left him with no other choice. He reluctantly escorted the two women out to his car, frowning when Nicole chose to sit in the back. She remained quiet on the drive home, letting Jenny chatter on endlessly about hairstyles, clothes and her recent vacation to some exotic island. But when they pulled up to Nicole's house, the way Shane jumped out of the car to walk Nicole up the front steps, left no doubt in Jenny's mind that he had not listened to a single word she had said.

Nicole had made a feeble attempt to reach her front door without being followed, but now was faced with addressing her host so as not to be rude. "Thank you for dinner, Shane," was all she said, placing her key in the lock.

"Very clever, Nicole. Bringing Jenny along made you feel safe, didn't it?" He halted her entrance into the house with one strong squeeze of her arm. "When you play games with me, you play with fire. I'd hate to see you get burned." He flashed his pearly white teeth at her, lingering just long enough to instill a small amount of fear in the young woman. Then he was gone, and Nicole felt the rapid beat of her heart begin to slow. Her hope of a wonderful evening had turned into a major disaster. Exhausted, she poured herself a brandy and slumped into her favorite chair. "May you rot in hell, Mr. Anderson," she mumbled, taking a large swallow.

After sitting there for five minutes, finishing her drink, a light rapping sounded at the front door. "Who is it?" she called, unaccustomed to late night visitors. "Cristoff," came the solid reply, prompting Nicole to get to her feet. She quickly unlatched the door. "Sorry," he said, "but I saw Shane leave and I had some news to tell you. Mind if I sit down?" She motioned with her hand and they both went over to the sofa.

"I do own a telephone, you know," she quipped.

"I thought you might let the answering machine pick up

the call and I didn't want to just leave a message." It was half true. He really stopped by to see for himself how her date with Shane had gone. He knew Nicole could mask her emotions over the phone; but, in person, he'd be able to read her expression. Already, he could tell she had had too much to drink, if not at Shane's, then at home.

"So, what's so important, Cristoff?" He smelled of scotch—not a good sign.

"I took Daniel out this evening for a few drinks and pumped him for more details about Dr. Bohman and the medicine. He had no additional information than last time we had talked."

"You call that 'news'?"

"There's more. When I told him that Justin was hiring Charlie King to do some snooping around, Daniel started asking a bunch of questions about him."

Nicole made a downward motion with her hand. "Oh, he's just checking him out, that's all. Daniel wanted to find out if this detective is worth the money. He's like that, Cristoff."

"Well, Danny did argue against it. He said we were foolish to even bother, since he had previously used a detective to search for Dr. Bohman."

"Daniel thinks whoever he hires is always the best. You probably insulted him, made him feel as if he didn't do a good enough job."

Cristoff shrugged his shoulders. "I didn't mean to offend him, if I did." He looked back at the raven-haired beauty, noticing her glassy eyes. "You didn't have too many drinks tonight, did you?"

"No."

"How was your date with Shane?"

"Why do you drink, Cristoff?" She had blurted out the question without thinking, something she was prone to do when under the influence of alcohol. But she was not sorry she had asked.

"Because I like to," came the deliberate response. "Now tell me about your date."

"What's the real reason? Did some girl break your heart once and you can't get over it?"

"Stop changing the subject, Nicole. Did you or did you not enjoy your evening?"

Wrapping a long strand of hair around her finger, she pouted. "It was horrible. The food was good. Shane went to a lot of trouble. But, well... you know..."

"No, I don't. Explain."

She cocked her head sideways. "Why? Why do you want to know? It's Justin, isn't it? Always Justin! He made you ask."

"Boy, you're temperamental tonight. No. Justin did not ask me to inquire. I, myself, was interested. So, are you going to tell me, or not?"

She tilted her chin upwards. "I don't want to talk about it."

"Okay, fine." The ranch hand got up and headed for the door. "See you in the morning, then."

"Wait," she called, going after him. "You never told me why you drink?"

Clearly annoyed, he replied in a clipped tone, "Didn't anyone ever tell you? An alcoholic doesn't need a reason to drink." He let the words sink in, amazed she was finally without comment, then quietly countered, "Why do you drink, Nicole?"

He could have heard a pin drop. She hung her head like a punished child. "I suppose I shouldn't, but Philip got me into the routine of having brandy after dinner. I rather enjoy it, now, although I'm not addicted, Cristoff. There is a difference. I didn't intend to hurt your feelings by inquiring. I just thought perhaps I could be of some help." Her eyes were large and expressive as she met his gaze, full of kindness and compassion.

Cristoff softened his tone. "No one can help me, Nicole. I have to help myself. I've already decreased the amount of alcohol I consume. You don't see me drunk every day, do you?" She shook her head. "So, don't worry about me. You have enough troubles of your own."

"But tell me something, Cristoff," she implored, still

curious. "Have you ever had your heart broken?"

"No, I haven't."

"Truly?"

"Never. There's a secret to that, you know." A hint of sadness laced his words. "I simply don't allow myself to get close to anyone. It's rather easy."

"I don't believe you. It's not easy. How can you bed different women and not feel any attachment?"

"They all look alike after a while, Nicole."

"You just use them. Have you ever thought of what it does to these women? Good grief, Cristoff! It's cruel to play with someone else's emotions."

"You make me sound like such a heel, Nicole. I have a great deal of respect for the opposite sex. I make sure I tell them what to expect, before I get involved."

"How kind," she drawled.

"No matter how it sounds, I don't lead them on. I'm very honest with the girls."

"Heartbreaker."

"Don't call me that. Besides, if my dates were displeased, why would they ask to see me again?"

"A masochistic streak?" She cracked a smile, lightening the mood. "All right. I won't torment you any longer." A sudden thought entered her head. "Cristoff. Can I ask you a rather personal question?"

He gave her a wary look. "More personal than this discussion?" She nodded. "I suppose it doesn't surprise me. Go ahead."

She began to fidget. "Um... when guys kiss on the first date... well... do they usually wait for a mutual sign of affection, or do they just overpower the female?"

"That's an odd thing to ask. I guess it depends. If you know the girl wants it, you just initiate the action."

"Like I did with you up in the hayloft?"

That certainly put color in his face. He couldn't believe she would remind him of the incident. "Yeah," he replied. "You assumed I'd reciprocate the action. What is all this leading to anyway, Nicole? Did something happen with Shane tonight and you're a bit confused?" She started to wring her hands, which Cristoff knew was never a good sign. "He didn't take advantage of you, did he?"

"Not really," she reasoned. "He kissed me while we were dancing, but… he held the back of my head so I couldn't resist him. I thought he was being a brute."

Cristoff gave her a stern look. "So, what exactly did you do to him, Nicole?"

"I..." Her eyes darted about the room, nervously. "sort of whacked him in the head with the heel of my hand."

"You what?" Cristoff snickered.

"Well, first, he had his hand on my thigh and I waited for him to remove it, but he didn't. So, I raised my hand to his throat and applied a little pressure as a warning."

"And he still attempted to kiss you?"

She nodded. "But now that I think back on it, maybe I was overreacting."

"Had you done anything to lead him on?"

"Absolutely not!" she defended. "In fact, he knew I was very nervous."

"Then, he's at fault," Cristoff firmly replied. "Justin and I were afraid he might get fresh with you. But you insisted on dating him." He emphasized the word "insisted". "At least you handled the situation well. I was wondering why you came home so early. It looked like someone else was in the car."

"Jenny Duvall. I invited her along on the ride home."

Cristoff hooted with laughter. "I can imagine how Shane took that suggestion."

"You won't tell anyone, will you?" she pleaded. "I mean, don't tell Justin. He'd never let me forget it."

"My lips are sealed. I won't say a word." He chuckled, again.

"Stop laughing. You're giving me a complex. I'll never go on another date." She looked so pathetic, he felt sorry for her.

"You just haven't met the right kind of man, my girl. You need a real gentleman. Unfortunately, I believe they are a dying breed." He lifted her chin with one finger. "Chin up, Nicole. All is not hopeless." Then he smiled, kissed her forehead, and departed, leaving Nicole a little less depressed than before. She turned in for the night, looking forward to a much calmer day upon the morrow.

CHAPTER ELEVEN

She was mistaken.

The morning began with a heated discussion with Justin over his sister. He had taken Nicole into a private area of the stable to voice his concern about Jan's recent collection of boyfriends. "It was only a few nights ago that the two of you went out," he frowned, "and now she has men calling her at all hours of the night!"

"And you think this is my fault?" Nicole argued.

"It most certainly is!"

"Your sister is getting the attention she wants. She has a level head. You should be happy for her."

"Happy?" he scoffed. "She has a date book now, for crying out loud, filled until next month! She'll be out every evening."

"If I had to live with you, I'd be out every evening, too," murmured Nicole.

"Fine. Go ahead and make fun. If she was your sister, you'd be worried." He stormed down the aisle, grabbed some grooming supplies and entered the nearest horse's stall. Nicole took her time to leisurely stroll the same path, stopping when she reached his location.

"I'm sorry if your sister has decided to assert her independence."

"Sorry doesn't fix it," he snapped, increasing his brush

strokes. He suddenly glanced in her direction. "How was your date last night?"

Nicole felt his eyes upon her, trying to interpret her expression, so she sported a glowing smile. "Oh, what an evening! Shane is so romantic. There were red roses, champagne, a main dish of lobster... and we danced..." She twirled around in the aisle like a prima ballerina. "Did I mention how romantic he is?"

"Yes," came the answering growl. "I guess you came home late, then?"

"I didn't look at the clock," she confessed, staging a long yawn. "I'm sure it was late."

"After midnight?" he pressed.

"Oh, well after midnight," she fibbed, a dreamy smile still on her lips.

"Well, that's funny," he smirked. "You must have been hiding in a closet when I showed up at Shane's place around nine-thirty, then." He watched her smile begin to dim.

"How dare you check up on me!" she fumed.

"Don't flatter yourself. I wasn't checking up on you. I had left my jacket over there a few nights ago and stopped by to retrieve it."

"And you simply had to stop by on the night I was to go there for dinner?"

"Well..." He hemmed and hawed. "If Shane had stepped out of line with you and I conveniently happened to drop in, you'd be thanking me instead of fussing."

"Oh, yes," she sneered. "You're my knight in shining armor, now aren't you? Exactly why is my private life so interesting to you, Justin? Don't you have anything better to do? Seems to me there must be a huge void in your love life. Why don't you ask Cristoff to lend you a few of his leftover bimbos? You could—"

"That's enough!" Justin bellowed, bolting out of the stall to silence her. Instinctively, Nicole took to flight, racing up the aisle and out the exit with lightning speed. She never stopped to consider how stupid she looked, running from her own employee, nor did she realize Justin posed no threat at all. What could he do to her? Verbally scold her? Certainly not strike her. So, why did she feel the need to escape? She couldn't answer that question, but still headed for the safety of her own house. Glancing over her shoulder, she saw him closing the distance. Why was he continuing to pursue her? What did he hope to accomplish? This new thought made her curious, but not curious enough to slow the pace. She ran like her life depended on it. And she was fast, too.

But not fast enough. Justin took hold of her sleeve and pulled. The two tumbled onto the lawn in a tangled heap, rolling a few feet before finally coming to a stop. When they did, Justin made sure he was on top of his victim, who now began to struggle and shout. He never intended to end up in a fight with the bewitching beauty, yet found himself pinning her arms to the ground just so he could carry on a conversation with her.

"Will you just shut up and listen to me?" he yelled. "Just give me one minute, Nicole! And stop that damn screaming; it's making me deaf!" They were both gasping for air, their hearts pounding from the chase. Cristoff and Jan appeared on the scene after hearing Nicole's frantic cry. However, Cristoff convinced Justin's sister to leave the two of them alone and let them work out their own problems.

Taking several deep breaths, the powerful blond looked long and hard at the captive female beneath him. Although he'd never tell her so, the event had been quite exhilarating. His gaze slowly left her eyes, traveling straight down her nose to her mouth, where it settled upon the lips so moist and soft, they reminded him of summer rose petals sprinkled with morning dew. He inwardly groaned and closed his eyes, almost certain he'd regret his next sentence. When he opened his eyes again, Nicole saw a new emotion in their depths. "Nicole," he whispered, biting his lip. "I don't want any of Cristoff's bimbos. All I want is you. All I ever wanted was you." He grew silent then, releasing his hold on her wrists, but making no move to roll off.

Nicole blinked twice, opened her mouth to say something, then promptly shut it again. There was no appropriate response to such a confession. She was absolutely stunned. Yet, she reassured herself that he had merely said he wanted her—not that he loved her. This brought a little relief to her shocked senses. She could handle someone being attracted to her. No problem. She nervously licked her lips. "Thank you for your honesty, Justin."

Two creases appeared between his brows. "Is that it? Just 'thank you for your honesty'?"

"What did you expect me to say?"

"'I want you, too,' would have sounded nice!" He continued to stare down at the perplexed female.

"But I don't," she sheepishly said, hating to admit it. Thoroughly embarrassed, Justin's face went red.

"Oh," he quietly mumbled, feeling like a fool. He quickly got to his feet, then offered his hand to assist her. Nicole accepted the kind gesture and brushed off her clothes. "I'm sorry," she said. "I hope this won't affect our working relationship."

"Not at all," came the cool reply as he began to walk towards the barn. She could see by the slump of his shoulders she had wounded his pride. Nicole felt lower than a snake. Perhaps there was some way to make it up to him? Maybe if she gave him the rest of the day off?

"What did you say to him, Nicole?" Jan asked, after watching her brother grab his lunch and leave. "I've never seen him look so miserable! Why did he go? Is he sick? He wouldn't tell me anything."

"He has a bruised ego, that's all," Nicole replied, plopping down in an office chair. She then explained what had happened between them a short while ago. "I didn't want to hurt him," Nicole defended.

Jan just shook her head, repeating, "Poor Justin." She glanced over at Nicole. "He must really be in love with you."

"He's not in love. If he was, he would have said so. Wanting someone and loving someone are entirely two different matters. He'll recover, I'm sure. You wait and see. This is the weekend, so he'll probably go into town and find some pretty girl to make him forget all about me, which shouldn't be too hard to do."

Jan studied her boss for a moment, then asked, "What is it you don't like about him, Nicole?"

"I do like him. I just don't want him. We argue too much. Besides, I've never quite forgotten our battle on the beach when we were strangers. Any man who throws a woman to the ground is on a power trip. I've had enough of that breed, thank you."

"Do you mean Philip?"

Nicole nodded, noticing the look of pity in Jan's eyes. Ever since Nicole had told her about the abusive past, the girl had carefully avoided the topic. Nicole did, however, keep the information on the wild parties a secret from her. Just then, the phone rang, causing both girls to jump. "It's Daniel," Jan said, after answering it. "He wants to speak with you."

Nicole picked up the receiver, waiting until Jan walked back to her desk in the adjoining room. A door separated the two offices, which Jan quietly closed. "Yes, Daniel. How are you?"

"Fine," said the voice on the other end. "Did Cristoff tell you he spoke with me last night?"

"Yes."

"Well, I think I have a solution to your flashback problem. With your consent, I'd like to bring a doctor with me to your house and induce the hallucinations. We can draw a sample of your blood at that point and have it analyzed to see what exactly is going on during this crucial time. Then, perhaps Dr. Stanton can locate a medicine to eliminate the problem. What do you think? Shall we try it?"

"This is awful sudden," Nicole said, a bit reluctant.

"It's up to you when you want to do it," he offered, then added, "If you want to do it. Perhaps you'd feel more relaxed if Cristoff were present. Feel free to invite him over. Just let me know in advance when you're ready."

Nicole hesitated a moment, but decided sooner was better. "Can you come tomorrow night?"

"Sure. If Dr. Stanton can't make it, I'll call. Is seven o'clock all right?"

"Fine."

"We'll see you then, my dear. Take care."

She hung up the phone and went in search of Cristoff, finding him outside, repairing a fence. After relaying the information to him, she noticed he was even less enthused about the idea than she was. "What's bothering you, Cristoff?" she quizzed.

"I don't know." He shook his head. "I just spoke with Danny last night. How could he have found this doctor so quick? Why didn't he think of it before?"

"You mean, before you told him of the detective?"

"Yeah. What are the chances he's trying to deter us from snooping around?"

"Boy, you're paranoid!" she said.

"No. I'm cautious. We have to look at this from every angle, Nicole."

"If you think he's trying to prevent us from using a detective, just throw a monkeywrench in his plan. Even though we're going through the experiment tomorrow night, tell him you're still using Charlie King. We'll see how he reacts."

"Good idea." The wind had kicked up, so he bowed his head to keep any dirt from flying into his eyes. "Where's Justin? There are two more horses that need to be exercised."

Nicole's back went stiff. "I-I gave him the day off." Still squinting, Cristoff angled his face to stare at her, clearly unhappy with her decision. "I had to, Cristoff. He was extremely upset."

The ranch hand put his hands on his hips. "Does this have anything to do with you?"

"Sort of." Upon hearing him softly curse, she grimaced.

"So, what did you do now?"

"I rejected him, as kindly as possible, though."

"He tried asking you out on a date, again?"

"Not exactly."

"Then what?"

"He just said he wanted me. Then, he became angry when I couldn't express the same desire."

"So, you felt guilty and gave him the day off. That's just great. Now, I have to take time out to exercise the horses."

"No. I'll do it. I was going to look at the financial books, but that can wait until later." She turned to leave, unaware the ranch hand who watched her was growing angrier by the minute. He couldn't believe she had just ruined any chance of Justin getting together with her. So much for matchmaking! Unless... Perhaps he could patch things up between them. First, he'd have to talk to Justin.

He went back to fixing the wooden fence, glancing up from time to time to view Nicole on horseback. She looked like a goddess upon the chestnut stallion, the wind whipping her long, dark hair about her lovely face as if it was jealous of her beauty. He became fixated on the image, his hammer slowly slipping through his fingers to fall onto his big toe. Cristoff barely felt it. He was caught up in the moment, and suddenly realized the trouble which lay ahead when they hired a new horse trainer. If it was a man, he'd no doubt become infatuated with the raven-haired temptress. And what if they needed more employees? Cristoff could not be everywhere at once, in order to protect Nicole. He simply had to fix things between her and Justin.

Picking up the hammer, he finished the job as quickly as possible, then headed to his house to call the blond. Unfortunately, Aaron answered and said Justin was nowhere to be found, but he'd leave a message for his brother to contact Cristoff. Yet, in the following hours, no call came, not even on Cristoff's answering machine. After work, he ate dinner and hung around his house for another hour before calling, again. This time, Jan picked up the phone, explaining that Aaron had gone out earlier to search for his twin. He found him in a local bar, chatting to several women. Justin insisted that Aaron leave him alone, so the twin returned home. "Nicole said this would happen," exclaimed Jan. "She was right. I don't even know if he's coming home tonight, Cristoff, but I'll leave another message for him, if he does." They ended the conversation, and Cristoff toyed with the idea of going after his friend. He decided it would prove futile; Justin was probably drunk by now and beyond reasoning.

Walking to a side window, the ranch hand peered out across the grounds. His vision was drawn to the stable area, where a bright shaft of light streamed out around the half-closed door. He glanced at his watch. "Nicole doesn't usually visit the barn at this hour." Deciding it was better to be safe than sorry, he went to check up on her. Sliding open the huge door, he called her name. No answer. He cautiously advanced down the aisle, stopping to look inside each stall as he did so, until he reached the office. Hoping she had merely fallen asleep at her desk, he ventured inside the room, then moved on to the adjoining room where Jan usually worked. There was no sign of Nicole. He picked up the phone and dialed her private line inside her house. Again, no answer. Now Cristoff was really getting worried. He jogged back to the breeding area and scanned the surroundings. As a last resort, he headed up the ladder to the hayloft and, lo and behold, found the object of his search.

"I didn't want you to find me," she confessed, her tone quiet and melancholy. She was sitting with her back against a bale of hay, which she had carefully positioned so that she was facing the far end of the barn. Although she couldn't see the ranch hand because he was behind her, she had heard him ascend the ladder. The glow of light from down below barely reached the narrow opening in the floor of the hayloft, making it difficult for Cristoff to see her expression when he reached her. He gave his eyes a minute to adjust to the dimness.

"Why are you up here?" he quizzed.

"Came to watch the stars." She continued staring out into the night sky, following the slow procession of clouds drifting by. "Why are you up here?"

"I saw the light on and was concerned. Are you all right?"

He squatted beside the young woman, now able to see her more clearly. She looked depressed.

"Wonderful," she said, flatly. "Don't bother yourself with me, Cristoff. Shouldn't you be in town having a good time?"

"Want to talk about what's troubling you?" He took her hand and gave it a light squeeze. "Hey. I'm your friend, remember? Maybe I can be of some help."

"Only if you're a magician and can start this day all over again." She emitted a long, drawn out sigh. "I feel terrible about Justin. I want to make it up to him, but don't know how."

"You were just being honest, Nicole."

"I've been thoughtless. I didn't even remember to thank him for scrubbing the office floor."

"But that chore was more of a punishment, not a favor he was doing for you."

"Still..." She turned to focus on Cristoff. "I guess I'm also nervous about tomorrow night."

"I figured that." He watched her face darken as clouds overshadowed the moon. "But you know I'll be right there with you, making sure everything goes smoothly."

"I really appreciate it, Cristoff."

"Now, in regards to Justin..." The moonlight resurfaced, allowing him to catch her frowning. "Don't make faces. This is important. If you want to improve the relationship, you simply must give him a chance. Go out with him. It won't kill you. Besides, he's a gentleman."

She held up her hand. "That's still debatable."

"If he's aggressive with you it's because he doesn't know how to control the conflicting desires he feels for you. No man expects to be hit by cupid's arrow."

She outright laughed. "You and Jan are way off base. He's not in love with me."

"How do you know?"

"He didn't say so."

"A man usually doesn't. Justin probably can't even admit it to himself."

Nicole eyed the 25 year-old suspiciously. "I can't believe

you're preaching about love when you plainly told me you've never experienced it. And since we're on the subject, even if Justin did love me, it wouldn't change a thing because I don't love him."

"You haven't given him a chance, Nicole. You might fall in love with him."

"And is that what you want?"

He shifted uneasily, unable to respond. Up until now, he always thought that was what he wanted. But something in Nicole's tone made him hesitate to say so. She had practically spat the words at him, almost as if she were angry. "Cristoff," she said, leaning forward to better read his face. Her voice became whispery soft. "Do you want me to marry Justin?"

He looked away and nervously ran his fingers through his thick hair. "Yes," he replied, still avoiding her gaze. "Yes, I do. I know he'd be good for you. There. I said it. Now you understand why I've been throwing the two of you together."

"Oh, I understand, all right. But I suspect a different reason." He gave her a puzzled look. "Must I show you, Cristoff?"

"Show me what? I haven't the foggiest notion what you're hinting at." Still baffled by her double talk, he was easily caught off guard when she kissed him. It was a soft, sensuous kiss, clearly meant to prove a point. He just didn't know what that point was. "Stop it," he demanded, pushing her off him. "What the hell has got into you? Have you been drinking?"

"No," she smiled, not the least bit discouraged. "And I forgive you for being angry. I expected it."

"What?" He scrunched up his face in complete bewilderment.

"I understand you now, Cristoff. You want me to marry Justin so it will put me off limits to you. You don't like being drawn to me, do you?"

"Of all the egotistical—"

"Of course you're in denial," she interjected. "It's hard for you to admit you can't control your own impulses."

"I can so!"

"Oh? You lost your temper last time I kissed you. Care to explain why?"

He couldn't. He couldn't even think up a good reason. He stalled for time, growing more skittish by the minute. "I have to leave," he suddenly said.

"Of course you do. I expected that, too. You're rather an easy puzzle to piece together, my friend."

Cristoff could feel his anger mounting with each labored breath. She was treading in the danger zone, where she had no business being.

"You run away from me because what I say hits too close to home," she continued. "You don't like someone telling you you're easy to read and you don't like anyone tapping into your true feelings. But, for goodness sakes, Cristoff, it's difficult for me to just sit by and watch you torture yourself over and over. At least have the courage to be honest with yourself."

As he felt the remainder of his masculinity crush beneath her heel, something inside the ranch hand snapped. He cupped her face with one rough hand and firmly squeezed, his voice a low growl. "I asked you a question the last time we were here, Nicole, and I'm going to ask you again. What the devil do you want from me?!"

"I only want the truth," she quietly said, "which you seem to avoid."

"Okay," he hissed, curling his lips to reveal several white teeth. "I'll tell you the truth. Yes, I'm attracted to you. Yes, you scare the hell out of me. And no, you are wrong when it comes to my ability to control my impulses; because, if I did not have some degree of self-restraint, I would have tossed you in the hay a long, long, long time ago." She could feel his hand trembling as it continued to exert pressure on her skin, his eyes full of pain at the disclosure of his most private feelings. "Now," he jeered, "are you satisfied?"

"Yes. Yes, I am," she bravely said, slowly wrapping her slender fingers around his wrist so he would loosen his grip. He complied, but not before stating, "You need a strong man to keep you in line, Nicole. I can see where Philip may have been provoked."

Her heart nearly stopped, she was so wounded. He might as well have said she deserved every single beating. Tears stung her eyes as she stared at the ranch hand. "How can you be so cruel?" she softly cried, unable to understand the vicious backlash.

Ashamed, he hung his head. "I'm sorry," he whispered, moving to wipe away the tears. "I didn't mean it." He slipped his arms around the slender body and pulled her close, his hand stroking the long hair when she rested her head near his shoulder. Cristoff felt a burning sensation begin in his abdomen. Was it no wonder? His stomach was tied in a million knots. He couldn't remember the last time he had been this upset. "You and I both know there was no justification for what Philip did to you. It was wrong for me to imply otherwise. Please don't cry, Nicole. It's just that..." He looked up at the ceiling, his voice full of despair. "I don't like discussing my feelings with anyone. You know that, yet you still prodded me. You wouldn't let up."

"Because I needed to know," she sniffed, lifting her head. "I'm attracted to you, too, Cristoff. Haven't you noticed?"

"You simply feel comfortable around me," he corrected. "There's nothing more to it than that. Hell, Nicole, we work with each other every day. There's bound to be some sort of attraction."

"But it doesn't end there," she continued, needing to tell him everything. "At night, when I'm alone in my room..." She paused, embarrassed to her toes.

"Yes?"

"... I think of you."

Cristoff's eyebrows shot up. "You do? How?"

The young woman grew shy, dropping her gaze to some imaginary spot on the floor. "I think of how it feels when I'm in your arms." There was a quiver in her voice.

She definitely had his attention now. His words no more than a whisper, Cristoff eagerly ventured, "And how exactly do you feel when you're in my arms?"

Nicole sighed. "Warm. Secure. And a thousand butterflies fluttering in my stomach." She watched him nervously scratch his chin, thinking that perhaps she had said too much.

She had no idea Cristoff was in a state of acute distress, his many emotions suddenly colliding. Although he had previously frowned upon a relationship between the two of them, at this very minute his mind was screaming for him to surrender to his carnal desires. It would be so easy...

A red alert went off in his brain, but unlike before, this time he ignored it. He let out a long exhale, his hazel eyes smoldering with lust. He no longer cared that she was his boss, no longer worried about his future stake in the ranch. Tonight... tonight he was fed up with pretending no bond existed between them. He had proof she truly cared. He was going to grab the prize and run with it. She was beautiful, she was almost financially secure, and she knew him better than any other person in his entire life. There were times she had actually guessed his thoughts—more times than he cared to admit. Why shouldn't he involve himself? He'd think of the consequences later.

"Cristoff," she whispered, her hungry eyes pleading. He loved the way his name sounded on her lips, how she gazed at him with those large, expressive eyes. Acting out his heart's desire, he now brought his mouth to hers, all the suppressed passion exploding in one, solitary kiss. The mutual affection between them blossomed then, making them oblivious to their surroundings, totally enveloping them in the sweet innocence of a friendship that extended far beyond its cautious borders.

Cristoff took it slow. He wanted nothing to ruin this night. Gone was the need for reckless abandon. Instead, he showered her with a hundred kisses, allowing his mouth to linger at the pulse point of her throat before traveling back up to her sweet, soft lips. She clung to him like a lost child, a bit frightened, yet excited. While enjoying his delicious assault on her senses, she embraced the thought of returning the pleasure.

Nicole's idea of pleasure, however, was quite different from his. She assumed that hugging and kissing would be enough to satisfy him tonight. After all, this was the first time she had engaged in such a display of affection since the death of her husband. Thus, she prolonged the tantalizing kisses, torturing Cristoff with her hungry mouth until he nearly cried out in frustration. Every time his hands wandered, she took hold of them with her own, deliberately conveying her objection. It drove the ranch hand crazy, prompting him to try another method of persuasion. Gently, he moved her onto her back. "I won't hurt you," he solemnly promised, undoing her coat so she could feel his hard body against her.

It was then, Cristoff saw him.

Standing two feet away, legs braced apart, strong arms folded across his massive chest, Justin sported a look of utter disgust. Like an animal caught in a trap, the ranch hand suddenly froze. This was one confrontation he would have given anything to avoid. He slowly lifted his head, his body following suit, the sound of Nicole's heavy breathing still ringing in his ears.

"Cristoff?" Nicole whispered, coming up on her elbows. "What is it?" Her gaze followed his as she twisted to see, the brown eyes widening with alarm at the sight of the stranger in the shadows. Nicole nearly fainted.

"Don't mind me," drawled the gruff male voice, silent rage gnawing a hole through his middle. The fact that he smelled like a brewery put his opponent on guard.

"Justin," Cristoff nervously chuckled, jumping up. "What brings you here?"

"You left a message for me to call you. When there wasn't any answer I went to your house and knocked on the door. Then I saw the barn light on." He watched Nicole tiptoe past him to turn on the main lights in the loft. All three of them squinted for a few seconds, waiting to adjust.

"How long have you been standing there?" she quizzed.

He studied her briefly, his eyes full of pain. "Long enough," he stiffly replied, wishing he had remained in town. It hurt too much to look at her now after seeing the two of them together. How could he have been so naive? He longed to forget the episode, and turned his attention back to Cristoff. "Why did you call my house?"

"Oh," Cristoff stalled. "Yeah, uh, um, actually, well, the problem already corrected itself, so, uh, I don't need to speak with you, after all." He stole a quick glance at the blond, then swiftly looked away, not realizing that although Justin was intoxicated, he still was perceptive enough to put two and two together.

"You know, Cristoff," he said slowly, stepping towards the ranch hand, "if you want to mess around with Nicole, that's your business. But what I really, really despise, is when a friend can't be trusted. You pretended you wanted Nicole and me to be together." His cold, blue eyes narrowed with contempt while his voice became an angry snarl. "What's worse is that you kept encouraging me to go after her. You kept pushing, and pushing," his hands shoved Cristoff backwards, "... pushing me, until, like a witless fool, I swallowed my pride and confessed how much I desired her. Do you have any idea how I feel right now, after watching the two of you writhing on the floor?"

Nicole stepped between them. "You shouldn't have been sneaking around, Justin."

"Sneaking?" he snorted. "Oh, sure. Blame me. Your loud moaning could wake the dead! And you wonder why you didn't hear me?"

"That's enough, Justin," Cristoff broke in. "Why don't we go over to my house and talk this out?"

A low, throaty laugh escaped the blond as he shook his head. "No thanks."

Cristoff persisted, feeling a twinge of guilt. "Things aren't always how they appear to be. What occurred here tonight, just sort of happened. It wasn't planned. Besides, we were only kissing." Justin's head moved back an inch, as if the words had actually struck him. He had only disdain now for his friend. Cristoff grew defensive. "What are you so upset about, anyway? I heard you were in town with several women. You must have got over your rejection pretty quick."

"It wasn't what you're thinking."

"How do we know?" piped Nicole.

Just hearing her voice made Justin's blood turn to acid. He walked up to the alluring beauty and took her by the arm. "If you're so damn curious, my dear, I'll be happy to fill you in on the details, but not until Cristoff leaves."

"I'm not going anywhere," came the answering reply. Cristoff folded his arms for emphasis. Nicole freed herself from the masculine grip, ordering, "Go home, Justin. Sleep it off."

He gazed long and hard at the raven-haired temptress before his eyes darted to Cristoff and a twisted smile pierced his lips. "Sure. I'll leave you two lovebirds alone." He silently made his way to the ladder, paused, then climbed down, vanishing into the light below. Cristoff nervously cleared his throat. Suddenly, he felt awkward. Although Justin was gone, he had definitely changed the mood of the evening. Nicole noticed it, too. She looked terribly uncomfortable. "I have some things to do in the house. I'll see you tomorrow, Cristoff."

"Wait," he said, taking her by the arm. "I--"

"Yes?"

Cristoff hesitated, then gradually released his hold. "... never mind. Good night, Nicole." He could do nothing but quietly watch her leave.

Nicole made her way out into the night and across the lawn. She was dismayed to find herself engulfed in a deep, gut-wrenching sadness, her mind recalling the bitterness in Justin's voice. She had no reason to feel sorry for Justin; after all, they weren't dating. She had been honest with him. If anyone should feel bad right now, it should be Cristoff. But even Cristoff had explained that what had occurred tonight wasn't planned. Still, she didn't want the two men to be at odds with each other. Perhaps it would be best to wait and see what Cristoff said in the morning. She'd help him patch things up with Justin.

When morning arrived, however, it was clear that Cristoff was not in the best frame of mind. He was thoroughly intoxicated, unable to pull himself up off the living room floor where he had spent the last nine hours. Nicole had known something was wrong when he hadn't shown up at the barn to feed the horses. Upon finding him stretched out on the rug, her worst guess had become reality. He wouldn't budge, wouldn't speak, wouldn't even open his eyes. His only response was a weak grunt. Disgusted, Nicole eventually left. She caught up on some housework and laundry while the morning gave way to the afternoon. It had begun to rain, a torrential downpour, prompting her to put the horses in the barn early. She was soaked by the time she finished, so she grabbed a shower and made preparations for dinner. When it was time to eat, however, Nicole had little appetite. Her nerves were playing havoc with her stomach. She dialed Cristoff's phone number, but there was no answer, and gradually she forced herself to accept the fact that he would not be able to fulfill his promise of coming over when Daniel arrived.

Nicole panicked. She felt uneasy being unchaperoned with this new doctor and Daniel. She desperately needed someone with her—even if it was Justin. The thought allayed her fears. That was it. She'd ask Justin. Nicole reached for the phone, then changed her mind. It would be too easy for him to just hang up on her when she called. She'd have to go there, in person, and arrange for them to speak privately so Jan and Aaron would not overhear.

Quickly, the young woman peeled off her clothes. She was smart enough to realize it would take more than just words to win the blond over. She slipped into her sexiest dress, a zebra striped outfit that fit like a second skin, clinging provocatively to every feminine curve. After reapplying some strawberry oil to her wrists and pulse point, she stepped into a pair of high heels, grabbed an umbrella and hurried out the door. All she could do was pray he'd be home. A slight burning sensation began in her stomach as she pulled up in the driveway and walked towards the house.

Holding her breath, the 21 year-old solidly knocked on the large, wooden door. When it finally opened, she came face to face with Justin's twin. "Hello, Aaron," she said. "May I please speak with Justin?"

The man who greeted her remained silent, his eyes traveling up and down the slender figure like a scanning device. His mouth twitched slightly at her adept talent of perceiving he was not his brother; in fact, it rather annoyed him for some odd reason. When he had had his fill of the gorgeous female, he smiled his approval, saying, "So you're the little vixen who's driving Justin to drink?"

Nicole ignored the remark. "If you haven't noticed, it's raining. May I come in?"

"By all means," he grinned, swinging the door open wide. She shook out the umbrella, then allowed him to take it from her. "It'll be in the kitchen," he said. "Would you like something to drink?"

"No, thank you. All I want is to speak with your brother, please. He is here, isn't he?"

"Oh, he's here," Aaron smirked. "But I don't think you should talk to him, not in his condition."

"I have to," she stressed. "It's urgent."

Not the least bit anxious to do her bidding, Aaron lingered in the room, staring down the front of her dress. "Oh, I'm sure it's urgent, all right," he leered.

Nicole felt her blood pressure rising. The insolent oaf! "Fine," she seethed through clenched teeth. "Is your sister home?" Aaron shook his head. "Then, I'll find Justin, myself!" She started for the stairs, but halted when Aaron called, "I wouldn't go up there. He's zonked out on his bed, asleep." She took two more steps. "In the nude."

Nicole froze, seriously reconsidering until she saw Aaron's cocky grin. A couple of quick leaps and she was up in the hallway, glancing in each room. It only took a second to find him. It took a hundred seconds to tear her gaze away from the marblesque, muscular form lying on its stomach across the crimson-colored bedspread.

"Like what you see?" mouthed the amused giant, beginning to turn over. Startled and embarrassed to the roots of her hair, Nicole ducked back from the entrance to a more modest position in the hall. "I heard your voice downstairs," he continued. "Wish I could say I'm glad to see you, but I'm not. Go back home, Nicole. Leave me alone. I've had enough angst for one day."

"Please put some clothes on, Justin," she begged. "I have to speak with you, privately."

"I said leave me alone."

"It's important. It's about Daniel. He's coming over tonight for a special reason."

"To sample some of your wares?"

Nicole bit back an angry retort. "If you'd just get dressed, we could discuss this. Believe me, if I could have avoided coming over here, I would have. Doesn't that show you how desperate I am?" Too late, she realized she had now insulted him.

"Well, if that doesn't win me over, nothing will!" mocked the blond.

"What I meant was, I know you don't want to see me. I didn't mean—"

"Save your breath," he growled. She heard the bed squeak and the sound of heavy footsteps walking to another area of the room. A closet door was opened before the faint sound of clothes hangers clinking reached her ears. A few minutes later, he appeared by her side, totally unprepared for the lovely vision captivating his senses when she turned to face him. She opened her mouth to speak, then closed it, puzzled by the frustration in his eyes. Indeed, Justin was more edgy now than when she had seen him in the stable. There was a definite hardening of his expression, his generous mouth tightening to a grim line, a crease between the thick, golden brows, a stiffening of his square jaw. These were not hopeful signs. Good grief! thought Nicole. I've now offended him with my choice of clothes. Is there any way to please this man?

He saw her mouth working, saw her trying to regain her voice, and decided to remedy the situation, himself, by suggesting, "Why don't we go out to your car?" She quickly nodded before following his lead down the stairs. "My umbrella is in the kitchen," she said. He retrieved it and opened the door. Even though the rain had stopped, Nicole carried the umbrella out to her car anyway, setting it behind the front seat as they got into the vehicle.

She told him about Daniel and Dr. Stanton, explaining the dilemma she was in now that she could not count on Cristoff being present for the experiment. When she finished, her eyes pleaded for his compassion. "I don't want to face them alone," she confessed, desperation in her voice.

"You won't have to," he solidly replied.

Nicole touched his arm. "Thank you. Thank you so much, Justin. I was hoping you'd understand."

"You were truly confident, huh?" he dryly remarked. "Is that why you had to get all dressed up to come over here?" Her gaze slid to the floor. "I would like an answer to a question that's been bothering me, Nicole." He turned his head to look out the window, not really wanting her beauty to cloud his judgment.

"I owe you that much," she quietly replied.

A slight pause ensued. He shifted uncomfortably in the seat, stretching one long leg out to its full extent. "Have you... slept with Cristoff?"

Nicole's answer was swift and firm. "No."

"Never?"

"Never. What you witnessed in the hayloft was the most affection we have ever demonstrated. Do you believe me?"

He swung his head around to stare deeply into her eyes, relief flooding his face at the intense sincerity in those depths. He knew he could trust her word, and somehow that made everything all right.

"If it makes you feel better," she mumbled, "I haven't slept with anyone since Philip's death."

"Because you're afraid of men?"

"No. Because I have no intention of doing so."

He gave her an incredulous look. "You're going to remain chaste for the rest of your life?"

"I didn't say that." She appeared somewhat embarrassed. "I would prefer being married before I engage in that type of behavior. I have certain beliefs... religious beliefs, corny as that may sound."

The blond giant openly chuckled, rolling his eyes heavenward. "This isn't the eighteenth century, Nicole."

"It was foolish for me to think a man could possibly understand." A frown tugged at her lips, but she felt the importance of explaining her position. "To me, making love is a joining of the spirit. It's deeper than mere physical interaction. A piece of my heart remains with the man I sleep with, just as a piece of his heart will remain with me. How can I form that type of bond from a one-night stand and not feel let down afterwards? I'm just not the kind of person who can turn off her emotions." She glanced up to find him thoughtfully studying her, his vivid blue eyes suddenly turning deep cobalt. Apparently, her words had moved him, moved him enough to actually consider what she had said. She also noticed something in those depths she had never seen before—respect.

"You never cease to amaze me, Nicole." The corners of his mouth stretched into a lazy smile. "I just wonder if Cristoff has heard your little speech?"

"Well, not exactly." She frowned when Justin began to lightly chuckle, then added, "I'm sure he'll understand my position on the subject."

Justin's chuckle rumbled deeper. "Oh, yes. Cristoff will understand!"

"Well, why wouldn't he?"

"Why, indeed!" laughed the blond, reaching for the door handle. "What time did you say I should be there tonight?"

"Before seven," she replied.

"I'll see you then. Uh, I advise you to change into something a little less provocative, though."

"I will. Oh, and... thank you, Justin."

She started the car, watching until he had disappeared inside the house. "I have nothing to worry about now," she smiled to herself.

CHAPTER TWELVE

An ominous feeling lurked in the shadows of the dimly lit room as Nicole leaned back in her favorite chair. Despite Justin being present, the young woman grew uneasy in the company of her guests, constantly running her hand over the material of the armchair, smoothing out imaginary wrinkles. Although Daniel had suggested darkening the room to help induce any hallucinations, Nicole now got up and reversed the dimmer switch. As the bright pool of light spread across the carpet, she felt little relief. A sinking feeling in the pit of her stomach had already alerted her to the future results of this experiment—it would prove futile. There would be no antidote, no miracle cure. Nicole's instinct was always right. And this very minute, she felt the unmistakable presence of evil in the room. Since she had never experienced that before with Daniel, she could only assume it was directed towards the doctor. The question was: Why? She studied the distinguished man in his early fifties, and noticed subtle signs of anxiety. This piqued her curiosity even more. She began to question him about his background, sensing a mental defensive shield surfacing as her interrogation continued. It was evident he did not enjoy the prying. Daniel seemed to pick up on this, too, and came to his rescue, saying, "Drink up, Nicole. The sooner the alcohol takes effect, the sooner we can leave. Why don't we change the atmosphere and play cards for a while?"

"Good idea," spoke Justin, rising from the sofa. "Nicole?"

"Sure." She reached into a drawer to extract the playing cards, then joined the men at her dining room table. The foursome played pinochle for the next hour until it became obvious Nicole's ability to concentrate had started to waiver. The time lapse between drinks had shortened. She was gulping sweet brandy like sugar water. Concerned for her health, Justin suggested she slow down. He received a wicked smile for the effort. Then, out of the blue, Nicole announced, "Justin thinks he can boss me around just because I saw him naked."

The room went deathly silent. Daniel's eyes darted to the blond, who, in turn, covered his embarrassment by making light of the situation. "I think the brandy is finally working, don't you, Dr. Stanton?" He joined the doctor in a quiet chuckle. Nicole laughed, too, suddenly feeling quite cheerful.

"We need music," she said, rising from her seat.

"Music is fine," Daniel replied, "but poetry would be even nicer, wouldn't it, Nicole?" Justin saw him lock eyes with her.

"Yes," the woman answered. "Poetry is wonderful."

"Do you know what poem I'd like to hear?" Daniel continued. "Remember the poem about the man with fire in his eyes?" Nicole hesitated, then slowly nodded. "Would you recite that for me, please?"

Eyes still glued to Philip's brother, she recalled the verse:

A vision slowly rises,
On a foggy, blue horizon,
Comes a man with eyes of fire;
Secret whisper, one desire;
Captivating all with stories;
Buried treasure, conquests, glories,
Far countries, bloody battles,
Royal brains he has rattled;
Nearly slain, but by a breath,
Eluded twice the jaws of death;
Spears the night in youthful ardor,
Careful not to play the martyr;

Slaying vice with saving grace,
Years of torment on his face;
Spots the object of his quest,
And finally lays his soul to rest.

As if in a trance, the dark-haired princess walked purposefully towards Daniel, leaned down, and kissed him fully on the lips. A smug grin lit his face as he pulled her onto his lap.

Across the table, Justin had seen enough. He jumped up from his chair, pointing an accusing finger at the 26 year-old. "What the devil are you doing, Daniel?" he demanded.

"Sit down, Justin!" It was an order, a very terse order. Both men exchanged hostile glares. "The needle, Dr. Stanton? I believe she's ready, now." Daniel rubbed the small of Nicole's back. "You don't mind if we take a little blood from you, my dear, do you?" The compliant girl numbly shook her head.

"Put your arm out on the table," the doctor said. "Make a fist. That's right. Good. Now relax." Justin stared in wonder, still trying to figure out what had just occurred a few seconds ago.

"Why the poem?" he quizzed Daniel.

"It holds meaning for Nicole. Tell him, Nicole, why you like that verse." Still sitting in Daniel's lap, she turned her head towards Justin, her face expressionless as she stated, "I read those words in a book… just before Daniel took me upstairs and made love to me." She barely blinked at the blond, her gaze so robotic it sent chills down his spine. There was no shame in her remark, no guilt in her eyes.

Justin was appalled. He stared at her while Daniel slowly smirked. It was evident the creep thoroughly enjoyed the effect this new bit of news had on the masculine blond. Daniel only regretted he hadn't the time to go into further detail of the incident. Glancing at his watch, he coaxed Nicole to get up. "I'm afraid we have to be going."

"No," she pouted, hanging on to his arm. "Don't go, yet."

Daniel gently chided her. "Let go, sweetheart." She did. "Sit down at the table and play cards with Justin, like a good little girl." She promptly obeyed, now shuffling the deck, oblivious to the fact that the masculine blond had jumped from his chair and was heading straight for Philip's brother.

"Not so fast!" Justin growled, his eyes shooting daggers. "Don't think that just because you toyed with Nicole like a puppet on a string, that you can manipulate her whenever the mood strikes you! You can be sure I'll tell her what happened here tonight, and she won't be very pleased, of that I am most certain!"

"Calm down, old chap," grinned Daniel. "You're taking this much too hard. If I hadn't played my daring game we'd never be sure she had achieved a high enough alcohol level. If Nicole were in a normal state of mind, she'd have never acted the way she did. This was simply a test, nothing more." The two men warily eyed one another. "Have fun, Justin. She's all yours. Enjoy."

"Wait a minute," the blond commanded. "When will we know the results of the testing?"

"A few days. I'll give a call. In the meantime, make sure she stays inside tonight. We wouldn't want her to stray while in this, ah, condition... now, would we?" He gave a knowing wink, a wicked grin spreading slowly up his cheeks. Before Justin could comment, he and the doctor slipped quickly out the front door.

Justin turned to look at Nicole, who still sat at the table, shuffling cards. What the heck was he supposed to do with her now? He knew what he'd like to do with her, but, after the speech she gave in her car earlier, he couldn't bring himself to take advantage of her. It was tempting though, especially when he realized she'd have no recollection of it in the morning. Leave it to Nicole; the night she should hallucinate, she loses her inhibitions instead. Thank goodness he had been here tonight. He didn't trust Daniel, not one bit. The way that man gloated over his affair with Nicole was simply nauseating. Another sickening thought entered his mind. What if Cristoff had been wrong? What if Daniel had slept with Nicole more than just once? By his actions tonight, he gave the impression he had repeated this scene before—how else would he have known to make Nicole recite the poem? And if Daniel had been Nicole's frequent lover, this would provide a motive to kill Philip. Justin strained his brain to recall what Cristoff had said was Daniel's alibi.

"Don't you want to play cards?" purred Nicole. He hadn't even noticed her walking towards him. Two feminine arms encircled his neck as she seductively smiled.

He carefully removed her hold on him. "Why don't you go upstairs and get some sleep?" he suggested. He knew she'd obey, but he wasn't prepared for her to insist he come with her. "No. I can't. I have to leave now, Nicole."

"Please," she implored, trying to kiss him. "I'm so lonely."

"Go upstairs. Now." The harshness in his voice startled her. She looked like she would cry. "Don't cry, either," he firmly ordered. "Do you hear me?"

"I'll go upstairs," she pouted, "after I find Cristoff. He'll keep me company."

Justin ran his fingers through his hair. He hadn't even considered Nicole running over to Cristoff's house, and the condition Cristoff was in would definitely lead to… He pushed the thought out of his mind. Daniel was right. He had to make sure Nicole stayed in the house, at least until the effects of the alcohol wore off. "You run on upstairs and get ready for bed. After you're under the covers, call me. I'll sit in your room until you fall asleep, okay?"

"Okay," she smiled, her chocolate brown eyes fixed upon him as she climbed the stairs. Justin let out a weary exhale. How could he be sure she would remain indoors unless he stayed here tonight? He knew Nicole had extra bedrooms, so sleeping over was a possibility. But would he hear her if she got up in the middle of the night? He was a pretty sound sleeper. Perhaps he could lay on the floor of her room. Naa. Knowing his luck, she'd probably step on one of his vital organs and maim him for life.

Continuing to ponder his choices, he leafed through a magazine. One of the new car advertisements showed a young bride and groom standing beside an expensive luxury vehicle. At first glance, the female resembled Nicole. Upon closer scrutiny, however, he saw the obvious differences in appearance. He tried to picture the temptress in such formal attire. She would prove a beautiful bride, but Justin pitied the man who would wed her. Boy, was she a handful!

"I'm ready!" called a faint voice from upstairs. Justin put the magazine away and headed up to her room, glad she was finally in bed, where she belonged. He pulled up a chair and sat down. "Close your eyes and go to sleep," he instructed.

"No goodnight kiss?"

"No. Now, be a good girl and do what you're told."

"Meanie," she whispered, her vision still deliberately focused on him. He could picture her as a child laying there, her big brown eyes looking up at her father. She must have stolen his heart, just as she was stealing his, now. He hated to admit it, but he was helpless at shaking the attraction he felt for her. It was more than physical; it was as if she belonged with him. Why couldn't she feel it, too?

He watched the sleeping beauty's eyelids close. He heard her breathing deepen and silently wished he were there beside her. All of his previous anger from last night had vanished. A deep longing stirred within him, and for once in his life, Justin realized he was teetering on the edge of love. It scared him half to death. He had never felt this way before. He wasn't so sure he wanted to, either. It left him frustrated—extremely frustrated. He thought about it for another fifteen minutes, then found himself dozing off.

One hour later, he was awakened by a whimpering sound. Nicole was making odd noises and thrashing about in bed, apparently experiencing a nightmare. Justin quickly switched on the hall light, which gave off just enough illumination he could see her amidst the rumpled covers. She was groaning like a tortured animal, wrestling with a nearby pillow, which unfortunately was taking a real beating. The bedspread was tightly wound around her legs, producing enough bondage to keep her from rolling off the edge of the bed.

Not knowing what to do, Justin called out to her in a soft voice, but to no avail. He repeated her name, louder this time, hoping to get her attention. She still did not respond. Finally he went to her, pulled her into his arms and gently rocked her back and forth. "It's just a dream, Nicole," he soothed. "Wake up. You're dreaming." Her eyelids fluttered in recognition, then slowly opened.

Justin felt his heart plummet. The fear in her eyes was so intense she looked as if any minute now she could go into shock. Perspiration lined her forehead, the soft, raven-colored hair damp and clinging. She clutched at him, all the while staring deep into his eyes. And then he heard her lungs expel a long rush of air, like a tea kettle after the flame is turned off.

"Justin," she whispered, her throat sore and scratchy. "You're here."

He tried to lighten the mood. "You're so hot I could fry eggs on your shoulders." He saw her give a weak smile. "Do you want to talk about the dream?"

"No." She lowered her head, trying to erase the nightmare from her mind. "Will you stay?"

"Yes," he replied, breaking away to stand and fix the twisted covers.

"You're welcome to use the adjoining bedroom?"

"I just might do that."

"Help yourself to anything in the kitchen."

"Thank you for the offer. You go on back to sleep. Morning comes early, you know?" But he had no sooner said the words when he noticed she had already closed her eyes. Within minutes, her breathing had deepened again. Justin sat back down in the chair to keep an eye on her. After twenty minutes, he, too, dozed off again, awakening shortly with a terrible neck ache. He massaged the muscles around his collarbone, desperately wanting to lie down. Finally stretching out on the floor near the door, he fell into a heavy slumber. It was when he got up around midnight to use the bathroom, he found himself returning to Nicole's bed, his senses groggy from sleep. He threw back the covers and comfortably sighed as his head touched the wonderfully soft pillow. He had no idea what he had just done—no idea at all, until five o'clock in the morning.

Whomp! Justin grunted with pain as his body slammed onto the hard floor. Kneeling on the bed, looking over the edge at him was Nicole, her mouth moving furiously while she shouted accusations at the dazed man. Justin had never heard a woman yell so loud. "Boy, have you got a set of lungs on you!" he exclaimed, picking himself up off the floor. He ignored the constant screaming and rubbed his left hip. Had she really kicked him out of bed? The thought almost amused him.

"You pig!" yelled Nicole, livid with rage.

"Hold your horses," Justin replied. "It's not what you think. I didn't touch you. Nothing happened here last night."

"You expect me to believe that?" she screeched. "I found you in bed with me!"

"I must have crawled in when I was half asleep. Don't you remember me sitting in the chair?"

"No. I don't!"

"Well, you'll just have to trust my word, then."

"Trust you?!" she bellowed, shaking her fist. "Trust you?!" She catapulted off the bed, taking him by surprise with a quick lunge. He caught her by the shoulders.

"I tried to sleep on the floor, Nicole. I wouldn't use the spare bedroom because you were having nightmares. I was afraid I wouldn't hear you if you called out. Honestly, I must have slipped into your bed in the middle of the night. Nothing happened between us. I was too tired. So were you."

The angry frown softened. She seemed to understand. "I guess I'll never know, will I?" she quietly said. "You do sound like you're telling the truth. But, then, I believed Daniel when he claimed he had never touched me. He was a liar."

"And still is, as far as I'm concerned," Justin mentioned, drawing a questioning look from Nicole. "We need to talk about what occurred last night." Nicole sensed the urgency of his tone. She sighed.

"All right. Allow me some time to change clothes. I'll meet you in the kitchen. We can discuss things over breakfast."

Pleased with the offer, the blond took one last look at her in the short, cotton nightgown before departing. When she rejoined him five minutes later, he noticed she had brushed out the tangles from her long hair and reapplied a small amount of makeup. He had the urge to tell her she could have remained how he first saw her—it wouldn't have mattered. In his eyes, nothing could detract from her beauty. But he kept the thought to himself, having no desire to sound like an infatuated schoolboy.

Together, they cooked breakfast, then sat down to eat. "So, go ahead," Nicole prompted. "Tell me the bad news about last night."

Justin took a sip of orange juice. "First of all, you didn't hallucinate."

"Oh? Then the project failed, correct?"

"Not exactly. You lost your inhibitions, instead."

Nicole's hand flew to her mouth in horror. "Tell me I didn't dance on the table!"

"No, nothing like that. You, um, recited a special poem for Daniel, at his request." He stopped eating to watch her expression. "When you finished, you calmly walked over to him and gave the guy a rather generous kiss."

Nicole gasped, unable to believe her ears. Justin stiffly smiled. "I'm glad I'm not the only one who was surprised."

"I can't imagine doing such a thing!" she defended, ashamed.

"Daniel took great pleasure in it. He made you explain your actions to me. Want to hear what you said?"

"I'm almost afraid to ask."

"You said you had read that exact poem right before Daniel made love to you." His words hung like lead weights around her neck, he could tell. Nicole was trying her best to control the repulsion she felt. "Then the good doctor extracted some blood and the two of them left. I asked Daniel when you'd know the results. He said in a few days."

"It doesn't matter," Nicole said, quietly.

"What doesn't matter?"

"The results. They won't produce a solution."

"How can you be so pessimistic?"

"I know," she firmly replied, meeting his gaze. "My intuition is never wrong. What's more, I had a terrible feeling last night about Dr. Stanton. This may sound crazy to you, Justin, but I don't think he's a legitimate doctor. I'd go so far as to suggest your detective check out his credentials while he's investigating everyone else for us."

"You feel that strongly about him, huh?" the blond quizzed, rubbing his chin. "Look. I have to be honest with you, Nicole. I know this is a delicate subject to bring up, but we have no choice. After witnessing this episode last night, I had the distinct impression that Daniel has repeated this scene before." Nicole threw him a baffled look. "What I mean is, what are the chances he has used the poem previously to get you into bed?" Ready to defend himself if she should throw an object at him, Justin was amazed to see her take the question so calmly. She studied the piece of toast on her plate, not the least bit angry. In fact, she appeared rather sad.

"I suppose anything is possible," she mumbled, emotion welling up in her eyes.

"I didn't want to upset you."

"No. That's all right. We have to consider all possibilities, not just those that fit in nicely. I just dread the thought that..." Her voice faded like a dying song. Justin went to her then, slipping his hands onto her shoulders to gently massage away the hurt, the anguish. She buried her face in her hands, openly crying before him, hating herself for the inability to control her own actions during the dark days of her past.

"No one's condemning you, Nicole," Justin whispered. "Don't condemn yourself. We don't even know if Daniel was your lover. I'm just trying to piece this all together. If he was your lover, he would have a motive for murdering Philip."

"Philip?" she said, drying her tears. "I can't believe Daniel would do such a thing. No matter how much I despise him now, Daniel is not a jealous person. If he killed Philip out of jealousy, why hasn't he pursued me? It's the same old question, over and over."

"Think about it, though. If he did pursue you as a lover, he'd end up a prime suspect. Don't you see? He has to lie low."

"You're forgetting one thing, Justin. Even if this far-fetched notion is correct, even if we know in our hearts that it's true, we have no proof, no evidence. There has to be evidence to get a conviction."

"I know," he quietly said. "Unless we can get Daniel to crack."

Nicole cocked her head. "Do you have a plan?"

"Perhaps."

He leaned against the kitchen sink now, deep in thought, then suggested, "If Daniel was to believe you were engaged to be married, he just might lose his cool."

"You have a point. We would know, once and for all, whether he's jealous or not. He keeps saying I'm not his type, but that could be blarney."

"Precisely."

"One problem, though. We'd have to make this appear as the real thing—wedding date and all. How can we pull it off?"

"First, we have to find you a groom."

"Cristoff would be the most likely candidate. Daniel knows I've been skittish around men since Philip. He knows Cristoff and I are good friends."

"Can't use Cristoff," Justin argued. "When he drinks, I'm sure he goes into town. If he was caught at the brothel, for instance, the whole charade would be over."

Nicole reluctantly agreed. "He's not dependable." She sat there, contemplating her other options, making Justin so frustrated he wanted to scream out the obvious. Finally, she shyly glanced in his direction. "Oh, no. It wouldn't work."

"Why not?" he crowed.

"We don't get along very well."

"Perhaps if we tried harder—"

"No!" Nicole's fist slammed onto the table, making the silverware rattle. "How convenient of you to think up this idea just to get close to me."

"I'd be a liar if I denied that accusation. But, you have to admit, this is a great idea."

The young woman grimaced as if in pain. "I refuse to allow you to be the groom."

"Then you'd better find a replacement, and quick. It's going to take plenty of time for you to develop a bond with someone else and trick them into proposing."

Nicole threw back her head and groaned. Why was he always right? She didn't have it in her to falsely lead on an unsuspecting stranger. She'd never pull it off. Studying the masculine blond through half-closed eyes, she firmly stated, "You're not moving in here."

Justin grinned, triumphantly. He had won the battle. "Should we let Cristoff in on the secret?"

She shook her head. "Can't take the chance of him spilling the beans if Daniel threatens him. It'd be better if he truly believed the engagement."

"What about a wedding date? How about two months from now?"

Nicole folded her arms. "One week."

"You're crazy! No one gets married in one week!"

"If you think I'm playing this charade for two full months, think again. One week, Justin. We need to put the pressure on Daniel."

"How am I going to find someone to marry us in a week?"

"Relax. There isn't really going to be a wedding, remember? We'll have a major fight and call the whole thing off a half hour before the ceremony. Daniel will have certainly made his move by then, if he's going to."

"But it has to look real, Nicole. We still have to schedule the ceremony."

"True." She gave the matter some thought. "We'll call a Justice of the Peace, if we have to."

"What about rings?"

"We won't need them—no ceremony, remember?"

Justin differed. "At least an engagement ring, Nicole. Who will believe I proposed if there isn't a ring?"

"Oh, all right. We'll go into town Monday morning. I'll withdraw some cash as soon as the bank opens and you can get the ring."

"No," came the stern reply. "I'll pay for the ring."

"Don't start acting macho. I have plenty of money to cover the expense. Besides, we'll be returning the ring in a week."

"I'm paying for the ring," he insisted, a spark of challenge in his eyes.

Nicole threw up her hands, giving in. "Have it your way. We just can't mention the engagement until the ring is on my finger. We'll set the wedding date one week from Monday. We do have to come up with the same story on how you proposed, in case anyone asks."

"We'll just say it happened last night. Jan and Aaron know I didn't come home."

"Great!"

He could see a tiny fleck of excitement shining in her eyes. It pleased him, immensely. "You do understand, though, that we'll have to be openly demonstrative in public? A few kisses, that sort of thing."

"I've always wanted to be an actress," she wryly replied, as if showing affection would never be more than a well-rehearsed act. Justin was willing to bet differently.

"Don't you think we should practice, Nicole? After all, you don't want to appear too stiff the first time we do it in public."

"I'll pass on that suggestion. You won't have to worry about me." She got up and cleared the table. "Oh, dear. What if Daniel asks if I told my parents?"

"Tell him you think it'd be too much of a shock for them; you prefer having a small ceremony and notifying them afterwards. It's your second marriage, so no one should question it."

"Very clever," she agreed. Suddenly, her tone turned serious. She reached out to touch his arm. "Justin, if your theory about Daniel is correct, your life might be in danger. I'd never forgive myself if anything happened to you."

"How sweet," he beamed, flashing his perfectly straight

teeth. “No need to worry. I live with my siblings, remember? It’d be kind of difficult for Daniel to just walk in and blow me away.”

“Still, you’d better keep an eye peeled for any strange cars or people following you around.”

“It’s very touching to see you so concerned, Mrs. Tyler,” he drawled, lifting her hand to his lips for a kiss. She ignored the warm gesture and picked up the coffee pot to pour some coffee into two mugs. They spent the next twenty minutes working out more details for the story.

At Nicole’s suggestion, Justin then walked over to Cristoff’s house to see how he was doing. Cristoff invited him in, asking if Justin would like to join him at the kitchen table for a hearty breakfast. The blond politely declined, mentioning, “I really came over to apologize for how I acted Friday night. I wasn’t myself. After all, you and Nicole were only sharing a harmless kiss.” He carefully watched his friend, who appeared very pleased by the apology. Justin silently wondered how the ranch hand would take the news of his impending engagement. It would prove quite interesting. “So… you’re feeling okay, Cristoff?”

“Nicole sent you, didn’t she?” he instantly asked. Justin couldn’t deny the obvious. “I was pretty messed up yesterday.” Cristoff stared at his french toast. “I wonder how she made out with Daniel last night?”

“She did just fine.”

“Is that what she said?”

“No. That’s what I say,” came the solid reply. “I was there.”

Cristoff suddenly stopped chewing. “Last night?”

Justin nodded, adding, “All night.” He saw a flash of jealousy in his friend’s eyes before the ranch hand averted his gaze.

“Didn’t see your jeep,” Cristoff muttered, resuming to eat.

“It was parked behind the barn. I thought you might get upset if you saw the vehicle there all night, since you were drunk. I didn’t want any fighting between us.”

“I don’t want to fight with you.”

"And I don't want to fight with you, either, Cristoff. You're my friend."

The ranch hand finished his meal and leaned back in his chair. "So, what happened last night?"

Justin took a deep breath, folded his arms, and gladly filled him in on the details, careful not to mention his plan with Nicole. Cristoff thought for a moment, then asked, "Do you really believe Daniel was her lover?"

"Why not?" Justin quipped. "I just don't understand why he'd be so careless as to clue me in on it. It was as if he wanted me to know. It certainly put a smile on his face."

"Daniel's a crafty son of a gun. He doesn't do anything without a deliberate reason. He's trying to get under your skin. Did you say anything to offend him?"

"No. Just played a harmless game of cards."

Cristoff slowly rolled his head from side to side to loosen the stiff muscles in his neck. "So, what time did you leave?"

Justin continued to watch him. "I didn't."

Cristoff's reaction was immediate. The corner of his mouth twitched ever so slightly. Hazel eyes locked with his, a forced smile slowly twisting its way up the handsome cheeks. "At least one of us got lucky last night." He continued to stare at the blond, attempting to read his expression, but Justin exhibited no response at all. It rather aggravated Cristoff, whose head now was pounding from his racing heart. He winced from the pain, using his fingers to gently rub the temple area above his ears.

Justin got up. "I'd better go. You don't look too well. Hope you feel better, Cristoff. Call me, if there's anything I can do."

"Yeah," mumbled the ranch hand, making no move to see his friend to the door. "See you on Monday." He waited until he heard the front door close before walking to the liquor cabinet. One shaky hand reached for the bottle of scotch inside. This was his undoing; this was the ruin of his future dream—this one, stinking bottle of alcohol. If it weren't for this addiction, he would have been the one protecting Nicole last night; he would have been the one in her bed. His whole body began to tremble with rage. He wanted to scream at the top of his lungs, a bloodcurdling, agonized scream, to release the pressure building inside.

But he couldn't.

Upon seeing his reflection in a nearby mirror, he glared at the bloodshot eyes, the boyish face, the unkempt hair. "Damn you!" he yelled, still clutching the bottle of scotch in his hand. "Damn you!" he shouted again, this time rushing to the liquor cabinet and grabbing as many bottles as he could handle. He took them to the kitchen, opened each one and poured its contents down the sink. When he was finished, and every last one of the containers was drained, he stuffed the empty bottles into the trashcan.

Still, his self-hatred festered. Rapidly moving from room to room, he frantically searched until he had confiscated all the extra bottles, then dumped them, too. Evil thoughts, like poison, raced through his brain, tormenting him, beckoning to him with their wicked suggestions. Lost in the cold abyss of insanity, he grabbed an empty scotch bottle and broke it across the edge of the kitchen sink. Mouth quivering, hands violently trembling, he set down the jagged piece to rip open the front of his shirt. Then he picked up the sharp glass, stared at the pointed end, and began to slowly carve Nicole's name on his chest, watching with morbid curiosity as the crimson blood flowed freely down his stomach. It wasn't until his skin puckered from the last, calculated stroke, the exhausted ranch hand finally found peace.

No longer jealous, no longer angry, he calmly held a towel over the wounded area, donned a new shirt, then drove himself to the hospital. Once there, he claimed he had no insurance, so Nicole could not discover what he had done. He had never allowed her to glimpse his dark side, and he would make sure she never did. He had to stay sober now, had to be on his toes. A bond was already forming between the temptress and Justin; he could feel it. A week ago, he would have gladly welcomed it. A week ago, he had not been passionately kissing her. Now, he needed to gain control of his emotions and prove to Nicole she could once again depend on him. He had to win her back.

Thus, when Nicole told him Monday afternoon of her engagement to Justin, Cristoff kept his temper in check. "I hope you'll be happy," was all he said, never giving a clue as to his true feelings. Just that morning, however, he had placed a beautiful assortment of red and white roses in her office with a note of apology. Nicole had thanked him immediately, yet neglected to mention her engagement at that time. Cristoff found this rather odd, considering how people in love are anxious to tell their peers right away. He decided he'd speak with her later, after Justin had gone home.

Yet, when quitting time arrived, Justin remained. Cristoff lingered around until it was clear that the blond had no intention of departing, then the ranch hand reluctantly retreated to his own house to make supper. Nicole was alone in her office when her fiancé appeared, a lazy smile on his face. "Hello, darling," he purred, his voice low and husky.

Nicole glanced up at the towering form. "You can cool the act. Everyone's gone home."

"What act?" he charmed, seating himself on the edge of her desk. "You were a very bad girl today, Nicole." A mischievous twinkle shone in his blue eyes. "I attempted to kiss you several different times and you cleverly avoided me."

"I was in a hurry. This was a busy day."

"Tsk, tsk! You can come up with a better excuse than that. I think we should discuss this over dinner."

"I don't." She took a stack of papers she had been looking at and shoved them in a drawer.

"Cristoff will never believe we're in love if we don't spend time together. Are you listening to me?"

"Yeah." She blew a bubble with the gum in her mouth as she looked at him. It made him grin.

"Sometimes I could just wring your neck."

"Ditto." She blew another bubble, this one much too large for her to handle. It popped all over her face. Justin laughed while she said, "I told Cristoff this afternoon. He isn't buying it. He's much too calm. I think he's suspicious because I didn't tell him this morning."

"Why didn't you?"

"Because we didn't have the ring!"

"Oh." He grew silent.

"I guess you'd better stay for dinner," she reasoned. "It'll add credibility to the story."

"Good. What are we having?"

"Leftovers." She smiled at the disappointment he displayed. "Better get used to it. I don't eat out very often." She got up from her chair. "Come on. I have to lock up."

As she closed up the barn, Justin casually asked, "Did you notice anything odd about Cristoff today?" Nicole shook her head. They walked across the lawn towards the house. "I saw him grimace a few times, like he was in some sort of pain."

"Oh? When did this happen?"

"When he lifted anything with weight—actually, whenever he had to use his arms for long periods of time."

"It wasn't chest pains, was it?" she said with alarm.

"I don't know. I asked him if he was okay. He said he was fine. But he was awful quiet today."

"Yes, he was, come to think of it. Should we invite him over to dine with us?"

"No." His response was swift and firm.

"Did you see the gorgeous roses he gave me?"

Justin scowled. "Why do women always get excited over a lousy bunch of flowers?"

"Because they're so pretty. They smell good, too. It's romantic. But, of course, you wouldn't understand that aspect."

He gave her a funny look as they entered the house and began to set the table. "I can be romantic if I want to," he proudly announced.

"Oh, yeah? When was the last time you were romantic?" He paused, much too long for his own good. Nicole gave a sarcastic "Ha!" He frowned.

"I gave you the ring, didn't I?"

"You call that romantic?" she scoffed. "You shoved the

box in my hand and said, 'Here. Put it on.'" She stared at the heart-shaped diamond sparkling on her finger. "I still don't understand why you insisted on getting a rock this big? I told you to buy the cheapest one in the store."

"Then everyone would think I'm cheap!" he argued, choosing to change the subject. "Can I go upstairs and wash up?"

"Sure." She waited until he disappeared before bringing out the leftovers, which consisted of lasagna, garlic bread, mixed vegetables, and salad. When he returned, he was pleasantly surprised.

"Wow! This is my kind of leftovers. Did you make the lasagna, yourself?"

"Of course." She reheated the lasagna and vegetables, allowing him to stand beside her as she did so. "Don't drool into the pot," she joked, poking him in the side. He nudged closer, planting a soft kiss on the back of her neck.

"Mm. What's that perfume you're wearing? Old Leather?"

She giggled. "Behave yourself. Hey, when does your detective come back from his business trip?"

"He's already back. He called me last night. I gave him the information he needs to start our investigation. He's supposed to get to work on it tomorrow. Have you heard from Daniel?"

"Not today." She set the food on the table and bowed her head.

"You say grace?"

"Yes. Don't you?"

He hesitated. "Oh, sure. I say grace."

"What do you say?" she pursued, not believing him one bit.

"Uh... thanks for the food, God."

She uttered a tiny chuckle and shook her head. Then she said her prayer, blessing herself as she did so. When she finished, she asked, "What religion are you?"

"None," came the irritated reply. He clearly did not like the topic. She let it drop, trying to find some other subject.

"How's your horse, Justin? You never mention him. Does he get ridden?"

"Jan usually rides Nugget. I used to, but I'm too tired after working here all day."

"Speaking of Jan, she gave me this huge hug this afternoon and squealed with delight at the idea of us becoming sisters-in-law."

Justin bit into the garlic bread. "She was pretty excited when I told her. I wish I could say the same for Aaron. I called him on the phone to tell him the news. I called Shane at work. Both of them sounded as if I had just signed my own death certificate. They tried talking me out of it."

"No kidding?"

"I expected as much from Shane, but not Aaron. I thought he'd be happy for me."

"Give them time. It's natural for them to be objectionable. After all, we haven't known each other very long."

"This food is delicious! You're a good cook, darling."

"I wish you'd stop calling me that. Otherwise, I'll have to come up with something just as offensive to call you, and believe me, it won't be pleasant." He took that as a warning, yet still smiled. This was the most civilized conversation he had had with her since the day they had met. She wasn't quite as ferocious as he thought she'd be.

"I have a great suggestion," he suddenly said, his thoughts taking a different turn. "After dinner, let's call Daniel and make our announcement. I'll get on the extension so I can hear his reaction, too."

"I have a better idea," she snickered. "Let's drive over to his house and do it in person. I want to see his face."

"Yes," he agreed. "And flash the ring around, right under his nose."

"I can hardly wait!" she squeaked, downing the rest of her food.

"It's impolite to gulp your food," he scolded. "Can't have you puking all over his expensive rugs."

"How do you know they're expensive?"

"Daniel has that snobby air about him. Know what I mean?" He pinched his nose, thrust his chin upwards, and imitated royalty announcing snacks of scones and cucumber sandwiches. Nicole could not help but laugh. She didn't know Justin could act so silly.

"Hurry up and eat. I'm going to call and see if Daniel's home."

"Wait a minute," he protested. "Don't we get dessert?"

"You men! All you think about is food. Okay. After we come back from Daniel's you can have dessert. Happy?"

"Very!" he grinned, patting his stomach. He wouldn't dare tell her that his happiness had nothing to do with food. He was ecstatic she implied they were returning here after their visit to Daniel. He had assumed she would simply end the evening. He mentally congratulated himself for mentioning dessert.

CHAPTER THIRTEEN

Nicole phoned Daniel's residence to make sure he was in. Then, they rapidly cleared the table and set off for his house in Justin's jeep, with Nicole giving directions. Daniel greeted them at the door, his inquisitive eyes burning a hole straight through Justin as he entered the magnificent mansion. He offered to take their jackets, but Nicole insisted they weren't able to stay.

"We just stopped in to tell you some news," she cheerfully beamed, waving her left hand in front of his eyes. "Look! I'm engaged!"

Justin eyed Philip's brother with mild amusement when he grabbed Nicole's hand to catch a better look at the diamond. "Yesss," Daniel drawled, finally releasing her. "Who's the lucky guy?"

Justin's faint smile disappeared. "Certainly not you," he politely replied. "I guess that leaves me as the lucky groom."

"Ohhhh." Daniel feigned surprise. Then he touched Nicole's arm. "May I have a word with you, in private?"

"Well..." Nicole faltered, glancing at Justin. He nodded for her to go ahead. Thus, she reluctantly followed Daniel to another area of the house, somewhere far, far away. It seemed to take forever to get there, but once they were inside the little room, he quickly closed the door.

"Have you gone mad, Nicole?!" he blurted, quite upset. "Justin is your stable boy, for heaven's sake!" He paced the floor like a caged tiger, pressing the heel of his hand against his forehead. "How long have you known him? One month? Two weeks? Good grief, Nicole! I had no idea you ever wanted to marry again."

"Why, Daniel!" she exclaimed, pretending to be hurt. "How can you talk this way? I'm in love with Justin!"

"Love!" he fumed, grasping her by the shoulders. "What the devil do you know about love? You married an abusive idiot, for crying out loud! I'm sorry to sound so harsh, but you're making a grave mistake. Justin is not the right man for you."

She innocently batted her lashes. "Then, who is, Daniel?"

He paused, considering the question. "I don't know, but it's certainly not Justin! He's just an overgrown farm boy. What level of schooling has he completed? What did he do before he worked for you?"

"You sound like a concerned father," she remarked, carefully choosing her words.

"I just don't want you to ruin your future. I'm begging you to reconsider his proposal. When did the two of you plan to wed?"

It was all Nicole could do to keep from grinning. "Next week," she meekly replied, watching as Daniel's face paled.

"What?!" he bellowed, taking hold of her shoulders, again. "Are you daft? This is absurd! Next week? What the devil is going on in your mind?"

"We simply can't wait," she sighed.

"You can't do this! You just can't!" he railed, back to pacing the floor.

Nicole swallowed a laugh. "Are you finished, Daniel? Justin and I have a lot of planning to do. We really should be going. By the way, do you have the results of the blood sample?"

"Not yet." He stopped pacing and faced her, his expression dark and foreboding. "You'll regret this, Nicole," he solemnly promised. "Mark my words. You barely know the man. Why can't the two of you wait a few months? Or better yet, let him move in with you. See if you're compatible. I won't stand and watch you get hurt again. Just say you'll think about what I've said?"

"I'll definitely think about it, of that you can be sure," she affirmed.

"All right, then. That's the most I can hope for." He escorted her out of the room and back to her patient fiancé, who was strolling about the waiting area, studying the decor.

"Sweetheart!" Justin exclaimed, anxiously pulling her into his arms. "I thought perhaps you had got lost."

The young woman simply smiled, then turned and said goodbye to her brother-in-law. Daniel mumbled a faint farewell, his brooding eyes lingering on the masculine male sweeping her out the door. He had to put a stop to the wedding. He simply had to! He shuddered at the thought of her marrying the macho blond. There had to be some way to end this foolishness. "Of course, there's a way," he murmured, cracking a smile. "How could I ever be so blind?"

While Daniel schemed, Nicole briefed Justin about their private conversation.

"He called me a farm boy, huh?" frowned the blond. "He's just jealous of my rugged good looks."

"He's jealous, all right," she agreed. "At least, he appears to be. He was ranting and raving like a wild man. Your theory may be correct, Justin."

They pulled up to her house and went inside, where Nicole removed a carton of ice cream from the freezer and dished a few scoops into a bowl for her guest. "There is one thing I don't understand, though," she recalled. "He suggested we live together before getting married, which doesn't sound like a man who is jealous. You'd think he wouldn't want you near me. Apparently, all he is concerned about is the actual wedding. Odd, isn't it?"

"Unless he just doesn't like me," Justin replied. He took another spoon of ice cream, letting it slowly melt in his mouth. "I can't imagine anyone not liking me, can you?"

"Oh, please," she groaned. Nicole leaned back in her chair, stretched her arms and yawned.

"I get the hint," he commented. "I'll be leaving, shortly. Let me help you clean up the dishes."

"No. I can do it."

"I insist. Don't argue, dear." She handed him the dishrag and filled the sink with hot water. Pulling a kitchen towel out of the drawer, she patiently waited to start drying the silverware.

"Cristoff says he's been trying to find a good trainer for you," Justin commented.

"I don't think he's had much luck. He hasn't sent anyone to me for a final interview."

"He said no one seems to have enough qualifications or experience."

"I know. There's also the problem of not being able to pay a high wage."

"I don't understand," he said, looking confused. "If you're concerned about affording the salary, why did you hire Jan and me at such a high rate?"

"I'd like all my employees to be paid well. My mistake was not foreseeing the future. I didn't count on hiring Charlie King to investigate so many people."

"I told you I could pay for that."

"Loaded with money, are you? Or do you have a private stash somewhere?" He grinned. "Well, do you?"

"What I have is none of your business."

"Oh, but, darling! We're engaged. Everything you have is already mine!"

He smugly smiled. "And vice versa?" He had dropped the washrag in the sink, dried his hands on a towel, and now slowly advanced in her direction.

"Of course not," Nicole replied. "What's mine is mine." She backed up a step.

"You don't play fair. Now, if what's mine is yours, then what's yours is mine, and I'm going to claim some of what's mine, right this very minute." His voice had deepened, his blue eyes twinkled, and Nicole's heart began to slam against her ribs at the prospect of what he was alluding to. She reached for the nearest pot and waved it at him.

"Put that down, sweetheart," he coaxed. "I wouldn't want you to whack yourself in the head with it."

"How kind!" she mocked. "It's not my head you should be worried about." She saw him stop in his tracks to reconsider. He turned to resume the task of washing dishes.

Nicole gave a victorious smile. "I'm glad you took the threat seriously."

"It wasn't your threat that changed my mind," he revealed, staring directly into her brown eyes. "When I decide to kiss you, it will be a mutual agreement. I have no desire to force my intentions upon you. I respect your wishes."

Nicole stared at the powerful blond, dumbfounded. She hadn't the faintest idea what to say. Was this guy for real? Quietly, she reached for the dishtowel to continue her chore. Silence filled the room while the couple's thoughts lingered on the possibility of such a kiss. The notion renewed Nicole's energy. She suddenly felt more alive than she had in years; it was the excitement of the unknown, the tempting thought of what a kiss with Justin might feel like. Would it be different than kissing Cristoff? She wondered...

"A penny for your thoughts?" Justin rinsed out the sink and put down the washrag.

"Nothing," Nicole answered. "It was nothing."

"Oh, it was something," he stated, walking into the living room. He grabbed his jacket, slipped both arms into the sleeves and zipped it up. "You don't have to tell me. It was probably the same thing I was thinking." His lips curved into a wide smile.

The dark-haired princess ventured nearer. "And what were you thinking?"

"Nothing," he shrugged, then laughed. They looked into each other's eyes and, for a moment, felt the same magnetic pull that had been present the first time they had met. Try as he might, Justin could not tear himself away. Cobalt blue eyes, the color of December skies, penetrated Nicole's very soul. "Thank you for dinner," he whispered in a deep, sexy voice.

"You're welcome," she breathed, allowing herself to step closer. She watched him slowly bend towards her, pausing, as if unsure, then continuing slowly, slowly, slowly. She thought he'd never reach her, but he did, his lips brushing lightly over hers like the fluttering wings of a dove; their feathery touch teasing, beckoning. Against her better judgment she gave in, lost amidst the rapture of one, gentle, lingering kiss. Nicole had never been kissed like this, never knew that a man so masculine, so powerful, could have lips so wonderfully soft. There was no sudden assault, no passionate bruising, no domineering hold. No. Justin's kiss was a light summer breeze upon a cool placid lake. It skimmed the surface, gently rippling the waters, with no intention of creating a major disturbance. Nicole sensed the unspoken promise of pleasure in its caress, and, as her eyes opened to gaze into his, she finally saw his compassion, his sensitivity, his unselfishness—all the virtues she had missed before.

It completely unnerved her. She drew away, afraid of any further discoveries. Her eyes, like warm, melting chocolate, stared down at the floor until Justin could stand it no longer. He raised her proud chin with one, long finger. "What is it, Nicole?" he breathed. "Don't say you didn't enjoy it, because we both know differently."

"It's you," she admitted, her voice barely audible. "You're nothing like I imagined." He took it to mean that she was disappointed in him, but Nicole saw the dejection in his eyes and suddenly smiled. "No. You have it all wrong. What I meant was... you're more than I imagined." Justin's eyes lit up like bonfires; his heart leapt up to his throat. Nicole decided to quit while they were ahead. "I'll see you in the morning," she said, her gaze never wavering.

"Yes," he replied, finally pulling away. After opening the door, he paused. "Sleep well, Nicole. Please call if you ever need to talk. It doesn't matter what hour of the night it is. I'll always make time for you." She graced him with another smile, a radiant smile, which made the blood race through his veins.

He departed then, his head in the clouds as he slowly drove off the property.

Nicole quietly closed the front door and sighed. She could get lost in a man like that. The thought frightened her, immensely. She would have to guard against such future moments, keeping her emotions wrapped tightly inside. The glitter of her ring caught her eye. He had said he wanted her. Why? she wondered—as a notch on his bedpost? Somehow that didn't seem to fit Justin. Was he truly in love with her, or was it merely pity? He was determined to solve the problem of her past. Was she just a charity case to him? Did she make him feel like a martyr? Some men thrived on rescuing damsels in distress. But that was not love. It gave her much to think about as she lay in bed that night.

When morning dawned, the questions returned, and Nicole struggled through the early hours in a half-daze as she pondered all suitable answers. Justin had greeted her with a friendly peck on the cheek before beginning his chores. Jan was out sick, so Nicole spent most of the morning in the office. She was filing papers when Cristoff strolled in and quietly closed the door.

"Something on your mind?" she called, closing a cabinet drawer. He appeared quite confident, his shoulders thrown back like a marching soldier. She almost expected him to salute her. But the ranch hand was clearly on a mission—his own mission.

"I sent Justin into town for some supplies," he began, casually stepping towards her. "So... when's the big day?"

Nicole stared at the papers in her hand. "Next Monday." She glanced up to find him silently studying her.

"So soon? That doesn't sound like you, Nicole. You were able to find a priest on short notice?"

"No. We're using a Justice of the Peace."

Now he drew closer, cocking his head sideways, hazel eyes penetrating her own until she grew uneasy. Knowing she had to hold her ground, she stared back with just as much determination. Cristoff faintly smiled, relief flooding his face.

"You're joking, right?" he challenged. "You're not getting married, Nicole."

"Oh, yes I am!" she stated emphatically.

He shook his head. "No, you're not. You and Justin are up to something. You can't fool me. I'll believe this wedding when I see it."

"Make sure you wear your good suit."

He uttered a tiny chuckle. "Give it up, girl. I'm on to you. For one thing, you'd never marry on such short notice, especially to a man you said you didn't like."

"I fell in love."

"Uh, huh. Secondly, you'd never get married by a Justice of the Peace. You're deeply religious. You'd insist on a priest, no matter how long you'd have to wait." Nicole frowned, unable to come up with a logical reply. She should have known she couldn't fool Cristoff. "So, why don't you tell me what's really going on here?" he continued. "Does this have something to do with Daniel?" The young woman frowned again. "Ahh. This is all for his benefit, isn't it?"

Nicole stuck to her guns. "All I can say is, I'm marrying Justin on Monday."

"What time?"

"I don't know, yet."

"Where?"

"I guess at the courthouse."

"Do your parents know?"

"I'll tell them, afterwards."

"You don't lie very well. You never did." His smile broadened. She was glad to see he wasn't laughing at her; no, he had a certain calmness in his eyes she had never noticed before. "I'll keep your little secret, though. I'll play along. I've quit drinking, you know?"

Her eyes widened. "You have?"

"Yep."

"For good?"

"We'll see. You won't find any liquor in my house. I'm turning over a new leaf."

"What brought this on?"

She sensed a sudden change in his mood even though he still held on to his smile. "I've been wanting to for some time now. I just needed a little push."

"You don't want to tell me, huh?" He shook his head. "That's okay." She patted him on the back. "I'm proud of you. Hey, listen. I'm taking an hour off to go over and check on Jan. Do you mind holding down the fort for a while?"

"No problem."

"Thanks. If the veterinarian arrives before I get back, the horses are due for their shots." She scooted past him and headed out the door. Cristoff plopped down in the office chair, leaned back and smiled. She wasn't getting married. He still had time. His fingers sought out the stitched wound under his shirt, then he closed his eyes, reliving their passionate embrace in the hayloft. When the ringing of the phone jarred him back to reality, Cristoff could not repress the happiness welling up inside.

"Desert Wind Arabians!" he cheerfully sang.

"Cristoff? Is that you?" spoke the voice on the other end.

"Well, hello, Danny, boy."

"You sound on top of the world today."

"Yes. Yes, I am. What can I do for you?"

"I need to talk to Nicole. Is she around?"

"She just stepped out for an hour. Want to leave a message, or should I have her call you?"

"I wanted to let her know the results of the blood test. We can't find anything... anything abnormal, that is. I hate to be the bearer of bad news, but it looks like we're back to the drawing board."

"She's going to be real disappointed."

"That makes two of us. Hey, Cristoff? Since I've got you on the phone, what's your opinion of Nicole's engagement?"

"Justin's a great guy."

"Uh, huh. So, you don't think it's a bit odd that they're getting married next week?"

"There's nothing I can do about it."

"Can't you talk to your friend? Justin seems like a reasonable guy. Maybe you could convince him to delay the date?"

"I don't think so. I'd rather not get involved." He could hear Daniel huffing on the other end.

"Come on, Cristoff! This is Nicole we're talking about! Why is Justin moving so fast? Does he need money? Is he trying to get his name on the deed to the ranch?"

"He's not like that. They seem to be in love, Dan. Have you ever heard of the word?"

"Fine! You may not see anything wrong with this match made in heaven, but I do. Furthermore, I plan to do something about it."

"Like what?"

"Never mind. I'll talk to you later." Cristoff heard a click, then the receiver went silent. He hung up the phone, curious as to Daniel's scheme.

"Nice going, Danny," he grinned. "You've given me the opportunity to play the good guy. All I have to do is alert Nicole to your intentions. It'll definitely score me some points." He could hardly wait until she returned from her errand.

Nicole, however, had just arrived at Justin's house. Upon seeing Aaron open the door, she promptly greeted him, told him why she had come, and politely inquired, "Are you off from work today?"

He gave her a dead stare. "My hours vary."

"I don't believe Justin mentioned what line of work you are in?"

"Investments," he replied curtly, not wishing to go into further detail. She didn't press the issue. "Jan's upstairs."

"Do you mind?" Nicole pointed towards the direction.

"You're asking me?" he mocked. "I expected you to just bolt up the stairs like last time!"

"Yes, well, last time, you weren't very civil towards me." He had no response to that statement. She chose not to wait for one, briskly ascending the wooden staircase.

"Nicole," Jan murmured, her voice so weak that Nicole had

to step closer. "What are you doing here?"

"I came to see if I could do anything for you, Jan. You look like you're in terrible pain."

"I am. I can't talk too much; it hurts so bad."

"I understand. How can I help?"

"There's nothing..." Her voice faded as tears trickled down her cheeks. Nicole handed her a tissue, then pulled up a chair.

"Don't say another word. You just rest. I'm going to sit here a while, in case you need something." While Nicole remained by Jan's side, she silently prayed for the healing of her headache, wondering why with so much modern medicine, no one could find a drug to help the poor girl? Perhaps she could persuade her to visit a special facility dedicated to the treatment of headaches, if there was one. Nicole would have to look into it. It just wasn't fair that Jan had to suffer like this. She appeared so pale and fragile lying there, so totally helpless against the sickness consuming her body. Nicole wished she could absorb some of the pain for her. She waited until Jan fell asleep before tiptoeing out of the room. Downstairs, she glanced around for Aaron but couldn't find him. She did see a gigantic pile of dishes in the kitchen sink, prompting her to get the detergent out of the cupboard and a dishrag. She was busy washing the soiled plates, when Justin's twin entered the room.

"Don't you have more important things to do?" he muttered, grabbing the rag from her.

She snatched it back. "Were you waiting for your sister to recuperate so she could do the housework?"

"It'd get done. Who made you boss?"

"I want to help. Anything wrong with that?"

"Certainly not. I have a ton of laundry you can tackle when you're through here." He seated himself on a kitchen chair and lit a cigarette, tossing the burnt match into the dishwater. Nicole held her breath, counted to ten, then dropped the rag into the sink and turned to confront her antagonizer.

"What exactly is your problem, Aaron?" she fumed. "Have you always had a bad attitude, or are you holding some kind of a grudge against me?"

He sneered. "Surprised I'm not like my twin? You couldn't pay me to be that gullible."

"Gullible? He's anything but gullible!"

"Yeah, right," Aaron scoffed. "He got taken in by you, didn't he?"

She put her hands on her hips. "So, that's what this is all about!"

"I sure don't know what he sees in you. You're just another pretty face out to make a buck."

"Pardon?"

"Don't act coy with me." He had put down the cigarette and was standing now, shoulders thrown back, drawing himself up to his full height in order to intimidate the young woman. Nicole found the gesture amusing.

"You'll have to do better than that to scare me off," she said, pulling out a kitchen chair. Aaron could not believe she climbed aboard the object so she could tower above him. "You're not such a big man now, are you?" she taunted. The smug smile on her face was too much for the blond. His foot gave a powerful shove to kick the chair out from under her, sending the raven-haired beauty tumbling forward into his arms. As Nicole heard him begin to laugh, she was struck by the wickedness of his tone.

"So... evil twins really do exist," she jeered, writhing in his arms to free herself. He held her even tighter, pressing the slender body against him while his laughter increased.

"You're despicable!" she spat.

"And you," he grinned, releasing her, "you fight like a wildcat! Your eyes even glow like a panther at night. I think I'll call you 'Cat'." It was bizarre but her anger actually excited him. He was almost inclined to call a truce. "Tell you what, Cat. When you're through with Justin, I'll show you what a real man is like."

"I'll tell Justin you said that," Nicole promised. "Although I'm sure he's used to you bullying his girlfriends."

"Just the gold diggers."

"I'm no gold digger. I own a ranch, in case you've

forgotten."

"Oh, come on!" he scoffed. "You're just starting out, profits are low. You simply can't wait to get your hands on Justin's money!"

"This house?" she quipped, looking around. "I don't want your house."

Aaron stared at her with pure disdain. Then his expression changed to mild confusion. Suddenly, his eyebrows raised with surprise. "You don't know," he murmured, almost incredulous. "He didn't tell you."

"Tell me what?" demanded Nicole.

Aaron lightly chuckled. "I can't believe it. He honestly didn't tell you!"

"What didn't he tell me?" she repeated, irked.

"Justin," the blond laughed, "is filthy rich."

Nicole's jaw dropped. She couldn't believe her ears. Rich? Not Justin. Not the man who mucked her stalls. "You're lying," she accused, when her mind screamed he wasn't.

Aaron picked up his cigarette, taking a long drag. His eyes danced merrily, clearly enjoying the awkwardness of the moment. "An eccentric old aunt," he explained, "left him a huge inheritance." He expelled a long rush of smoke into the air. "He used to spend weekends at her house when he was a boy, doing odd jobs for her. It paid off, didn't it? I'm surprised he kept it a secret from you." He studied the young beauty before him, re-evaluating her. So, she wasn't a gold digger. It made a difference. It made him curious. "What exactly is your reason for marrying my brother?"

"I love him," she stated, but not convincingly enough for Aaron.

"You're a skittish thing," he mused, "not at all like his other girlfriends." Nicole returned to the sink to finish up the dishes, aware of Aaron's eyes firmly fixed on her. She heard him snuff out the last of his cigarette, then say, "You're not a party girl, are you?"

"No."

"Do you drink?"

"Occasionally, not that it's any of your business."

"What do you do for fun?"

Nicole hesitated. "I paint."

"Really?" His interest was piqued. "What kind of painting?"

"Oil or water color. I do both, mostly horses."

He approached her then, just as she let out the water in the sink and neatly folded the washrag. "An artist; imagine that," he drawled. He suddenly raised his hand to brush back a few loose strands of her hair, but upon seeing Nicole flinch, he stopped. "I wasn't going to hurt you."

"You just surprised me, that's all," she mumbled, turning to rush from the room. "I have to check on Jan." Before she could leave, however, Aaron caught her by the arm and gave a solid jerk, causing Nicole to pivot back around. Anger flashed in her eyes. He suddenly let go and smiled.

"You're a spooky one, Cat."

It wasn't so much what he said, as how he said it. There was an underlying tone to his voice, which made her believe he found her to be a fascinating specimen of the female gender. The last thing Nicole wanted was this guy's interest. He made her skin crawl. She hurried upstairs to look in on Jan, then promptly left the house.

When she arrived at the ranch, Cristoff came to greet her and fill her in on Daniel's phone call. When he relayed the news of the test results, Nicole grew quiet. "I'm sorry," Cristoff said, trying to comfort her.

"I didn't expect them to find anything," she replied. "What else did Daniel say? You look like you're about to burst."

"He's real upset over the wedding. He says he's going to do something about it, Nicole."

"Well, that's what we're waiting for."

Just then, a familiar form walked down the aisle. "Dr. Brown," Nicole called. "How nice to see you." She left Cristoff to greet the veterinarian. Out of the corner of her eye, she saw Justin pull up outside, so she did the best she could to hurry the horses' shots so she could speak to her fiancé. When the task was finally completed, the phone began to ring. It was a new client, a very talkative man who kept Nicole tied up on the phone for half of an hour. After hanging up the receiver, she looked around for Justin. The only person she saw was Cristoff. "Cristoff, do you know where my fiancé went?"

"He's out riding. Do you want me to try to find him?"

"No, that's okay." She glanced at her watch. "He'll be coming in soon."

"I've been meaning to ask you," Cristoff said. "Would you like to join me for dinner tonight?"

"Thanks, but Justin and I are going out. Would you like to tag along?"

"Naa. How about tomorrow night?"

He was staring at his shoes when she looked at him, and, for once, Nicole noticed he had a shy side. It struck her as funny, though she didn't dare laugh. She had never seen Cristoff look so darn cute. "Sure," she grinned. "I'll have dinner with you tomorrow. We can't eat out, though. Since Justin and I are engaged, it wouldn't look right to have me dining out with another man."

He finally met her gaze. "I understand. I'm cooking. Is five o'clock too early?"

"That will be fine, Cristoff. I'll bring dessert. By the way, a new client is coming for a tour tomorrow. His name is Westervelt. He says he's a friend of Daniel's. I'd like you to accompany us during the tour."

"Westervelt must be part of Danny's scheme."

"Perhaps, although I can't imagine how a new client could drive a wedge between Justin and me?" The sudden neighing of horses outside drew their attention. Justin had returned on King Arthur. Cristoff headed towards the pasture to start bringing in the other horses for their evening meal, accompanied by Nicole. "How'd it go?" she called to her fiancé.

"Fine," Justin answered. "But I had a devil of a time getting him to accept the bit when he was bridled."

"Next time, go into the tack room and get the jar of molasses. Spread some on the bit. He gets fussy every now and then." Justin nodded and proceeded to cool off the large Arabian. Cristoff and Nicole finished bringing in the animals, made sure they had food and water, then closed up the barn.

"I'm going to run home and grab a shower, Nicole," Justin said. "What if I stop by in an hour to pick you up for dinner?"

"Sure. Tell Jan I hope she's feeling better. She was asleep when I last saw her today."

"You went over to my house?"

"I was concerned about her. You don't mind, do you?"

Justin frowned. "I would prefer it if you'd wait until I could accompany you."

"Oh. I'm sorry. I had no idea you felt that way."

"It's not your fault. It's just that..." He paused, trying to find a nice way to say it. "Aaron can sometimes—"

"Be a bully," she finished for him. "I found out."

"He has a short fuse."

"He's pure evil, if you ask me."

"Not really. He just likes to give that impression. Did the two of you fight?"

"Not much. Why don't you go ahead home now. We can finish this conversation later."

"Trying to get rid of me, are you?" he teased, pulling her into his arms.

"You can let go, Justin. Cristoff knows we're not truly engaged."

"What?" His eyes hardened at the thought. Couldn't she keep one tiny secret from Cristoff?

"He confronted me this morning. It's no use trying to fool him."

"How did he guess?"

"He knows I'd never get married by a Justice of the Peace. He also knows I'd never get married on the spur of the moment. I attempted to deny his accusations, but he stuck by his theory. The good news is, he's sober, Justin. He's given up drinking. He can be trusted now."

"So he says," drawled the blond. He gazed off in the distance, reflecting upon this new information. Overhead, storm clouds loomed into view. "I'd better get going. It looks like rain." He turned for a goodbye kiss and was met by Nicole's rouged cheek. He let it slide, knowing the time would come when she would willingly offer more. When he had departed, Nicole hurried inside to get a quick shower. He returned in an hour, as promised, and they drove to a restaurant in town.

"Daniel called today," she mentioned, sipping a glass of water. "They couldn't find anything abnormal in my blood."

"Just like you had said."

"Cristoff told me Daniel has a scheme to break us up. A new client is coming tomorrow who claims to be one of his friends."

Justin swallowed a bite of roast beef. "Daniel works pretty quick. He was just over my house last night, offering to buy me off."

Nicole's eyes grew large. "What?"

"Yeah. He offered me ten thousand dollars to leave you alone."

"The nerve of him!"

"I told him you were worth much more than that. I got the price up to thirty thousand. Can you believe it?" He chuckled.

"Thirty thousand!" Nicole gave a low whistle. "He's going to crack, isn't he?"

"Time will tell. One thing's for sure: He definitely doesn't want us together. I had another visitor last night. Shane. He brought two girls with him, hoping to entice me to do who-knows-what." Justin smiled at the shock on Nicole's face. "Shane keeps reminding me of what I'll be missing if I marry you."

Nicole picked at her broiled flounder. "So, did you go out with him?"

"Don't be ridiculous. I'm engaged, remember?"

She gazed up at him with doe-like eyes. "Did you want to?"

He grinned. "How sweet of you to wonder."

"I don't care," she quickly defended, resuming eating. She watched him lean across the table, whispering, "You certainly do care, darling, and just for your information... I had no desire at all to be with either of those women."

"I'm having dinner with Cristoff tomorrow evening." Nicole stuffed a forkful of food in her mouth to keep quiet. Why, in the world, had she blurted that out? It was totally inappropriate. What's more, Justin was now staring at her like she had two heads. His jaw was clenching, his fingers curling around his utensils as if brandishing a weapon. "Just a harmless, friendly dinner," she casually added, trying to smooth over the mistake.

"I forbid it." The words were stated like a true husband.

Nicole snickered. "You forbid it? Who do you think you are?"

"Your fiancé, or has that tiny detail slipped your mind?"

"I shouldn't have said anything. Sorry."

"You can't have dinner with him, Nicole. We're engaged!"

"No one is going to see us. Relax! We're old friends, remember?" Justin pushed his plate off to the side. She quizzed, "Aren't you hungry?"

"I've suddenly lost my appetite."

"Boy! I never pegged you to be the jealous type."

"We had a plan, Nicole. I'd appreciate it if you'd stick to the rules. You could just as well have dinner with Cristoff next week, after this is all over. What if Daniel stops by?"

"We'll invite him to join us. I don't know."

"Are there any other surprises I should know about?"

"No, but now that you've brought the topic up... Are there any surprises you haven't told me?" She closely studied him, waiting for him to reveal the secret of his recent wealth. He remained quiet, offering no reply. "Justin," she prodded, finishing her meal. "Is there anything about you I should know?"

"Such as?"

"Anything which might affect our relationship: old flames, bad habits, secret inheritances?" She saw the blood rush to his face. He clenched his fist.

"Wait until I get my hands on that brother of mine!"

Nicole folded her arms. "Why didn't you tell me?"

"Why should I? Would it have made a difference?"

"No. But I felt like a fool when Aaron assumed I knew. Here we are, engaged, and I don't even know you're wealthy! Talk about blowing our cover!"

"Keep your voice down," he commanded, motioning for the check. After paying for dinner, he swiftly ushered Nicole out to his jeep and drove her home, refusing to discuss the issue any further.

"What have you got to be mad about?" she quipped, walking up the front steps. "I'm the one who was in the dark. Why are you even working for me, Justin? Will you answer me that? You have plenty of money to do whatever you want to do with your life. I can't imagine why you took this job? A rich man like you—"

Before she could finish, he grabbed her by the shoulders and roughly kissed the soft lips that had tantalized him all evening. Nicole had not been prepared for the assault, had not expected this type of behavior from him, and didn't appreciate the sudden surprise. She broke all contact and reached for the door.

"I'm sorry, Nicole," she heard him say, his voice sad. "I didn't know the issue of money was so important to you."

She turned around. "I don't care about the money. I don't understand why you thought you couldn't tell me. When you were first offered a job here, you made me feel like dirt when I tried to fire you. You said you had just given notice to your boss; you sounded so upset, as if your carpenter job was extremely important to your financial welfare. Now I find it wasn't. You played me. I applaud your acting ability and how easy it is for you to lie. I'm hurt, that's all. Stupid of me, isn't it?"

She wheeled back around and flew inside the house, shutting the door before he could say another word. It began to rain, then; yet Justin continued to stand on the front porch, letting the cold droplets stream down his face while he tried to figure out what had just occurred. He was never very good at understanding women, and Nicole was certainly more complex than most. All he knew was that a well-planned evening had just been ruined. He had Aaron to thank for that. Climbing back into his jeep, he took off for home, where a bitter argument ensued between the two brothers.

CHAPTER FOURTEEN

Nicole had only been asleep one hour when a series of loud raps sounded on the front door. Throwing on a lemon-colored robe, she hurried downstairs and asked for the identity of the visitor. "Justin!" boomed the tall figure dressed in a raincoat and hat. He looked more like a gangster in the attire, his hat strategically tilted down over his brow. The minute he stepped inside, she discovered why.

"Aaron!" Nicole gasped. "What are you doing here? Why are you impersonating Justin?"

He swiftly moved forward, cornering her against the wall. "I doubt you'd open the door for anyone else," he bitterly said, his steel-blue eyes laced with contempt. "You did a very stupid thing today, telling Justin about our discussion. He took out his anger on me after your dinner date this evening."

"I'm sorry. I only confronted him with the truth. How was I to know he'd—"

"Shut up!" Aaron snapped, giving her a good hard shake. Fear gripped Nicole's heart when she saw the wildness in his eyes, for she had seen that exact same look just before Philip would beat her. She began to tremble, protectively raising her arms to shield her face. Aaron eased his hold. "I'm warning you," he growled. "Whatever you and I discuss, including this little visit, remains between you and I. If you cause one more problem between Justin and myself, I will make sure you live to regret it. Do you understand?" Nicole numbly nodded. "Good girl." He suddenly smiled, an evil smile. He took his index finger and slowly trailed it down her throat to the open vee of her bathrobe.

That one, solitary movement caused something to snap inside Nicole. Her fear transformed into blinding rage—rage at being taken advantage of, rage at being intimidated, rage at having to cringe in the corner like a frightened child. She hurled herself at the stunned man, clawing at his face, punching, kicking, shrieking like a banshee, then jumped on top of him to knock him to the floor. It was all Aaron could do to get his breath. He had no inkling she'd go berserk on him. He was left with no other choice but to defend himself. Fortunately, just as he made his move to strike back, Cristoff burst through the door to pull Nicole off of him. It was no easy task. Nicole had taken a few swings at Cristoff before realizing who he was. She was hysterical, yelling and shouting, calling Aaron names, daring him to come within arms' reach.

"What went on here?!" Cristoff demanded, struggling to keep Nicole subdued.

"She's crazy!" roared the blond. "I didn't do anything to provoke her. She just attacked me like a nut!"

"Then why are you here?" Cristoff argued, furious. "I saw your car outside. Good thing I decided to check on things!"

"We had a disagreement, that's all." He wiped his face with his hand, alarmed to find blood on his fingers. "She mauled me!" He pointed an accusing finger at the seething woman. "You're going to pay for this! Oh, I promise! You're going to pay, big time!"

"What are you gonna do?" she jeered. "Hit me, big fellow? Will that make you a man?" Her leg swung out to kick him as he stormed past to leave. In the nick of time, Cristoff yanked her away. Outside, the sound of Aaron's car could be heard speeding off the property. Cristoff closed the door, then wheeled around to face Nicole.

"You could have been badly hurt!" he yelled, angrier than

a hornet. "What the devil's wrong with you? Can't you see he's bigger than you? Didn't you notice his muscles—not to mention his temper?"

"Get out of my house," Nicole muttered.

"That's the thanks I get, huh?" He noticed she was gasping for air, desperately trying to compose herself, yet her eyes... her eyes were on fire. He had never seen anything like it. It was as if she had become another person, a complete stranger. The large, expressive eyes had narrowed to two, tiny slits and were glaring at him with all the ferocity of a Bengal tiger. It was then that he realized he had not even asked for her side of the story. "What did he do to you, Nicole?"

"Nothing. Leave me alone." She was still breathing heavy, her fists repeatedly clenching and unclenching at her sides. He watched her walk to the liquor cabinet and guzzle some brandy, straight from the bottle. "Unless you care to stay for a drink," she taunted, shoving the bottle towards him. Cristoff now knew something was definitely wrong with her, but felt unable to break through the barrier she had built around herself.

"I'm calling Justin," he quietly said, turning to leave. "Maybe he can figure you out."

"Don't bother," she sneered. "I just had a fight with him earlier this evening. Did you know he's rich, Cristoff?" A peculiar sounding laugh bubbled up from her throat. "I've got me another rich man to play with. Of all the luck, huh? Just what I need—someone with wealth. And we all know that wealth buys power, now doesn't it? A rich man can beat his wife any time of the day. A rich man can lock her up in the nuthouse if he wants to."

"Stop, Nicole," Cristoff begged, going to her. "Don't do this to yourself. He isn't worth it."

"That's right!" she smiled, a vagueness in her eyes. "No man is worth it." The smile slowly vanished as she stared across the room, spellbound by her own reflection in the mirror. Cristoff took a chance and cautiously pried the brandy bottle from her fingers. After doing so, he gently guided her towards the sofa.

"Sit down and rest, Nicole. I'll fix you a cup of tea." He thought she was only half-listening until she reached for his hand to pull him near.

"Please," she whispered, her dark eyes pleading, "don't tell Justin. Don't say a word."

Cristoff carefully avoided an answer. "We have to discuss what happened tonight. You do know that, don't you, Nicole?" She nodded, filling with tears. He left her then to boil some water. When he returned, she was calmly sitting with her hands folded in her lap, her gaze downcast. With a small amount of coaxing she finally opened up to him and spoke of Aaron's visit. She no longer cried, no longer felt helpless or angry. She definitely had no regrets for her actions. In fact, what had occurred a few minutes ago now seemed like an overrated play. She felt no emotion at all when she spoke of it.

The tea kettle whistled, breaking Cristoff's concentration. He entered the kitchen, set a tea bag in a steaming mug and brought it into the living room with the sugar bowl. "I can understand why you flew off the handle, Nicole. Aaron threatened you. You panicked. I think it was a natural reaction for a woman who has suffered past abuse."

"You do?" Her voice was that of a child seeking reassurance.

"Of course," he soothed, placing an arm around her shoulders so he could give her an affectionate squeeze.

"You don't think I overreacted?"

"Well, you have to think of the consequences of your actions. If I hadn't come over in time, you might have been seriously injured. You've got to control your temper, Nicole." She leaned forward to fix her tea while he continued, "You may not agree with me, honey, but I suggest you tell Justin about this."

Nicole's response was automatic, a resounding "No!" filling the room.

Cristoff gently persuaded her. "Aaron threatened you. You have to let Justin know. He'd want to know."

"It would just cause more problems between them."

"Justin could talk to his brother."

"He won't. He'll fight with him; that's why Aaron came over here in the first place. No. I don't want you to tell Justin. Promise me, Cristoff."

"All right. But if you see Aaron's car outside anytime in the future, you call me, do you hear?"

Nicole calmly sipped her tea and smiled. "You're my bodyguard, Cristoff."

"It can't be like this forever, honey. You have to start looking out for yourself—either that, or get a husband." His words brought Justin to mind, making him frown.

"You'll make a wonderful husband some day, Cristoff." She gazed fondly at the handsome ranch hand, picturing him in a tuxedo.

"I prefer the single life," he replied. "Being tied down to one person makes me shudder."

"That'll change when the right woman comes along. You won't be able to stand the thought of her with another man, so, one day you'll pop over to the jewelry store and purchase a precious diamond ring to bind her to your heart forever."

"Like Justin did?"

"That ring is a mere prop, remember?"

Cristoff lifted her left hand. "That's an awful big rock to use in a play."

"I told him to buy the cheapest. He's so pigheaded."

Cristoff said nothing, deciding this would be a good time to make his exit. If he remained much longer, looking at her in that robe, he'd have a high level of frustration to contend with. He rose from the sofa. "You'll be okay if I leave, won't you?"

"Yes. Thank you, Cristoff. It seems I'm always thanking you, these days. I wish there was some way to repay your kindness?"

He let that statement pass without comment, biting his tongue to keep from making suggestions. "Coming to dinner tomorrow will be thanks enough." He winked, then walked to the door. She watched him depart, knowing she was very lucky to have him as a friend. After Nicole finished her tea, she returned to her bedroom for some much needed sleep, hoping the following day would bring relief from the recent turmoil in her life.

She was wrong. Jan was still out sick, which forced Nicole to leave Cristoff in charge of the incoming calls while she escorted Mr. Westervelt on his tour. She thought of using the answering machine, but lately the phone had been ringing with possible clients. Mr. Westervelt was extremely happy with the arrangements, using every chance he had to flirt with Nicole. It soon became obvious his interest in the breeding business was not limited to horses. When he finally made a pass at her, she called it quits and politely ended the tour. One hour later, Daniel appeared with a tall stranger.

"Nicole, I'd like you to meet John Gaites. He's new in town, so I thought perhaps I'd introduce him to some of the local horse breeders. He owns several Arabian mares he hopes to breed."

"Nice to meet you, Mr. Gaites," Nicole politely said. She turned to Daniel. "I do hope Mr. Gaites has more of an interest in the equine industry than Mr. Westervelt did?"

"Oh?" Daniel remarked. "Didn't you strike a deal with Westervelt?"

"Not the kind he wanted. May I speak to you, in private, Daniel?"

"Certainly. Will you excuse us, John?"

The stranger nodded, studying the inside of the stable area as the pair walked into Nicole's office. Cristoff took the cue and left, quietly closing the door behind him. Nicole wasted no time. "What are you up to, Daniel?" Folding her arms, Nicole looked ready to give him a sound lecture.

"I'm drumming up business for you. You should be grateful."

"You're trying to fix me up! Did you think I'd be stupid enough to fall for it?"

"Well," he drawled, "I was hoping you could be John's escort at an important social function tomorrow night. You see, he's new in town and—"

"Yes. Yes. I know! He doesn't know many local women, right?" She rolled her eyes heavenward. "How could you?! I'm engaged!"

"Not if I can help it," he muttered. Losing his patience, Daniel approached her with another offer. "What type of man do you want? I'll find him. I'll get you someone reserved, well-established. You'll have security."

"I want Justin. What is it about the man that bothers you?"

"I think he's after your money."

"Think again. Justin is very wealthy. He's only working for me out of the kindness of his heart. You can even ask his brother or sister."

"Have you seen his so-called wealth?"

"I trust his word."

"Call the National Bank on Broadway Street," boomed a third voice from the doorway. Justin stood like a marble statue, solid and unmoving, his vivid blue eyes zeroing in on Daniel like a combat missile. "I won't apologize for interrupting. Anything you have to say to Nicole, you can say with me in the room."

Completely flustered, Daniel's face reddened. "See here, MacFierson! I will find out the reason behind your sudden proposal to Nicole, and when I do, I will make things most unpleasant for you."

Justin gave him a drop-dead stare. "I can hardly wait." His rudeness had the desired effect; Daniel sailed out of the room in such an uproar he forgot to tell Nicole goodbye. She and Justin could hear John Gaites running after him, repeatedly calling his name. "Who was that?" the blond inquired.

"A prospective blind date," Nicole said, studying Justin. Considering this was the first time she had seen him today, she felt quite awkward. He saw her walk to the desk, open a drawer and withdraw a piece of colored paper. Then she casually pulled off the engagement ring, handing it to him with the paper. "It's your check," she said, still waiting for him to take it. "I don't think you should waste your time working for me when there are better things awaiting you out in the world. Besides, we no longer have to pretend we're getting married. I found out a short while ago that Daniel is not jealous. He's been trying to fix me up with suitable bachelors. We had him pegged all wrong, so... I'm releasing you from any obligations."

"How thoughtful," Justin remarked, dryly. He took the ring, but not the check. "Since when do you dictate what I am to do with my life? I don't recall complaining about my job. Perhaps I haven't lived up to your expectations?"

"You've been a wonderful employee. I couldn't ask for a more dedicated worker."

"Then why fire me? You seemed content until you discovered I had money. I don't understand people like you. I don't understand why money has to change a relationship?"

"You weren't married to Philip, either."

"Philip is an exception, Nicole. Not all men are like him, and frankly, I don't think it's fair to compare me to him. Just because he abused his wealth, doesn't mean I will. Look at the vehicle I drive—an inexpensive jeep, not a race car. Look at the clothes I wear. Have I given any indication I've been corrupted by my inheritance? No. I'll tell you what I think, Nicole." He walked up to the young beauty, his eyes turning cold. "I think you're using my money as an excuse to end our friendship, a friendship that scares the daylights out of you." He raised a hand to silence her protest. "You once said I was more than you had imagined. You're attracted to me, whether you'll admit it or not."

"I'm also attracted to Cristoff," she defended. "So what?"

"But for some reason, you're more frightened of our relationship."

"I wonder why?" she said in a cynical voice. "Could it have anything to do with being manhandled by you down at the beach?"

"That was a long time ago. Something's happened since then, something since our kiss at your house, something that changed your mind virtually overnight." He recognized fear in her eyes. "What is it, Nicole? What has happened to you?"

She thrust the check towards him, again. "Here. Take it and go. Please."

"Not until I get to the bottom of this." A picture of Aaron flashed across his mind, the twin's face covered by long scratches. When Jan and Justin had questioned him, he claimed to have had a wild romp with a local whore. Justin had never given it another thought until now. His stomach turned over as he laid his hands upon Nicole's shoulders. "Did Aaron visit you?" he whispered, desperate for a denial.

"Why would your brother come to my house?" she quizzed, deliberately meeting his gaze.

"Did he, Nicole?" Justin's voice, full of despair, demanded the truth. "Answer me!"

"No."

He lifted her chin, staring deep into her eyes. "You're lying! Why? Why would you lie to me?" His face contorted in a mixture of rage and frustration as he sought the answer in those haunting, brown eyes. The blond suddenly groaned in anguish. "He threatened you, didn't he? Damn him! I have to put an end to his meddling." Wheeling around to leave, he was stopped by Nicole's firm hold on his arm.

"No, Justin! Don't. I'm afraid he'll come back. I'm afraid he'll hurt me." She hated to admit her fear, but he left her no choice. "He was upset that you had been furious with him. He only wanted to make sure I didn't put you at odds with him again."

"I want to know what he said," Justin commanded. "I want to know everything!" Upon seeing him struggle to control his own rage, she thought it best to oblige. She would, however, alter a few minor details so Aaron would appear less menacing.

She underestimated Justin's intelligence. He was not so easily fooled. "You've conveniently left something out of your story," he accused. "I assumed you knew by now that I despise playing games. I always thought you did, too. Don't disappoint me, Nicole. Don't make me beat the truth out of my brother." Blue eyes narrowed with determination, Nicole could see he was deadly serious. She avoided his gaze and reluctantly added the missing details, sensing Justin's fury when he heard how Aaron had provoked her attack. When she finally peered up at him, the vein in his forehead was enlarged and throbbing.

"Don't do anything stupid," she implored. "Aaron doesn't want to fight with you."

"Then he shouldn't threaten my fiancée. Don't worry. I'll make sure he never sets foot inside your house again."

"Leave it be. I'm begging you."

"You're that frightened, are you?" He noticed her hands slightly shaking. It made him all the more enraged. "I'll kill him," he growled, taking three strides towards the office door.

"Justin!" Nicole went after him, panic in her voice. "Please! He'll come after me. I know he will. He won't rest until he's gotten even. I know his type. He won't hesitate to beat me. Please!" She was frantic, tugging on his sleeve, causing such a scene that Cristoff flew out of the tack room and ran up the aisle to find out what was going on.

Justin saw the terror in her eyes. He stopped in his tracks, having a change of heart. How could he put her through this? "All right, Nicole. You win. I promise I won't stir up trouble. You needn't worry." His words were convincing enough, but Justin wanted something in return. "I'll do things your way, if you keep me employed."

Cristoff reached them, a hundred questions forming. "What's wrong? Are you okay, Nicole? Did he hurt you? Why were you yelling?"

"It's already settled," Justin replied.

Nicole looked at Cristoff. "I told Justin about Aaron. He was going to confront him, that's why I was upset."

"I told you it's settled," Justin repeated. "I'm not going to say a word to my brother. Cristoff, will you excuse us? We have some unfinished business." The ranch hand waited, taking his cue from Nicole to leave them alone. After patiently standing by until Cristoff was far down the corridor, Justin turned back to Nicole. "Will you let me stay?"

"Why? Why do you want to be a hired hand?"

"I want to help out," he explained. "If you're still hung

up on the issue of money, why don't you consider forming a partnership with me? My funds could buy better stallions, plus pay for a professional trainer."

"Oh, no," she adamantly stated, shaking her head. "The last thing I need is to be bossed around by a man!"

"Partners can't boss each other around; they're equal."

She scoffed. "And what happens when we disagree?"

"We compromise."

"I'd like to see that happen. No. I don't want a partnership. I'll struggle on my own, sink or swim. If I fail, you'll be welcomed to buy me out."

Justin surrendered with a shrug. "Have it your way, then, Mrs. Tyler. Let me stay employed, though. I really enjoy this type of work. I love the horses. I love the labor. I even love the smell of leather and grime." His words made her smile. "I'll take a cut in pay, to help you out."

"I can't accept that," she said. "But... you can stay." And as she made the last statement, she shyly approached him, giving him a warm hug. It surprised and pleased the handsome blond, who never took her signs of affection lightly. Each tiny gesture was to be treasured, sustaining him until the day he could break down her protective defenses. He had emerged victorious from this one, minor battle. And in the future, he would settle for no less.

"Oh, I almost forgot!" Nicole exclaimed. "I called some places this morning and found a headache clinic for your sister. It's about forty minutes from here. Do you think she'd go?"

"I'll have to ask."

"They said they'd need her for about six hours of testing, which includes allergy tests. I'd be glad to take her there, myself."

"I'll tell her you offered and see what she says. That was very considerate of you to check into this. I had no idea there was such a thing as a special clinic. Thank you, Nicole." His gratitude was genuine, his warm smile contagious. The phone began to ring again, forcing the two to end their conversation. When Nicole was through with the call, she saddled The

General for his daily exercise, trotting off into the nearby woods.

She had only been in the forest for five minutes when her stallion picked up the scent of another horse. He planted all four hooves, flared his delicate nostrils and quivered. "Easy, boy," Nicole soothed, gently stroking the snow-white neck. She was unsure whether the object of his attention was man or beast. After a few seconds, however, The General took one step forward, which gave her reason to believe the intruder was another horse. Since horses never roamed this area alone, she assumed there was also a rider, and called, "Who's there? You're on private property."

Immediately, a rustling could be heard close by. Crisp, autumn leaves crackled under the weight of an emerging palomino and rider. "I thought you'd never get here, Cat," Aaron grinned. "I've been waiting most of the day, although I did have to make a hasty departure when I saw Justin heading this direction."

Nicole calmed herself, realizing she had nothing to fear as long as they remained on horseback. She was sure The General could outrun the palomino. He was her fastest Arabian on the ranch. "Don't you have anything better to do than go stalking?" she quipped.

He urged Nugget closer, careful to keep some distance between his gelding and the white stallion. "I'd have driven to your house, but I don't think you would have agreed to see me."

"And I don't care to see you now." She turned The General to leave.

"Wait, Cat. I want to apologize for the other night." He saw her continue to turn the Arabian until the horse had come full circle and was facing him again.

"What did you say?"

He nudged Nugget forward a few steps. "I want to apologize. I let my temper get out of control. I'm sorry for scaring you."

She noticed the long scratches on his face, but felt no remorse. "I hope you're not expecting an apology from me, because it won't happen. You're a brute, Aaron MacFierson. You're devious and cruel."

"Cruel?" he repeated. "No, no, Cat. You just overreacted to my warning. You cowered in the corner like a child."

Nicole gave a scornful laugh. "Tell me, Aaron, did a child put those six inch marks on your face?" She watched his jaw clamp shut, the muscles tightening in anger.

"Damn, you're difficult to make peace with!" He forced the palomino to advance until they were side by side. "I'm offering a truce, in case you haven't noticed. If my brother wants you for a wife, so be it."

"This is your lucky day, Aaron. I've called off the wedding. Justin and I are no longer engaged." His shock at the announcement was evident, relief washing over his face.

"It's for the better," he remarked.

One sable brow arched high. "Better for whom? You?"

Without waiting for a response, she dug her heels into The General's sides, pushing him into a full gallop far, far away from Justin's twin. From where he sat perched upon the palomino, Aaron watched the graceful woman guide her stallion out onto the beach, her raven-colored hair streaming behind her as the pair raced against the wind. She looked like a princess in a fairy tale, her sudden beauty catching him by surprise. He grinned, finally seeing why Justin had fallen head over heels for her. She was feisty, she had character, and, yes, she did have beauty. She was definitely unlike any other female he had known. But was she good enough for his brother? Aaron pulled out a cigarette, ignited it, then continued to watch the temptress. Apparently, she assumed he had left. She had slowed The General to a brisk walk, turned him and was now heading in Aaron's direction.

"Damn, you're gorgeous," murmured the blond, his lustful eyes studying each slender curve. It took every ounce of his willpower to tear his gaze away, but he had to do it. She was gaining too much ground. If she found him waiting for her, there'd be a whole new slew of questions to answer. He pulled on the reins, quietly urging Nugget towards home.

Nicole continued riding for an hour before heading back to the ranch, where she cooled out The General. Since it was close to quitting time, she ventured into the office to check for phone messages. "Justin," she called, seeing him pass by the doorway. He backed up to step inside. "I had a surprise visit from Aaron today, in the woods. He gave me an apology."

"In the woods?"

"He was on your palomino... said he'd been waiting there all day. Strange, isn't it? I can't imagine any sane person lurking in the woods, waiting to catch a moment with me. Doesn't he work?"

Ignoring the question, he remarked, "Aaron made an apology? You're sure?"

"He even said the word." She saw Justin's brows draw together, perplexed. "Is something wrong?"

"Aaron has never apologized for anything in his entire life—not to me, not to Jan."

"Maybe he had a change of heart. It happens."

"Not with Aaron," came the firm reply. "If you run into him again, turn around and come back to the ranch. I'd prefer if you kept your distance from him."

"As if I haven't? I can't help it if he's stalking around in the woods."

"Just be careful."

Feeling a lecture coming on, Nicole conveniently found an excuse to leave. She returned when she was sure Justin had gone for the day. The horses needed to be brought in and fed, so she grabbed several lead ropes before heading out to the pasture, where she met Cristoff.

"You haven't forgotten our dinner, have you?" he asked.

"A free meal? No way. Why don't you go home, Cristoff? I'll take care of the horses."

"Thanks," he replied, making a beeline for his house.

A half hour later, Nicole was knocking on his door, a peach cake roll in her hands for dessert. She had awakened extra early this morning to bake it especially for him. "Come in," smiled the ranch hand. For a moment, Nicole thought she had the wrong house. Usually attired in blue jeans and a sweatshirt, Cristoff now wore an expensive gold satin shirt with black dress pants.

"Did I under-dress?" she asked, feeling out of place. She had thrown on a violet velour top and jeans.

"No. You look lovely, as usual," he charmed, taking the dessert from her. "What have we here?"

"Peach cake roll. I hope you like it."

"Mm. Smells delicious."

After walking into the kitchen to place the dessert on the table, Cristoff motioned for her to sit in the dining room until he had brought out all the food. Her mouth watered at the sight of steak, baked potatoes, corn on the cob, string beans and salad.

"I bought a bottle of champagne for you, even though I'm not drinking," he mentioned.

"Oh, no, Cristoff. I couldn't possibly drink in front of you."

"But I already bought it," he argued. "If you won't have any, then you must take it home with you."

"Only if you allow me to pay for it."

"No. Take it as a gift. Please." Embarrassed, she began to blush, bowing her head so he wouldn't notice. Cristoff assumed she was saying her grace before meals, except that when she raised her head again, her skin was deep pink. He smiled. "What can I get you to drink, Nicole?"

"What are you having?"

"Ginger ale."

"I'll have the same."

"You're not nervous, are you?"

"Not at all," she blurted, a little too quickly. The truth was, she was extremely nervous.

"I want you to relax tonight," he said. "Use this evening as an escape from the hassles of the day. Enjoy our time together. There's no pressure, no time limit, no conflicts allowed." His words brought a smile to her lips. Oh, how she wanted to forget all the problems plaguing her! It would be so nice to just sit back and relax. She sighed, feeling the warmth of his gaze upon her.

"Did I tell you, you look stunning, Cristoff?" He shook his head. "Well, you do. I don't believe I've seen you look more handsome. Sobriety agrees with you." She raised her glass in a toast.

"Let's not talk about me," Cristoff commented. "I'd much rather discuss you. When was the last time you painted?"

"Feels like years," she laughed.

"You're a bit rusty, ay? Perhaps we can get you back into the swing of things." There was a mischievous twinkle in his eyes as he held her gaze.

"What are you up to, Cristoff?"

"I'll show you, after dinner."

Her curiosity piqued, Nicole swiftly ate her meal, anxious to have the mystery solved. This was promising to be a very interesting evening...

Justin shared those exact same thoughts. He and Shane had just pulled up to a fancy restaurant on the other side of town, decked out in their best suits. As they got out of the car, a long white limousine stopped at the restaurant's front door. "Look at that," Shane motioned, impressed. "That could be you, you know? Why don't you ever do those kinds of things, buddy?"

"Just to be noticed?" snorted Justin. "I'm not the type." His eyes scanned the couple exiting the vehicle. "Well, bless my hide!" He gestured for Shane to follow before hurrying across the parking lot. "It's him, all right," muttered the blond.

Shane was confused. "Who?"

"Nicole's brother-in-law, Daniel Tyler."

"Look at the babe on his arm!" Shane whistled.

"First class." They followed the couple inside, but at a safe distance. Justin had no desire to converse with Daniel. He'd rather observe the pair, which is what he did. Luckily, his table was across the room from Daniel, allowing him to view them discreetly.

"What's the big fascination?" quizzed Shane. "Are we spies tonight?"

Justin met his friend's gaze with melancholy eyes. "I can't

even go out without something or someone reminding me of her..."

"Nicole?" Shane studied the blond more closely. "Hey, what's wrong? Did you two have a fight? Is that why you agreed to come here with me? Does this guy, Daniel, have something to do with it?"

"It's a long story," Justin replied, ordering a drink. He carefully chose his words. "Nicole and I thought Daniel was interested in her, so we pretended we were engaged in order to provoke him."

Shane's eyebrows raised. "That's the craziest thing I've ever heard. Are you serious? Do you mean to tell me you never intended to marry the girl?"

"It was all staged," Justin answered.

"Why didn't you two just go out on a few dates? Seems to me, getting engaged was overdoing it." Shane shook his head. "I can't believe this!"

"Daniel kept checking up on Nicole. He's a sneaky guy. We felt it would take something extreme to get a response out of him."

"And?"

"He took the bait, but not like we expected. He wasn't jealous."

"Obviously," noted Shane as he watched Daniel nuzzle his redheaded girlfriend's neck.

"Daniel tried to find other suitors for Nicole. Apparently, he doesn't like me."

Shane's green eyes darted back to Justin. The waitress had returned, staring with surprise as Justin downed most of his tequila drink the minute she handed it to him. "Easy, buddy," Shane warned. "What's eating you? You're not yourself tonight."

Justin felt the slow burn of the liquor hit his empty stomach. "Nicole is having dinner with Cristoff this evening."

"So? You just said you're not really engaged." Justin signaled the waitress for another drink. Shane frowned. "You're going to get smashed, aren't you, Justin?" The blond said nothing. Shane gave a long-winded exhale. "She's not worth it, buddy."

"Oh, yeah? It was only a week or two ago that you tried dating her."

"What a mistake that was! I made one tiny pass at her and she nearly bit my head off." His remark made Justin smile. He had wanted to know what had gone on between the two that night; now he knew, nothing had gone on. He glanced over at Daniel, again, who appeared on very intimate terms with the redhead. If the man wasn't interested in Nicole, why did he object so strongly to Justin's engagement? Perhaps he didn't like the fact that Justin had sent a detective out to investigate Philip's friends? The question ate at him all evening. He could barely concentrate on what Shane was gabbing about, his mind was so preoccupied. Plus, he was upset over Nicole's dinner date. He could imagine what Cristoff was doing with the young beauty at this very minute. "I hope you won't be disappointed, Shane, if I call it an early night?"

"I thought we were going to shoot some pool later?"

"I forgot. Can I get a raincheck on it?"

Shane fidgeted, clearly agitated. "Nicole has you running in circles. You haven't even listened to a word I have said tonight. Why can't you just forget her, Justin?" The minute he looked into those blue eyes, he knew the answer. "Damn! You're in love with her!"

Now it was Justin's turn to become agitated. "I wouldn't know what love was if it kicked me in the pants." He downed the rest of his drink and paid the check.

"You're paying my share of the tab?" exclaimed Shane. "You're definitely in love!"

The blond cast him a sideways glance, then pushed back his chair. "I need to ask a favor of you, Shane. Could you drive me to Cristoff's house before you take me home? I'd drive my own car over there except that I'm feeling the tequila right about now."

"I wouldn't visit Cristoff and Nicole, if I were you, Justin. You'll be seeing them tomorrow. Can't it wait?"

"No," he snapped, walking out onto the parking lot. "I have to see Nicole tonight."

Shane tried to convince him, otherwise. "She won't appreciate the fact that you've been drinking. I know women. They don't like a man visiting them after he's had a few drinks."

"Just take me there," the blond insisted. "I want to break up this little affair of theirs."

"Be reasonable. Cristoff lives next door. You can't police them twenty-four hours a day! Let them have their fling. You know Cristoff isn't going to date her for long. Last time we were all together, he claimed he only takes a girl out once or twice before he drops her. He'll tire of Nicole, just like he tires of all the other babes. You'll probably tire of her, too. Then you'll look back on this and kick yourself for getting so wrapped up in the broad."

"Don't call her that. She's a lady."

Shane rolled his eyes. There had to be some way to straighten out his friend. They drove for a while in silence, then Shane said, "Julie told me she wants to go out with you."

"Not interested," Justin replied, folding his arms.

"You have become so boring." He had pulled up to Cristoff's house and stopped the car.

"If I'm so boring," Justin remarked, "then maybe we shouldn't spend so much time together." He closed the car door, silently approaching the porch steps. Looking up, he noticed an upstairs bedroom light on. "Just great," he grumbled. "Wonder if I should count how many minutes it takes for them to answer the door?" He gave four solid raps with his knuckles. To his relief, both Cristoff and Nicole appeared at the door. He stared at Nicole, mumbling a faint hello as he studied her clothes. They didn't look rumpled or untidy—a very good sign. Then his eyes focused on Cristoff and he felt the familiar pangs of jealousy burn a hole through his stomach, or was that the tequila?

"Justin," Nicole repeated for a third time. "What are you doing here?"

"Fancy threads," the blond commented, examining the gold cuff of Cristoff's sleeve. Blue eyes met hazel, and Justin was again reminded of the ranch hand's boyish good looks. He appeared more together than Justin had ever seen him; his thick, caramel-colored hair neatly styled away from his handsome face; his gaze determined, confident; the deeply tanned skin was shiny and flawless.

"Justin!" Cristoff called, giving his shoulder a good shake. "Are you okay? Have you been drinking?"

The sound of his voice brought the blond back to earth. "Huh? Yeah. I'm okay." His eyes sought out Nicole, again. "I just wanted to tell you I saw Daniel a short while ago. He was with a redhead. He brought her to the restaurant in a limousine. Can you believe it?" He cracked a smile. "He seemed quite fond of her."

"Did you speak to him?" Nicole asked.

"Didn't want to. I guess this proves he isn't interested in you. Anyway..." He focused his attention back on Cristoff. "I just thought I'd tell you."

"Thanks for the information," Cristoff responded. "See you tomorrow, Justin." He was about to close the door when Nicole stopped him.

"Wait, Cristoff. Justin? May I have a word with you, outside?" Cristoff took a deep breath, placing his hands in his pockets while he patiently watched his date step onto the porch with his friend. Realizing Cristoff was within earshot, Nicole motioned for Justin to follow her down the steps and off to the side.

Once there, she took his hand in hers. "Justin. What is the real reason you came by?"

"I just told you," he sniffed. There was a slight chill in the air.

"You've been drinking, haven't you? I can smell it."

"What's it to you?"

"I'm concerned, that's all. Is something troubling you? You look worried."

"Why do you care?"

She silently counted to ten before saying, "I do care about you. I just thought you might have come over here to talk about what's troubling you. If you did, I'm willing to listen." He could barely see her dark brown eyes in the dimness of the porch light, but he sensed she was truly sincere. He swallowed a smile and put on the most pitiful expression he could muster.

"I do have a terrible problem," he frowned, shaking his head. "But it'll take too much of your time to discuss it. It's very complex."

"I'll make time," she offered. "We can walk to my house. Cristoff will understand." She looked at the vehicle parked nearby. "Is that Shane's car?"

"Yeah. He's waiting for me, but I'd rather get this problem off my chest; otherwise, I don't think I'll sleep tonight. I can't talk to Shane about it. It's kind of personal. I need a woman's view."

"Sure," she quietly agreed. "Why don't you tell Shane to go on home. I can drive you to your house later. Let me go inside and explain this all to Cristoff."

"He'll be mad at me," Justin pouted.

"No, he won't. I'll talk to him."

But Justin was correct. Cristoff was mad, more than mad. He was furious. "You know he's trying to ruin our evening!" Cristoff fumed.

"You're wrong," Nicole argued. "He has a problem he needs to discuss."

"Oh, I'm sure of that!" Cristoff replied, dryly.

"I can't believe you'd be so uncompassionate. This isn't like you, Cristoff."

"Open your eyes, Nicole. He doesn't want us to be together. This is all part of some scheme he's dreamed up."

"Think what you want. I'm going to help him. I'll be back afterwards; if you want me to, that is." Angry eyes clashed with his. Cristoff knew she was beyond understanding.

"Of course I want you to return," he said. "I'll wait for you." She departed then. From his window, he watched the young woman walk with Justin across the lawn to her house.

He gave the nearby wall a solid pounding with his fist. The pain felt good, but it didn't change the circumstances. Everything had seemed so perfect up until now. After dinner, he had led Nicole upstairs to a spare bedroom which he had converted into his own private studio. He could still see the excitement in her eyes when she discovered the easel and blank canvas along with numerous tubes of paint. He wanted to learn to paint, he had told her, before shyly asking her to teach him the art. She was so elated he thought she would burst. They had only been painting a few hours when Justin had arrived. Now the virile blond was accompanying Nicole to her house in an attempt to keep her away from Cristoff, he was sure of it.

And Cristoff was right. Justin was silently patting himself on the back for gaining Nicole's sympathy. It had been so easy, he almost felt guilty. But, here she was, eager to listen to his imaginary problem, anxious to provide a solution.

"How can I help you?" she asked, seating herself beside him on the firm sofa. He had a million answers to that question, but chose, instead, to say, "My sister's birthday is coming up and I'd like to buy her something very special. The problem is, I'm not good at picking out presents for the opposite sex. I was hoping you could give me some ideas? This has to be a terrific gift; money's no object." As he finished the explanation, he noticed a sudden change in Nicole's expression. Her eyes locked with his, boring a hole straight through.

"A solid iron frying pan," she flatly said.

Justin cracked a smile. "Why would she want an iron frying pan?"

"Every girl should have one." Nicole rose from the couch. "It proves a handy weapon when some conniving weasel ruins a perfectly enjoyable evening!" She whirled around and dashed into the next room to retrieve her purse and car keys. "Let's go, Justin. I'm driving you home."

"But, but—" He acted stupid, still refusing to accept the fact that his plan had failed.

"Don't even try playing me for a fool again!" she warned, yanking him up from the sofa. "Jan celebrated her birthday prior to the two of you being hired. I guess it didn't occur to you that I look at the employment applications?"

He frowned. "Okay. I made the whole thing up. It was only because I wanted to see you tonight." She pulled him out the door and down the steps. "Is it a crime to vie for your attention?"

"It is when you lie to me."

"You recently lied to me, too, remember? You said Aaron hadn't come to your house."

"Get in the truck."

"Can't we take the Shelby?"

"No! We're not out on a date, in case you haven't noticed."

"If you'll just spend an hour with me, I promise I'll never lie to you, again?"

"You're lucky I haven't made you call a cab." She started the engine. "Don't give me that neglected look, either. None of this would have happened if you hadn't been drinking."

"You're beautiful when you're mad."

"Shut up." She floored the truck, zooming off the property in reckless haste. "You had better be on time for work tomorrow."

"Yes, ma'am." The blond slouched in his seat, staring out the window into the darkness. A few minutes later, they were in his own driveway.

"Get out," Nicole ordered, throwing open the passenger side door. From where she stood on the ground, hands on her hips, she could see he had no intention of moving. "If you don't, you'll no longer be employed at the ranch."

That moved him, his muscular form sliding out of the seat to stand in front of the bewitching beauty. "You enjoy throwing that up to me, don't you? Everything boils down to me obeying your command or suffering the consequence of being fired. What happens when I'm no longer employed by you, Nicole? What threat will you use then?"

"The police," she simply said, almost smiling. "Restraint orders come in very handy for that purpose."

Her reply upset him. Justin fought back an angry retort,

turned on his heel and stomped up the porch steps. When he slammed the front door so hard that she jumped, Nicole knew she had struck a nerve. "Too bad," she muttered, restarting the truck. "That's what he gets for lying." She drove back home, unable to shake the mild depression setting in.

CHAPTER FIFTEEN

When she knocked on Cristoff's door, he already knew her state of mind. "His little scheme failed, didn't it?" he inquired.

Nicole whisked past him and began to pace the floor. "He's starting to get on my nerves, Cristoff."

"We could always hire someone to replace him?"

"I've seen him ride. He's excellent."

"There are a lot of good riders in this vicinity."

"He's patient with the problem horses, too."

"You're making excuses," Cristoff softly said.

She stopped pacing, glanced over at him, then half-smiled. "I suppose I am."

"You like him."

"I suppose I do, a little."

"A lot."

"A little."

"A lot."

"He drives me nuts." She gave a frustrated sigh.

"You drive him nuts," Cristoff commented.

Nicole bowed her head and grinned. "My relationship with Justin is the complete opposite of my relationship with you."

"How so?"

"With you, I'm so relaxed. You're easy to talk to." Dark, chocolate brown eyes warmed his heart. "With Justin, I'm tense, highly excitable, foul-tempered."

"Come on." He took her hand. "Let's go back upstairs and paint. You need to get your mind off Justin."

"Yes," she agreed, following him up the steps to the studio room. She picked up the wet brush and palette, all the while studying the colorful canvas before her. "The sky should never be one color, Cristoff. A blue sky has many different hues. Watch what happens when I mix slight variations of blue." Dabbing her brush into a small mound of wet paint, she was about to mark the canvas when she felt Cristoff move her long hair behind her shoulders so he could nibble on her neck. "Cristoff," she giggled, shying away. He followed her movement, his mouth finding the ticklish spot near her collarbone. She laughed again, putting down the brush and palette to better defend herself. Cristoff caught her hands in his, a friendly smile on his face. He grew unusually quiet. She couldn't discern if he was simply being playful, or if his actions implied something deeper. It wasn't until she gazed into his eyes that she noticed the intensity of his passion.

"You tricked me," she faintly murmured, almost in disbelief. "All this," her view swept the entire room, "was done to manipulate me." She jerked her hands free of his.

"No, Nicole. It was no trick. I wanted you to teach me how to paint. I still do."

"Then why kiss me?"

"I wanted to show you how happy I am to have you here with me. Please." He stepped towards her, but Nicole backed away. "I won't kiss you, anymore. I'll respect your wishes. Just... don't leave, Nicole. I wanted tonight to be our night, something special. I was hoping to cheer you up. Is that so wrong?"

"No." She thought over his words. "I guess I overreacted. I'm sorry, Cristoff." She watched him pick up the brush and palette. "Please," he said, offering them to her. Nicole gave a slight smile, then took the objects and continued the lesson.

Cristoff adopted a very business-like attitude the rest of the evening, enabling Nicole to eventually relax. Thus, when it was finally time for her to depart, she felt a twinge of guilt for her earlier accusation. The pair stood at the door: Nicole with the champagne bottle under her arm; Cristoff with his hands in his pockets, making no move to show any sign of affection which might be misread.

"I had a wonderful evening," she said. "Really." Her host vaguely smiled, unsure of her sincerity. Sensing his skepticism, Nicole stepped forward and kissed him on the mouth. Cristoff, however, did not return the gesture. He remained very still, almost indifferent. "You're angry," she remarked.

Cristoff folded his arms. "What makes you think that?"

"Look how you reacted to my kiss."

He gave a short, cynical laugh. "I honestly don't understand you, Nicole. If I kiss you, you get upset. If I don't kiss you, you get upset. What do you expect from a man?" He waved his hand through the air. "We're not robots waiting to be programmed by you. We're living, breathing, flesh and blood." He grabbed her free hand, placing the palm of it against his cheek, his hazel eyes flashing. "See? I'm only human, Nicole. And you are, too. It's normal for us to have desires." Slowly sliding her hand down to his mouth, he softly kissed the slender palm, all the while locking eyes with the young beauty, his lips lingering against the sensitive skin before moving on to the pulse point of her wrist. His seductive ploy lured Nicole's buried sensuality up to the surface in a single flash. Passion burned in her eyes, the heat of it nearly scorching him as he fought to hold on to the moment. He had her exactly where he wanted her now, teetering at the fine line that divided lust and morality.

She eased the bottle of champagne onto the floor. Cristoff held his breath, knowing she must be the one to initiate the next move. Don't disappoint me, he silently begged. Come on, Nicole. Take a chance. While his heart raced, the young beauty moved forward and lightly caressed his lips with her own. Cristoff's arms encircled her, drawing her closer, a tiny sigh of relief escaping him when he felt no resistance. Her kiss deepened as she uttered a soft moan of pleasure. This is too easy, he thought, congratulating himself while their tongues intertwined.

Then he noticed Nicole's fingers had unbuttoned his shirt, slipped inside, and were scanning the width of his muscular chest. He winced, silently cursing as the slender fingers found his stitches.

Nicole tore her mouth from his, looked down and gasped.

She stared in horror at the puckered gashes, halting Cristoff's efforts to rebutton the gold shirt. There was no use hiding it now. She had already seen the wound, and as her mind rapidly pieced together the letters, her hand flew to her mouth to stifle another gasp. Cristoff's arms dropped to his sides, with no further need to cover the area. The damage was done.

"I can explain," he said, reaching out to the startled woman. Nicole backed away, eyes darting from the engraved name, up to his face, then back down again. "Will you at least listen to what I have to say?" he pleaded. "I was drunk when it happened. I didn't know what I was doing." He gave an innocent, little laugh. "I was bored, you know?"

His worried smile slowly vanished when he saw Nicole reach for the door. He called out, but she flew down the steps, running across the large lawn as if a posse were after her. Realizing how badly he had frightened her, Cristoff became desperate. With haste, he rebuttoned the shirt and took off after her, banging on her front door. "Nicole! Let me in! We need to talk. Please!" He knocked until his knuckles bled, then pounded the wooden object with his fist. "Nicole!" His voice became frantic, his panic mixed with anger. "The key," he mumbled, charging back across the grass to his house where he searched for the key she had given him in case of an emergency. Finding it, he returned and shoved it into the keyhole. The doorknob turned, yet no entrance could be gained. He then realized she had locked the inside deadbolt, for which he had no key.

"Damn it! Open this door!" he shouted, slamming his body against the sturdy piece. "Don't shut me out! I have... to talk..."

His voice began to fade. "... to you..." He slumped against the frame, despondent and exhausted.

Nicole turned out the lights, went upstairs and crawled into bed, hoping he'd think she was asleep and leave. Although she felt sorry for Cristoff, she could not bring herself to speak to him right now. She was in shock, her emotions a jumbled mess. She lay there in the darkness, wondering what to believe, thinking how close she had come to being intimate with him tonight. That scared her, too. She had always prided herself with the knowledge she had absolute control over her desires. This evening, she had thrown herself at Cristoff, desperate for attention, any kind of attention. It repulsed her, this weakness of hers. She hated herself. Yet, she could not deny the excitement which prompted her despicable actions. She had actually experienced lust; she had actually craved a man's body, even though her past relations with Philip had been full of fear and abuse. It seemed so bizarre to suddenly discover one's own sexuality at the age of 21.

She rolled onto her side, pondering the matter until sleep overcame her. Not even waking to change into a nightgown, Nicole slumbered in her regular clothes, dreaming of Cristoff and his scarred chest. In her vision, he was standing at the edge of the bed, silently staring down at her restless body. His presence was so real, it jarred her from her sleep. Nicole gradually opened her eyes and caught her breath. The distinct silhouette of a man stood immobile by her bed, his head tilted downwards. Had it not been for the shaft of moonlight on his clothes, Nicole would have screamed her lungs out. As it was, she recognized Cristoff's attire and bolted upright.

"How'd you get in here?" she demanded, her relief slowly changing to fear.

"The window," he calmly replied.

Nicole glanced across the room to the opened window, where the top of a ladder was visible. "You can't run from me now, Nicole," he continued. "We have to talk."

Nicole licked her lips, frantically searching for some way to get rid of him. "We can talk in the morning. I need my sleep, so do you."

"This can't wait until morning." Through the dimness of the room, he could see her slowly moving towards the opposite side of the bed. He had no idea where she was headed, but his instinct told him she was probably going to reach for an object to use as a weapon. Thus, Cristoff solidly warned her, "Don't try anything. I don't trust you, Nicole. You're frightened, I'm sure. But if you continue to put distance between us, I'll be forced to subdue you. It'd be a shame to have to hold you down just to talk to you. I thought we were friends."

"Yes. Yes, we are," she nervously answered, still inching her way across the mattress.

"You're so stubborn," he muttered, switching on the light to reveal her actions. Nicole froze, watching as Cristoff casually strolled around the bed to the nightstand. Pulling open the drawer, he lifted out her gun, holding it high in the air. "Is this what you wanted? I can't believe you thought you had to arm yourself against me." He pointed the weapon directly at her. "Is it loaded?" Nicole's heart jumped to her throat, pounding so fiercely her whole head began to throb. "Why, Nicole... is that fear I see in your eyes? Perhaps this will make you feel better." He aimed the gun at his temple, his finger still on the trigger.

"Cristoff! Stop! It's loaded!"

"Well, that got a response out of you," he smiled. "You probably wish I'd pull the trigger."

"Don't be ridiculous!" Nicole answered. "I care about you."

"Even after tonight?" he challenged.

"Yes. Of course. Put the gun down, will you? You're making me nervous." She was surprised to see him obey, placing the object back in the drawer.

"Now, will you talk to me, Nicole?" he begged, the sadness in his voice evident.

Nicole pitied him. "Yes, Cristoff." She motioned for him to sit beside her. She wasn't prepared, though, for the pain she saw in his eyes when moonlight illuminated them; it caused her to let down her defenses and become the compassionate friend he so desperately needed.

"I never meant for you to see the wound," he began. "I was ashamed of it, myself. I told you the truth when I said it was done during a time I was drunk. I'm not crazy or insane. I didn't even want to force my way into your room, except that I knew you wouldn't speak to me until tomorrow; and, by tomorrow, your overactive mind would have jumped to all sorts of conclusions. I certainly didn't want to frighten you, but I know I have and I am deeply sorry." He gazed at her with true sincerity. Nicole touched his hand.

"Why did you hurt yourself, Cristoff?"

"I was angry I had let you down. I knew you were depending on me to be with you when Daniel and Dr. Stanton came to your house that Saturday."

"This is why you stopped drinking, isn't it?"

"Not my injury," he explained. "I stopped drinking when I made a decision to be the type of person you could rely on."

Nicole drew her brows together. "Our relationship means that much to you?"

"Yes." Baring his soul to another person was the most difficult thing he had ever done, yet, it felt good to have this out in the open.

"Oh, Cristoff," she sighed, gently brushing back a lock of hair from his eyes. "For a minute, I thought you had really gone off the deep end." She still wasn't one hundred percent sure he hadn't, but she knew better than to say so.

The ranch hand got to his feet. "I'll leave you alone, now. I apologize again for scaring you, but I had to talk to you, Nicole. You do understand, don't you?"

She slightly nodded.

"If you don't mind, I'd prefer to exit by using the front door. Don't worry. I'll take care of the ladder. Goodnight, Nicole."

"Goodnight," she echoed, still in a half daze. As he silently slipped from the room, the young woman ventured over to the bedroom window to shut it. She then proceeded downstairs to relock the door. Despite the confidential talk they had had, Nicole was beginning to wonder about Cristoff.

Erratic behavior was not like him. She did not need a degree in psychiatry to realize that any time a person mutilates their body it is a sign of mental disturbance. She prayed this was a one time incident. But then she remembered him pointing the gun at his head, asking if she wished him dead.

Nicole paced the floor of her bedroom, unsure what to do. Should she tell Justin, in hopes he could persuade Cristoff to get help? She certainly couldn't be the one to confront Cristoff since he had often told her to see a shrink and she had refused. On the other hand, Cristoff might become upset with her if she did mention this to Justin. "What to do?" she mumbled, wringing her hands. She finally made her decision a half hour later. She would wait and see if sobriety ended the irrational behavior. Yes, that was a good idea. Satisfied, Nicole changed her clothes, washed up, and climbed into bed.

The next morning, Cristoff appeared in the stable with his usual sunny disposition. It was as if nothing had ever happened last night. He presented her with the champagne bottle she had left at his house, then went about his business. After Nicole put the liquor away, she entered the office to check for messages.

"Nicole!" called Jan, rushing to her side. Before Nicole could get a word out, Justin's sister embraced her with a tight hug. "I'm so sorry that you and Justin have split up! Is there anything I can do?"

"Yeah. Relax," came the calm reply. "Didn't he tell you we staged the engagement?"

"No." Jan looked baffled.

"We just wanted to see if my brother-in-law had his heart set on me. Sorry we couldn't let you in on the secret."

"Oh." Jan sounded disappointed. "Well, does he?"

Nicole shook her head. "We were wrong. Daniel isn't interested in me."

"What made you think he was?"

"It's a long story."

Jan's expression turned sad. "Gee. I was hoping you and Justin were really going to get hitched."

Nicole frowned, deciding to change the subject. "Did he tell you about the headache clinic?"

"Oh, yes! I'm so excited! I'm going to make an appointment. Do you mind if Justin takes off from work to drive me there?"

"Not at all." She was about to comment further, when Justin barged into the room, grabbed Nicole by the arm and pulled her towards the door, saying, "Excuse us, Jan. I need your boss for a minute."

"How dare you yank me out of my office!" stormed Nicole, fighting to free herself.

"I'm sorry, honey, but this can't wait." His lowered voice signaled his distress. "We've got problems, bad problems. Let's talk inside your house. Where's Cristoff? Is he around?"

"I think he's saddling one of the horses. Want me to call him?"

"No. It's better if he's kept in the dark for now." He hurried her across the grass and up the porch steps. "I would have talked in your office, but I can't risk anyone hearing us."

"What? What is it?" she asked, closing the front door behind them.

"Lock it. Can't take the chance of Cristoff walking in."

She quickly obeyed, then turned to him. "Justin, what has happened?" His fearful expression alarmed her.

"It's our detective, Charlie King. He's disappeared." Nicole stared in disbelief. "I received a call last night from his wife. She said he hadn't come home. The last time anyone saw him was nine o'clock yesterday morning."

"Did she call the local hospitals? The police?"

"She's called every possible place she can think of."

"Maybe he stopped somewhere after work yesterday?"

"Not Charlie. He's a family man, has a good marriage and three kids. He loves them more than anything in the world. He always calls home if he's going to be late."

"Justin, you don't think... You don't suspect—"

"Foul play?" He looked her straight in the eyes. "I sure do. That's what has me so worried."

Nicole held her head. "I just can't believe this! Perhaps his car broke down somewhere."

"Charlie's oldest son already combed the area for the vehicle. That's vanished, too."

She laid her finger against her bottom lip. "He started our case two days ago, didn't he?"

"Yep. That's why his wife called me. She's filing a missing person's report this morning, Nicole, and she asked me to go to the sheriff's office and offer whatever information I can. It's going to be difficult to scoot around the issue of why we needed Charlie to investigate."

"I hadn't even thought of that," Nicole murmured.

"We can avoid mentioning some of the details. All we have to say is that he was checking out possible murder suspects in regards to Philip. But..." He went to her, placing a hand on each shoulder. "If they find any of his notes about the case, well, it could prove very embarrassing for you." The compassion in his eyes helped soothe her frazzled nerves.

"I can't worry about it, Justin. Whatever we have to do to find Charlie, regardless of the consequences, we should do it. Perhaps Cristoff has some suggestions."

"I wouldn't mention this to him." Justin gave her a steady stare. "I don't know how to say this, Nicole, but... I'm highly suspicious of both, Cristoff and Daniel."

"What?"

"You heard me. They were the only two people who knew about the detective, besides you and me. Either one of them could have had a hand in this."

"Oh, please!" she scoffed, walking to the window. "You know right well that any of the men being investigated could be suspected."

"And if any of them did something to Charlie, it would draw attention straight to them."

"I don't understand what you're getting at?"

"Then let me tell you my best guess." He joined her at the window. "If foul play is involved with Charlie's disappearance, I don't think it had anything to do with questioning men about the type of pills Philip used on you. I believe our suspect is your husband's killer and he felt threatened, so he hired someone to dispose of Charlie."

"Hired someone?"

"I doubt the suspect would do the deed himself, considering it would draw more attention to him."

"You believe it was a conspiracy."

"More than likely. Nicole," he said, studying her again. "Is there anything you've forgotten to tell me which could shed some light on this case? Think hard. Has Daniel been by recently?"

"No."

"What about Cristoff? Has he acted any different than usual?"

Nicole bit her lip. What to say? "Of course he's a little different now that he's sober."

"Funny how he chose this specific time to quit drinking. Wonder why he suddenly felt the need to have a clear head?"

Nicole's eyes darted to the far side of the room. "I would suspect Daniel before I suspected Cristoff," she quickly replied.

"That's because you're fond of Cristoff."

She met his hard stare. "So what if I am?"

"I don't want to argue, Nicole. I just think that we should be extremely careful. I'm concerned about your safety. Who knows what could happen? If someone hurt Charlie, they're going to go after whoever sent him. Depending on which one of us they think hired him, we could be in danger, too." He let the next statement slide out of his mouth as swiftly as possible. "I'm hiring a bodyguard for you."

Nicole's jaw dropped. "What? Without my consent? I think not!" Defiantly folding her arms, she dared him to differ.

"It's for your own good."

"You are out of your mind! Charlie hasn't even been listed as missing, yet. There's no proof of foul play. Aren't you putting the cart before the horse?"

"I'd rather be safe than sorry. If anything ever happened to you..."

Nicole arched a brow. "Yes?"

"There would go the ranch and everything you've worked for," he finished, frowning.

"I see," she dryly replied. "When and if I ever need a bodyguard, however, I'll hire one, myself, thank you."

"Don't be pigheaded!"

"You should be quite familiar with that term."

Justin held in his anger. "Don't be surprised if the sheriff wants to talk to you today."

"Maybe I should accompany you this morning and get the interrogation over with?"

"Good idea." He drew in a deep breath. "What will we tell Cristoff?"

"The truth." Ignoring Justin's scowl, she continued. "He'll eventually find out, anyway. Besides, I truly think he's innocent."

"Let's not get into that discussion again!"

Just then, a knock sounded at the front door. Nicole hurried to open it, meeting the puzzled gaze of Cristoff. "You threw the deadbolt?" he quizzed, eyeing Justin with suspicion. "I need you to look at King Arthur's heel, Nicole. It's bruised and swollen."

"In a minute, Cristoff. Come in," she said. "Justin and I have something to tell you. I had locked the door so Daniel could not walk in unexpectantly." Cristoff's curious expression turned serious.

"What is it, Nicole?" he asked.

Despite Justin's opposition, Nicole informed the ranch hand of the detective's disappearance. It was apparent Cristoff was just as shocked as Nicole was at the news. His brows drew together as he searched for an explanation. Finally, he said, "I should never have told Daniel. I bet he had something to do with this."

Justin cocked his head, studying the ranch hand. "You're a little quick to judge him, aren't you?"

"You weren't there the night I told him about Charlie," Cristoff pointed out. "He had been staring at his drink; then, when I mentioned the detective, his eyes darted to mine and narrowed. I'll never forget that look; it was as if you could see the wheels turning in his head."

"Why didn't you mention this to us before?" Justin challenged.

"I shrugged it off. How was I to know Charlie would suddenly vanish?" Cristoff's eyes lit up. He snapped his fingers. "There was another time Daniel acted a bit odd, when I told him Nicole was experiencing flashbacks. At first, he refused to believe it. However, when I finally convinced him, he became real worried. In fact, he seemed to take more of an interest in the matter than I had expected."

"Perhaps he was concerned for my welfare," Nicole reasoned.

"Yes, but why, Nicole? Why is he always so concerned about you? We've asked ourselves that over and over. I don't believe it's just loyalty. Don't you find his doting quite unusual?"

"Especially when it came to our engagement," spoke Justin. "Maybe he didn't want you becoming too involved with me because he knew I was the one who hired Charlie?"

Nicole pressed her hands against the sides of her head. "All this guessing is giving me a headache."

"But we have to discuss it," Justin said, glancing at his watch. "Damn. We have to leave for town, Nicole."

The young beauty agreed. "We'll have to continue our talk later. Hold down the fort, will you, Cristoff?" He nodded, following the pair outside.

When they had left the property, he began mucking a few stalls but found it difficult to concentrate on the chore. Philip's murder weighed heavily on his mind.

"Need a hand?" Jan called, grabbing a pitchfork. "The phone's quiet and I finished my paperwork. I don't have anything to do right now." She stabbed a mound of soiled straw, sifted through it and tossed the remainder into a wheelbarrow. Cristoff paused a moment, straightened up, then ran the back of his hand across his sweaty forehead. "Hey, are you sick?" Jan asked, approaching him. "You're perspiring like it was eighty degrees in here." She felt his forehead. "You're not warm, though." She glanced at his hand. "You're trembling, Cristoff!"

"I skipped breakfast, that's all," he replied. "I'll go in the house and make something to eat. I'll be okay." He departed before she could question him further, glad to be away from her scrutinizing stare. Inside his house, he sat down, trying to relax, wishing he hadn't given up the booze. He could sure use a drink right now.

"I've got to stay sober," he told himself, making a ham sandwich. He ate while he walked upstairs, stopping at the door of the studio room to gaze at the picture Nicole had helped him paint. An artist, he was not. The sloppiness of his work caused him to shake his head with disappointment. Nicole had said he shouldn't get discouraged; no one became a great painter overnight. He had to agree with her. He was in no hurry to advance, either; his lack of skill was a good excuse to prolong the art lessons.

The telephone rang as he finished off the sandwich. It was Nicole. After Jan told her of his unusual symptoms, Nicole had become concerned, needing reassurance.

"I'm okay," he told her. "I just needed to eat. How did everything go with the sheriff?"

"Nerve-racking," she answered. "Fortunately, he believed we only hired Charlie to investigate Philip's murder. Nothing was said of the poker parties or dope."

"Let's hope those details remain undiscovered."

"Yes." She paused. "I feel so emotionally exhausted."

"I guess so, after answering all those questions. Why don't you and I take a leisurely trail ride? I stumbled across some new paths at the southern end of the woods."

"I'd love to, Cristoff, but there are several more stalls which need to be cleaned."

"I'll do it when we get back. I don't mind. Come on, Nicole. When was the last time you rode just for the sheer pleasure of it?"

Nicole gave a wistful sigh. She couldn't even remember the last time she took a peaceful walk in the woods. Being close to nature always calmed her restless spirit. "You've talked me into it. Okay. I'll saddle The General."

"Good! See you in the barn." He hung up the receiver and smiled, thinking someone had to make the girl get some relaxation. Last night had been meant to take her mind off her problems, but the discovery of his injury had ruined that. He had another chance now to build a few good memories with the young beauty.

His wish was granted. It proved a perfect day for riding, the autumn breeze crisp and stimulating, the falling leaves transforming into a million swirling dancers in their brightly colored dresses. Sensing the change of season, the horses pranced with renewed vigor, snorting and shying at imaginary monsters. Their playful antics made Nicole laugh.

"It's wonderful to hear that sound," Cristoff commented, nudging his chestnut stallion closer.

"What sound?" Nicole asked.

"Your laughter. I've missed it. I think The General has, too. Look. He tosses his head every time you chuckle."

She grinned. "So, where are these new trails, Cristoff?"

"Not far. If we canter, we'll save some time." She nodded, following his lead when his mount broke into an easy lope. The General, however, had other ideas. Full of energy, he suddenly charged into a full blown gallop, nearly running right over the stallion ahead of him. Nicole seesawed frantically on the reins, jerking his head into his massive chest, determined to cut off his wind so he'd be forced to slow down. It took several minutes to get him under control, but when she did, Cristoff pulled back to a trot, saying, "He thinks he's a racehorse, Nicole. I always said that stallion should be tried on the track."

"The racing world would have a fit," she replied, gulping in the chilled air. "It will be a long time before anyone accepts Arabian racing. Maybe some day in the future." They looked at each other and smiled, their cheeks red from windburn.

Cristoff led her up a narrow path, weaving through a dense mass of pine trees whose fresh scent reminded Nicole of Christmas. Deeply inhaling the sweet aroma, she pictured the beautiful scenery layered in dazzling white snow. As they continued to proceed, several deer, startled by the intrusion, gracefully bounded for safer territory. Cristoff glanced over at Nicole, saying, "If you died and came back to earth as an animal, I bet you'd be a deer."

Nicole shyly smiled. "That's an odd thing to say."

"Every time I see a doe, I think of you. You're beautiful, graceful, you startle easily, and you're always running from something."

Nicole halted The General. "Me? Running? From what?"

"Not what. Who." He pulled up his steed and dismounted, helping her to do the same. "You run from me. You run from Justin."

"I don't recall running," she politely argued.

"But you do. You still won't let anyone get close to you."

"I almost did, last night. I would have, if I hadn't discovered your injury."

"You used the wound as an excuse," he quietly said, gazing into her eyes. "Sure, you were shocked. But you could have put it behind you, if you had really wanted to."

"Easy for you to say. How would you feel if you saw your name carved into my flesh?"

"No doubt I'd be upset. But if I truly wanted you, I'd get over it."

"Are you implying I didn't want you?" He made no reply. Nicole became flustered. "Well, I did! I did want you. I wanted you very much!"

He lifted his shoulders. "Okay." He stepped forward and kissed her, his one hand still holding his horse's reins as both arms encircled the raven-haired temptress. Nicole stiffened until he released her. The disappointment in Cristoff's eyes was obvious. "See?" he said. "You don't really want me."

"You caught me off guard," Nicole countered, angry when he slowly shook his head. "Besides, I decided last night that I wouldn't allow my desires to control me."

"That scares the hell out of you, doesn't it?" he challenged. It was Nicole's turn to grow silent. Cristoff uttered a frustrated sigh. "It's like I told you before, sweetheart, we're only human. There's nothing wrong with experiencing desire."

"Oh, yes there is!" she quickly exclaimed. "Desire probably accounts for most pregnancies in this world. Desire can turn a mild-mannered person into a murderer. Desire drives some people insane. Desire—"

"You made your point," Cristoff interjected with a frown. "You should have been a nun."

Nicole smiled. "I thought of it when I was younger, but I have too much passion locked inside of me." She stared back at him with eyes as big as saucers, looking quite the innocent after such a profound statement.

Cristoff could not help himself. "If stifling passion is the problem, my girl, then why don't you simply let it out?"

"Because I prefer being rational. Can we change the subject, please?" They began to walk the dirt path, both scrambling for other topics. Finally, Cristoff informed her he needed to relieve himself, so Nicole sat down beneath a tall oak tree while she waited, holding the reins of both horses. When he returned, he seated himself beside her, propping his back up against the tree. He took in the lovely autumn scenery. "I suppose there isn't much time left for exploring," he said.

"No." Nicole leaned back, feeling disappointed. "I wish we could stay here the rest of the day. But, of course, that wouldn't be fair to Justin or Jan."

"We could always say we got lost?"

"You might fool Jan, but I doubt Justin would buy that excuse."

"So what? You're the boss. You can do anything you want."

Nicole gave a lame chuckle. "I wish."

Cristoff touched her arm. "I know! Why don't we come back here this weekend? We could even camp out."

"I don't think I'd like being here overnight. Knowing my luck, there'd be a serial killer in this part of the woods."

"Then let's just make a day of it—the two of us. What do you say?"

"Well..." She tapped her toe as she considered the offer.

"Okay." Cristoff was so delighted by her response, he slapped his thigh and whooped, terrifying both horses by the sudden outburst. The chestnut stallion's head jerked up with alarm, yanking the reins right out of Cristoff's hand. Nicole would have grabbed at the dangling leather, but The General had also startled and was giving her a good struggle now, pulling backwards in his attempt to free himself. Nicole was yanked forward onto her knees as she continued to hold on. Cristoff's mount quickly darted down the trail, leaving the ranch hand free to assist Nicole, which he promptly did. Together, they quieted the white Arab, although it was no easy task.

"I'm so sorry," Cristoff said. "I should have known better."

"Forget it. These horses shouldn't spook so easily. Good grief! We ride noisy tractors right under their noses and they don't even snort. One little shout of joy and you'd think they were caught in a forest fire." She glanced over at the embarrassed ranch hand. "Come on." She hoisted herself up into the saddle. "Climb up behind me. It was time to head home, anyway."

"Talk to The General, first. I'm not anxious to eat dirt. I hate being thrown."

Nicole leaned forward to pat the stallion's muscular neck. "It's okay, General. You know Cristoff. He's no stranger. Be a good sport and let him join us for the ride home." After much hesitation, Cristoff hoisted himself up behind Nicole, stiffening when he saw the horse's ears pin back. "Relax, Cristoff," Nicole murmured. "He feels the tension." She remembered the time Shane had ridden home with her, astride The General. Her horse had behaved very well that afternoon, despite Shane being a complete stranger. Then she realized why. Shane had been at ease on the stallion, not knowing the horse's temperament. Cristoff, on the other hand, was a little fearful of The General. He knew how wild the animal could be.

"Do you mind if I hold on?" he politely asked.

Nicole laughed as her steed began a brisk walk. "Did you think I'd expect you to ride with your arms dangling at your sides? Really, Cristoff. Of course, you should hold on."

Nicole urged The General into an easy trot, watching the lovely scenery of colors float past them as Cristoff searched his surroundings for something special to remember this day by. When they entered a small, open area, he asked her to pull up. After she did so, Cristoff slid down to the ground and made his way over to a patch of vibrant wildflowers, where he carefully selected certain ones. Nicole patiently waited while he gathered the colorful bouquet, feeling quite honored to be the recipient of such a wonderful gift. "Oh, Cristoff," she smiled. "How sweet of you."

He climbed back on board the Arabian, grinning with pride. "Wait, Nicole." Reaching around the temptress, he pulled one long stem from the bunch she was holding. It was a vivid violet-colored flower. "This will only take a minute. Turn your head to the side." He isolated three small sections of her hair before carefully braiding the flower's stem in with the different strands. "This way, the flower won't fall out so easily." Satisfied with the result, he remarked, "Now you look like a forest princess."

"I didn't know you could be so romantic, Cristoff," she playfully teased. Her smile matched his, as The General continued on his way.

Back at the ranch, Justin saw them approaching. When Cristoff's horse had returned without its rider, he had almost ridden out after them. But upon seeing the couple now, he was glad he hadn't. It would have proved embarrassing. From where he stood near the house, cooling out one of the horses he had just exercised, he could plainly see neither Cristoff nor Nicole needed his help. "What the hell's in her hair?" he grumbled, squinting into the sunlight. They were still a good distance away, yet Justin not only saw the wildflowers, he also noticed the way Cristoff was nibbling at the base of Nicole's neck. She, in turn, was giggling. "I think I'm gonna puke," Justin spat. He couldn't bear to watch any longer. If it wasn't for Aaron's car racing up the driveway, he would have made a hasty exit. As it was, he stayed put, knowing Aaron's news had to be important in order for him to interrupt Justin's work.

Aaron threw his car into park and jumped out. "It's Mrs. King," he said to Justin. "She just called the house, looking for you. She said it was urgent you contact her, right away."

"Thanks," Justin replied, his eyes riveted once again on the approaching couple on horseback. Aaron followed his gaze, then grinned.

"It didn't take her long to get over you, now did it?"

"Shut your mouth," growled Justin. "I have enough problems on my mind."

"Easy, brother. Don't get mad with me. I was just mentioning the obvious. Jan says Nicole told her that Cristoff converted one of his bedrooms into an art studio. She's teaching him how to paint. And I bet that isn't the only thing she's teaching him." His taunting drew a solid pounding on his shoulder from Justin, who didn't find the jest at all amusing. Aaron dodged the next intended blow and snickered. "You could take a few tips from Cristoff, Justin. See how he's showing interest in everything Nicole likes to do? People in love do things like that."

Justin scowled. "Don't stand here and tell me what people in love do. I know what they do!"

"Then why aren't you the one up there, sitting so close to Little Miss Hot Pants that she's practically in your lap?" In response, Justin turned on his heel to leave, but his twin caught hold of his arm, saying, "A little advice, brother—the Lippizan stallions are appearing at the Arena either this month or next month. Why don't you buy two tickets and ask her to accompany you? No horse-crazy female would pass up the offer."

Justin shook off his hand. "Maybe." His tone gave no promise, however, as he continued towards the barn. Aaron walked back to his car, lit a cigarette, then casually leaned against the vehicle as he waited for Nicole. When the couple arrived, Cristoff quickly dismounted and called to the twin. "Hey, Aaron. What brings you here?"

"I had to give Justin a message," Aaron replied before walking up to The General. His hands reached up for Nicole's waist to help her dismount, but she cleverly avoided the gesture by hopping off the opposite side. A lopsided grin pricked the corners of Aaron's mouth as his eyes narrowed. The lit cigarette now dangled precariously at the edge of his bottom lip while he studied the raven-haired beauty. "Still don't trust me, eh?" Nicole ignored him, promptly leading The General towards the barn to be unsaddled. Aaron chuckled.

"So, how have you been?" Cristoff asked.

"All right." The blond took a long drag of nicotine. "I see you have a new girlfriend."

"Who? Nicole?"

"Haven't seen you over at Carla's."

"I've been busy."

"So I see." The lopsided grin reappeared. "So... how is she?"

"Nicole?"

Aaron nodded.

"She's okay. Why?"

The blond shook his head. "No, no. I mean... how is she?" Upon seeing Cristoff's puzzled expression, Aaron loudly swore. "In bed! How is she in bed? You have slept with her, haven't you?"

"If I had, you wouldn't think I'd be broadcasting it, would you? Did Justin put you up to this?" He waited for the blond to finish grinding his cigarette butt into the dirt.

"No. Justin didn't have anything to do with the question. I was curious, that's all. You two look pretty close."

"I like to think so," Cristoff proudly responded. "I'd stay and chat but I have some stalls to clean."

"Don't work too hard," called the blond. They parted company, and Cristoff entered the barn.

"Oh, good. There you are," Nicole said, rushing to him. "Justin got a call from Mrs. King. She found some of Charlie's notes and asked if Justin wanted to see them before she gave them to the police. We're going over there now, so would you mind sticking around here until we get back?"

"Sure. I have to clean the stalls, anyhow."

"Thanks, Cristoff. Jan is still here. I don't think we'll be too long."

"Good luck," he said, just as Justin came up the aisle. The blond quickly ushered Nicole outside to his jeep, where the two seated themselves and exchanged nervous glances.

"I'm glad you came along," Justin admitted.

"Considering everything Mrs. King has gone through these past couple of days, it would be very cold of me not to express my sympathy and gratitude. She didn't have to offer you the chance to look over those notes."

"She feels she owes it to us since Charlie was working on our case. Deep down, I believe she's hoping we might discover some helpful clue amidst the writing."

"It could happen." Nicole bit her nails, then sat on her hands to prevent any further damage.

"You're pretty nervous, aren't you?" Justin asked.

"Aren't you?"

"Yeah. Who knows what might be mentioned in those notes." Too skittish to talk, Nicole quietly looked out the window. When they pulled up to the large, individual house, both hurried up the pathway to the porch. Mrs. King had been watching for them and quickly opened the door. "Justin," she called in a sweet voice. "So glad you could come. And you must be Mrs. Tyler?"

Nicole held out her hand. "I am so sorry about your husband, Mrs. King. If there's anything I can do to help, please tell me." The short, plump woman politely smiled; but it was a sad smile. The result of many hours of crying was evident by her swollen eyes. It broke Nicole's heart.

"In here," Mrs. King said, leading them to her husband's study. "I don't understand why he'd leave the notes under a pile of papers. You'd think he'd take them with him?"

Justin began to glance down a page. "These might just be scribbled thoughts... brain storming, I think they call it." He had to squint to decipher some of the words. "I can barely read it."

"I know," Mrs. King replied. "I always said Charlie should have been a doctor. His handwriting is horrible." She gave a tiny laugh, then began to snivel. Immediately Nicole went to her side, placing an arm around the woman's shoulders.

"Why don't we sit and talk, Mrs. King?" she offered. She pointed to various pictures decorating the walls. "Are these your children?"

"Oh, yes! Beautiful, aren't they?" Nicole politely smiled as each child's history was revealed to her. It provided an opportunity for Mrs. King to brag a little, but more importantly, it kept her mind off of Charlie. Thus, Nicole prolonged the conversation until Justin had finally finished with the notes.

"Did you find anything important?" Mrs. King queried as he joined them.

"I don't think so. Is your husband's appointment book still here?"

"No. He always carried it with him."

"Did he ever keep a log of his calls or places he visited?"

"Not at home. I'm sure he had that information at the office, but the police would have confiscated it by now."

"What about the calls he made from home?"

"The deputy already went through his trashcan in the study. He dumped everything into a bag and took it with him."

"There's really nothing else that can help us, then. I'm sorry, Mrs. King."

"That's all right," the kind woman replied. "I'm sure Charlie will show up soon. Our son's birthday is tomorrow, and Charlie never misses a birthday." Eyes filling with tears, she weakly smiled. Nicole was also on the verge of tears but held them in.

"I'll say a prayer for his safe return," she offered as she and Justin walked to the door. "Thank you, again, for allowing us to look over the notes."

"You're welcome."

While Nicole and Justin stepped off the porch, a sinking feeling struck them in the pit of their stomachs. "Even the deputy knows he's not coming back," Nicole sadly remarked. "When we were told that the deputy emptied his trashcan, I knew Charlie's case was being treated as a murder."

Justin's throat constricted. "I know." He opened the passenger side door and waited for Nicole to get situated. When he entered on the other side and started the jeep, he said, "The notes were mainly background information on Philip's poker buddies, their wives' names, children's names, street addresses. He did list the fact that Dr. Bohman does not exist."

"Then who supplied Philip with the drugs?"

"I have no idea, unless Dr. Bohman was a fake name given to one of the poker players. But Charlie didn't draw that connection in his notes. The only other items of interest were some scribbling about a government link and then a bank name."

"Daniel works for the government. I guess Charlie was just getting around to investigating him. Perhaps the bank name was where he does his banking?"

"So, why didn't Charlie just write down Daniel's name? Why would he make a note of a government connection?"

"Who knows?" Nicole frowned. "But I can tell you, first hand, there was no talk about government issues at my house."

"At least not that you can remember," remarked the blond. "I think I've got an idea..."

CHAPTER SIXTEEN

"It's no use," muttered Cristoff, shaking his head. "Maureen won't talk to me." He ventured towards the liquor cabinet in Nicole's living room, turned, then walked away. "Sorry. Just a habit."

"Well, what do we do now?" Nicole quizzed, hands on her hips. It had been such an excellent idea. If Cristoff could speak to Daniel's ex-wife, perhaps they could get a little information about his personality and line of work during the few days prior to Philip's murder. The project had bombed, however. Maureen wanted nothing to do with any of Daniel's acquaintances, including Cristoff and Nicole.

"Has she remarried?" Justin asked.

"No."

Nicole added, "Daniel told me she has a new boyfriend, though."

"No problem," smiled the blond. "I'll simply date her."

"Absolutely not!" Nicole snapped. Then, aware of two pairs of eyes twinkling with amusement, she began to stutter. "I-I mean, it isn't a very good idea." Her cheeks tinged a lovely pink as she sought some way to justify her remark. "You would be leading her on, using her."

Cristoff raised a brow, surprised by the sudden display of jealousy. Justin defended himself. "It will be worth it if this provides us with the information we need. I'll just take her out a few times, then casually ask her if she's been married, etc."

Cristoff agreed. "I think it will work. Maureen is a talker, especially after a couple of drinks."

"Give me her address, Cristoff, and I'll do the rest." Cristoff grabbed a piece of paper, scribbled the information and handed it to the blond.

"And how do you plan to introduce yourself?" Nicole quizzed.

Justin looked at Cristoff. "Do you know which clubs she goes to?"

Cristoff thought for a moment. "Daniel used to take her to the Midnight Lounge."

"But she has a boyfriend now," Nicole interjected, folding her arms with satisfaction.

Justin's lips formed a wolfish grin. "I've never let a boyfriend stand in my way before." Cristoff stifled a laugh as they watched Nicole's face pale with disgust. She was taking this pretty hard, poor girl. In fact, Cristoff could practically see the revenge lurking behind those dark eyes. She would definitely get even with Justin for that last statement, and Cristoff couldn't wait to hear the comforting sounds of them fighting again. Naturally, he'd offer his services if she wanted to provoke the blond's jealousy.

"I guess you'll do whatever you want," Nicole stated.

"I always do," Justin replied. Blue eyes clashed with brown.

"Now that this has been settled," broke in Cristoff, "I believe Nicole and I should discuss another very important topic—a horse trainer."

"Yes. I agree," spoke the irritable female. "I'll see you at work tomorrow, Justin."

The quick dismissal annoyed the blond, but he hid the fact, saying, instead, "I guess Jan forgot to tell you. I'm taking her to the headache clinic tomorrow."

"Oh. Then I suppose I'll see you on Monday. Call me if there's any news on Charlie." He stared at the restless beauty, saw that she was still burning with jealousy over Maureen, and smugly smiled.

After he departed, Cristoff sifted through Nicole's newspaper rack. "Where are the Arabian magazines?"

"In the closet. They're too thick for the rack." She quickly retrieved a few, then curled up on the sofa with Cristoff. While they leafed through the advertisements, Nicole jotted down various names of trainers. However, after an hour of searching, the additions to the list dwindled. Cristoff glanced down at the notes. "You can scratch off half of those names," he glumly said. "I can tell by who they've worked for that their prices will be over our heads."

"And none of the applicants you've interviewed were qualified?"

"The ones who were qualified didn't seem to have the patience. I put them on some of our newer horses to test them. If we could raise the salary we're offering, we'd have a better pick." Nicole remembered Justin's offer to help with the ranch's finances, but refused to give it more than a passing thought. If she borrowed his money, she'd feel obligated to his every demand. She grabbed another magazine and flipped the pages. Suddenly, she froze. Her bottom jaw dropped. "I don't believe this!" she whispered. Her hand clutched Cristoff's arm. He leaned over to view the page before turning his gaze to Nicole. They looked at each other in a state of confusion, then slowly angled their vision back to the opened book. There, as plain as day, on a colorful page, stood the elegantly attired form of Shane, his hand calmly resting on the withers of a Reserve Champion stallion.

"Bless my hide!" Cristoff exclaimed in a voice full of wonder. "What's the date on this magazine?"

"Four years ago." She studied the picture. "Why did Shane deliberately avoid mentioning this to me when we talked? You'd think he'd brag to impress me, or at least offer some suggestions in the training of my horses? But, not a word... not a word was ever said about his background with Arabians."

"I have a more interesting question," pressed the ranch hand. "Why did Justin keep this information from us? He knows we're looking for a trainer." They exchanged inquisitive glances.

"Why don't you ask him, Monday morning?"

"We could call him right now."

"No, no." Nicole stroked her chin. "Give me a few days to think about this. There must be some obvious reason Justin didn't tell us."

Cristoff shut the book. "Well, we've sure struck a gold mine, haven't we? I mean, Shane is the answer to our dilemma. I doubt he'd charge you very much to work with the horses, since he likes you."

"Oh, no," stated Nicole, emphatically. "It's out of the question."

"Are you crazy? You couldn't ask for a better opportunity! He's a professional; plus, he'll probably jump at the snap of your fingers."

"You don't understand. The last time I spoke to him, we didn't exactly end the evening on a friendly note."

"So? Swallow your pride. Let's be realistic. You can't afford a high salary. Shane can be bribed."

"The answer is still no." Nicole rose from the sofa, gathering the thick magazines in her arms.

Cristoff threw up his hands in defeat. "All right. Tomorrow, you call around and find out what kind of price these other trainers are asking. You'll reconsider." He went to the door to leave. "You're making a big mistake, Nicole." She didn't realize how accurate his words were.

Nicole spent the entire next day phoning trainers, to no avail; either they were still obligated to a former contract, or their price was unreasonable. With a reluctant sigh, Nicole sat back in the office chair to contemplate other choices. The thought of hiring Shane made her bristle. Could she put up with seeing him at the ranch every day? How much conflict would it cause with Justin and Cristoff? Then, of course, there was the problem of getting enough nerve up to ask Shane. Sensing her predicament, he'd probably decline the offer just to teach her a lesson. "He'll laugh in my face," she grumbled, her eyes falling upon Shane's phone number, which Cristoff had conveniently written on her office note pad. Pushing the item aside, she got up and tended to the horses.

It was six o'clock when she finally decided to give Shane a chance. Yet, the minute she heard his voice, she became speechless.

"Hello? Hello?" called the young male, an edge to his tone.

"I'm sorry, Shane," Nicole sheepishly replied. "Did I call at a bad time? I could try back, later?"

"Who is this?" It suddenly dawned on him. "Nicole?"

"Yes," she squeaked.

Shane's voice changed into a softer, sweeter tone. "I'm surprised to hear from you. I was under the impression you didn't want to speak to me, again."

Nicole could picture him smiling arrogantly, knowing she must be desperate in order to phone him. "I'm sorry our time together ended on a rather sour note," she apologized. "I was under a lot of stress, back then."

"Oh?" His green eyes began to glitter. "Are you saying we should try, again?"

"Well, uh, not exactly. I..." It was becoming difficult to conceal the nervousness in her voice. "... I need to discuss a business proposition with you."

"Sounds important. What if I stop over so we can talk about it in person?"

"I'd prefer we meet at Holly's Tavern."

"Not a good idea, too noisy. Why don't you come over here, instead?" Nicole gritted her teeth. The last place she wanted to be was in his apartment. Yet, she was the one who needed the favor, and if it meant being alone with the randy smooth talker, she had better play the game his way.

"All right," she agreed. "Give me a few minutes."

"Not too long, though. I don't like to be kept waiting."

Nicole bit her tongue and hung up the receiver. "This is only a business deal," she reminded herself as she pulled on a tight black dress. The temptress realized she had to look her best tonight; Shane always surrounded himself with beautiful women. She had to catch his eye, had to hypnotize him with her feminine charms until he no longer could think rationally. Advancing to the mirror, she mussed up her hair so the wild waves fell in no particular pattern. Pulling the clinging dress slightly downwards, she smirked. "Okay, Mr. Anderson. I may look a little wicked, but I have a feeling that this is right up your alley." She picked up her purse and jacket, then hurried out the door.

Standing in the hallway of his boarding house, however, she almost changed her mind. She was jittery, her heart racing with anxiety. She hated doing this, hated resorting to drastic measures to acquire someone's services, someone she wasn't even sure was worth it. But it was too late now to leave, for the apartment door was already opening.

"Hello, Shane."

"Good to see you, Nicole," he purred, as her eyes met his. His appearance was striking; his emerald eyes sparkling, coal-black hair neatly styled, broad shoulders straining against a gorgeous tan velour shirt—or maybe it was just the effect of the dim light inside the room, casting a tantalizing glow upon his masculine form, reminding her how alluring he could be. Cristoff and Justin could produce the same response in Nicole, but Shane had a certain charisma, an air of mystery, which the other two lacked. He was the type of man a girl never trusted; yet, oddly enough, was always drawn to. She noticed he was staring at her also, a wistful look in his eye. Then suddenly remembering his manners, he invited her inside. As he took her jacket, Nicole noticed he seemed unusually mellow. She had never seen him so calm. His gaze was steady and deliberate, his voice now a rich timbre as he offered her a drink.

"Some wine, perhaps," she answered, needing something to quiet her nerves. She was becoming more restless by the minute.

"You've aroused my curiosity," he admitted. "I can't imagine you coming over to my apartment," he let his eyes roam up and down the slender body, "dressed like this, just to talk business." He motioned towards the sofa. "Would you like to sit down?"

"Thank you." Nicole seated herself on the plush material, inwardly fuming when Shane's gaze focused on the hem of her slinky dress sliding provocatively upwards to expose most of her thigh.

"This business must be pretty important, hmmm?" he smirked, inching closer. Ignoring him, Nicole gracefully tilted the wine glass to her lips, allowing the sweet, dark red liquid to flow slowly over her tongue. She had been in his presence less than five minutes and had already managed to arouse him. Mesmerized, Shane watched the muscles of her throat expand, then constrict with each swallow. He would have never guessed that sipping wine could be so stimulating. His mind toyed with several erotic ideas, which he quickly dismissed. Instead, he took a few strands of her long hair and wrapped them around his finger. "You're playing games, Nicole, and you know what I told you about playing with me."

"Oh, I remember," she said in a sultry voice. "You're made of fire, and I'll get burned." She finished the wine and set the glass down, feeling much more relaxed now. "So, I'll get straight to the point, Shane. I need a favor." She paused, studying the handsome face. "I'd like you to train my horses... and show them."

For a brief second, she saw apprehension flash through those lucid green eyes. Shane tossed his head back and emitted a soft rumble of laughter. "Nicole, what makes you think I can train horses?"

"I know you can," she said, doggedly. "I saw your picture in one of my magazines."

He paused, collecting his thoughts. "A friend of mine asked me to stand in for the shot. It was publicity for the horse, not me."

"Then there was a misprint, also?" she quizzed, arching a sable brow. "It definitely listed you as the stallion's trainer."

"Misprints happen."

"Not of this caliber. What is the big secret? Why didn't you tell me, Shane?"

"There was no need to. I don't train anymore."

"Why not?"

"I've lost interest."

"I don't believe you."

"You can believe whatever you want." His tone turned cold, causing Nicole to rethink her strategy. In a gesture of understanding, she reached out and touched his hand.

"I'm sure you had your reasons, Shane. I don't mean to pry. What I'm asking now is for you to reconsider your decision. I need help. I can't attract breeders when my horses have no awards."

"Sorry." Shane got to his feet. "Find someone else." He walked to the liquor cabinet, poured a small glass of scotch and downed it, then filled the glass a second time as he began to brood. Nicole's heart sank. She had to find some way to make him change his mind. Going to him, she pleaded, "Please, Shane. You're my only hope. I already contacted other trainers, but I can't afford their wages."

"I'm sure Justin would give you the money."

"I don't want his money."

Her statement made him smile. "Well, that's a first. I've never heard a woman refuse a man's money before." His green eyes studied her. "What makes you think I won't charge you an excessive price?"

"Perhaps we could strike a deal," she suggested.

"A deal?" Two black brows lifted like raven's wings. "This should prove interesting."

"I will pay you what I can afford, plus a modest share of the profits."

A sinister laugh reverberated deep in his throat. "Try again, sweetheart." He downed the second drink, then a third. It had barely fazed him. She felt those emerald eyes focusing upon her and silently cursed.

"All right," she said with much reluctance. "I'll... be your escort on social occasions."

"Hmmm."

Intertwining his fingers, Shane stretched his arms towards the ceiling, palms up, and yawned. He then casually strolled over to the large sofa, seated himself in a half-reclining position against one end, and smugly smiled the type of smile Nicole loathed. Before the words had left his mouth, she knew what was coming.

"Persuade me," he challenged, in a slow drawl.

Nicole's lips drew tight. A lump formed in her throat. Well, she told herself, what did she expect? He was a normal, hot-blooded male. She had come to his apartment, dressed like a streetwalker. Did she really think Shane would not respond?

I can do this, she silently said. I can play the part; it's for the ranch, for my future.

But as the temptress slowly advanced towards her impatient host, she became plagued by her nagging conscience. She had no idea Shane saw the struggle in her eyes. He held her gaze in a hypnotic stare, quietly beckoning, "Am I that unappealing, Nicole?", compelling her to move forward, his sensual voice lingering in the air.

"You're anything but unappealing," she admitted, sliding her hands up the strong arms to his shoulders. He had the sudden urge to pull her towards him, to crush the sexy female against his hard body, but he refrained, allowing her time to rethink her actions. For, as much as Shane desired Nicole, he could not erase from his mind the sound of her anguished cries on the day of their picnic. Her screams had revealed Philip's abuse—a topic Shane was only too familiar with. He had dated a girl with an abusive past. It had destroyed their relationship. His former girlfriend had merely tolerated his touch—intimacy had been out of the question. It had ripped him apart, knowing he was powerless against her fears.

And now, looking at Nicole, beautiful as she was, he saw the same fear. He was actually shocked when she merged her mouth with his. The girl had guts. He had simply called her bluff with his suggestive behavior, never expecting her to comply. Yet, here she was, lying softly in his arms, playing the willing servant for... what? A horse trainer?

"You surprise me," he whispered, cupping her face in his hands. He wanted to read her eyes but she avoided his gaze. Without a word she gently removed the masculine hands from her cheeks, then resumed kissing him, her tongue intertwining with his in a dance of eroticism. In the midst of the foreplay, however, he guessed her intentions: She would lead him on, waiting until he reached the peak of his frustration before she finally pulled away, promising to finish the act after he agreed to train the horses.

Rage washed over him. How could he have been so stupid?! One large hand reached up, entangled itself in the mass of dark hair and slowly pulled Nicole's head backwards until her lips were forced to leave his. He spoke now, his tone low and threatening, "I warned you not to play with me."

"I'm not playing," she insisted.

"Yes, you are. Did you really think you could pull it off? I admit you're a good actress. I just wonder how far you were planning to take this?"

Nicole held a steady stare. "I don't know what you're talking about."

"I called your bluff once; I'm going to call it again." He tightened his hold on her. "Finish what you started, Nicole."

"First, sign an agreement to train my horses."

"No."

Nicole winced. Her plan had backfired. "I see I'm wasting my time," she admitted, making a move to get up. Shane's athletic arms easily thwarted the attempt. She threw him a questioning look.

"I said," Shane slowly repeated, "finish... what... you started..."

A moment of silence passed between them. Nicole's mind flitted back and forth, sifting through attack strategies. Like a defenseless doe caught in a trap, she simply stared at the man holding her captive. Despite her previous courage and scheming, despite the sarcasm that often laced her words, Shane saw a glimmer of innocence in those large, brown eyes.

Somehow, within a fleeting minute, she had become a helpless little girl. It spoiled the game. His desire rapidly diminishing, he released her and rose from the sofa. "We both know you can't finish what you started, Nicole. In fact, I'll wager five hundred dollars you haven't been intimate with a man since Philip's death."

"Do you honestly believe I'm going to discuss my private life with you?" she hissed, walking to a nearby closet to fetch her jacket.

"I knew a girl like you, once," he absently said. "She'd been abused, too. What a pity. Never did enjoy a man's company after that."

Nicole smirked. "When I do meet a real man, Shane, my passion will ignite just as quickly as my temper."

"And what is your description of a real man, pray tell?"

The young beauty tossed a few long strands of hair backwards, thrusted her chin out and snapped, "Certainly not you." Her cutting remark did more damage than she had expected. Shane's nostrils flared angrily. What a disastrous evening! She couldn't wait to leave. With great haste, she grabbed hold of the doorknob and flung herself straight through the doorway and into the arms of Justin MacFierson, who yelped with pain as her forehead smashed his nose. For a moment both parties stood stunned, rubbing a soothing hand over injured areas, staring with righteous indignation. Nicole was furious.

"How dare you!" she accused, searching for some crime to charge him with. "How dare you eavesdrop on our conversation!"

"What?" Justin bellowed. "I wasn't eavesdropping! I was about to knock on the door; that is, until you barreled into me! No wonder women cause more car accidents." He caught sight of the short hem of her tight, black dress, high heels and smudged lipstick. A lead weight dropped into the pit of his stomach. Nicole noticed the repetitious clenching of his jaw and cleverly changed the subject, inquiring, "How did Jan do at the headache clinic?"

"Fine," Justin muttered, giving her a cold, hard stare. "She now has medicine."

"Justin!" called Shane. "What brings you here this fine evening?" His dazzling smile drew Justin's eyes to the faint trace of lipstick on his mouth.

"We already know what brought him here," scoffed Nicole. "He obviously saw my car in the parking lot and has come to spy on me!"

Fed up with her accusations, Justin decided to humor her. "Shucks!" he exclaimed in an over-dramatized voice, placing the back of his hand against his forehead to feign a swoon. "You've found me out! And all this time I thought I had covered my tracks so well. Oh! What shall I do now? Ah! I know..." He yanked her into his arms, knocking the breath from her lungs as he savagely kissed her. Then he tossed her to the side, deeply sighing, "I feel so much better now."

Humiliated, Nicole glowered. "You pig," she spat, hitting him with her purse before marching down the hall. She would get even with him later. It was bad enough he had made a fool of her, but now his laughter bounced from wall to wall as she descended the long staircase. "Ape!" she muttered, listening to his voice fade as he entered his friend's apartment.

Suddenly she stopped and turned. What excuse would Shane give Justin for her visit? Surely, Justin would ask. If Shane told him the truth, perhaps they'd discuss Nicole's offer. She tiptoed back upstairs and pressed an eager ear against the wooden door. It never occurred to Nicole she was now doing exactly what she had accused Justin of doing—eavesdropping. She considered it as merely acquiring information. Fortunate for her, the acoustics were excellent. The crisp, clear sound of Justin's voice alerted her that he had not ventured far from the door.

"You never mentioned to me that you were dating Nicole, again?" the blond quipped.

"I'm not," Shane answered. "It was her idea to meet. Care for a drink?"

"No, thanks. I want a clear head for this one. Why would

Nicole come to see you?" Justin's eyes, like slivers of blue ice, slowly chipped away at the truth.

Upon seeing the dark scowl lining his friend's face, Shane donned a cheery smile. "Lighten up, buddy. If anyone has cause to worry, it's me, not you. It seems your boss caught a glimpse of me in one of her horse magazines and got the bright idea I'd train her horses. Of course, I declined the offer."

"At what point?"

Shane appeared puzzled. "What do you mean?"

"When did you decide against her proposal—before or after she seduced you?"

Outside the door, Nicole nearly screamed with rage. She wanted to strangle Justin with her bare hands.

"I don't consider kissing to be much of a seduction," Shane cleverly replied. "That's all we did—kiss. She wouldn't go any further than that, Justin. Hell, you should know."

At this comment, Justin cocked his head to the side and doggedly studied his friend. "Know what?"

Shane laughed. "It's obvious, isn't it? She does have an uncanny knack for acting, but one look in those eyes and it was Mandy, all over again."

"She's nothing like Mandy."

"That's where you're wrong." A long pause ensued, during which time Shane approached the blond to lay his hand on his shoulder. "Justin, you're the only one I've ever spoken with about Mandy. I've been through this, remember? Girls who are like Mandy and Nicole turn out to be nothing more than a tease, even though they don't do it on purpose. They can't get over their abuse, at least not without professional help. I can't just stand by and watch Nicole rip your heart out. I know what it's like. I care about you, buddy."

Justin searched his friend's face, saw the compassion and slowly nodded. "I understand your point of view, Shane. Thanks for the advice." He walked across the room to pour himself a drink, now. Swirling the liquid around in the glass, he calmly stared at the vortex. "However, I have a different opinion of the little lady, based on my own experiences with her."

Nicole pressed her ear more firmly against the cold wood.

"I've seen her with Cristoff," he continued. "When I spied them making out, up in the hayloft, she was anything but inhibited."

"But you didn't see very much," Shane countered. "You told me they were just kissing."

Justin downed his drink, then wiped the back of his hand across his mouth. "I know a writhing body when I see one." The memory made him wince. He chose a less painful topic. "If she shows up here again to ask for your help, tell her I'll gladly pay for an experienced trainer."

"I already suggested that. She doesn't want your money. Can you believe it?"

"Well, we can't have her pestering you. She might get suspicious as to your reasons for refusing. The last thing we need is for her to start playing detective."

"You're telling me! If she ever found out about Davis, she'd probably blackmail me into showing her Arabians."

Justin's response was muffled by the ring of Shane's telephone, but it was just as well, for Nicole was so wound up at the moment she couldn't hear anything but the loud swooshing sound of her blood pressure skyrocketing. So that was the big secret! Shane had a dark past. Nicole pressed her hand to her heart, as if that would slow the rapid pounding. All she needed now was to do a little research with old newspapers and magazines at the library. How hard could that be? Lost in her thoughts, she was completely caught unawares when the door she had been leaning against suddenly jerked open. Two strong hands broke her fall, then roughly pulled her inside.

CHAPTER SEVENTEEN

"What the hell do you think you are doing?" shot Shane. His threatening glare matched Justin's, much to Nicole's dismay. Both men stood with legs braced apart, arms folded boldly across their chests. Flustered, the raven-haired beauty glanced hopefully at Justin, but found no hint of compassion.

"I... I was coming back to reconsider your offer, Shane, when I heard voices. So, I waited out in the hall."

"With your ear pressed to my door?" he quipped. "Lucky for me, I have nosy neighbors. You can imagine my surprise when the lady across the hall called to notify me of a certain young woman listening outside my door."

Nicole gave an innocent shrug of her shoulders.

"Sit down, Mata Hari," ordered Justin. "You're going to be here for a while."

"I most certainly am not! I have important things to do and—" She gasped as she was lifted off the floor like a weightless toy and plopped onto the sofa. Standing before the flabbergasted female, Justin shook his finger in warning. "Don't you dare move!"

Exasperated, Nicole muttered, "For heaven's sake! What crime have I committed?"

"Eavesdropping," he reminded her, taking great delight in turning the tables. "Something you accused me of only a minute ago!"

"I was acquiring much needed information. There's a difference." If she didn't look so solemn, Justin would have burst out laughing; as it was, he merely smiled. Nicole misread the sign and rose to leave. Both men grabbed an arm. "Not so fast," Shane said. "What did you hear?"

"Muffled voices," she lied.

"Saying what?"

"How would I know?"

"Oh, you know, all right!" interjected Justin.

"Know what?" Nicole faked.

Shane cursed and left her in Justin's hands while he paced the floor.

Nicole innocently batted her thick lashes. "I really don't understand what the fuss is all about?"

"Cut the act," Justin muttered. "It's pathetic. When you trade fighting for flirting, I know you're up to something."

Nicole gave him the evil eye, then pulled her arm out of his grasp and strutted over to Shane. "You!" she scolded, waving her finger in his face. "You have no right discussing my personal life like a tabloid reporter," she swung around to point at Justin, "and to him, of all people! Why, I've known alley cats with more manners than you. You're nothing more than vermin, you... you snake! And another thing..."

Shane listened to the shrieking, the ranting and raving, until he could endure it no longer. Covering his ears with his hands, he pleaded to Justin, "Make her shut up!" and walked from the room, at which time Justin quietly stepped forward and clamped a firm hand over Nicole's noisy mouth. Only when silence prevailed did Shane reappear, none too happy with the situation. "What are we going to do with her?" he coolly asked.

"We could tie a nice, hefty rock around her neck and pitch her into the ocean, but with all that air inside of her I doubt she'd sink."

Nicole glared. "Are you implying I'm a windbag?"

"You said it, not me; although I will admit I prefer the

more docile side of your nature."

"Quit the bickering!" Shane shouted, fed up. "I'm not playing games here, Justin. What the devil do we do with her?"

"I have a suggestion," Nicole offered sweetly, stepping towards the handsome man. "Try bargaining. It seems to me, you, Mr. Anderson, are the one who is at a great disadvantage. Now that I know you have a dark secret, it won't take long for me to dig up some old articles at the library. Our local papers usually carry horseshow information. When I discover who this 'Davis' person is, and I will, I'll solve the mystery."

"But you'll never be able to prove anything," Shane argued, to which Nicole uttered a sly chuckle.

"Money buys proof. You'd be surprised how many hidden witnesses suddenly pop out of the woodwork when a wad of cash is waved under their nose." Upon seeing the deep stain of crimson creeping up Shane's face, Nicole protectively stepped behind Justin.

Shane threw his friend a withering look. "I have you to thank for this! If you hadn't become involved with Nancy Drew here, I'd be having a peaceful evening!"

"You're the one who let her into your apartment," Justin reminded. "I only stopped by to show you my new car."

"New car?" Nicole repeated. Ignoring her, the blond continued. "So, I suggest you strike a bargain, like Nicole offered; otherwise, she'll dig up all the dirt she can find on you."

"Yes," beamed Nicole. "I most certainly will. So, will you train and show my horses, Shane?"

Shane turned to Justin. "I thought you didn't want me to handle her horses?"

"We don't have much choice at this point. But you'll have to explain to Nicole the risks involved."

"What risks?" she quizzed. "No one said anything about risks."

"Tell her," Justin relented, throwing up his hands.

Shane shifted uneasily, eyeing the curious brunette. "What the hell," he mumbled. He slid his hands inside his pockets.

"I used to show horses for the Bennetts at Enchanted Oaks Farm."

"No one likes to compete against the Bennetts," Nicole nodded. "I've read about their success."

Shane continued. "They did have one unyielding rival—Fox Run Farms. It was like the Hatfields and the McCoys, each trying to outdo the other. No stake was too high. We had just won the Regionals and were getting ready for the Nationals when Bill Davis, the trainer from Fox Run, starts threatening me." He paused. "At first, I didn't take him seriously. Then... things started happening. One morning, I found the windows of my car shot out. Another day, someone broke into my apartment. I called the police and told them who I suspected, but Davis always had a convenient alibi. Finally, a week later, he approached me with an offer."

"And you took it," Nicole concluded. "He paid you to lose the Nationals." Her sweeping gaze was filled with disdain. "How could you?"

"Yes, I took the bribe," Shane admitted, "only because I was roughed up two days prior to the offer. Four men with lead pipes proved extremely convincing. My only thought was to get out of the business as quickly as possible."

Like a candle whose flame is suddenly snuffed out with one huge gust of wind, Nicole felt her hopes rapidly diminish. This was definitely not the type of trainer she wanted. "Great," she grumbled. "I'm back to square one." She placed the tip of her finger against her cheek and pondered the dilemma. "I never guessed that competing could be so violent."

"I do miss working with Arabians, though," Shane added.

"I'm surprised," said Nicole. "Your father raised you on Thoroughbreds."

"I suppose this was my way of rebelling." He dropped his gaze to the floor. "It sure caused a rift when dad found out. He barely spoke to me."

"So why did you continue working with Arabians?"

Emerald eyes sparkled as they met hers. "There's something about an Arabian, you know? The way they hold their tails up like flags, the beauty of each fluid movement... the dished face and compact body; but most of all, their spirit. I knew an Arab once that let a two year-old put her hand in its mouth, he was so gentle. Throw a saddle on him though, and voila! Presto change-o! Instant fire. Not skittish, mind you; he just came alive with a rider on his back. He was so full of energy and fire. And smart? He could find electric fence wires on the ground before I even saw them. He saved my neck several times." Nicole noticed the whole time Shane was talking, a radiant smile magically lifted the corners of his mouth. She could see the excitement in his eyes, the same excitement she had felt the first time she had seen an Arabian in action. It softened her opinion of him.

"Come work for me," she softly said. "If you won't show my horses, at least train them for me. Please?"

He glanced at Justin. "I don't know."

The blond nodded. "She's a good boss. Besides, you told me you were bored working at the bank. I can assure you there is never a dull moment at the ranch."

"But I must tell you, up front," Nicole added, "Cristoff is the foreman. You'll be taking orders not only from me, but him as well."

Shane didn't like that aspect at all, but kept his feelings to himself. He could deal with Cristoff. What seemed more important was being able to keep close tabs on Justin's relationship with Nicole. Justin was like a brother to him. There was no way in hell he was going to let this woman destroy him. He would do whatever was necessary to keep the two of them apart. "It's a deal," he finally said, extending his hand. Nicole gladly shook it, an easy smile sliding up her cheeks. "Now if you boys will kindly excuse me, I think I'll leave you to enjoy the rest of your evening. Our work day starts at seven, Shane. I assume you'll be giving two weeks notice to your present employer?"

"Yes. But if he asks me to leave on the same day, can I begin work at Desert Wind the following morning?"

"Sure."

Pleased, Nicole said her goodbyes, then departed. Once in her car, however, a state of melancholy began to set in as she recalled the men's earlier conversation. The fact that Shane so openly discussed her inability to be intimate deeply disturbed Nicole. Cristoff had confronted her with the same accusation. Were her emotions that easy to read? What if they were right? Perhaps saving herself for the next man she married was only an excuse to avoid closeness? She needed a woman's perspective. Yes. She'd talk to Jan. Jan was smart. Maybe she could offer a more objective view?

Wrapped up in her own problems, Nicole never noticed the dark sedan following in the far distance. It turned off just prior to Nicole entering Jan's driveway. After getting out of her car, her eyes briefly scanned the surroundings. She uttered a sigh of relief. Aaron's car was nowhere in sight. "Thank God for small favors," she mumbled, knocking on the front door.

"Nicole!" Jan exclaimed, ushering her inside. "What a surprise."

"I hope I haven't imposed," the brunette replied.

"No. Not at all. Let me take your jacket. Would you like something to drink?"

"No, thank you." They both sat down on the sofa. "Justin said things went well at the headache clinic. How do you feel?"

"Pretty good. The testing was extensive but at least I have medicine now. What a relief! You can't imagine how happy I am."

"I'm so glad for you, Jan."

"You said you spoke to Justin? When was this?"

"A short while ago. Why?"

"Did the two of you go out?"

"No. Actually, we sort of bumped into each other."

"Oh." The blonde looked disappointed. "I was hoping you two were getting back together. I don't like this new woman Justin's dating."

Nicole seemed puzzled for a moment, then suddenly remembered. "Who? Maureen?"

"How did you know her name?"

"Oh, uh... Justin's mentioned her to Cristoff."

"Yeah, well, I don't like her, not one bit. She's been over here twice already."

"Oh, has she?"

"And she's bossing me as if I'm her little sister! To top it off, she has Justin wrapped around her little finger."

"Does she?"

"Yeah. She's the reason he sold his jeep and bought that new Ferrari."

"Ferrari!" exclaimed Nicole, her eyes opening wide. "And he says he's untouched by his wealth. Wait 'til I talk to him… "

"It won't do any good. He's totally smitten with her. It's driving me nuts. Can't you seduce him, or something?" Nicole blinked with surprise at Jan's candor. "Oh, sorry, Nicole. I'm desperate, can't you tell?"

The dark-haired beauty gazed at her friend with affection. She knew Jan could be trusted with the truth, so she confided in her and explained the real reason Justin was dating Maureen. However, Nicole still kept Philip's wild parties a secret from the girl, only mentioning that Justin, Cristoff, and herself were trying to discern if Daniel was the actual killer. "If Daniel ever shows up at the ranch," Nicole warned, "find Cristoff or Justin, immediately. I don't want him on my property unescorted. Actually, I don't want him on my property at all."

"What if he's innocent?" Jan asked.

"I've thought about that myself. Still, I have to take precautions. You should, too."

"This explains so much," Jan remarked. "Justin has been interrogating my boyfriends as if they were on trial. It's so embarrassing. I suppose he's just trying to protect me."

"We all have to be careful, Jan. If you notice anything peculiar, especially at the ranch, please let us know." The worried look overshadowing Jan's expression prompted Nicole to steer the conversation to a more pleasant topic. "I guess with your new medicine, you feel like an entirely new woman, huh?"

Jan's face brightened. "Oh, yes! I have a whole new outlook

on life. My future looks promising." She sighed and gazed fondly at her friend. "So many times, when I was ill in bed, I thought death was right around the corner. The pain was that bad. I'd stare at the clock for hours, waiting for time to slip by... waiting, waiting, waiting. After the second day of pain, like a miracle, the headache would finally drift away. It's amazing how your body can rebound from such severe trauma. Anyway, once the pain had lifted, I'd ease out of bed to walk to the window." Jan's face turned radiant. "And the beauty of that first day without pain never ceases to astound me. As I would look out the window, all the leaves on the trees would be such a vivid green they almost seemed unnatural. Even the varying shades of brown on a sparrow's wing were etched in fine detail, the color crisp and vibrant. Then I'd go through the house to the opposite rooms to gaze out at the ocean. I can't even begin to describe the deep blues and greens of the water, or the way its surface shone like glass when the sun's rays fell upon it. It was..."

"Like a painting?" smiled Nicole.

"Yes! Exactly! And I shall never forget it. Never." She touched Nicole's hand. "So you see, Nicole, through the tragedy of pain and suffering came a deeper perception of the beauty of life. Ironic, isn't it?"

"What I find amazing," Nicole replied, "is that you found something positive in such an experience. You're very wise, Jan. I think any man who chooses to spend the rest of his life with you will be very lucky, indeed."

The blonde grinned with pride. Not wishing to spoil Jan's happiness, Nicole decided to abandon the thought of burdening the girl with her own worries about intimacy. Perhaps some other day she'd discuss her problems with Justin's sister. The decision turned out to be a good one, for at that exact moment, Aaron stumbled into the house, a blonde-haired girl on his arm.

"I think I'll be going," murmured Nicole, getting to her feet.

"Don't go because of Aaron," Jan replied.

"Oh, please!" mocked Justin's brother. "Don't leave because of me, Cat. Can't you see I'm preoccupied?" His words were followed by a loud giggle from his voluptuous lady friend, whom he easily tossed over his shoulder like a caveman before bounding upstairs. The laughter and carryings on from up above proved too much for even Jan.

"I'm leaving, too," she said, handing Nicole her jacket.

"Want to come over my place for a while, Jan?" Then, upon hearing shrieking and more laughter, she added, "What the heck. Go grab some pajamas and you can spend the night."

"Thanks a million!" beamed the blonde as she hurried up to her bedroom. Within minutes she returned, taking some time to scribble a quick note so Justin would know where she was. Then the two women headed out the door and hopped into Nicole's sports car.

"I have popcorn," Nicole said when they pulled up to the ranch. "And, of course, you can help yourself to anything in the refrigerator." Walking towards the porch steps, she caught sight of a moving shadow near the right side of the house. Instantly, her hand grabbed Jan's and she motioned for silence. Both women froze. Glancing at the tenant house, Nicole noticed Cristoff's lights were on, so she gestured for the two of them to walk in that direction. Needless to say, by the time they arrived at their destination, neither one could contain their fear.

"Are you sure it wasn't an animal?" Cristoff inquired after bringing them inside.

"It was a person, Cristoff," Nicole insisted. "I'm positive. It was a very large person, too. Has anyone been at the ranch this evening?" He shook his head before walking to his gun collection. Unlocking the doors, he pulled out his shotgun and loaded it.

"We could just call the sheriff, you know," Nicole suggested.

"He'd be pretty mad if he had to come all the way out here for a wandering deer."

"It wasn't a deer!"

"Okay, okay. Stay here while I have a look."

Cristoff headed out the door and across the lawn towards the adjacent house, carefully searching the darkness for signs of movement. It took thirty minutes to thoroughly scan the house and barn. Once he was sure it was safe, he went back home. "Your door's still locked," he assured Nicole. "Whatever you saw is gone."

"But, Cristoff," Nicole said, "Daniel told me, himself, that he was dropped off at a distance when he wanted to gain entry onto the property. Are you positive no one was in the barn?"

"The horses would have given some indication of an intruder," he reminded her. "If you're still worried about going home, then don't."

"Don't go home?"

"Sleep over at Jan's house."

"We could do that," Jan offered.

"With Aaron and his girlfriend carrying on down the hall?" scoffed Nicole.

Cristoff looked at the two women and let out a long exhale. "You're both welcome to spend the night here and I'll stay at your house, Nicole. That way, if there is a prowler skulking around," he held up the shotgun, "he'll be taken by surprise."

"I hate to inconvenience you, Cristoff."

"It's no problem. Make yourselves comfortable." He grabbed his keys and was about to leave when Nicole stopped him. "I forgot to tell you," she said. "I hired Shane."

Cristoff glanced down at the short hem of her dress. "Did it take much bribing?"

"Justin convinced him," she replied, sternly.

"Did he mention why his experience was kept secret?"

"He doesn't like the show circuit. He is willing to train for us, though. I told him he'd also have to take orders from you."

"I'll go easy on him. Things will work out." He turned to go, calling over his shoulder, "Have fun, girls."

After the door closed, Nicole threw the deadbolt. Jan peered around at the surroundings, commenting, "He's a pretty good housekeeper, for a man. There's hardly any dust in this room."

"I've never noticed," laughed Nicole. "But then, I have a habit of overlooking obvious things. One time, Cristoff repainted the whole house a different color. I completely overlooked it. He was quite disappointed, to say the least."

"Has he ever shown you his photo collection?" Jan asked.

"What photo collection?"

"He used to be a real camera buff when he was a teenager. He has a zillion albums filled with pictures. I'm surprised you didn't know. In fact..." Jan opened a closet door. "I bet he has them stashed away in one of these closets."

"Jan! You can't rummage through Cristoff's belongings!"

The blonde smiled. "Oh, he won't mind. We're old friends, remember? Besides, how do you think he's going to amuse himself at your house?"

Nicole's jaw dropped. "Are you insinuating that he might root through my stuff?"

"Of course he will," Jan laughed. "He's probably checking out your negligees this very minute."

Alarmed at the thought, Nicole quickly put her jacket on again, saying, "Come on! I'd rather spend the night at my own house." She grabbed Jan's hand and pulled her towards the door, giving the poor girl barely enough time to snatch her own coat and purse as they hurried outside.

"I was only joking!" Jan giggled as they ran across the lawn.

"Joke or no joke, I definitely feel uneasy about having Cristoff alone in my house—not that I have anything to hide, mind you."

"You're a very private person, aren't you?"

"Aren't you?" Nicole countered.

"No. My brothers look through my stuff all the time."

"And it doesn't bother you?"

"Nope."

"Well," Nicole said, rapping on her front door before placing her key in the lock, "Cristoff is not my brother." The door swung open and they stepped inside. "Cristoff? It's just us. I've changed my mind. We're sleeping here tonight."

"Oh, okay." He was sitting in front of the television, a bottle of soda in his hand. "Are you sure?" She nodded. "Well," he said, getting up to go to the door, "don't be afraid to call me if you hear anything." As if on cue, the phone rang. Cristoff hesitated. Nicole picked up the receiver and was surprised to hear Justin on the other end. As the phone conversation continued, Jan and Cristoff waited patiently nearby, noticing the slight tremor in Nicole's voice.

"There's trouble," she said, hanging up the receiver. "Justin wouldn't go into details over the phone but he said it was urgent we all meet. He's on his way over."

"I don't understand," spoke Jan. "What kind of trouble?"

"Serious enough for him to call," Cristoff commented. "Apparently it can't wait until morning."

Jan looked bewildered. "But why does he need to speak with all of us?"

"Maybe it has something to do with Daniel," Nicole guessed. Cristoff nodded, then glanced out the window to look for headlights. In a matter of minutes, a vehicle appeared, but not the one Cristoff expected. He quickly pulled the forend of the shotgun towards him to prepare for firing. "This isn't a jeep approaching, I know that much."

"Wait!" called Nicole. "Justin bought a Ferrari. He doesn't have his jeep anymore."

Upon hearing her words, Cristoff relaxed and put the gun aside. "Good thing you told me. When did he purchase a race car?"

"Today, after we went to the headache clinic," Jan answered, watching as Nicole quickly opened the front door for her brother.

"Nice car," Cristoff called to his friend. "I almost shot you. I thought you were an intruder."

"A little trigger-happy tonight, aren't you?" Justin casually said, removing his coat.

"That's because we had a bit of excitement earlier," spoke Nicole. "When Jan and I left your place to come here, I saw someone sneaking around the side of the house."

Justin's back stiffened. The intense look in his eyes made her stomach churn. "Justin?" she half whispered, almost afraid to inquire.

"You're in danger," he quietly said. "I'm in danger." He gazed at Nicole for what seemed like an eternity before continuing. "I didn't want to alarm you, but I have no choice, now. Someone took a shot at me today, after I dropped off Jan." Justin's sister gasped, then reached for his hand. "They blew out one of my tires; either they're a lousy shot or they never intended to kill me in the first place. I've also noticed someone following me on different occasions. I decided to buy the Ferrari so I could give the culprit a run for his money."

"Then," broke in Jan, "Maureen had nothing to do with you buying the new car?"

Justin cocked his head to the side. "Whatever gave you that hair-brained idea?" His sister shrugged.

"By the way," mentioned Nicole, "I decided it was best to tell Jan about our suspicions concerning Daniel, especially since you two live and work together. It'd be difficult to keep everything a secret, plus she was upset over you dating Maureen."

Justin nodded. "I truly hoped to shield all of you from further trouble, but after I left Shane's tonight, I was followed again. Thankfully, I lost the creep on a side road. However, I've given the situation some serious thought. Tomorrow, there will be a bodyguard for you, Nicole." He held up his hand to quiet her. "It's a done deal. I don't want to hear any arguments about it. Hopefully, we won't need the protection for long. I'm also hiring security guards for the ranch."

Nicole was furious. "You have no right! This is my property!"

"Shh!" Cristoff grabbed her arm, trying to silence her. "Listen to what Justin has to say before losing your cool."

"Thank you, Cristoff," the blond said. "I'm taking a drive to Daniel's place. I'm going to lie and tell him I've decided to let Philip's murder case rest."

"But there's already an investigation into Charlie King's disappearance."

"I know, but that isn't my doing. If Daniel believes I've dropped any interest in this, maybe he'll stop sending his men after me."

"If they are his men," Jan pointed out. "You still don't know."

"No, I don't. But I'm going to assume they are, and speak with Daniel. His reaction will provide whatever proof I need." He turned towards Cristoff. "Do you want a bodyguard?"

"Don't insult me," he frowned. "I know how to shoot."

"So do I," Nicole quickly said.

Justin stared at the young beauty, long and hard. "So you do. I don't care. I'm not taking the chance of anything happening to you or my sister."

"What about Aaron?" Cristoff asked.

"Justin!" cried Jan. "What if they mistake Aaron for you?"

"I suppose I'll have to hire a bodyguard for him, too, until this blows over."

Nicole lifted a brow. "Why don't you just send him away on vacation for two weeks? It'd probably be cheaper."

"Not a bad idea. Maybe Jan would like to go with him?"

"No, thanks," his sister replied. "I couldn't stand the thought of not knowing what was going on back here."

Justin frowned. "If you insist on remaining here, Jan, I can't have you living at our house. It's too risky."

Nicole slyly smirked. "Just hire security guards. Why even stop there? Build a fortress, complete with a moat and alligators."

"I'm glad you're taking this so lightly," Justin sneered. "Of course, no one's fired a bullet at you... yet." Finally, Nicole grew quiet. Justin continued. "Since I'm suspicious of Daniel, and he works for the government, I prefer any future discussions about our situation to be done in private, not on the telephone. Even if our phones aren't bugged, the government has access to all telephone lines."

Nicole shook her head. "You're really blowing this out of

proportion, Justin. Do you actually believe Daniel thinks our conversations are that important?"

"It's his only way of keeping track of us. I think my line's already been tampered with. I called in a carry-out order for some food the other night. When I arrived at the restaurant, a man greeted me in the parking lot and issued a warning."

"What did he say?" Jan asked.

"I'd rather not repeat his exact words, but this is the reason I'm hiring a bodyguard for Nicole. He should be here by tomorrow afternoon. As for you, Jan, I'd feel much safer if you lived with our cousin for a while."

"But I have a job!" she protested.

"The ranch isn't as busy as I thought it would be," Nicole stated. "You should listen to your brother. I completely agree with him on this issue."

"Miracle of miracles," Justin scoffed.

Ignoring him, Nicole inquired, "What should we do about tonight?"

"Good question. You did say you thought someone was prowling around. Perhaps I could call the sheriff and bribe one of his men to come out and keep watch until morning?"

"Ahh. The power of money."

"And this is one of the advantages of having it," he argued.

The upper corner of Nicole's lip rose with disdain. "Save yourself the expense. Cristoff will protect me." The ranch hand proudly smiled.

"I'll stay here, too!" chirped Jan.

"No, you won't, young lady." Justin's tone was commanding. "I'm dropping you off home so you can start packing. I'll use a public phone to call our cousin before I go to Daniel's. I'll tell her there's a stalker on the loose over here and I'd feel safer if you were out of the vicinity. When I'm finished with Daniel, I'll come by to pick you up, so be ready." Jan threw her brother a mean look as she said her goodbyes to Nicole. After grabbing his coat, Justin opened the door to exit, stopped, and suddenly turned to face the raven-haired beauty. "Keep your gun with you at all times until the bodyguard arrives tomorrow."

"Justin." Her hand touched his shoulder. "I hope you are right about Daniel and he'll back off once you mention you're dropping the case. I'm sorry you ever became mixed up in all of this. I no longer care who murdered Philip. Let it go. Nothing is worth the loss of another life. If I had been close to Philip, perhaps I'd think differently."

Justin looked incredulous. "How can you sleep at night, knowing his murderer is still out there? What if he kills again? What if he killed Charlie? Don't you care about Charlie's family?"

"Perhaps Charlie isn't dead."

"We'll find out soon enough, won't we?" A touch of anger in his voice, Justin pivoted and flew out the door with his sister, leaving Nicole in a state of distress.

Cristoff quickly came to the rescue, softly squeezing her hand. "There, there. You have to forgive the harshness of his words, Nicole. After all, he was shot at today."

"That's what scares me, Cristoff," she quietly said. "I don't want to lose him. I don't want to lose you, either." She looked towards the liquor cabinet.

"Go ahead," he said, reading her mind. "Have a glass of brandy. It won't bother me." Upon seeing her reluctance, he poured the drink, himself, offering it to her.

Nicole warmly smiled. "I wonder if Justin is as nervous as I am?"

"I wonder..." echoed the ranch hand.

He wasn't. The masculine blond was too furious. He had a hundred things he'd like to say to Daniel, yet refrained, knowing self-control was the key to outsmarting the man. He drove up to the enormous iron gate and announced his arrival into the intercom, feeling an overwhelming urge to just pummel Tyler's face into a bloody mess. Upon gaining entrance onto the property, however, he calmed himself and politely smiled at the man opening the front door. "I hope I haven't kept you up past your bedtime, Daniel?"

"I think we're too old for childish banter, don't you?"

drawled Tyler, gesturing for him to enter. "I'm glad you finally decided to come clean."

"Come clean?"

"Yes. I find your game-playing very tiresome."

"Ditto." Justin searched his brown eyes, noting how different they were from Nicole's. His lacked compassion, at least for now, and exhibited a hardness often associated with cold-blooded killers. How fitting, thought the blond. "I won't beat around the bush, Daniel. I only stopped by to let you know I'm pulling out of your brother's murder investigation. I no longer have the time nor the interest. My only concern is Nicole. She clearly stated she doesn't care who murdered Philip."

"I find that hard to believe," Daniel coolly replied. "After all, she was his wife."

"Ask her, yourself. Go ahead. Pick up the phone. She practically ordered me to give up the search for his killer. So, I am. If you want to pursue the matter, however, of course feel free to do so." Icy blue eyes twinkled with anticipation as he closely scrutinized his host. But Daniel, a stoic expression on his face, simply stared back, never moving, never speaking, not even a blink. Justin couldn't help but wonder what was going through his mind.

Odder still, Daniel then took a few steps towards him, slowly walking a pattern around the powerful blond, his hands clasped behind his back. He reminded Justin of a circling vulture about to swoop down upon roadkill. "Why come to me at all?" Daniel asked. "Why didn't you just say this over the phone?"

"I prefer dealing with people, face to face. It's more personal that way, don't you think?" His humor had little effect on the host. "Anyway, there's no more need to have me followed or shot at. So do tell your men, although they did provide some rather interesting entertainment, their services are no longer required, okay?"

"And you'll call off your men, too?" Daniel countered.

Justin squarely met his gaze. "What men?"

"The ones who broke through my security system," Daniel fumed, losing all patience, "the ones following me everywhere I go. Don't play stupid, Justin. I'm not in the mood!" His voice had risen to a feverish pitch, bringing the butler quickly into the room.

"Is everything all right, sir?" William asked.

"Yes!" shouted Daniel. "You're excused, William!"

"As you wish, sir." The butler politely bowed his head and exited.

Now it was Justin's turn to approach Daniel, his sky-blue eyes narrowing. "Do you mean to tell me that you've been followed, too?"

"As if you didn't know!" Daniel sneered. "Why do you think I sent those men after you?"

"To kill me."

"If I had wanted you dead, you wouldn't be standing here now. I told them not to injure you, just scare you. Apparently, you don't scare too easily."

"I haven't hired any men to trail you," Justin insisted, adamantly.

"Well, if you didn't hire them, then..." Daniel's face suddenly paled. He nervously cleared his throat, his eyes darting back and forth across the room as his mind began to race.

"Perhaps the sheriff found cause to have you investigated," suggested Justin, watching with curiosity.

"Yes. Yes. You could be right," Daniel quickly said, a slight quiver in his voice. "Thank you for stopping by. Give Nicole my regards. Do you know the way out, or shall I have William show you to the door?" The sudden polite brush-off evoked another curious stare from the blond. Daniel was certainly in a rush to be rid of him. Stranger still, before Justin left the room, Daniel called out to him, saying, "Justin. Whatever happens, I'd never do anything to hurt Nicole. You do know that, don't you?" The words stopped Justin in his tracks. Slowly turning to face the fidgety male, he tersely replied, "Where you're concerned, Daniel, I'm not sure of anything." He then left the mansion, hopped in his car and sped down the driveway.

The instant he was gone, Daniel called William's name. "Take the suitcases," he barked, "and pack as many of my belongings as possible." He grabbed a piece of paper and a pen, hastily scribbling various names and telephone numbers. Shoving the paper towards William, he instructed, "Then call these people. Tell them I want to see them here within an hour. Tell them I'll make it worth their while. When you are finished, get your own things together, William. I'm sending you and your family on a nice, long vacation."

"But, sir—"

"All expenses paid, plus plenty of spending money. Would you like that, William?" Flustered, the butler found himself speechless. "Any island of your choice," smiled Daniel. "But you must leave by tomorrow morning. I'll arrange the flight. You just tell me where you'd like to go." Ever the obedient servant, William politely nodded. He knew all too well the sound of trouble knocking at the door. He also knew Daniel Tyler...

CHAPTER EIGHTEEN

"MacFierson, isn't it?" Dave Carraway swivelled the large office chair around until he faced the tall visitor. "You were called in on the Charlie King case?"

"Yes. Hello, deputy."

"Call me Dave. What can I do for you at this late hour?"

"I was driving through town and thought I'd stop in to check if there's been any news on the case?"

"Nope. Not a clue. I think we have your phone number on file. If I hear anything I'll give you a buzz."

"Can you tell me if you've turned it over to a special investigative unit?"

"That wouldn't be public information."

"Oh." Justin looked at the short, balding man and cracked a smile. "You guys never cease to amaze me, always one step ahead of the average person. I don't know whose idea it was to check up on Daniel Tyler, but I must say they deserve a promotion. Yes, indeed. I just came from Daniel's house a few minutes ago."

"Is that so?" Carraway gave him his full attention, now.

"The man is shaking in his boots!" grinned Justin. "The way you guys follow him around... he's ready to crack, I know it. And getting past his security system? Brilliant! I wouldn't be surprised if Tyler walked in here tomorrow morning and confessed."

"Really," drawled Carraway, leaning back in the oversized chair. "That would be quite a surprise—considering he isn't suspected of anything."

Justin held his grin. "You're joking, right?" He bent forward, lowering his voice to a whisper. "It's okay. I won't tell anyone about the investigation. I just wanted you to know he's ready to crack. You guys are doing a bang-up job!" He patted the deputy's shoulder. "Congratulations."

"MacFierson, I assure you we're not doing anything of the kind, especially not to one of the wealthiest citizens of this town. The Special Forces Unit has enough work on their hands, already. Even if we wanted to, we couldn't spare the manpower. We've been getting extra assistance from other precincts."

"Sorry to hear that," Justin remarked. "I'm sure better times are on the horizon." His smile weakened. "I didn't mean to take up this much of your time, deputy. You enjoy your evening, now." With a nod of his head, Justin turned and departed, the plastic smile slowly fading as he jumped into the Ferrari to head out to the ranch.

By the time he knocked on Nicole's door, worry lines deeply creased his brow. "None of this makes any sense!" he exclaimed, sailing past the young woman to the other side of the room. Turning on his heel, he purposely strode back, eyes fixed on the gaping beauty. "Did I say hello?"

"No."

"Then, hello." He channeled his gaze towards Cristoff, who, up until this time, had been enjoying a peaceful evening with Nicole. The ranch hand sat forward, asking, "What happened at Daniel's?"

"Not what I expected, that's for sure!"

Nicole locked the front door, then spun around. "Will you please stop pacing and tell us what's going on?"

"I was correct in assuming Daniel had me followed. His reason, however, threw me for a loop. He said he did it because I was having him followed!"

"What?" blurted Nicole.

"I told him I wasn't the one behind it. Then, his face went completely white. I suggested that perhaps the sheriff was having him investigated."

"Good guess," Cristoff commented.

"Wrong. I spoke to Deputy Carraway, afterwards. No one is checking up on Daniel."

Nicole crinkled her nose. "This is weird."

"At least this puts you in the clear," Cristoff said. "You don't have to worry about someone trying to kill you."

Justin's palm slapped his forehead. "Damn! I should have asked Daniel if he also sent the prowler that Nicole saw."

"What if the intruder I saw has nothing to do with Daniel's men?" Nicole quizzed. Cristoff and Justin exchanged worried glances. "Use my phone and call him, Justin," she suggested, which he promptly did. The butler, however, told him that Daniel was extremely busy and could not be disturbed, despite Justin's pleas for William to ask Daniel one simple question. In frustration, the blond let fly several vulgar expletives before slamming down the receiver. Throwing Nicole a sideways glance, he muttered, "Sorry," and resumed pacing. Nicole frowned, then asked, "Aren't you forgetting something, Justin?"

The blond came to a standstill. "Jan! I have to pick her up."

"But she's not in danger anymore, right? You just told us that Daniel is no longer threatening you."

"I can't trust Daniel's word, except..." He looked again at Nicole. "When I was leaving, he did remind me that he'd never hurt you. I wonder why he mentioned it?"

Cristoff interjected. "I think Daniel knows something we don't. I say, let's get Shane and Aaron to join us, Justin, and beat the truth out of him!"

Nicole folded her arms. "Oh, isn't that a typical male response!"

"Works for me," the ranch hand replied.

Justin headed for the door. "I'm still sending Jan over to our cousin's house and I'm still going to get rid of Aaron for a few weeks. Call it intuition, but I have a bad feeling." He suddenly turned. "Nicole? Could I speak to you, outside, for a moment?"

She quickly joined him on the porch, closing the front door behind her. "Yes?" He listened to her voice as if for the first time, his heart thump, thump, thumping inside his chest at the pleasant sound. Though the lighting around the house was dim, he still saw her eyes and gazed warmly into their dark depths. "When Cristoff mentioned Shane's name," he began, "I remembered there was something I've been wanting to tell you." Taking hold of her hand, he gently rubbed his thumb back and forth over the soft skin. "I don't know why I have the sudden urge to say this now, but, um... well... Do you recall the conversation you overheard at Shane's apartment?"

"Like yesterday," she frowned. "Actually, I was trying to forget it."

"Well," he continued, "those things that Shane said, about you having a problem with intimacy... I just want you to know that I don't believe it. Please don't think I agree with him. In my heart, I realize the time will come when you'll fall in love again, and when you do, I'm sure you'll be the type of wife who stays married for fifty years and has a house full of laughing children." He gradually let go of her hand. "That's all I wanted to say." Staring deep into her eyes, he was surprised to find them shimmering with tears.

"I'd like to think I'd be a good wife," she softly said. "But I doubt there'd be a house full of children."

"I'm sure you're mistaken. You'd make a great mother."

She bowed her head and half-whispered, "I can't have children, Justin." The confession was so painful she couldn't meet his gaze. Justin had to forcefully, but gently, lift her chin. The anguish in her eyes stirred him.

"Just because you didn't become pregnant while you were with Philip, doesn't mean you can't have children, Nicole."

She shook her head, dabbing at the corners of her eyes with her fingertips. Justin handed her a handkerchief. "I found out just before Philip died. He wanted a son so badly. Although I didn't enjoy most of our times together, I thought perhaps I could win his affection by becoming pregnant. Stupid, I know. When it never happened, we both visited doctors. We checked out okay, but the doctor claimed the problem was more likely to be mine. I never quite understood that?"

"I'm so sorry," Justin whispered, embracing her.

"Philip was devastated. I remember thinking he'd take out his anger on me, but he didn't. In fact, he was kinder to me in our last days together than he had ever been. He even tried to comfort me. But I felt so guilty, so depressed; I decided to arrange a visit to Maryland to see my parents. That's why I left. It was the last time I ever saw my husband alive." Composing herself, Nicole pulled away. "I apologize for blubbering like a crybaby. Jan is probably worried sick over you. You had better be going."

"Don't apologize," Justin replied, his hands lightly grasping her shoulders. There was more, much more he desired to tell her, yet he knew time did not allow it. His stomach started to burn as a dark, foreboding feeling crept silently back inside. Watching her in the halo of the porch light, she appeared angelic, and a deep longing stirred within him. He took Nicole in his arms and kissed her, his mouth pressing firmly against hers in an ardent display of passion, two strong arms enfolding her, molding her against his warm body. When he finally released her, it was not without noticing the same spark of passion in her own eyes, which made parting all the more painful. "Would you like to go with me?" he quietly asked.

Nicole shook her head. "I'm exhausted. Besides, Cristoff is waiting for me. I feel obligated to remain here."

Yet, something deep inside was compelling her to reconsider. She opened her mouth as if to say something, then just as quickly closed it. Disappointed, Justin turned to leave.

"Call me tomorrow, Justin. Perhaps we can have dinner together?"

"Sure," he replied, walking to his car. Once behind the steering wheel, however, Justin had the uncanny feeling the promise would never be fulfilled. His premonition irked him all evening, especially after Jan had been dropped off at their cousin's house.

He drove home, turned off the engine and sat parked in the driveway for a full ten minutes, trying to discern the strange sensation within him. Throughout his childhood, he had witnessed such oddities between his own parents, when one of them sensed something wrong about the other. It always proved to be a correct assumption. When his father had had a bad day at work, his mother often fixed one of his favorite meals before he came home. He and Aaron used to joke about their mother's extrasensory perception and avoid dad like the plague when they saw mom fixing one of those special dinners.

Now, sitting outside his own house, he silently wondered if this was what his mother had experienced. She had often told him to act on his intuition. "Okay, mom," he murmured. "I'm going."

The Ferrari cut through the blackness of the night like a blaze of lightning until it once again stopped in front of Nicole Tyler's house. Inside, Cristoff heard the car door slam and bolted from the sofa, gun in hand. He relaxed at the sight of Justin walking towards the steps. When he let his friend in, the masculine blond shyly glanced around the room, unsure how to explain his reason for the late night visit.

"Nicole's asleep," Cristoff bluntly said. "What's wrong?"

"I don't know," Justin replied. He ran his fingers through his thick, golden mane. "I just don't feel right about tonight. I thought maybe Nicole could use some extra protection."

Cristoff eyed the blond, warily. "Protection from whom? The prowler... or me?" His remark drew Justin's gaze like a magnet.

"Cristoff?" called a soft, feminine voice from upstairs. "Who is it?"

"Justin," snapped the ranch hand. Both men turned to find Nicole descending the staircase, her slender fingers still tying the big sash around her lemon-colored robe. Just the sight of her made Justin suck in his breath. She looked like a fairy princess floating down the stairs, her shiny black hair tumbling down her back, her skin so tan and smooth, long shapely legs extending with each graceful movement. How he envied that robe!

"Justin!" Nicole called a second time. "I asked you a question."

"I... uh... didn't hear you."

She was directly in front of him now, her chocolate brown eyes holding him spellbound. "Why are you here?"

"Um..." He searched for a reason, any reason, but found his thinking muddled by her presence.

"Extra protection," offered Cristoff, giving his friend a sour look.

Justin returned it with one of his own. "I'll speak for myself, thank you, Cristoff." Sapphire blue eyes penetrated Nicole's. "I can't give you a good explanation, except that I'm concerned for your welfare. I—"

He was stopped by Nicole's hand suddenly clutching his arm. "You feel it, too?" she whispered, her eyes widening with alarm. "You do, don't you?" He gave a slight nod.

"What the devil are you two talking about?" Cristoff demanded. "Did I miss something in the past five minutes?"

"Justin," Nicole continued. "Will you stay?"

"Yes."

Much to Cristoff's confusion, the couple embraced, arms tightly wound around each other like two long-lost lovers. It provoked his anger. "Don't feed her fears!" he accused Justin. "She was fine just a half hour ago."

"I'm not feeding her fears," Justin argued. "We both sense danger. It's best we all stick together."

Pulling Nicole away from the blond, Cristoff quipped, "Don't you see what he's doing? He's taking advantage of your vulnerability. He knows you're scared. Don't be a dope and play into his hands, Nicole!"

Justin concealed a grin. "Why, Cristoff! What an impolite thing to say."

"Yes, Cristoff!" Nicole said in a clipped tone. "What has got into you?" The ranch hand threw Justin a hostile glare, the type which said, "I know what you're up to and I don't like it, one bit!" Justin artfully flashed him a smile.

Nicole tugged at the edge of her robe to pull it tighter. She headed towards the stairs. "With both of you here, I'll have nothing to worry about." Then, glancing over her shoulder, she added, "I think," and hurried up the steps to her bedroom.

Below, both men stared at each other until Justin finally broke the silence. "I see I didn't interrupt anything between the two of you, tonight."

"I don't prey on frightened women," growled Cristoff.

"Believe it or not, neither do I. So, let's make the best of it, shall we? Any good movies on TV?" Cristoff flung the TV guide at him, hitting him square in the face.

"Sorry, old friend," he smirked, settling into a chair. Justin made no comment. The rest of the evening passed in silence.

When morning arrived, Nicole and Cristoff were up at dawn, tiptoeing through the rooms so as not to awaken Justin, who was still peacefully snoring on the living room couch. They quietly made breakfast, ate, then strolled out to the barn to care for the horses. "It's going to be a pretty day," Cristoff remarked upon seeing the vivid blue sky. "You haven't forgotten our trail ride today, have you?"

"No. What should we do about Justin?"

"Let him sleep. We can leave a note. He said the bodyguard won't be here until this afternoon. If we head out early, we'll have plenty of time to ride."

"Should I bring my pistol?"

"Naa. We'll be safe on the horses. How can anyone sneak up on us on the trail? No one even knows which way we're riding."

"True." Nicole finished feeding the horses. Together, she and Cristoff walked each animal outside to the pasture. "We can groom them after we come back."

"I suggest we bring a sandwich along. Why don't you tack up our mounts while I go home and fix the food?"

"Peanut butter and jelly, I presume?"

"What else? Lunchmeat will spoil."

"Make sure you bring a thermos of water, then."

"I will. See you, shortly." They parted company. Nicole re-entered the house to write Justin a note before saddling King Arthur and The General. Then she and Cristoff left for the trails, Nicole's pistol strapped to her waist, beneath her coat. She wasn't taking any chances, despite Cristoff's assurance of their safety. Little did she know, he was also wearing a hidden piece under his coat.

It was chilly that morning as they started out, so the horses were urged into a brisk trot to get their blood pumping. Quite a distance was covered within two hours. They slowed the animals to a walk every now and then, allowing them to catch their breath, at the same time allowing Nicole and Cristoff to study the beauty of the scenery. One spot in particular caught their eye, prompting them to draw to a halt and dismount.

"This would be a nice area to eat our sandwiches," Cristoff suggested, leading his stallion to a nearby tree. Nicole agreed. They took off the horses' bridles, slipped on their halters, attached lead ropes and securely tied them. Placing her hands at the base of her spine, Nicole leaned backwards to stretch the tight muscles. "Need a massage?" coaxed the ranch hand.

"It's not that bad," she smiled, sitting under a tall oak tree. While they ate, Nicole scanned the premises. Ahead of them lay a large, grassy area dotted with brilliant wildflowers, which continued across to the next borderline of trees. She assumed there was an opening somewhere across the field that led to another set of trails. "Have you been this far?" she asked, turning to Cristoff.

He sat cross-legged, finishing the last bite of sandwich. Briefly raising his head, he glanced around. "Yep. This is where I wanted to take you. Wait a few minutes and you'll see why." Puzzled, Nicole took a sip of water to wash down the bread, then resumed studying the surroundings. Gazing upwards, she noticed quite a few clouds had moved in over the last hour. They didn't appear to be rain clouds, though. Overhead, sparrows gathered on several branches and broke into song. "Why is it," Cristoff smiled, "the birds always seem to know where you are? It's amazing how they appear directly above us when we stop riding." Nicole simply laughed. Her laughter gradually faded, however, once the sun broke through the clouds.

Within seconds, the entire area magically transformed into a vision of paradise, the beauty of which took Nicole's breath away. Each separate group of wildflowers was illuminated with color so intense it almost hurt the eyes to gaze upon it. If she unfocused her vision ever so slightly, the grassland became an unending carpet of swirling colors. But that was only part of the picture. Across the grounds where the next border of trees began, another miracle appeared; the sun's rays filtered down from the heavens like sparkling stardust, its particles forming a glorious golden beam which highlighted the next section of trails.

Struck with awe, Nicole's eyes now focused like the lens of a camera as she mentally snapped pictures of each radiant section, afraid to lose this precious moment of artistry. "Jan's first day," she whispered, excitedly.

"What?" asked Cristoff.

"I was remembering something Jan had told me, how the outdoors looked so wonderful the first day after one of her migraines disappeared. Now I understand." She grasped Cristoff's hand. "Oh! Have you ever seen anything so beautiful in all your life?"

A wistful look passed through his eyes. "Yes," he quietly said, turning towards her. "Yes, I have..."

Still reeling from the ecstasy of it all, Nicole didn't quite catch on until she glanced in his direction. By then, it was too late. His mouth was upon hers, his tongue slowly sliding between her lips, his hands entangled in her hair. Not wishing to scare her, Cristoff gradually lightened his hold, drawing just far enough away so he could murmur, "Wouldn't this be an ideal place to make love, Nicole?"

She took tiny gulps of air. "Maybe." Her heart leaped into her throat. "For someone who is married." She winced after saying it, realizing how stupid it sounded, but she didn't know any other way to get her meaning across without hurting his feelings.

"Look at me, Nicole," he said, and she noticed his breathing was becoming more ragged. "Out here, there are no interruptions, no one to come knocking on the door, no telephone to ring. We're alone. Can't we seize the moment? When we return to the ranch, you'll have a bodyguard, security guards and who knows what else? There won't be any privacy. It will never be as peaceful as where we are now. Lose yourself in the beauty of it, Nicole. Treasure this one day."

She bowed her head and smiled, but it was a cynical smile. "You know, Cristoff, I heard a similar speech in the back seat of a car once."

"But I'm not a teenager, out for a joy ride."

"Oh, no?" She lifted one dark brow.

Anger flashed in his hazel eyes. Cristoff jumped to his feet, picked up his horse's bridle and began unbuckling the halter, unaware Nicole had followed. "I'm sorry," she said, reaching out. He pushed her hand away, continuing with the task of bridling King Arthur.

"Cristoff. Please."

He swung up into the saddle and stared down at the fretting female. "Please what?" he grumbled.

"Please forgive me. Don't stay mad."

His eyes hardened. "I'm getting a little tired of you suspecting the worst in me. You must think every man who pays you the least bit of attention is trying to get you into bed!"

"Well," she sheepishly replied, "You did ask me to make love to you."

"No, I didn't," he cleverly pointed out. "I said this would be an ideal place to make love."

"Well, you implied—"

"You assumed that's what I meant." He was grasping for straws, trying to outwit the flustered female. "I thought we could just enjoy the moment with some nice kisses." For emphasis, he added, "Don't you think I know you well enough by now to forget about asking you to sleep with me? I was only trying to be romantic, for crying out loud. Is that a crime?"

"Well, no, but—"

"Right away, you jump to conclusions! As always. Why don't you get on your horse, Nicole? I see no reason to continue this outing." Looking down at her, he could tell she was quite upset. Good! She deserved it. Any minute now, she'd be right where he wanted her—eager to make amends. Hopefully, he wouldn't have to wait very long.

"I said I was sorry," she repeated in a low voice. As the words left her lips, however, something odd occurred. A sudden feeling of panic swept over her. Cristoff saw the expression of terror on her face and quickly dismounted.

"Are you okay? Are you sick, Nicole?" He watched the color drain from her tan skin; her hands began to tremble. "Nicole?"

Like a helpless child, she stared at him. "It's just like the day of Philip's murder," she breathed, clutching his arm. "Something's happened at the ranch, Cristoff. I just know it. We've got to get back!" Without further explanation, she scooped up their belongings, tacked up The General, and mounted. Cristoff had learned over the years not to doubt Nicole's gut feelings. He urged King Arthur into a gallop. They fled down the trails at a reckless pace, pausing only long enough to give their horses their wind before taking off again. During the times they had to slow to a walk, Nicole fought to control her fears, but the fear of the unknown was always the worst type of fear for her. Unfortunately, her anxiety was sensed by The General, who pranced and fought against any restraint. It was all Nicole could do to stay astride him while they ducked low branches and jumped fallen trees.

By the time they reached home, both horses' necks were lathered with sweat. Cristoff jumped off King Arthur, handing his reins to Nicole. "You wait here while I check your house. Justin's car is gone, so at least we don't have to worry about him."

"You'll need a gun," she stated.

"I already have one." He sprinted towards Nicole's house and vanished inside. She nervously looked around. At least the stable wasn't on fire. But she noticed the horses in the pastures were anxiously walking around, peering over the fence in different directions. Not a good sign. While waiting, Nicole tied King Arthur and The General to an iron hitching post by her home and undid their saddles. After handwalking them for five minutes, she peered anxiously at her house. Cristoff had not come out, yet. What in the world was keeping him? She decided he must have used the back entrance to go to the barn so he could make sure that area was safe, too. Thus, she returned to handwalking her two stallions.

When another five minutes passed without any sign of the ranch hand, Nicole began to worry. With haste, she unbridled both stallions and set them free in a nearby pasture. Since she did not feel safe going inside the barn, she let the saddles remain on the ground. She was about to shout Cristoff's name, but her instinct warned her against it. Her heart began to hammer beneath her ribs. Oh, God, she thought, please direct me, tell me what to do! She wasn't chancing walking over to Cristoff's house to use the phone because she no longer felt secure on the property. Reaching inside her pocket, she withdrew the keys to the Shelby. She'd go to Justin's house. He'd know what to do.

Suddenly, two men wearing ski masks flew out of her house in hot pursuit. Unbeknownst to Nicole, they had patiently waited for her to release the stallions, unwilling to take the risk of her escaping by hopping astride one of the beasts. Out of the corner of her eye, Nicole saw what was coming and made a mad dash for the safety of her vehicle. She was a fast runner, something neither of her attackers had counted on, and easily reached the door handle. But by the time she jabbed the key into the lock, her luck had expired. Nicole knew she'd be caught. She quickly withdrew her pistol and leveled it at the assailants.

"She's got a piece!" came a shout. The taller of the two began to talk. "Easy, baby. We just want you to know you're outnumbered here. Both of us have semi-automatics, so there's no use getting your hopes up." Perspiration lining her brow,

Nicole crouched in a ready position, both arms extended, her hands firmly wrapped around the gun. She watched with horror as they slowly withdrew large weapons from their coats. "If you shoot us, honey, I can guarantee you won't live to see tomorrow."

"Who are you?" she hissed. "What do you want?"

They took a step forward.

"Hold it! I swear I'll shoot! I don't care which one of you I hit; it'll be worth it. Where's Cristoff?"

"If you're referring to the guy who was with you, he's alive, so is the blond." spoke the man on the left.

They had Justin, too? Nicole suddenly felt sick to her stomach. At least they had stopped moving towards her. Maybe they weren't too eager to test her shooting ability? She decided to try her luck. "Throw down your guns!" she yelled. To her dismay, they snickered. "I said, throw down—"

She was cut off in mid-sentence by a pair of gloved hands grabbing her from behind. Nicole screamed. Her pistol discharged, just as a cloth was placed over her mouth and nose. Her struggling ceased. Everything went black...

CHAPTER NINETEEN

When Nicole gradually awakened, her body ached and her stomach felt queasy. Although she knew she was lying on top of a bed, she didn't know whose bed, nor was she anxious to find out. So, she refrained from opening her eyes, choosing instead to remain very still and quiet, focusing on the events leading up to her abduction. She vaguely remembered trying to get to her car in order to drive to Justin's house.

But, even if she had made it over to Justin's house, he would not have been able to help her. He had been ambushed while she and Cristoff were trail riding, his Ferrari moved to behind the barn, parked next to the attackers' van. Cristoff and Justin had been tied and gagged inside Nicole's house. She had been caught in a no-win situation.

The young woman now focused on her present dilemma, half-opening her dark eyes. They slowly rolled from left to right, moving across the pastel painted walls to a closed white door, which she already presumed was locked. Easing her upper torso forward, she managed to sit on the edge of the bed. It was covered in a beautiful floral comforter, giving her cause to suspect her abductors did have a tiny ounce of compassion. Curious, she lifted the top of the spread off a pillow. To her amazement, gold satin sheets matched the fabric of her pillowcase, whose edges were embroidered with tiny, pastel flowers. Expensive, was the first word to come to her mind. Whoever held her captive had good taste.

Despite the nausea, she got to her feet to slowly walk the room's perimeter. She did have a window, thank God. Unfortunately, it had bars on the outside. Nicole frowned. There was no other furniture in the room except the queen-sized bed. She did find a closet but it was empty, not even a hanger dangled from the rod. As a matter of convenience, she discovered the room did have its own private bathroom, complete with a linen closet filled with towels and washcloths. There was soap, too, and a mirror over the sink. The medicine cabinet, however, was empty. Nicole groaned. Her abductor had enough intelligence to make sure there were no sharp objects she could use for a weapon. Now she understood why there were no coat hangers in the closet. She exited the bathroom and looked up at the ceiling. Two light bulbs without any glass globes would provide whatever lighting she needed. The young woman smiled. All she had to do was move the bed towards the center of the room, climb aboard, then unscrew the fixture. A smashed light bulb would provide enough of a jagged edge to neatly cut a man's jugular. So... she did have a weapon, after all.

Before Nicole could fashion a plan, however, she had to figure out how many men were holding her hostage, plus what location she had been taken to. It would be to no avail to escape, then discover she was on some remote island with foreigners who spoke a different language. I've got to think this through, she told herself, just as the sound of footsteps reached her ears. Tiptoeing to the bed, she resumed her original position on top of the floral spread, thankful the mattress and box spring hadn't squeaked, and closed her eyes. If her hearing was accurate, there was only one man entering the room. Outside the doorway, another called, "Is she awake?", prompting this intruder to bend over and lift one of her eyelids. She tried like the dickens to stare straight ahead without any movement of her eyeball, praying he'd be fooled. It must have worked, because, assuming she was still unconscious, the man's fingers moved to slowly comb through her long, thick hair.

Nicole sprang up from the bed, nearly knocking the man backwards, and grabbed his throat with both hands.

"She's awake!" he sputtered, struggling to subdue the ferocious feline so he could catch his breath. Nicole's hold on him tightened. Suddenly, several pairs of hands were pulling her off the half-choked victim. She was tossed back onto the bed, where she quickly got to her feet, standing upon the comforter so she could flee their grasp if they pursued her. But they didn't. Except for the man she had nearly strangled, the rest were quite content to stand still and chuckle. She felt like a caged panther in a zoo being gawked at by strangers.

"Easy, baby," grinned one of the five, his words giving away his identity.

"You!" she hissed through clenched teeth. "You were at my ranch." Tigress eyes darting from one man to the next, she felt all hope drain from her body. These men were built like football players! They were huge, much too big for her to tackle. No wonder they laughed at her ability to choke one of their friends. It was probably the only time a female had managed to get the upper hand with the guy. Realizing the disadvantage facing her, Nicole simmered down; she had better save her energy.

"Call the boss. Tell him she's awake," said the largest of the five. At their reluctance to move, he shouted, "Out!", gesturing with his finger until each one filed out of the room.

Upon noticing he was also going to depart, Nicole quickly called, "Wait! Who's your boss? Where am I? Why am I here?" She may as well have been talking to the wall. He turned his back on the distraught female without so much as a grunt. Nicole slowly sank down into a lotus position on the bed. Things could be worse. They could have raped her. Actually, they were quite restrained, except for the guy she strangled. For whatever reason, they had kept her alive. Although a million questions filtered through her mind, the raven-haired beauty was left with no choice but to bide her time while she waited for this so-called "boss" to materialize.

Within minutes, however, the door reopened. The largest football player had returned, an emerald dress draped over his arm. "Get a bath and put this on," he ordered, laying the item on the bed.

"Why?" Nicole asked.

"Because you smell like a horse."

She eyed this man with the close-cropped black hair and mustache. "What if I refuse?"

Two gray eyes crinkled at the outer corners. "Then we'll just have to do it for you. Is that what you want, Miss?" Furious, Nicole looked for something to throw at the ogre, then remembered the room was bare. Reading her thoughts, Old Gray Eyes grinned again, giving her a mock salute before exiting. She heard a key turn in the lock. "Creep!" she murmured, fingering the soft material of the dress. She walked inside the bathroom, ran the tap water until the temperature suited her and turned on the shower.

It was one of the quickest showers she had ever taken; she wasn't risking anyone barging in unexpectedly. After wrapping her wet hair in a towel, she searched for an electric hair dryer. There was none. "Great!" she fumed, walking barefoot to the bedroom door. The green dress she had put on was disgustingly skimpy, with an opening that nearly reached her waist. She shivered, pulling the material tightly closed over her breasts. She made a fist and rapped on the door. "Hey!" she shouted. "Any of you ever heard of a hair dryer? I need one. I'm freezing!" She anxiously waited, but heard no reply.

Nicole sat on the edge of the bed, wrapping the comforter around her to keep warm. She considered putting her dirty clothes back on, but didn't want to test the patience of her captors. Looking towards the window, she realized the sun was setting. Had that much time already passed? How long had she been unconscious? Long enough to travel to this hellhouse, she thought. So, four to five hours must have elapsed between the time she was kidnapped and the time she awakened in the bedroom.

The sound of a key in the lock broke her concentration. Gray Eyes cautiously stepped into the room. Behind him, walked Daniel. Nicole leaped to her feet. "You!" she cried, pointing a finger. "I knew this was your doing, Daniel. Did you really think you could get away with it?"

"I have," he simply stated. He could see she was madder than hell.

"Is this your idea of a dress?" she hissed, nodding towards the thin material.

Daniel brought his hand up, pretending to scratch an itch on his upper lip, but Nicole knew he was covering a smile. "My apologies," he offered. "Switch picked out the dress. I do believe it was his way of getting even with you for the nasty gash you put in his shoulder." During his statement, he gestured towards Gray Eyes, who quickly glared at the alluring young woman. Nicole noticed a slight bulge beneath his shirt at his right shoulder, and assumed that was where her bullet had grazed him when her pistol had discharged.

"I'm sorry, Switch," she politely said. "I meant for the bullet to lodge in your head."

"Why, you...!" The huge giant lunged forward, only to be halted by Daniel's swift intervention.

"You can exchange snipes later," he said, still grasping Switch's arm. "Right now, there are other things to discuss." He cautiously measured the hostility in Nicole's eyes. "Actually, perhaps we had better talk later." He held out his hand. "Here's the hair dryer you wanted. However, someone has to be here when you use it. I can't chance you transforming it into a weapon." He addressed the bodyguard. "Switch? Go find Nicole something more proper to wear." The football player grunted, then departed, at which time Daniel began to admonish the young woman before him. "I wouldn't antagonize my men, if I were you. They don't take too kindly to insults, especially from the inferior sex."

"Inferior?" scoffed Nicole.

"That's how they view you. Go dry your hair. We'll talk afterwards. You're certainly not going anywhere," he casually added, watching her stomp into the bathroom to plug in the equipment. While he waited, Daniel walked over to the bed and straightened the comforter, staring down at the satin sheets. He hoped she liked them; he had chosen them especially for her, picturing the beautiful contrast the warm shade of gold would have against her tan skin and dark hair.

His fantasy was terminated by the appearance of his bodyguard. A pair of jeans, a blouse, undergarments, and a silk nightgown were handed to Daniel for his inspection. "And these are what you found at her house?" he inquired, to which the other man nodded. The sound of the hair dryer clicked off. "Take the dryer from her and give her everything but the nightgown. I'll leave that on the bed for later." From his seated position on the bed, Daniel watched the exchange of clothes for the hair dryer take place in the bathroom. He didn't miss the slight hesitation as she contemplated using the weapon. As soon as Switch left her, she slammed the bathroom door shut so she could take off the dress.

When she re-entered the bedroom, wearing the jeans and blouse, she politely asked Daniel to make the guard leave them so they could talk privately, but Daniel balked.

"I don't trust you," he clearly stated. "Not yet, at least."

"Afraid I'll scratch your eyes out?" she smirked.

"If that was my fear, I'd have you bound and gagged. Actually, I just may consider the option."

"Beast!" she shrieked, flinging herself at the startled man. Two seconds later, her arms were painfully pinned to her sides as Switch held her in a bear hug. Daniel quickly rose. "I'll come back when you gain control of your temper," he tersely said, striding from the room. Switch stepped towards the door to follow.

"You can come back when hell freezes over!" she yelled, running after them. Blinded by her own rage, she ran directly into Switch, who hadn't quite made it out of the bedroom yet. He pivoted, placed one hand above her chest and gave a massive shove, causing the young woman to topple backwards onto the floor. Shaken, but undaunted, Nicole challenged him.

"You're not so tough, you big ape! Pushing women around is child's play. Under all that muscle you're probably a sniveling nerd. I bet you cry like a baby in the dentist chair! What kind of stupid name is 'Switch', anyway?"

The huge man kicked the door shut, turned, and proceeded towards her with predatory eyes. "Uh, oh," Nicole murmured. Instinct dictating, she jumped onto the bed for height advantage. Realizing the guard had not followed him, Daniel returned to the bedroom, only to find his hostage jumping up and down on the expensive mattress as if it were a trampoline. Switch was at the foot of the bed, ready to spring forward to nab the beauty. He would have, too, if Daniel hadn't stopped him.

"Switch! You lay one finger on that woman and you'll be out of a job!" As the giant's face turned towards his boss, Nicole seized the moment. Using a sidekick while suspended in mid-air, she whacked him in the head with her bare foot. The unexpected blow knocked Switch backwards into the wall, stunning him for several seconds. Too bad, thought Nicole. She had wanted to knock him unconscious. She watched with mild curiosity as the dazed man shook his head to clear it.

Daniel's face went absolutely white. "Jendrick! O'Hara! Get in here!" he shouted. At first, Nicole thought he had called in extra help to subdue her. She soon realized, however, the guards were not for her, but Switch. They had a devil of a time restraining him as he lunged towards her. Before they managed to push the giant out of the room, he gave Nicole a silent promise with his dark, hooded eyes, planting the seed of fear deep in her heart. Daniel proved even less forgiving, loudly cursing and swearing at her before finally storming from the room. The slamming of the door nearly broke her eardrums.

"I guess this means that dinner is out of the question!" she called after the fleeing man. Nicole pouted. Her stomach began to growl; all the excitement had stimulated her ravenous appetite. She waited several minutes before approaching the bedroom door to quietly rap. "Daniel?" she said in a much calmer voice. "Daniel? I'm hungry. Can I have something to eat, please? I'll be good. I promise." She pressed an ear to the door. Someone sneezed. "Hey," she called. "Will you get Daniel for me? I need to speak with him." There was no response, only silence. Nicole knocked on the wood again, this time a little louder.

"Who's out there? Can you hear me? I want to speak with Daniel!"

Again, no reply. Nicole grew impatient. She counted to ten, trying to suppress the fresh spark of anger, but failed in the effort. Making a fist, she repeatedly slammed it against the door. "Someone is going to hear me," she dryly remarked, now increasing the volume of her attack by also kicking at the base of the door. "Daniel!" she shrieked, amidst the racket. "Daniel Michael Tyler!" Her piercing voice echoed down the hall, prompting several pairs of footsteps to quickly ascend the long staircase. Upon hearing the key hit the lock, Nicole triumphantly smiled. She backed away from the opening door. To her dismay, Daniel was not one of the men who entered.

The first football player had shoulder-length, curly brown hair, a beard, and hazel eyes. The second one had short, red hair, a mustache, and green eyes. They were the same two guards who had restrained Switch. "Daniel and Switch left," spoke the brown-haired fellow. "I suggest you quit your screaming, or else I'll have to gag you."

"I just want some food," pleaded Nicole.

"She wants food, Jendrick!" the red-haired guy chuckled. "Maybe we should let Switch fix her something to eat when he gets back?" The two men laughed.

Nicole grew fearful. "I don't want Switch to make my meal. He'll probably sprinkle poison over it." She studied the amused males, carefully assessing their vulnerability. Choosing Jendrick, she slowly stepped towards him, saying, "Look, I have money back home. I'm sure Cristoff will send you some if I ask him. So please, would you be so kind as to fix me some supper?"

"Hear that, O'Hara?" Jendrick elbowed the other. "She's finally making a peace offer."

"Don't think Daniel would approve," warned the redhead.

"But Daniel isn't here right now, is he?" Two pairs of eyes leered at the young woman like hungry wolves.

Nicole backed away. "Forget what I said. I'll wait until Daniel returns. I'd like to be left alone, please," she stated.

"What are you afraid of, sweetie?" Jendrick coaxed, inching towards her. "We won't hurt you, will we, Johnny?"

"Course not," grinned the redhead. "We won't even leave a mark on that supple, young body." They crept forward like one huge praying mantis, forcing Nicole against the side wall.

"No way!" boomed a third voice from behind. Both men swung around to face the guard who had been posted outside Nicole's door. She groaned. He was the brown-haired fellow she had nearly strangled. "If anyone gets the dame, it's me! She owes me. You two can have her after I'm through."

Johnny O'Hara snickered. "You wimp! You couldn't even handle her when she was unconscious!"

"Why, you—!"

To Nicole's delight, a brawl ensued, providing her with ample reason to seek safety elsewhere. And she did. She flew out of the room, via the open door which was now unattended, and sprinted down the long hallway to the staircase. She had no idea where the front door was, but she ran down the steps anyway, taking two at a time, keeping a careful eye on each wooden step so she wouldn't trip.

She had successfully reached the halfway point, when she smashed into a solid brick wall. Apparently, Daniel and Switch had just returned to the house, heard the uproar, and bounded full speed up the long staircase. Needless to say, Switch had no inkling a woman would come sailing down at the exact same moment. The two collided, then rolled back down the remaining steps, landing in a tangled heap at the bottom. Daniel, who had been several steps behind Switch, had managed to turn and escape the human bowling ball heading his way. Now, looking at them, he shook his head with exasperation. To think that only a few minutes ago, he had assured Switch that Nicole would no longer antagonize the man. Daniel cursed like a drunken sailor.

Switch cursed, too, but in Spanish. He roughly shoved Nicole's leg off of his own.

"Ow!" she shrieked, hitting him alongside his head with the palm of her hand. "Wait a minute, you big oaf! Can't you see we're entwined? Why don't you just break my leg?!" He was about to voice his approval of that request, but the ferocious feline was cussing up a storm of her own, using her own vocabulary as a substitute for the more common expletives, using words such as "fudge", "darn", and "blasted". Hearing that type of talk, combined with such anger, made Switch suddenly bust out laughing. It was a deep, rumbling laugh; the kind you'd expect from a man who was six feet, five inches tall. Nicole stopped her ranting to stare at the giant.

In the meantime, the three guards from upstairs quickly descended the steps. By the looks of them, Daniel already knew what had happened. "I can't believe the three of you could not guard one, single, slender female!" he growled. "I will have your last paychecks ready for you by tomorrow morning." The trio simultaneously glared at Nicole, who by now had finally disentangled herself from Switch. Since there was no chance for escaping at the present time, the raven-haired princess simply stood and straightened her clothes, as if nothing unordinary at all had occurred. She even had the nerve to stare Daniel straight in the eye and announce, "None of this would have happened if you had just fixed me something to eat before you left."

Daniel could not believe his ears. He slowly walked towards the brazen female, several methods of torture forming in his mind. "There will be no food for you, tonight," he quietly hissed through clenched teeth. "There may not be any breakfast for you, either!"

"But," Nicole protested, "you promised Justin you wouldn't hurt me."

"That was before I found out what a little hellion you are. Now go back upstairs and get in your room." He turned to the only bodyguard left he could trust. "Switch? Make sure she obeys."

"I don't want him near me!" Nicole vehemently protested. "Where's the other guy... the fifth abductor? Let him be my guard."

"You're in no position to issue orders!" Daniel barked. "Damn it, Nicole! You're enough to drive a man insane!" It was obvious by the quiver in his voice, Daniel had lost it. He pointed one, shaky index finger at her and threatened, "Get up those damn stairs before I do something I'll regret!"

Taking the cue, Nicole fled. She ran inside the bedroom, slammed the door shut, and flung herself on the bed to cry. Darkness had settled in, but she no longer cared. She was tired and hungry and miserably unhappy. Picking herself up off the comforter, she went into the bathroom. There, she used the toilet paper to blow her nose. At least her tantrums had worked. She had irritated Daniel to the point where he'd probably be happy to get rid of her. How he'd get rid of her, was the only question. If he had wanted her killed, he certainly could have done it by now.

She walked back to the bedroom, her gaze falling upon the silk nightgown still laying on top of the bedspread. She tossed it onto the floor. She'd sleep in her clothes, tonight. Pulling the top sheet and comforter back, she noiselessly slipped into bed. Cramps stabbed her abdomen. The spill she had taken down the stairs only aggravated her hunger pains. Her head hurt, too. Tears filled her eyes as she stared up at the ceiling. "Oh, God," she whispered. "Please let Justin and Cristoff be all right." She thought of this morning, how she and Cristoff had visited that one special place on the trails where everything looked like paradise. She longed for the tranquillity. If she had it to do over again, she would have stayed there the whole day, just feasting her eyes upon the beauty of her surroundings. If she had it to do over again, she'd let Cristoff kiss her, passionately. She wouldn't find fault or criticize. She'd enjoy the romantic moment.

And Justin... She'd never have left him alone in her house, alone to face Daniel's men. She wondered what he was doing at this very minute, if he was thinking of her, trying to plan her rescue. She could picture him hiring a whole posse to find her. The thought evoked a smile. Nicole turned onto her side and slowly drifted off to sleep.

At least, that was what Daniel assumed when he opened the door two hours later. The room was pitch black. Instead of throwing on the overhead light, which might blind Nicole, he made his way to the bathroom, half-closing the bathroom door after flipping the bathroom light switch. It produced just enough light so he could easily see his surroundings. Motioning to Switch, he led the way over to Nicole's bed. Since she was mumbling out loud, he supposed she was talking in her sleep. He sank down on one bended knee and brushed the soft skin of her cheek with the back of his hand. With her dark hair fanning out across the gold satin pillow, she looked exquisite. "Nicole," he whispered in a kind, gentle voice. "Wake up, my dear." He suddenly realized she had been awake the whole time—the words being mumbled were nothing more than fervent praying. Still, she would not acknowledge him.

"Nicole," he tried again, this time, stroking the long, black hair. "God is not going to come to your rescue." He slowly shook his head. "Praying is useless."

"It brought me food, didn't it?" came the wry reply, for Nicole could smell the wonderful aroma floating in the air. She could also smell the strong odor of bourbon on Daniel's breath, reminding her that he was not immune to bouts of drinking.

"I've brought you dinner... beef stew." She eyed him, suspiciously. "There's no catch," he quickly said. "You need to keep your strength up." He turned his head to the side. "Leave us, Switch. I think she's too weak to fight right now." The guard hesitated, his eyes locking with Nicole's. Those gray eyes spoke a thousand words, none of which she liked. He was silently threatening her, again, she was sure of it. Even when the big-boned male had departed, she unconsciously shivered from his icy stare. "Come on, Nicole," Daniel coaxed, helping her to sit up. "Eat your food." He brought the tray closer, frowning when she blessed herself to say grace. When she was finished, he pointed to a crystal glass. "Brandy."

"What did you put in it?" she dryly remarked. "A little something to relax me, perhaps?"

His expression darkened. "No. But I can, if you so desire it?" Ignoring him, she took a bite of stew, savoring the rich flavor. "I will do what I have to in order to keep you safe, Nicole."

"I don't like the sound of this conversation," she said, swallowing another bite. "And I don't know why Switch has it in for me."

Daniel's voice took on a grave tone. "You can't imagine why he despises you, barring the fact that you've shot him in the shoulder, kicked him in the head, and knocked him down a flight of stairs?"

"He deserved it," she nonchalantly said, "except for the episode on the stairs… that was his own sheer clumsiness."

A low, cynical chuckle sounded in response. "You do think highly of yourself, don't you, Nicole? This arrogant attitude of yours is making a dangerous enemy. Even I don't cross Switch's path. If you continue this crusade of self-destruction, I will most assuredly take measures to stop you."

Nicole threw him a hostile look. "Why don't you just kill me, Daniel, and get it over with? I'd much rather be dead than spend my time with the likes of you."

The cruelty of her words hit him a stunning blow. The 26 year-old stared incredulously at the female before him. And then Daniel did something he had never done before in his entire life.

He struck a woman.

It was a deliberate, vicious slap, snapping Nicole's head sideways. Yet, as his opened palm cracked against her cheek, he instantly regretted it. The bourbon had weakened his self-control, leading him to violence. Not only furious with her, but himself, as well, the wealthy man quickly strode out of the room to prevent any further conflict.

Inside the dimly lit prison, Nicole sat quietly on the bed, not a whimper, not a moan, nor an anguished cry from the stinging of her flesh. A sudden loss of appetite caused her to place the tray across the room. Then, climbing back into bed, she curled into a ball, tucked the covers under her chin, and stared numbly into space until sleep eventually claimed her.

It was just after midnight when she felt the mattress sink considerably. The tip of a steel blade pressed lightly against her lower spine as she lay on her left side. Then the voice, the voice she dreaded, whispered softly in her ear, "You wanted to know why they call me 'Switch'? It's my blade, sweetheart, my weapon of choice." For emphasis, he gave her a tiny poke with the tip, making her wince. She was glad he didn't have the satisfaction of seeing her reaction.

"What do you want?" she quietly asked.

By now, he was smack up against her, the heat from his body like a blazing furnace. "Let's start with an apology."

"Fair enough. I'm sorry. Now leave me alone, before I scream my head off."

"Go ahead," he replied in a low voice. "Daniel is dead to the world from booze. The only other person who will hear you is Downing and he wouldn't dare tangle with me." His free hand moved her hair away from the nape of her neck as his hot mouth caressed the newly exposed skin. Nicole shivered. He playfully bit the back of her neck, briefly pressing his teeth into the soft flesh in a sensual, primitive way. "You're going to learn not to mess with me, princess. Most women learn right away, but you... no, you have to learn the hard way, don't you?"

Nicole was mildly surprised to discover her fear had vanished. In fact, the numbness she had felt earlier still prevailed, prompting her to coolly say, "Cut the sermon, Switch. If you're going to rape me, then let's get it over with."

"You don't fool me." He was grinning, still nibbling on her neck. "You're scared witless."

"That's quite some power trip you're on," she muttered. "I'm not scared at all. If you knew my past history, you'd realize there isn't anything you can do to me that hasn't been done before. I've been raped, exploited, institutionalized, knocked senseless, even beaten with a horse whip."

He smirked. "Nice try, but I ain't buyin' it."

"Then I'll prove it to you," she flatly said. "Run your hand across my lower back."

He hesitated, finding this a rather unusual request. She was the craziest dame he had ever come in contact with, that was for sure. To speed things along, Nicole reached back, took hold of his one hand, then guided it to the proper area. Switch suddenly stilled at the touch of the long scars beneath his fingertips. He estimated them to be about eight inches in length. He grew quiet, extremely quiet, as he tried to fathom why someone would do such a cruel thing to her. Then he remembered her foul temper. Finally, he said, "I guess you pushed one of your enemies a little too far."

"Not an enemy," she corrected. "My husband. I wasn't feisty then, either. I was quite the submissive, attentive wife. A lot of good it did me..." Her voice trailed off, bitterness, sorrow lacing her words. The distinct click of a retracting switchblade sounded from behind, yet, oddly enough, she felt no relief. Nicole felt nothing at all, just the same cold numbness spreading like cancer inside her.

Placing one hand on his victim, Switch gently rolled the young woman onto her back, his own body still beside her, propped up on an elbow. Nicole looked over at him, very calm, very serene. "Is Daniel... going to kill me?"

He heard the question, but chose not to answer. Instead, his finger lightly skimmed the bridge of her nose, then slowly traced the outline of her rose petal lips.

"I understand," she sadly said. "You're loyal to your employer."

"And your men are loyal to you," he wanted to say, recalling how difficult it had been to subdue Justin and Cristoff. "Loyal" was not the word. Her men were absolutely devoted. But Switch kept quiet, not wishing to remind her of any other man right now. He suddenly swooped down on her like a bird of prey, as if he would devour her, alive. His move had been anticipated; Nicole quickly rolled to the side. The switchblade clicked open again as a rough hand firmly jerked her back. "No games," he said. "This can either be pleasant or unpleasant, the choice is yours."

She answered him by slamming her knee into his groin. Switch gave a guttural howl. In an instant, her fingers wrapped around his in an attempt to gain control of the knife. But she was no match for him. The powerful giant quickly recovered to render her absolutely immobile. She was pinned to the mattress now, the tip of the knife against the pulsing artery of her throat. "If Daniel doesn't kill you," he breathed, "I surely might."

"Then do it," she spat, "and put me out of my misery." She held her breath and waited, expecting to feel the sharp stab of the blade. She even closed her eyes and silently whispered one last prayer.

But her courage fascinated Switch. He hesitated, staring down at her, immersed in his own thoughts and feelings. His thoughts went to the scars on her back, the words she had said, and suddenly his mind beheld the face of his own mother, bringing back a memory he had tried to forget for over 20 years. He was only a child then, a child who had ventured from his room upon hearing his mother screaming and crying. To his horror, there stood his alcoholic father, beating her senseless. To a young boy who loved his mother dearly, this was the worst thing imaginable. Hatred festered inside him from that day on, hatred for anyone who abused women. And now... now as he looked upon Nicole on the bed, he discovered he was no different than all the other males who felt it was their right to do as they pleased to a female. The realization of his actions began to make him feel sick.

A familiar, delicate sound jolted him back to reality... the sound of a gun being cocked.

"My, my," drawled Daniel from his position at the foot of their bed. "Isn't this a cozy arrangement?" His murderous glare ricocheted from Nicole to his hired man. Switch instantly rolled off her and sat up. Nicole, now relieved of his weight, lifted herself to a sitting position, also. With the gun's barrel leveled at Switch's chest, Daniel sternly addressed Nicole. "So, you managed to get three of my guards fired and now you've snagged the fourth."

"She was cold," Switch lied. "I was only helping to keep her warm. It's not what it looks like."

"I bet," snarled Daniel. He uncocked the gun, placing it in the waistband of his pants. His cold eyes flickered towards Switch. "Get out of her room. We have some things to discuss, you and I." Daniel then headed for the doorway, but suddenly turned back to face the two of them. A lecherous smile curled his lips. "Oh, and, Nicole? I'll make sure there will be someone to warm your bed from now on."

"I wouldn't be so anxious, if I were you," she snapped. "Pillows make wonderful weapons of suffocation." Her remark hit the spot. Daniel's smile quickly vanished. He stormed from the room in a fit of temper. Switch had jumped out of bed, and was about to join Daniel when he suddenly stopped in mid-stride to turn towards Nicole. Gray eyes focused briefly on the beautiful woman in bed as the moonlight through the window illuminated her face. Something caught his attention. He looked again, this time studying her more closely as he advanced. He took hold of her chin, tilting her face a different angle.

"You have a slight discoloration covering this whole cheek," he commented. "Someone hit you." His expression turned to stone. "Who?"

"I thought you heard," she replied. "I thought you were outside my door." The shadows on his face shielded his expression of disgust. Nicole felt something change between them in that moment. Did he suddenly have some respect for her? Or pity? She took a chance, quietly pleading, "I need you as an ally, Switch. Don't jeopardize my safety. If you're fired, I'll have no one, no one... I can pay you, I have money. I'll reward you if you let me go. Are you listening to me?"

With a grunt, he turned and marched from the room. Nicole was never any good at interpreting grunts and this one was no exception. If he had been able to violate her, his emotions could have become involved, then he might begin to feel protective towards her. But try as she might, Nicole could not fight the repulsion at the idea. She couldn't give herself to her abductors, not even to save her life. She had had enough abuse already. But, perhaps... if she played her cards right, maybe she could manipulate the big ogre. It was worth a try. She thought about it before falling back asleep.

CHAPTER TWENTY

When dawn bathed the room in warm rays of light, Nicole pulled herself out of bed to take a hot shower. To her dismay, she discovered several more bruises on her arms and legs from her fall down the stairs. Stepping into her clothes from yesterday, she yearned for freshly laundered attire. Now came the hair dryer problem. She rapped on the bedroom door. "I need the blow dryer," she called. "Is anybody out there?"

"Just a minute," came a gruff reply. The door eventually opened and the last football player stepped through. He was approximately her height, with long, light brown hair gathered into a ponytail, and olive eyes. His face wore no expression as he handed her the instrument. Trying to be polite, Nicole muttered, "Thank you," before heading into the bathroom. The guard followed, then watched as she proceeded to dry her hair. Nicole decided to ignore him. But when a noise sounded inside the bedroom, prompting the guard to look in that direction, she swiftly cracked him on top of the head with the dryer and ran. Assuming the noise they had heard in the bedroom was Switch bringing her breakfast, she had no qualms about her malicious attack upon the fifth guard. She assumed Switch would not thwart her attempt to escape.

But Switch was not in the bedroom.

Daniel was. What's more, he had witnessed the whole

charade. It was bad enough he had a hangover this morning, but having Nicole irritate him only fed the raging monster within him. "Oh, that was good!" he sneered, advancing towards the startled female. "That was very good, Nicole. Now see if you can get past me!" he viciously taunted, beckoning with both hands. Inside the bathroom, Nicole's victim came out of his daze.

"You win," she quietly said, her eyes never leaving her enemy. "I give up."

"You never give up," he hissed like a snake. "I know you too well." Staring over her head to his guard, he called, "Downing, get me the cuffs. I've had enough aggravation for one morning."

"No, Daniel! Please don't! I'll be good. I promise!"

"Of course you will," he grinned. "You'll have no other choice."

Frantic, Nicole considered fighting him, but quickly gave up the idea when she remembered Downing would come to his rescue. Perhaps Switch would restrain Downing? "Where's Switch?" she quizzed.

"Out, running an errand." He hardened his eyes. "I wouldn't count on his help, if I were you. As long as I have the cash to pay him, his loyalty is bought. And I have plenty of money, Nicole... lots and lots of it. I can keep you here for several years, if I so decide."

"But why?" she argued. "Why am I here, at all? How does this benefit you, Daniel?"

"The less you know, the better." His words stopped abruptly at the sight of Downing. "Cuff her hands behind her back." Expecting a struggle, the guard was relieved to find his victim cooperative.

"What do I do when I need to use the bathroom?" she inquired.

"You'll have to call one of us, but don't expect anymore hair dryer privileges."

"Will you at least give me some socks and shoes? Going barefoot makes me cold."

"No shoes; they can be used as a weapon. Perhaps slippers, if you're a good girl," he flatly replied. "I may even give you breakfast and a change of clothes."

"You can't be enjoying this, Daniel," she reasoned, noticing the dark circles under his eyes. "I'm sure you realize Justin will hunt you down."

"Maybe. He also may tire of spending money to look for you. It's not like you're his wife, my dear."

"How did you find out?"

"There was no marriage license drawn up."

"He'll rescue me," she vehemently stated. "I'm sure your name is on the deed to this house."

"Wrong. I'm not that stupid, Nicole. I'm borrowing this place from a friend who owes me a favor."

"A friend who puts bars on the windows?" she scoffed.

"I had that done prior to your arrival."

"So this was planned ahead of time, because you couldn't have had the work done on the window in just the past 24 hours. How long have you been planning my abduction?"

"Enough questions." He turned to leave.

"Justin will find me!" she called to his back, satisfied that his responses proved Justin had not been seriously hurt. He must be alive. That was good; that was very good!

When Switch appeared an hour later with breakfast, Nicole wanted to shout with glee. "I'm so happy to see you!" she grinned, watching him carefully place the tray near the bed. She turned her back towards him, waiting to be uncuffed.

"Aren't you hungry?" he asked.

"I'm starving. Hurry and get these things off me." She jiggled her hands with anticipation. The food smelled delicious.

"The cuffs have to stay," he announced, to which Nicole abruptly whirled back around.

"Why?" she demanded.

"Orders."

Their eyes locked for a few seconds. Nicole noticed the same coldness in their depths she had first seen upon her arrival. Her heart sank. Slowly, she sat on the bed. Daniel had been right. Switch's loyalty went to the highest bidder. The large guard jabbed a fork into some scrambled eggs, then placed it in her mouth.

"This would go a lot faster if you undid my hands," she bribed. "I won't say anything. You can just recuff me when I'm finished eating." Switch remained quiet, concentrating on getting the task over with as soon as possible.

Nicole changed her tactic. "My friend, Justin, is loaded with cash. He's very wealthy. I'm sure he would double whatever Daniel is paying you, if you'd help me escape. His phone number is 555-2139. Call him."

"Is that why you date him?" Switch snorted. "Because he's rich?"

"I'm not dating him," she protested.

"Then, why would he pay me to bring you home?"

She squirmed nervously. "Because he wants to date me," she finally said.

"Uh, huh."

It was the "uh, huh" that alerted her to his suspicions. "Really!" she insisted. "Justin is a nice guy, but we're not an item."

"Then, why was he sleeping on your couch?"

"Couch, not bed," she pointed out. "He had suspected Daniel was up to no good. Justin was afraid to leave me alone. He and Cristoff spent the night."

"Daniel's pretty wealthy. I doubt this friend of yours can meet my demands. He may even set me up."

Nicole felt all hope vanish. "Then do me one, small favor, Switch? Would you call Justin to make sure he's alive?"

"Oh, he's alive."

Nicole's eyes widened. "You've seen him?"

"I didn't say that. Look. Finish this last bite of toast. I've got to get out of here." She tried questioning him further, but he gave her the cold shoulder. Not knowing when she'd see him again, she tried one last time to fashion a plan. "Switch," she called. "Let's use a special signal between us." She paused, then said, "Scratch the top of your head when Daniel is out of the house. That way, I'll know only Downing is left on guard duty, besides you, of course."

Switch's next words were chillingly cold. "What makes you think I'll let you escape?"

Nicole blinked in surprise. Without another word, the tall man exited the room.

Nicole began to fret. "I've got to stay calm," she repeatedly told herself. "Think, Nicole. Think." She sat on the edge of the bed for a few moments, pulling against the handcuffs. It occurred to her that she might be slender enough to slip her hands through them. The effort soon proved to be painful and futile. "Maybe with a little soap?" She walked into the bathroom, positioned herself so she could turn on the faucet, then wet a bar of soap and rubbed it all over her hands. As luck would have it, Switch entered the room at that precise moment.

"I could have saved you the trouble," he announced, startling the young woman so badly, the bar of soap tumbled to the floor. He bent down and picked it up. "Turn around."

Still thinking of Switch as her friend, she obeyed without a peep. He rewarded her by unlocking the handcuffs. "Thank you," she smiled, facing him again.

"Rinse the soap off your hands," he commanded. Nicole noticed his tone was indifferent. There was no warmth in his eyes, no friendliness at all. She quickly did as she was told, then dried her wet hands on a towel. "Did you call Justin?" she asked, wondering if this was what brought about the change of events.

"No."

"But, I don't understand...?" Her words fell on deaf ears. Switch swiftly strode out of the room, cuffs in hand. As the bedroom door shut, she heard the all too familiar sound of the key turning in the lock. Perhaps he would return later and unlock it for her? Nicole smiled. Yes, that was it! Daniel must be leaving the house soon; when he did so, Switch would return to help her escape. She prayed he'd bring her her gun. The raven-haired princess beamed with excitement. Then she looked down at her feet. She still had no socks or shoes. "Well,

I've got to have socks and shoes if I'm going outside," she mumbled. She'd have to ask Switch to bring them when she saw him next time.

Her chance came within ten minutes. Shouting and cursing drew Nicole's attention towards the closed door. An argument was ensuing, a very loud argument. Male voices lingered downstairs before advancing up to the echoing hallway. There was more swearing, mostly from Daniel, as the men neared her bedroom. What on earth? thought Nicole, just as the door swung open, nearly hitting her, and Daniel was shoved through the opening, his hands cuffed behind him.

Nicole whooped with joy! A timely, sarcastic laugh bubbled up from her throat at the turn of events. "How does it feel?" she taunted, grinning from ear to ear. Without waiting for a response, she ran to Switch and embraced him. "Thank you! You won't regret this, I promise! Justin will pay you handsomely for your good deed."

Daniel gave a pathetic laugh. "Poor Nicole! Do you honestly think Switch did this for your benefit?"

Nicole's arms instantly dropped to her sides. She retreated a few steps to study the guard's face. It was expressionless.

"Do what you want to him," Switch flatly said before turning to exit the room.

Panic seized Nicole. "Wait!" she called, running to the door. "Switch! Please! I don't understand..."

Behind her, Daniel shook his head. "You are so naive, Nicole."

She pivoted, threw him a contemptuous look, then marched over to where he stood. "What's going on, Daniel?"

"You really haven't a clue, have you? I suppose it's time to enlighten you. Shall we sit?" Depressed, Nicole took a seat beside him on the bed. He looked worn, aged and tired. "I brought you here for your own safety," he began. "I have some enemies who are searching for me. I knew I had to leave the area and I was afraid they'd come to you to extract information."

"Why me?" Nicole quizzed.

"Well, they know Maureen has no further contact with me. You are still a relative. The men were tracking me, so I assume they knew I visited you."

"Who are these men?"

"I can't tell you, Nicole. If we should manage to get out of here, it'd be better if you weren't too informed."

"Better for me?" she dryly remarked. "You mean, better for you." She studied her brother-in-law, her dark brown eyes narrowing. "You've left out an awful lot of details, Daniel. You had planned to bring me here."

"For your own protection," he re-emphasized.

"Justin had hired a bodyguard for me. He was to arrive the same day I was kidnapped. There was no reason for you to snatch me off the ranch. How long did you intend on keeping me holed up in this joint?"

"Not long," he said. "I had already decided we would start a new life, with new identities, somewhere overseas."

"Together?"

"No. We'd have our own separate lives."

"I doubt it. You'd have to check up on me from time to time, just to make sure your enemies hadn't pinpointed my location. What did you do to anger these guys, anyway?"

"It's none of your concern."

"When I'm involved, it is my concern!" Silence passed between them. "Justin said there was a government connection." Nicole's eyes suddenly widened. "Daniel, did you embezzle money?"

"Of course not," he frowned. "I was rich even before Philip left me most of his wealth. There's no use guessing at the reason, Nicole. I told you you'd be better off not knowing. You'll be in less danger, that way."

"Oh, sure," she scoffed. "For all I know, you'd probably have dropped me off on some deserted island. I can't believe you thought we could assume new identities!"

"It would have worked, Nicole," he stated firmly. "If only Switch hadn't..." His voice trailed off, leaving the sentence unfinished.

"Hadn't what?"

He nervously glanced around the room. Sadness crept into his voice. "You're in more danger now than before, I'm afraid."

"What's that supposed to mean?"

Daniel sucked in his breath, trying to figure how to lessen the blow. "Before I left to come here, I closed out all my bank accounts, then reopened them in this area under a false name. I even had a special ID card made up."

"So?"

"Switch has one, too. He's been doing all my banking transactions. I wear a blond hairpiece if I go out of the house so I match the picture on my identification card. Since I'm still scared of being tracked, I figured it would be to my advantage to stay inside the house as much as possible. I simply sign my name to all the financial transactions and let Switch do the rest. I never guessed he'd double-cross me. I've known him for years."

Elbows on her knees, Nicole placed her head in her hands. "And you called me naive?"

"Nicole," he gazed at her with compassion, "I don't know how best to say this, but... I'm afraid you're going to be killed."

She instantly stiffened.

"They have no need for you," he explained. "You can identify them."

"Them?"

"Switch and Downing. They've joined forces."

"Now that they have your money, they have no need for you, either," she pointed out.

"But they do. If they withdrew my entire account, it would certainly draw attention. The bank would insist I show up, in person. It would prove risky for Switch to hold a gun on me in a public place. So, they're extracting my wealth, a little at a time, until they come to a decision on a final plan. If Switch decides to take up residence in another country and has a plane waiting, he can then force me to the bank to close out the accounts, grab the cash and run if anything goes wrong."

Nicole didn't like what she was hearing. It made sense.

Still, she shook her head, refusing to believe the obvious. "Switch won't kill me. He doesn't have the heart to do it."

She changed the subject. "Did you kill Charlie King?" Upon seeing his confused expression, she added, "The detective, Daniel. Justin hired him, remember?"

"Oh, yes, I remember now. Was he found dead?"

"He's missing."

Sadness crept into his eyes. "Probably the work of my enemies."

"But why? Charlie was on a mission for me, not you."

His gaze pierced her. "Was I part of your little investigation?" Nicole hung her head. "Well, then. Mr. King is probably dead. I assure you, though, I had no hand in it." She stared at him, her dark brown eyes full of questions—questions she no longer had the courage to ask.

"I don't want to discuss this anymore," she numbly said. "I have to plan my escape. Where are we, Daniel?"

The 26 year-old hesitated. "In a secluded area in West Virginia. We're surrounded by forest, except for a dirt path that leads out to the road. The nearest neighbor is miles away, I'm afraid." His expression turned to one of hope. "I'll do whatever it takes to help you, Nicole."

She rolled her eyes. "Now he says it! Where is my gun and the rest of my clothing?"

"The gun is in my desk drawer in a blue-colored bedroom, two doors up. Your clothing is in the same room, in a closet."

"Where are the keys to your car?"

"Also in the desk."

"Give me your shoe."

"What?"

"I said give me your shoe." She bent down, taking it off his foot. Filled with curiosity, Daniel looked on as she went inside the bathroom to begin wrapping a towel around the mirror on the front of the medicine cabinet. Swinging open the cabinet door, she took another towel and carefully covered any bare spots of glass. Taking a firm hold of Daniel's shoe, she smacked the heel against the center of the covered mirror. The linen cleverly muffled the sound. Nicole hit the object again, just to make sure it had broken. She then carefully unwrapped the towels, her slender fingers delicately choosing one, large sliver of triangular glass from the shattered pieces.

"Nice going," Daniel commented. He watched her place the filled towels in the closet. "Don't you think they're going to notice the missing mirror?"

Coming out of the bathroom, she half-closed the door, answering, "Not until it's too late." She held the piece of glass with a small hand towel. Daniel gulped, realizing it could have very easily have been his throat she had planned to slash, instead of the guard's. He was in awe of her ingenuity. "I was going to use a smashed light bulb," she added, "but it wouldn't prove as effective." She faced him. "Switch does have a gun on him, doesn't he?" Daniel nodded. "And Downing?" He nodded again. "Before I launch my attack, I'd like you to answer a few questions, Daniel." She saw him clench his jaw.

"Daniel, Justin and I know there is no Dr. Bohman. Why did you say there was?"

"There was," he insisted, a slight tremor in his voice when he noticed Nicole's eyes darting from him to the long sliver of sharp glass. Like a pro, she placed the tip against his cold, sweaty neck. "Okay," he relented. "There was no Dr. Bohman. I made up the name."

"Why?"

"Shh! Someone's coming," he whispered.

Upon hearing footsteps, Nicole quietly placed herself behind the door. The next few seconds felt like eternity while Nicole patiently waited for her captor to step past the entrance. Murder, even as a means of self-preservation, did not leave a pleasant taste in her mouth. A zillion thoughts raced through her brain as she contemplated her actions. What if she missed? What if she only wounded the man instead of severing an artery? After all, he did have a gun. Perhaps Daniel had been wrong. Perhaps Switch was going to release her. She felt sure he did care about her. But did he care enough to trust her? Questions, questions, and more questions flickered in and out of her mind, causing the young woman to hesitate as she stood poised to strike.

If Downing had been the man walking through the doorway, Nicole would have courageously done what was necessary. But it wasn't the outline of Downing that now filled the doorway.

Nicole's stomach churned.

She watched Switch innocently step into her trap. As he entered the room, pivoting to search for Nicole, she suddenly froze. His hawk-like eyes darted to the glint of glass in her hands. His reaction was immediate; he began to reach for his gun.

From that point on, everything became a blur to the terrified woman. She remained frozen, unable to think, unable to speak. Daniel panicked, realizing it was up to him now to initiate the attack. He flew across the room, reaching the guard and kicking him in the back of his knees, causing his legs to buckle beneath him. As the giant fell to a kneeling position, Daniel began to scream like a maniac. "Kill him! Kill him! Now, Nicole! Do it! Do it!!" He was practically jumping up and down.

But when Nicole saw Switch's face gazing up at her in astonishment, she could not find it in her heart to take his life. Her hand never moved, providing Switch the opportunity to finish drawing his weapon. Within seconds, the cold metal flashed before her eyes, the gleam of hard steel forcing an involuntary shudder.

Daniel had been right—Switch would surely kill her now.

She had forfeited her one chance of survival. She could only pray that death would come quickly. Unable to tear her gaze from the stormy gray eyes that were now transfixed upon her, Nicole bravely squared her shoulders. At that exact moment, some new emotion flashed across her attacker's face, and Switch suddenly pivoted, firing three precisely executed shots into the shrieking Daniel Tyler.

Nicole muffled a scream, the large chunk of mirror dropping to the floor while Daniel's lifeless body made its gruesome thud. Still in shock, she swayed unsteadily, unable to believe what her senses had just witnessed. The hideous sound of blood bubbling up in the dead man's throat made her want to retch. Switch took hold of her arm, jerking her towards the door and out into the hall. By this time, Downing entered the room, surveying the scene.

"Take the handcuffs off him and bring them to me. I'll also need some rope," Switch said to his partner. "Together, we'll clean up this mess and find something to wrap him in." He then directed his attention back to Nicole, who was sobbing uncontrollably. He wanted to yell at her and thank her at the same time. She could have killed him in the few precious seconds he had hesitated to draw his weapon. But she hadn't, which is precisely why Switch considered women the weaker sex. Today, it had been to his advantage.

When the wailing continued, his patience soon dwindled. "Nicole," he said in a hushed voice. "I thought you didn't like Daniel. After all, he did kill your husband."

The sobbing suddenly stopped.

"He what?" she sniffed.

"He murdered your husband."

Nicole stared at the man before her. "How do you know?"

"The other night when he had been drinking, he was yakking about the Feds being after him... then he said it was probably because he had killed your husband. So don't cry yourself ragged over the man."

Downing suddenly appeared, handing the cuffs to Switch. "I'm sorry I have to do this, Nicole." He reached for her wrists.

"Why?" she cried, anger and frustration evident.

"Just until we get Daniel taken care of." He ushered her to a new room with green walls, secured a rope around the cuffs and tied it to the base of the metal bedframe. He then left her.

Still in shock from the shooting, Nicole simply sat cross-legged on the carpet and cried. She had considered untying the knotted rope, but theorized that once she did so, she still had to contend with the problem of being handcuffed. She couldn't very well shoot a gun in this position; besides, she had already proven she couldn't kill Switch. Mixed emotions plaguing her, the young woman barely heard the male voices echoing down the hall. When it did register, however, she felt an icy chill run up her spine. Downing's voice, the louder of the two, was harsh and demanding.

"We have to get rid of her!" he insisted. "She saw you murder him. She knows what we look like."

"Keep your voice down!" Switch replied.

It was the only part of the conversation Nicole overheard. It was enough to fill her with new fear. Reluctant to admit it, she now knew she should have slashed Switch's throat. Hope for freedom was becoming scarce. Downing was right; they'd have no choice but to murder her, too, unless... Nicole racked her brain to come up with a good reason they should keep her alive. After half an hour of thinking, Switch entered the room. He purposely strode over to her and untied the rope, stating, "The other room's clean, now." Suddenly, he leaned very close, his voice lowering to a whisper. "Downing wants you dead. Please don't cause anymore trouble; if you do, I can't assure your safety."

Nicole nodded. "How did you convince him to let me live?"

"I told him we could always use you later, if the bank tellers grew suspicious. I mentioned you had a rich boyfriend who would probably pay a hefty ransom."

"Thank you," she murmured as he led her back to her original room and took off the cuffs. Nicole nervously glanced around after the key turned in the lock. A pair of socks and slippers were on top of the comforter. She quickly put them on, all the while trying to avoid looking towards the place where Daniel's body had lain. A morbid feeling overcame her, as if his spirit had decided to linger. "It's not my fault," she said out loud, knowing if she had killed Switch, Daniel might have remained alive. The air grew thick and clammy. She broke out in goose bumps. "It's not my fault you're dead," she repeated. Was her mind playing tricks? She could actually feel cold air on her cheek! Where was it coming from? There were no open windows. Terrified, Nicole ran to the bedroom door, beating on it with her fists. "Switch!" she yelled. "Switch! Please come here!"

Her plea was answered in a matter of seconds, Switch having been just down the hall. "He's still in the room!" Nicole frantically said, pointing in the direction where the dead body had been.

"Daniel's gone, Nicole."

"No. No, he isn't! His spirit is still here. I felt him. He touched my cheek..." Her fingers lightly stroked the area on her face. By the terror in her eyes, Switch knew something had occurred, but whether it was real or not, he could not say. What mattered was getting Nicole under control; she was delirious.

"If I take you to my room, will you promise not to try and escape?" She rapidly nodded. He led her back down the hall and into the green room again. "I'm not going to cuff you, in case you need to use the bathroom. It's in the far corner. Why don't you get some rest? Afterwards, I'll bring you some food." Without waiting for a reply, he then turned and left her. Thankful she no longer was in her old room, Nicole proceeded to remove the colorful slippers. She felt exhausted. What in the world would happen to her now? she thought as she stretched out on the bedcovers. Her mind began to race. Maybe she could make an escape while the two men were busy burying Daniel? No, she heard Switch lock the door here. Her eyes darted around the perimeter of the room... Ahh... a window! And without bars! Nicole leapt from the bed to race up to it. Peering out, she noticed the dense forest surrounding them. She also noticed she was two stories up from the ground; a jump would produce possible broken bones, which would then hinder her escape. Darn! Did she have time to tie the bedsheets together to make a safe ladder? If she got caught, it'd surely be the end of her. Nicole's heart began slamming against her ribs. What to do?

She stared out the window again, this time making sure her vision took in every tiny detail. But suddenly she saw movement between some trees. Her heart sank. It was Switch and Downing. That must be the place where they were digging the grave. Of all the rotten luck! There was no chance of her slipping out the window now without them eventually seeing her. So Nicole did the only thing left to do. She went to the bedroom door and tugged furiously at it, hoping to jar it open. But the door was not budging. If only she had a screwdriver! Nicole went to the desk in the room, opening drawers in search of some tool. A bureau stood nearby, so she searched that, also, but found nothing of use. Then her eyes fell upon the closet. Maybe? She grabbed a wire coat hanger out of it and tried wriggling it in the keyhole of the door.

Her hopes soon faded. It wasn't working. Frustrated, Nicole continued trying while her brain searched for other ways to escape. Time was not on her side. Every few minutes she had to run to the window to see if the men were finished yet. Perspiration lined her raven-colored brow. Why was this door not opening? Time continued to tick on while the frantic girl renewed her efforts. All to no avail. Tears in her eyes, Nicole finally gave up, put the coat hanger away, and sank down on the bed. Sounds reached her from below; the men had come back inside the house and were probably washing up. After a while, she heard the door to her room open. Switch entered, then slowly made his way over to the young beauty while he began stripping off his clothes.

Nicole's mouth went dry. He had better not be planning to have sex with her! Was he nuts? He had just killed a man within the past hour! What kind of monster was he? Nicole's heart raced like a Thoroughbred. What could she do? He had saved her life. He had also taken a life. He was a cold-blooded killer. He was no better than Daniel. Nicole's conscience tugged at her until she wanted to scream. Instinct dictated she should yield to Switch in order to remain alive. But she couldn't bring herself to do it. She just couldn't.

Guessing her thoughts, Switch grinned a crooked smile, saying, "Relax. I'm not going to touch you. I just need to change my clothes and rest a bit, too. I promise not to bother you."

And he was true to his word, much to Nicole's amazement. Something had definitely changed within him, although she wasn't quite sure how or why. He seemed more respectful from that day onward, never giving her reason to be afraid again. He even made an attempt to comfort her when she began having horrible nightmares about the day Daniel died. A twinge of guilt hit him as he watched her toss and turn in bed, she was so tormented by the trauma. But he couldn't undo the damage he had done, and for some reason that bothered him immensely now.

As the days passed, Nicole felt her resentment start to build, despite Switch's efforts to make her feel as comfortable as was possible. To be cautious, they placed her back in her original room with the bars on the window during the day; at nighttime, Switch brought her back to his room to sleep. Downing accepted her presence, albeit reluctantly. They even played cards together on occasion; and, even though she was never allowed to roam the house, Nicole was visited often in her room. She became a first rate actress, never showing the tiniest indication of her disgust for the men who were now accommodating some of her needs. Upon her request, Switch had even purchased canvas, paints, and an easel for her. While she busied herself, painting "Jan's First Day", her thoughts lingered elsewhere, pondering new ways to gain her freedom. Once, she tried to use the sharp end of her paintbrush to get the doorlock undone, but without success. Eventually, she realized she needed to allow her captors time to feel relaxed enough they weren't so cautious; then hopefully she could spring a plan into action, catching them off guard.

As time went on, the men did finally relax, living a lavish existence now that they had access to Daniel's money. Nicole could only assume they were forging Daniel's name on checks to pay for renting this house. There was no indication they intended to flee to another country or island somewhere, probably because they still couldn't extract too large of a sum of money at one time without generating suspicion. They squandered cash on new clothes, fine food and wine. Downing purchased expensive gifts for women who were barely worth a dime. Sometimes he brought them to the house, but always to a room far down the hall, away from Nicole's. Nicole secretly wished Switch would do the same and leave her alone for a night; he still made her sleep with him, handcuffed together, but it was only to make sure Downing would not creep into her room to violate her. Switch continued to keep his word and did not touch her. Nicole wondered why he trusted that she wouldn't smother him with a pillow while he slept. Perhaps he sensed she could not do it. He was right, of course. She couldn't do it; she still couldn't bring herself to kill someone.

Lately, however, it was becoming more and more difficult to pretend she was content. The yearning to be free was almost unbearable. She desperately missed Justin, Cristoff, Jan and the horses. She longed to hear the sound of her mother's voice on the phone. Her parents... the agony they must be going through... the thought tormented Nicole, night and day, renewing her attempts to fashion an escape plan.

But the weeks soon turned into months, without any opportunity for Nicole to put her plan into motion. She needed Downing to be alone in the house with her, but Switch was wary of that and made sure he was always around, too. If he needed to go out, he waited for when Downing was going out also, or he asked him to accompany him. Hope was quickly dwindling. Also, it was obvious Justin's detectives weren't having much luck finding her. Was it no wonder? Daniel was dead, and a dead man couldn't leave clues. What's worse was that Switch began to notice her restless behavior and was watching her like a hawk. He had grown attached to the bewitching beauty and was unwilling to let her slip through his fingers.

As their relationship continued, he started telling her about his family, his childhood, the tragedies in his life which deeply disturbed him. Nicole patiently listened, only offering advice when she was asked, mentally storing the useful information for the day she might use it against him. If he could have read her mind during those times, he would surely have killed her. Thus, Nicole kept her true feelings hidden. She did, however, toy with the thought of trying to take Switch's gun; but, if she did not succeed, it would be her last breath, and there was no guarantee she could finally pull the trigger. So... time slowly ticked on.

She often thought about Daniel and Philip, wondering what could have gone wrong between them. She still couldn't understand why Daniel would kill his brother? Philip never spoke badly about Daniel; they always appeared on good terms with each other. Daniel had plenty of money of his own, so it couldn't have been for money. What had happened while she was away in Maryland during that time? It was such a mystery. Her mind recalled the many times she was a victim at Philip's hands, and how now she was a victim again. But then her thoughts took a turn. Being a victim is a state of mind, she told herself. There are many people who survive worse tragedies and go on to do something productive with their lives. She nodded to herself, making an internal agreement to reflect on her life and change what needed changing. She reflected on her childhood, as an only child, recognizing the little ways her parents reinforced her individuality and helped her to develop a strong character. She remembered all the sacrifices they had made to improve her life.

Her mind moved on to the ranch, her friends and the interactions between them, and then... there was Justin. She felt a twinge of guilt stab her. Why had she been so darn rude to him? Here was a man who truly wanted to date her, to care about her; a man who hadn't let his riches go to his head, was afraid to even tell her he had money and seemed a bit embarrassed when she had found out. Yes, they got on each other's nerves at first, but Nicole had to admit that even when she was furious with him, she was strangely attracted to him at the same time. She often watched him quietly from the stable when he was out in the field working with one of her horses. He was so very gentle with the animals, so patient, so understanding. They all responded to him, wonderfully. Perhaps he really was a gentle man with only a macho tough exterior? The more she thought about him, the more she wanted to be with him again. She didn't like admitting how much she truly missed him. A gnawing ache began in her heart. "Oh Lord, please don't let me be in love with this man!" she breathed, as new fear swept over her. "It's too soon... too soon." She didn't want to be caged by a man again. No! She wiped the thought of him from her mind and began recklessly throwing paint on a new canvas…

CHAPTER TWENTY-ONE

Justin MacFierson opened his bloodshot eyes once more to study the detective reports, furious he had nodded off again. It seemed like only yesterday, Nicole's soft voice floated through the barn office. He could hardly believe how much time had gone by. Christmas came and went... New Year's, too... each passing holiday magnifying his frustration and grief. The guilt trip had almost driven him to the brink of madness. He kept wondering: if only he had taken her off the ranch that night, if only he had awakened early that morning, if only, if only...

"Why don't you go home and get some sleep?" Cristoff approached him, concerned. The past months had hit the ranch hand just as hard. Together, the two men spent each weekend searching for some small clue to give them hope.

"I can't sleep," Justin mumbled, running his fingers absently through his tangled hair; it was shoulder-length now, due to neglect.

"Jan says you've been having nightmares again."

"Jan has a big mouth."

"Go home, Justin. You can't think clearly when you're tired."

The blond slowly rose from his chair, blue eyes scanning the room. "When she's found, she'll be pleased we've kept the stable up."

"She'll be tickled pink," Cristoff assured him. "Shane has done a terrific job with the horses. Kevin and Billy have been great, too." He was referring to the two extra hired hands Justin brought on. Kevin was a tough guy, in his 30's, who showed Nicole's horses for them. Billy, an enthusiastic 18 year-old, traveled with Kevin as his assistant. When not on the road, the pair helped out in the barn. "Want to join me in town tomorrow night?"

Justin wearily shook his head.

"A roll in the hay might do you some good," Cristoff suggested. "Have you been dating at all?"

"I don't have time for it."

"You used to."

His words struck a sour note with the blond. When had he last dated?

Before he fell in love with Nicole.

Justin openly scowled and changed the subject. "I just can't believe no one can find a trace of Daniel—not even overseas. What did he do? Disappear into thin air? And why isn't his butler talking?"

Cristoff plopped down in a chair. "Tell me, again, what Maureen said to you."

The blond scratched his stubby whiskers. "She said she had hired a detective when she suspected Daniel was having an affair with Nicole. The detective reported that Daniel was traveling to the Tylers on the nights he claimed to be working late. Then, the day Maureen asked for a divorce, Daniel came home that evening smelling like strawberries. She knew Nicole wore strawberry perfume because she had met her. Maureen said the only detail of the story which never made any sense was why Daniel telephoned his coworkers from his house before he left for Nicole's?"

Cristoff broke in. "And that's when you theorized that the coworkers were the actual poker players in Philip's house."

"But the new detectives can't get any answers out of those guys. I still think they're linked with Daniel. Heck, they may have been the ones tracking him. If we could find some way to scare one of them into talking, we might finally get our lead."

"Can't we hire someone to do the dirty work?"

"If the detectives won't do it, I seriously doubt anyone else will take the risk."

"Then I guess we'll just have to tackle this, ourselves, won't we, and find out what these fellows are keeping mum about?"

Justin glanced at his friend and smiled. "Aaron and Shane could join us. They don't have to know anything about Nicole's past. We'll just question the coworkers about Daniel's whereabouts."

Cristoff anxiously rubbed his hands together. "When do we start?"

For all their enthusiasm, Cristoff and Justin had no idea what was in store for them. Expensive security systems protected the homes of Daniel's friends, not to mention guard dogs and iron gates. Trying to corner one of the coworkers proved just as frustrating. "What should we do?" quizzed Cristoff. "Force one of them into a back alley?"

Justin cursed, thoroughly frustrated.

"Oh, sure!" mocked Shane. "Let's sign our own death warrant by beating the hell out of them. I can just see a van full of Feds pulling up outside my building, waiting patiently for me to emerge." He violently shook his head. "No thanks!" The four men headed back to Aaron's car and got in. "There is an easier way to find Daniel."

"Now he tells us!" Aaron whined.

"I just thought of it," Shane countered. He hadn't truly wanted Justin to find Daniel and Nicole, but after watching his friend brood over the woman for such a long time, he decided it'd be best to end his agony. Besides, there was a good chance Nicole was dead; the sooner they found out, the sooner Justin could move on with his life. "When I worked at the bank, there was a coworker who owed me a big favor. If we knew which bank Daniel used, we should be able to locate where his money was transferred to."

"Assuming he's in this vicinity," Aaron argued.

Justin interjected. "Maureen said he was a stickler for routine, he hated change. She claimed he was very insecure. He didn't even like to travel when his job called for it. There's a good chance he isn't far from here, or from the state of Virginia. Shane, the bank name Charlie King had written down in his notes was the same one you worked for. Is there a chance we could see if Daniel had his account there? And if so, see if there was a large transfer of money approximately around the time of his disappearance?"

"I'll see what I can do," answered Shane.

"Daniel isn't stupid," Cristoff broke in. "He's not going to dump all his cash in one institution. It would be too easy to trace."

"True," Justin replied. "But if we found several banks in close proximity to each other, all with newly opened accounts with large sums of money on a specific date, I'd say Daniel couldn't be far away. Could your friend find that out, Shane?"

"Sure," Shane replied.

"Why didn't the police think of this?" Aaron quizzed.

"Maybe they did," Justin answered. "Maybe they don't want to mess with Daniel since he has a government connection."

"Maybe the Feds warned them to stay out of it," Cristoff suggested. The four men silently nodded. "Although I'd think if the Feds were following Danny, they'd have investigated his bank transactions long before we thought of it? Or even followed him to wherever he is? He could even be dead, for all we know."

"You know," spoke Shane, carefully choosing his words, "even if we do find Nicole, there's no telling how she'll react. We can only guess as to how they have treated her."

"What are you saying?" Justin challenged.

"Well," Shane made eye contact with him to drive the point home. "She isn't an ugly duckling, you know, and there might be several men with Daniel—"

"Shut up!" Justin thundered.

"I'm just trying to warn you," Shane continued, softening

his tone. “She may not even want to see another man, let alone be with one.” He watched Justin jerk his face towards the window to hide his expression. Shane quirked a slight smile. Cristoff switched the conversation to a safer topic. But while the others joined in a lively political debate, Justin remained quiet, his thoughts running amuck. He knew Nicole’s mental state was fragile. Yet, on the other hand, he knew she could be tough as nails when the occasion called for it. He was positive she would wreak havoc upon anyone who threatened her. But did she know how far to push her enemies? Sure, he told himself. Nicole has brains. She’s a smart girl.

His frustration slowly melted during the next few days as he patiently waited for Shane to bring him the banking information. Hope hung in the air like an elusive brass ring until Justin finally grasped it firmly in his hand. “Here it is!” he called excitedly, pointing to the scribbled notes from Shane’s coworker. “Kingston, West Virginia!” Shane, Aaron, and Cristoff huddled around, peering anxiously over his shoulder. “There’s the bank he transferred his money to, and here are two others in the nearby area with large deposits that same day!”

“It’s worth a try,” Cristoff grinned, slapping him on the back.

“I think I’ll give Charlie’s wife a call and see if I can borrow Charlie’s spare detective badge. I’ll need some fake identification, too, and a picture of Daniel. Then we can start asking the new accounts people some questions.”

“I’ve got a photo of Daniel with Philip,” Cristoff offered.

“Good enough. Let’s get a map and chart our trip.” He gazed fondly at Shane. “Thanks for your help, buddy.” Shane forced a tiny smile.

“Can I come along?” Aaron questioned.

“Sure. Anyone can. But I’m the only one going into the bank. The rest of you will have to wait in the car.”

“What about the ranch?” Cristoff quizzed. “We can’t just pack up and leave it.”

“No. We can’t,” Justin replied. He looked coolly at the ranch hand, hoping he’d offer to stay. But Cristoff had put so much time into searching for Nicole, Justin didn't have the heart to ask him to remain behind; it had been Cristoff who had spent endless hours on the weekends with Justin, traveling miles and miles in the hope of finding her. Besides, Cristoff was an expert gunman.

"I'll take care of the ranch," spoke Shane, much to Justin's surprise. "Kevin, Billy and Jan will help."

"Thanks," Justin replied. "I just didn't feel comfortable leaving the place in Kevin's hands. He's still a newcomer, and Jan, well... she's limited with what she can do. I appreciate this, Shane."

That settled, the four men now discussed strategy, coming to the conclusion that Justin would enter the bank in a disguise, show his badge and I.D. to the bank manager and ask to question the person who handled all new accounts. He'd then display a picture of Daniel, claiming he was a wanted criminal. After pinpointing what day Daniel usually came into the bank, Justin and the others could then lay a trap to snare him. Satisfied with their plan, Justin, Cristoff, and Aaron went home to pack what they might need, then said their goodbyes to Shane, Kevin, Billy and Jan before taking off for West Virginia. The journey took some hours, which only increased their anxiety.

Justin tried to keep his nerves under control when he finally stepped inside the bank. Everything seemed to be going as planned, until the person in charge of new accounts did not recognize Daniel's photo. "Are you sure you haven't seen him?" Justin persisted, watching the young man take another look.

"I'm sorry, sir," came the reply. "It's been some months since this account first opened. Perhaps one of the bank tellers has seen him." He walked across the room to a pretty girl with long, red hair. "Jeannie?" He placed the picture on her counter. "Do you recall seeing this fellow in the bank?" She paused, then shook her head. Daniel's photograph was given to the next teller, and so forth, until each girl had been given the opportunity to identify him.

"This doesn't make sense," Justin commented. "Are you

implying that this account has remained inactive since it was opened?"

"I can check that for you," Jeannie offered, punching in the account information into a machine. "It's active," she announced, "on a weekly basis—withdrawals only."

"Well, someone has to be making those transactions," Justin stated. "Aren't there any checks floating around?"

"No, sir."

"The withdrawals, are they retrieved on a certain day of the week?"

"Umm..." she glanced again at the account, then at a calendar. "Looks like Tuesdays, sir."

"Good. What about an address for this account?"

"We show P.O. Box 2014."

Justin withdrew a small notepad from his coat pocket and scribbled the information. "May I have the phone number listed for this account, please?"

The redhead smiled. "Yes, sir, Detective Laramie. Anything else I can do for you?" Her eyes sparkled. Justin knew that look all too well as he jotted down the telephone number.

"No, thank you. You've been a great help, already." He avoided her gaze while placing the notepad back in his pocket. With Daniel's phone number on his mind, he quickly left.

"Well?" Cristoff asked when the blond entered the car.

"No one recognized Daniel."

"He might be incognito," Aaron commented.

"True. I need to dial Information on this phone number they gave me, to see if I can get an address listing. They only showed a P.O. Box number for the account." He peeled off his fake disguise and handed it to Cristoff to put back in a bag. "Let's get to a pay phone so I can try this number."

Aaron started up the car's engine and they searched for the nearest phone. It only took Justin a few minutes to find out the number was a fake.

"Bloody hell," swore Cristoff. "Now what?"

"Well," thought Justin, "we do know the withdrawals are made on Tuesdays. So I suggest we come here tomorrow and wait to see a car enter the lot with a Virginia license plate instead of a West Virginia one."

"What if he's renting a car, though? Then he'd have this state's tag," Cristoff pointed out.

"We take our chances. Otherwise, we'd have to stake out the post office every day, not knowing when and if he ever goes there. I say we follow whatever car comes in here with a Virginia tag, even if it doesn't look like Daniel at the wheel. I'm thinking he would borrow someone else's vehicle, not rent one here, because Feds could just check car rental places if he truly believes he's being followed." Cristoff and Aaron agreed.

"So, that's tomorrow," mumbled Aaron. "What the hell do we do with ourselves the rest of the day? This place looks beat. Don't they have any bars here?"

"At this time of the day?" laughed Cristoff. "I knew we should have brought separate cars."

Justin jabbed a finger into Aaron's shoulder. "You're not going to a bar. The last thing I need is for you to get liquored up and ruin our chances of nabbing Daniel, tomorrow. I think we should go back to our hotel rooms, spend a quiet afternoon watching movies."

"Oh, goody," mocked Aaron with a frown. "What if I drop you two off at the hotel and I'll take a leisurely drive?"

"Forget it," Justin warned.

"I need a little action."

"No way. You'll fall asleep who knows where, then be late returning to the hotel. I know you like the back of my hand, Aaron. You're staying with us." Justin's twin mumbled something under his breath before cutting the steering wheel too sharp to the left, forcing the vehicle into a minor spin. A long stream of curses spilled from Justin's mouth, echoed by Cristoff.

"Did you or did you not want to come on this trip with me?!" boomed Justin.

"I know. I'm sorry," Aaron whined. "I didn't think it'd be so boring."

"Enjoy today. Tomorrow, you might find yourself at the

wrong end of a rifle!"

"That's right," Cristoff agreed. "We don't know how many men are with Daniel." Aaron grew silent, concentrating on his driving. Patience was not one of his virtues. He couldn't wait for morning to come so they could get this over with. He had only tagged along because he feared for his brother's safety. When it came to Nicole, Justin was often blinded by his own emotions. Cristoff seemed to have the same problem. If they did find Nicole, Aaron thought with amusement, she'd probably look like a hag by now; her tan skin faded, no makeup to hide any blemishes; dry, chapped lips, scraggly hair... The sight of her would probably jolt the two men back to reality. Yeah, he grinned, it would be worth the wait just to see the look of revulsion on their faces.

Nicole sensed something had happened. Her heart had quickened in the last five minutes, for no apparent reason. Downing had gone to the bank, leaving Switch to keep watch. On this particular day, however, they both felt edgy. Everything was quiet, but... she couldn't place her finger on it. She hovered near the window until Downing's car came into view, noting his reckless approach down the dirt driveway. Something was wrong. Yes, it certainly was. She raced to the bedroom door and placed an ear against it, straining to catch a few fragments of conversation. By the tone of Downing's voice, she knew he was furious. Curses spewed from his mouth like a man possessed.

"... I don't know who they are, but I can make a pretty good guess! It took forever to lose them... they had a black Plymouth Road Runner... no, I had to hit the brakes. They skidded and swerved to avoid ramming the back end of my Cadillac. They ran off the road... can't take any chances... where?... you know we can't withdraw all the money at one time... I suppose so..." Switch cursed, then stomped up the stairs. Inside her room, Nicole quickly moved to sit on the bed. The door flew open with a bang! "Sorry, Nicole," Switch muttered, cuffing her hands. This time, however, he took out another set of handcuffs from his back pocket.

"What's that for?" she quizzed, realizing they had bought another pair.

He gently pulled her towards the carpet, snapped one end of the cuffs around the metal links which separated her hands, then snapped the other end onto the side of the bedframe. "You'll have to yell when you need to use the bathroom."

"Why? What's going on?" she begged.

"I can't risk you getting near the window."

"What happened, Switch?"

Before he could answer, Robert Downing barged through the door, angrier than a hornet. "I warned you we should have moved out of here weeks ago! Did she tell you who they were?"

"I haven't asked her, yet," Switch calmly replied. He gazed at Nicole, his gray eyes silently pleading. "Do you know anyone with a black Plymouth Road Runner?"

"Why?" she quipped.

"Don't be difficult, Nicole."

"She knows who they are," Downing sneered. "It was her boyfriend."

"Does Justin own a Road Runner?" Switch tried again.

"No." At least Nicole was being truthful. It was Aaron who owned the car.

"Does one of his friends have a Road Runner?"

"No," she honestly answered. "None of his friends."

"She's lying!" growled Downing. "We have to get out of here, Switch—the sooner, the better. Those guys are gonna come snooping around, mark my words."

"If you think it's Justin," Nicole commented, "why don't you leave me here while the two of you make an escape? He's only looking for me, not you. Once he finds me, no one will track you."

Downing folded his arms, looking down his angular nose at the cuffed female. "Oh, and we should just trust blindly in you, huh? As if you wouldn't say a word!"

"I won't!" she earnestly promised. "Not a peep. I don't care if you steal Daniel's money. I don't care what you do, as long as I'm able to return to my ranch." Tears filled her eyes. "Please. Please leave me behind so I can go home."

"I should have killed you back when Switch shot Daniel."

Downing's cruel words sharply wounded his partner. Switch suddenly found himself caught in the middle. He realized keeping Nicole had been a bad idea, but he was attached to her now and couldn't bear to see her dead. "Actually," Downing continued, a malicious look in his eyes, "it's still feasible."

"It's stupid," Switch quickly said, facing him. "What will we gain by it?"

"One less person to identify us," Downing argued. "Until today, those guys in the Road Runner were probably looking for Daniel, not us. So we ditch my car, get another and split to the next state."

"But the money is here," Switch reminded him. "We can't close out the whole account, either. If we bring the girl, at least we can get some ransom money."

"What good's that? There has to be a dropoff point. Her boyfriend will probably have the cops stationed there for when we arrive. I say let's pull out as much cash as we can, ditch Nicole, and take off."

"Ditch... you mean, kill!"

The two men locked eyes, Downing cracking a smile and shaking his head. "Switch... don't be going soft on me, pal. We can get you a new woman to warm your bed."

"And when will the killing stop, Robert?"

"After she's cold and six feet under."

"Oh, like Daniel? I didn't exactly have a field day burying him. I don't want to go through it, again."

"Fine," Downing said. "I'll do it, myself." He reached for his gun.

"No."

Switch stood in front of Nicole's cringing body. "Give me one more night with her."

"We don't have a night," Robert snapped. "I'm telling you,

those guys might be scouring the area this very minute."

"Then give me a half hour," Switch reasoned. "One half hour won't make much of a difference."

Downing's eyes darted between Switch and Nicole as he considered the plea. "All right. Thirty minutes. After that, she comes with me." Nicole hung her head with relief, refusing to look at her future murderer as he waltzed out of the room. Instantly, Switch knelt down and unlocked the handcuffs. He expected to hear her sob, to see tears streaming down her cheeks, but Nicole could not cry. She was still in shock, unable to believe she had only a half hour to live. It felt like a nightmare. She hoped it was a nightmare. But, no, it had to be real because Switch's strong arms were lifting her fragile body from the floor to place her in the middle of the large bed.

"You've got to be kidding," she scoffed when he began to unbuckle his belt. He glanced down at her, bewildered, watching as the young beauty easily rolled towards the opposite side of the mattress, swung her legs over the edge and stood up. In one brief minute, she had already considered her options: She could surrender to Switch while coaxing him to eliminate his own partner, painting a more promising future with herself as the new business associate; or, she could refuse his advances and spend her last thirty minutes in peace. She chose the latter.

"Sorry, Switch," she coolly said. "I'm not in the mood for a last minute romp."

"I understand you're angry," he replied. "But there's nothing I can do about Downing. At least I've bought you some time. Let's make good use of it."

Nicole laughed, loud and deep. "Oh, no. I've had enough of pretending to enjoy your company. I'd appreciate being left alone."

Switch stared at the alluring female as if he had been shot between the eyes. "What did you say?" his voice cracked, stunned.

"I want to be alone!" she nearly shouted, clenching her fists so tight her knuckles turned white.

The huge man strode over to stand directly in front now, his gray eyes growing cold.

Nicole accused, "Did you really think I could enjoy sleeping with my own kidnapper? I was scared every night. Every night! And I resent you for that!" Her eyes flashed angrily at him, searing him like a branding iron. The fire was all-consuming.

"You, bitch," he breathed, feeling like a damn fool. "Just for that, I'm going to speed up your little death sentence. Downing!" he yelled, huffing as if he had just run a marathon.

"Go ahead," she mocked. "You don't abuse women, you just kill them. Right, Switch?"

"Switch!" called his partner, jerking the door open before colliding with the giant. "We've got trouble. They're here!"

"What?!" screeched Switch.

"I told you they wouldn't waste any time!" Downing shouted, throwing him a bullet-proof vest. "They're driving around the side of the house and will probably see the car parked in the back!" Justin, Cristoff and Aaron not only saw the car, but the upstairs window with the bars on it for security. That was all they needed.

Switch motioned towards Nicole. "Help me get her cuffed. We may need to use her as a hostage to make our getaway." The two men wrestled with Nicole, who now fought like a wildcat, scratching, kicking and biting her abductors while letting out a very loud, long scream in hopes that whoever was outside would hear her. She was no match for the two men, though. They subdued her as quickly as possible and connected her to the bedframe, just as a window smashed downstairs. Both drew their weapons and proceeded with caution. The minute they opened the bedroom door, however, Nicole yelled at the top of her lungs, "They have bullet-proof vests on, but there's only two of them!" Her sudden outburst brought Switch back into the room, mad as hell. He swiftly entered the bathroom, grabbed a washcloth and shoved it in her mouth, nearly choking her in the process. He then left with Downing.

The stalking began.

Nicole lowered her face towards her hands, removed the gag, and slid her body beneath the bed, out of range of flying bullets if they came back upstairs. It was there that she rapidly whispered numerous prayers for the safety of her rescuers. If Justin failed, Nicole was as good as dead. The rational side of her told her his chances of succeeding were slim; the guards were trained expert marksmen; plus, their reinforced vests would protect the area of the body that was easiest to hit. Justin and whomever he brought along would have to use a combination of skill and brains to outsmart their adversaries. The outlook seemed bleak, at best, but Nicole held on to a thread of hope. "God," she murmured, "if there are angels watching over us, we sure could use some help down here."

Suddenly, the sound of gunfire being exchanged ricocheted throughout the house. Nicole sucked in her breath, perspiration lining her brow. Her palms began to sweat. For once she wished her hearing wasn't so keen, for each bullet being fired made her body jerk in response. Her stomach cramped up, but she was forced to swallow the bile that rose in her throat. Another round of bullets discharged. A mixture of panic and fear now threatened to close off her throat, as if invisible hands were actually squeezing her slender neck. A million pictures flashed through her mind in the next five minutes—pictures of family, old friends, her childhood, events she had forgotten, small, insignificant pieces of conversation, toys she had played with as a young girl...

She was brought back to reality by a man's yelp of pain. Nicole frantically tried to decipher whose voice it was, desperately hoping it belonged to the enemy. She yanked on the cuffs, pulling and tugging until the metal scraped through several layers of skin. It occurred to her that perhaps she should just break her knuckles to free her hand, but realized she'd have to repeat the painful procedure to free the other. She wouldn't be of much help with two broken hands, yet it would release her from the bedframe and provide her with the opportunity to run if she could kick down the door.

Just as she decided to give it a try, someone crashed

through the wooden barrier. "Nicole!" called a familiar voice.

"Under here!" she replied, overjoyed at the sight of Justin rushing towards her. She inched out until her face showed from beneath the bed.

Then the unspeakable happened.

A shot rang out. The blond arched his back, his body twisting wildly as if someone else controlled it, his face contorting in agony. He fell forward, hitting the floor so hard his head bounced. Nicole's stomach lurched, yet she held on to her sanity, the survival instinct taking precedence over any emotion.

Glancing up, she saw Switch at the doorway. He relaxed his firing arm while Nicole ducked back under the bed. Downstairs, Downing shouted for him, but he hesitated, unsure of his victim's condition; he wanted to be positive the blond could not get up and surprise him from behind. He had decided to grab some more ammunition from the other room to shoot Justin again when he suddenly saw a woman's foot swiftly slide out from under the bed and skillfully kick Justin's fallen gun towards her hands. It happened so quickly, he didn't react until several seconds later. By then, it was too late. Nicole had the weapon in her cuffed hands and fired. Searing pain burned Switch's right wrist, automatically causing his fingers to open. His gun dropped to the floor. As he reached for it with the other hand, Nicole fired again, this time lodging a bullet into his left arm. The startled man gasped with fresh pain, surprise in his cold, gray eyes. Nicole pressed her luck, firing one last time. The bullet whizzed through the air, striking Switch smack in the forehead. Wide eyes frozen in astonishment, the giant finally fell... finally... finally.

At last... at last... Nicole closed her eyes, sickened by the sight; but she had no choice—it was either kill or be killed. She was thankful there were enough bullets left in Justin's gun to accomplish the task.

Justin... Nicole looked at the fallen figure, but his face was turned the opposite direction. Upon seeing some movement in his back, she realized he was still breathing. She wanted to go to him, to comfort him, to reassure him she'd do everything possible to get him to a hospital.

But Nicole couldn't go anywhere. She was still cuffed to the metal bedframe. Downstairs, the exchange of ammunition continued. Studying the Smith and Wesson, Nicole had to make another crucial decision: should she waste a bullet to break the cuffs, or save the bullet for self-defense? How many bullets were left? She managed to swing open the gun chamber. There were two. He must have reloaded when he was coming up the stairs. Pushing the chamber back in, she crawled out from under the bed, turned the gun upside down, carefully aimed, then fired at the linkage between the cuffs. It was a direct hit. She was finally free.

Racing to Justin, she knelt down and promised, "I'll get you help as soon as I can. Hang in there. Don't you dare die on me. You can't, you hear me? You can't... because... I think I might love you." As the words were spoken, the blond looked up at her with dazed blue eyes and cracked a tiny smile. It was then Nicole realized the injured man was not Justin—it was Aaron.

"Daniel," he whispered. "Where's Daniel?"

"He's dead," she replied. "Don't talk. Save your breath. And forget those other words I just said," she added, her face turning red. Leaning forward, she lightly kissed him on the cheek. "I have to help the others, but I'll be back."

Nicole cautiously made her way over to Switch's limp body to pick up his gun. It was empty. She searched his clothes for more ammunition but only found the key to the handcuffs, which she made good use of by unlocking each ring of metal surrounding her wrists. Where was he keeping the extra bullets? Precious time was ticking by. It could take five or ten minutes to search the other rooms for ammunition. Aaron needed help, now. She quickly glanced inside each room to find a phone. There were none. Nicole bit her lip. "My gun," she said, remembering where Daniel had placed it. She raced to the appropriate room, found the weapon, and groaned. It had been emptied. Tossing it, she headed back into the hallway.

She'd have to end the fighting downstairs in order to reach the telephone, if there was one. Nicole hurried to the top of the stairs. Below, occasional gunfire resonated. Heart pounding erratically, she tried to ascertain her enemy's hiding place. Realizing Downing was not in the room at the bottom of the staircase, she carefully removed her slippers.

Like a panther on the prowl, she slowly slinked noiselessly down the stairs, half-crouching, halting on every other step while her predator eyes darted from side to side, zeroing in on any moving object. She had the element of surprise on her side and took full advantage of it. Downing would not be expecting her. He might be able to keep her friends at bay, but she'd be approaching from the opposite direction. Unfortunately, this could put her directly in the line of fire from her friends. There was also the possibility Downing could turn and shoot her. If she got in too close, he could try to grab her to use as a hostage. Still, she continued.

Holding her breath, she neared the landing. The sound of someone reloading their gun reached her ears. They were in the next room, past an open set of double doors.

The 21 year-old put her back against the wall and inched her way towards the opening. Taking only a brief second to peek past the wall's edge, she saw Downing squatting behind a metal table that was turned on its side. The person he had been shooting at was hiding in the kitchen, taking pot shots whenever the opportunity presented itself. By the looks of it, whoever ran out of ammunition first was going to be the loser, and from her position at the wall she could see that Downing definitely had plenty of bullets.

Nicole cautiously raised the nose of her revolver, aligning it so the bullet would pass through the back of Downing's skull. Much to her dismay, her hand began to shake. Blast! she silently fumed. This has to be accurate... She concentrated on steadying her hand. Stop moving your head, Downing!

A bullet whizzed by, forcing her to jump back. Nicole gulped. That was too close! Mentally counting the minutes, she took aim again, knowing any further delay might cost Aaron his life. She calmed her nerves, took a deep breath, then slowly squeezed the trigger.

At that precise moment, Downing suddenly pivoted, glanced up at his surprise attacker, and fired.

The split-second event changed to slow motion for the woman who stood immobile, frozen at the spot where a second bullet now ripped through the air on its journey towards her.

Had it not been for Justin's shout of "Duck!", Nicole would have instantly died, the bullet striking her in the head. But her body obeyed his command in the nick of time, and Nicole found herself kneeling on all fours, too shocked to move. As if in a dream, a pair of hands pulled her upwards. A deep, masculine voice soothed her. Nicole thought she had been hit, for something wet was running down her cheek in little streamlets. When the fog slowly lifted, she realized it wasn't blood at all, but tears from Justin's eyes mingling with her own. He was holding her tightly, calling her name. "Where's the other guy?" he asked, his voice trembling.

"I... I killed him," she slowly replied.

"Daniel. Where's Daniel?"

"He's dead, too."

Then Nicole suddenly thought of Aaron and her senses became fully alert once more. "Aaron!" she exclaimed. "He's been hit, bad. We've got to get him to a hospital!" Acting on her words, Justin raced to the nearest phone to call an ambulance and the police. Nicole went back upstairs to check on the injured man, sighing with relief to find him still conscious.

"You're going to be all right," she soothed, taking his hand. "Justin's calling for an ambulance."

Aaron slowly blinked, his breathing ragged. "Is he..." He swallowed and licked his dry lips. "Is he okay?"

"He's fine. Don't talk, Aaron."

He ignored the request. "You... you saved my life."

"No. If it hadn't been for me, you'd have never come here in the first place and been shot. I'm so sorry." Nicole's eyes were brimming with tears. Aaron was touched.

“It’s okay, Cat.” He made a weak attempt to smile. “I needed a little excitement.” His hand slowly moved to cover hers. By then, Justin and Cristoff entered the room, Cristoff quickly going to Nicole while Justin comforted his brother. The relieved ranch hand wrapped one arm around Nicole, hugging her fiercely.

“Cristoff!” she exclaimed. “You’re hurt!”

“Just a flesh wound,” he replied. Nicole examined the blood-soaked fabric tied around his right upper arm. “Justin made me stay outside in the car after I was hit. Just as well, I suppose, because I’m not a very good shot with my left hand. Are you okay, Nicole?” He studied the weary female whose flaming red cheeks were the only indication of their past excitement. She bobbed her head up and down, then turned towards Aaron. Outside, the wail of sirens could be heard. Cristoff took Nicole’s hand. “Justin told me Daniel was dead,” he commented. “Is that true?”

Nicole silently nodded her head.

“I know you may not want to think about it, Nicole, but the police are going to ask you about each death.”

The young woman’s gaze fell to the numerous pools of blood seeping through the fibers of the carpet, so many endless puddles... Her body grew weak, her eyelids closed... Nicole slowly sank to the floor.

CHAPTER TWENTY-TWO

"Nicole?"

The sound of Cristoff's voice prompted two eyelids to flutter open. "How are you feeling?"

"Better," she faintly said, shifting her focus to survey the white surroundings. She had hoped that the next time she awakened, it would be in her own bed, at home. Hospitals did nothing to boost her spirits. Sleep had been a nice escape from the recent police interrogation she had endured. They had charged into her room, indifferent to her need for privacy.

"The investigating officers suggested I stay in West Virginia for the next few days, in case they have more questions," she quietly said.

"I know," Cristoff replied. "We've all been asked to stay. Who were the two guys in dark suits I saw leaving your room an hour ago?"

Nicole pulled herself up into a sitting position. "I don't know. I suppose they are another branch of police, but they asked only a couple questions—mostly about Daniel."

Cristoff instantly snapped to attention. "What kind of questions, Nicole?"

She paused, trying to recall. "They kept asking me what Daniel had told me."

"About what?"

She lifted her shoulders. “Beats me. They made me repeat everything he had said, over and over.” A worried look crossed Cristoff’s face, but Nicole ignored the urge to quiz him. She was too tired. Instead, she yawned and stretched. “How is your arm?”

“It’s fine, Nicole. I told you it was only a flesh wound.”

“What about Aaron?”

“He’s in the recovery room from surgery. He sure was lucky. The bullet missed his spine. The doctor says he’ll be okay, but he’ll have to take it easy for a month. Justin is going to remain here with him until he’s well enough to come home.”

Nicole’s thoughts turned to the ranch, but she no longer wanted to talk. “I’d like to go back to sleep, Cristoff, if you don’t mind?”

“Sure. I’ll come back in a few hours.” Rising from his chair, he leaned over to kiss her forehead. “There will be plenty of time for talking, later. Sleep well, Nicole.” He left her to enter the long corridor, his stride quickening as he neared the waiting room where Justin sat, reading a magazine. Since Cristoff was more familiar with Nicole’s temperament, Justin had suggested the ranch hand go in to her room alone to assess her mood. Then, Cristoff was to gently persuade Nicole to speak with the hospital’s psychiatrist.

The blond looked up, his voice filled with concern. “How is she?”

“Down. Real down.” Cristoff seated himself in the adjacent chair. “I couldn’t mention anything about the psychiatrist, Justin.”

“I was hoping you could warn her in advance, before the shrink walked in on her.”

“I know. I know. But she’s so depressed.”

“Then I suppose it’s a good thing that her doctor decided to send someone to evaluate her. I’m just glad I won’t be in the room when he arrives!”

“There are bigger problems on the horizon,” Cristoff said. Justin raised one brow. “Two men questioned her about Daniel. From the sound of it, they’re government agents. The only thing they were interested in was what information Daniel had leaked to her."

"Damn." An angry scowl lined Justin's face. He pitched the magazine back onto the table. Elbows on his knees, he rested his chin on the heels of both hands. "I don't know what the devil to do, Cristoff. Should I tell her the whole story, the information I pieced together recently, or keep my mouth shut to protect her from the truth?"

"It's a hard decision," Cristoff agreed. "I don't understand why the Feds won't leave her alone? What do they think she'll do when she finds out? She can't sue them. Besides, they've probably destroyed all the records. What are they so worried about?"

"Maybe this interrogation was just a follow-up procedure. Perhaps they'll stay away from her, now."

"Perhaps."

Both men looked at each other and frowned. Where the government was concerned, nothing could be certain. "I think I'll wait until she's home before I say anything," Justin finally said.

"Good idea."

"I just hope her parents don't run into those guys at some point, or we're going to have even more questions to answer!"

Cristoff knew Justin was right. "Her parents should be arriving soon. That's a long drive from Maryland, probably 7 hours or more. Hopefully, the sight of them will bring some comfort to Nicole."

Justin nodded in agreement, although his thoughts were elsewhere. "Why don't we head downstairs to the cafeteria to grab a bite to eat?"

"I was wondering when you were going to be hungry," grinned Cristoff as they both stood up. They headed for the dining area, where the two men enjoyed a peaceful meal together. Cristoff had some difficulty moving his right hand because of his injured arm, so he tried eating with his left hand, instead, which wasn't very easy. When the last morsels of food had been scraped from their plates, they checked in on

Aaron. Afterwards, Cristoff called the ranch to see how things were going. Then, both men started for Nicole's room. A well-dressed man in his 40's was just leaving as they approached. "Excuse me," he said. "Are you Nicole's relatives?"

"You must be Dr. Warren, the psychiatrist," Justin commented, holding out his hand in a friendly gesture.

"Yes. And you are?" They shook hands.

"Justin MacFierson. And this is Cristoff Colvert. We're close friends of Nicole. We also work with her at the ranch. She has no relatives here with her, sir."

"Ah, I see." The doctor stroked his small goatee. "May I have a word with you?"

"Of course." The three walked to another area down the corridor where it was more private. "Is Nicole okay?" Justin asked.

"That's what I needed to discuss," the doctor replied. Justin could sense the concern in his tone. "She's a very complex girl, and not very cooperative, I'm afraid. She practically threw me out of the room."

"We assumed that might happen," Cristoff remarked. "She was treated very badly by some doctors in an institution several years ago."

"So she told me," he commented. "Miss Tyler, however, did eventually put her fear and anger aside and allow me a few minutes to work with her."

"And?"

Dr. Warren paused, collecting his thoughts. "She's deeply depressed, which is typical after experiencing such trauma. The problem is, she won't express it. Oh, she'll tell you all the details of what occurred, but it's as if she's the narrator. There's no emotion in her voice."

"Could she still be in shock?"

"Yes. I've seen this happen before. Unfortunately, the longer she suppresses her feelings, the greater the danger when they finally surface."

"What do you mean?"

The doctor pursed his lips and briefly stared at the floor.

"When this occurs, some people merely go through a crying spell; others, well..." he glanced up, his eyes shifting from one man to the other, "others may become temporarily, uh, shall we say... uncontrollable."

Cristoff grew defensive. "Not Nicole. She's tougher than you think. She'll talk about her feelings when she decides the time is right. She's smart, you know?"

"This has nothing to do with intelligence," the doctor firmly stated. "I strongly suggest she make regular visits to a psychiatrist when she returns home."

"We'll see she does that," Cristoff said in a strict voice, knowing full well Nicole would do whatever she pleased.

Dr. Warren wordlessly studied the ranch hand for a few seconds with suspicious eyes. "Where are her parents? I'd like to speak to them."

"Uh..." Cristoff nervously glanced at his friend. "Her parents aren't in West Virginia."

"Fine. Give me their phone number," Dr. Warren commanded, prompting Justin to speak up.

"Nicole's parents are deceased, doctor. They passed away while Nicole was in captivity. We haven't told her, yet."

The older man's eyebrows lifted at this new information. His expression turned grave, his voice low and firm. "I strongly suggest you delay informing her of this as long as is humanly possible. She is in no condition to handle it. Put her in touch with another psychiatrist as soon as she returns home. It is imperative you follow this advice, is that understood?" The two men nodded. "Good. I've left some pills at the nurse's desk. Make sure Miss Tyler continues to take them when she leaves the hospital." Without waiting for a reply, Dr. Warren uttered a faint goodbye and quickly left their presence. Justin and Cristoff watched him leave, then helplessly looked at each other. It would not be easy walking into Nicole's room, now.

"Her parents died?" spoke Cristoff, half choking on the words in amusement.

"Well..." Justin coughed nervously. "If the doctor thought they were alive, he'd contact them and scare them so badly they'd insist on Nicole coming back to Maryland to live with them. We can't have that now, can we?"

Cristoff threw the blond an incredulous look, then wagged his head from side to side.

They delayed seeing her for another half hour. When they finally stepped through the doorway, the question they expected to hear, surfaced on her lips. "Where are my parents?"

"They should be here soon, Nicole" Cristoff answered. "You know it's a long drive to West Virginia from Maryland."

"Oh, yes," she remembered.

"Let me tell you about the ranch," Cristoff offered, quickly changing the subject. "I think you'll be quite pleased. Shane has already shown some of the stallions."

"Really?" Nicole perked up. Cristoff took the cue, expanding on the issue for the next 15 minutes to keep her smile intact. The horses had done well at the shows.

"Ribbons?" Nicole squeaked. "We have first place ribbons, already? It's not even Spring, yet! This is fabulous! What about the two new hires you mentioned? How are they doing?"

"Fine." Cristoff relayed a few tidbits of information about Kevin and Billy while Nicole eagerly listened. Then suddenly, out of the blue, Nicole switched topics in midstream, addressing Justin. "Is Downing dead?"

An immediate hush fell over the group. Nicole studied their expressions, trying to ascertain the answer.

"He died two hours ago," Justin calmly replied. Nicole showed no emotion. "Don't worry," he continued. "He admitted everything to the police."

His answer seemed to satisfy her as she quizzed, "Did he tell them where Daniel is buried?"

"If he did, they're keeping quiet about it."

"Oh." Nicole's gaze drifted downwards to the end of her bed. Cristoff nervously cleared his throat and carefully steered the conversation back to discussing horses. By her response to the questions being asked, Justin could tell she was only half-listening; her mind was far, far away.

"Since The General has been so unruly, we've simply lunged him, daily," Cristoff said while she slowly nodded. Her eyes suddenly fell upon Justin, again.

"My painting!" she blurted. "Did you bring my painting?"

"What painting?" the blond queried.

"The one from the room... the one I had made for your sister while I was being held hostage. Where is it?"

"I don't know."

"I have to have it!" she insisted.

"We'll get it for you. Don't worry."

"Please try," she implored. "It's very special." She lapsed into silence after speaking, thus ending their visit. Cristoff and Justin rose to leave. The blond glanced in her direction one more time, his heart thudding against his ribs. He leaned over the bed and kissed her forehead. "Rest well, Nicole. We'll be back soon." Dark eyes met his as she softly smiled, then watched the two men slowly walk out the door.

"Well," Cristoff sighed to his friend once they exited the room, "we have our work cut out for us. Nicole wants her painting."

"We're not going to be allowed on the murder scene," Justin said.

"Maybe one of the investigators will fetch it for us."

But when both men ventured back to the scene of the crime the next morning, they were stunned to find out the picture had been confiscated. "Why?" Justin demanded.

"Evidence," came the authority's reply.

"Evidence for what?"

"That information is confidential."

Cristoff looked perplexed. "The police know who killed Daniel. Robert Downing told them Switch did it. He also confirmed what occurred when we arrived at the house. What's the big mystery?"

"Can't say," came the firm reply.

Justin didn't like what he was hearing. "When can Nicole Tyler return home? She's going to be released today, you know."

"You'll have to speak with Detective Nichols."

"Who's he?"

"He's in charge of the investigation."

Cristoff and Justin exchanged frowns, then headed to the police precinct to find the detective, who proved to be very evasive of their questions. He strongly suggested, however, that all of them remain in town for at least a week. "Impossible," Justin objected. "Nicole and Cristoff have a ranch to run. I'll be here, though, with my brother."

"It's not going to look good," Detective Nichols remarked, "if anyone skips out."

Anger flashed in Cristoff's eyes. "No one is skipping out, least of all, Nicole! She has more scruples than any female I know. But we have a business to run, detective, and it isn't going to make much money if we're here in West Virginia! Now, unless you have a warrant for Nicole's arrest, I'm taking her back home." That said, the ranch hand turned on his heel and stormed out of the office, with Justin close behind. They jumped in the car, tension mounting.

"What the devil is going on, Cristoff?" Justin snorted. "I get the feeling we're not in the clear."

"I have the same feeling," Cristoff grumbled. "I have an idea, though. Let's get a newspaper and read about the incident."

They did. The article, however, gave no hint of the dark secret the police were harboring. The only new information they found was the discovery of Daniel's body in the woods behind the house. To their relief, the news listed Switch as the alleged murderer. Justin peered at his friend. "I'm going to keep tabs on any late breaking stories while I'm here. If anyone comes to the ranch to question Nicole, let me know."

They drove over to the hospital to visit Nicole, but found her preparing to leave. Her parents were standing by her side, assisting her.

"Good to see you, Mr and Mrs. Henderson!" chirped Cristoff. "I hope you were able to get a restful night's sleep last night?"

"As well as can be expected," smiled Mr. Henderson. "I

want to thank you for finding my daughter, Cristoff. I don't know what we'd have done without your help."

"Yes!" chimed in Nicole's mother. "Thank God for you and the others!"

"Oh, this is Justin, Mr. And Mrs. Henderson," Cristoff motioned towards his friend. "He's our close friend and played a big part in the rescue of your daughter. He organized it all."

"Then I must thank you, too!" the older man said to the blond.

Justin reached out to shake hands with the father, noticing how firm his grasp was for a man in his 40's. He had large, kind eyes, the same color as his daughter's, and stood over six feet tall, broad-shouldered, thinning brown hair. Nicole's mother was more petite, with sparkling blue eyes and wavy black hair. Her appearance was striking and would turn any man's head. There was a protective air about her that Justin sensed right away. This woman was not going to let her daughter go back to the ranch to stay, he could feel it. They would need much convincing. As if reading his mind, those dreaded words tumbled from her mouth.

"Darling?" spoke Mrs. Henderson to Nicole. "We really do think you should come home to Maryland with us while you recover. The ranch was never a safe place."

Cristoff and Justin held their tongue, but tension filled the air as they watched Nicole's body language. What would she do?

"Now, mom," she began, "you do know that all the bad people involved are dead? There's no reason to feel concerned about me. I'm perfectly safe at the ranch. Besides, I need to be within driving distance if I get called back here for further questioning. They aren't too happy with me leaving the area in the first place."

Both young men let out a tiny sigh of relief under their breath.

Mrs. Henderson gave her husband a worried look. As if on cue, he asked, "Couldn't your mother stay with you for a while, honey? I do have to go back to work, but she could remain at the ranch to make sure you're well taken care of?"

"Don't be silly, daddy. I'll be just fine." Nicole smiled lovingly at her mother, but hesitated when she saw tears brimming in those beautiful blue eyes. "Oh..." she stepped up to the older woman, giving her a warm affectionate hug. "If it makes you feel better, mom, I guess you could stay for a week or two? Would that be all right? We can buy you some clothes in town." Nicole gave her a generous smile.

"Thank you, darling!" beamed Mrs. Henderson. "I feel so much better now!"

Cristoff and Justin smiled politely at the trio. Justin had nothing to worry about now with Nicole's mom staying at the ranch; Cristoff couldn't make headway in his relationship with the dark-haired beauty as long as 'mom' was around. Plus, by the time Mrs. Henderson would be going back to Maryland, Justin would probably be out of West Virginia with Aaron and heading to Coltsville. The timing was great. He thoughtfully studied Nicole. She almost looked like her old self, although she only had slippers to wear with her clothes, but there still was a vagueness in her eyes.

She turned to Justin, "I need to buy shoes. Did you find my picture?"

"No. I'm sorry, Nicole. I'll check again tomorrow. When I find it, I'll mail it to you." She remained expressionless for a moment. He took a chance, approaching to lightly kiss her cheek. "Have a safe trip home. I'll call when they release Aaron."

"I saw him a few minutes ago to tell him goodbye. He looks so helpless. Take care of him, Justin."

"You know I will." Their gaze met, but only briefly. Nicole turned away.

Justin wanted to pull her into his arms, but he realized she had no knowledge of the torment he had gone through these past several months; the waiting, the hoping, longing just to touch her, to see her smile. It was pure hell. He had even fantasized about the day he'd find her, how he'd be the knight in shining armor, sweeping her off her feet to carry her into the sunset. Instead, Nicole had been the heroine, killing two men to save his skin, not to mention Aaron's. How ironic.

She was not the same person now. How could she be? He ached when he saw how she had emotionally detached herself from her surroundings. He shared her pain. He needed to help her, to be with her so she could lean on him. But his obligation to remain with Aaron had priority; thus, Cristoff would take his place. At such a crucial time in her life, Cristoff might easily win her favor, eliminating any chance for Justin to deepen their relationship. It frustrated him to no end. The only comfort was in knowing Mrs. Henderson would monopolize most of Nicole's time, instead of the ranch hand.

Cristoff glanced at his watch. "We probably should grab something to eat before starting the journey back home." He held out his hand to Justin, saying, "Good luck. Hopefully we'll see you soon." But his eyes were lying; Justin picked up on it. An uneasy feeling settled into the pit of his stomach as he watched them all walk down the long corridor and disappear around the corner.

The next two weeks dragged so slowly that by the time Justin and Aaron headed for home, both men were a bundle of nerves. Justin had called Nicole numerous times, but the conversation between them had been strained, at best; she was never in a talkative mood. In fact, she barely said anything, except that she decided not to attend Daniel's funeral. When he spoke to Cristoff, the ranch hand assured him Nicole was taking her medicine although he still could not convince her to see a psychiatrist. Mrs. Henderson even pleaded with her, and it was with much trepidation that the older woman finally left to return home to Maryland. Cristoff had always liked Nicole's mother, but he knew Nicole needed lots of freedom and would feel confined by her mother's overprotectedness. He saw her become more restless and agitated with each passing day. Just his luck that Mrs. Henderson left only the day before Justin was due to arrive!

Finally in Coltsville, Justin entered his house, made Aaron as comfortable as possible, then telephoned Nicole. There was no answer. He dialed Cristoff's number. "Cristoff? This is Justin. I just got in. Where's Nicole? I called her house but the phone kept ringing."

"She's probably in the barn. She's been spending a lot of time with The General. How's Aaron?"

"He's doing pretty well. He isn't supposed to lift anything for a while. I'm hiring a private nurse for him for during the day while Jan and I work."

"Oh, I bet he'll love that!" Cristoff replied. "Oh, by the way, Justin, if you're planning to see Nicole, I think I should warn you—she's a bit skittish."

"Skittish?"

"Yeah. Every little movement scares her. Actually, I think she's paranoid. She even bought a new gun."

"Hmm... doesn't sound good, no. I was about to head over there now, so see you in a few minutes?"

"Sure."

Hanging up the phone, Justin pondered the situation. If Nicole was skittish, Cristoff probably had had no luck pursuing her. "Poor Nicole," he said under his breath as he jumped into his Ferrari. Who knew what hell she was going through now? When Cristoff met him near Nicole's house, he was apprehensive. The two of them walked to the stable in silence. After sliding open the large door, Cristoff called, "It's just me, Nicole. I've brought someone to see you." A few more steps and Justin caught sight of the young beauty; she was in The General's stall, sitting on a pile of dry straw, looking sad and withdrawn.

"Hello, stranger," he greeted in a low, husky voice filled with emotion.

Nicole jumped up from her position, a radiant smile on her face. "Justin!" she cried, running two steps forward; then, checking herself, she hesitated, took a deep breath, and slowly strolled towards the handsome blond. She did not miss the amused sparkle in his eye, nor the tense shoulders now lowering as he relaxed. Allowing him to embrace her, she exclaimed, "It's so good to see you! Cristoff told me Charlie King was never found, so, silly me, I thought perhaps you might disappear, too!"

"Never," Justin replied, gently pulling away; he didn't want her to feel trapped within his arms.

"How is Aaron?"

"About the same as last time I talked to you. He's whining like a baby. He says to tell you to stop over sometime."

"Maybe I will. Let's go into the house. It's getting a little chilly out here." She threw Cristoff a sideways glance. "The three of us; like old times, eh?" She smiled. It warmed their hearts. Both men were lost in their own thoughts as they walked over to Nicole's house and went inside.

Just then the phone rang. Nicole politely excused herself to answer it. A few minutes of conversation ensued, after which she quickly hung up the receiver, then approached her friends. "This is odd," she said. "Daniel's lawyer just phoned, asking me to visit his office in a few hours. I didn't know lawyers had Saturday hours."

"Are you sure this person is who he claimed to be?" Justin quizzed.

"Why on earth would you think differently? Of course he's Daniel's lawyer. He said so."

"You'll have to forgive me, Nicole. I'm quite suspicious ever since the kidnapping. I hope you'll take someone with you." Her eyes met his and locked in a stare-down. "I only made the suggestion because I care about you," he firmly said. "You don't know what I went through while you were missing."

"Yes, I do," came the surprising reply. Her expression softened considerably; compassion emanated from the dark brown eyes. "Jan told me." She placed her warm hand on his arm. It occurred to him then that she had no idea how much her touch affected him. He desperately wanted to show her, but instead, he asked, "How have you been, Nicole?"

"I'm coping."

"You look as if you hadn't slept in days. Are you having

nightmares?"

She bowed her head. "I've been a little tense, that's all."

"Look, Nicole," he said, gently, "if you ever feel the need to discuss what happened while you were held captive—"

"No!" She rapidly shook her head. "There's nothing to discuss." There was a subtle warning in the finality of her words which Justin could not ignore.

He softened his tone. "Nicole... eventually, you will have to talk about it."

All conversation abruptly stopped at this point. Had he gone too far? Perhaps he had better drop the subject. Justin began to feel awkward. He scratched his knee. "Have you been bothered by reporters since your return?"

"Just the first day I arrived. They were swarming like hornets."

"Hard to avoid, huh?"

She cocked her head to the side, mildly amused. "You don't avoid them, Justin. You play to them. I gave them a story. It's the fastest way to get rid of them. Then I bragged about the Desert Wind stallions. It's smart advertising."

"I'll say. One thing that bothers me, though, is that anyone can walk onto this property. Did Cristoff mention a security system to you?"

"Security system?" She bristled. "I had enough of captivity the past several months; I certainly don't want to feel like a prisoner in my own home! No," she said, shaking her head, "I don't want a security system."

"It's to protect you," he insisted. "You don't even have to activate it during the day, if you don't want to. Just use it at night. You'll feel much safer."

"No. You'll feel much safer," she wryly replied. "With Daniel gone, I have nothing to be afraid of."

Justin let out a long exhale.

"Besides," she added, "I bought another gun last week, considering the police never returned mine. Did they return yours?"

"Come to think of it... no, but I'm glad our weapons were

properly registered."

"Well, anyway, I have no need for a security alarm."

Worry, like a dark shadow, flickered across Justin's face, much to Nicole's dismay. "What is it?" she pressed. "You know something I don't."

"You'll have to excuse me," Cristoff interrupted, quickly throwing on his coat. "I just remembered I left a pot of coffee perking on the stove!" Without so much as a glance in Justin's direction, he sailed out the front door, leaving his friend to fend for himself against Nicole's prying eyes.

With an exit like that, Justin was positive Nicole now surmised the seriousness of the situation. He had no choice but to level with her. "Do you remember two men in suits who questioned you while you were in the hospital?"

"Yes."

"They might have been government agents. Did they identify themselves?"

She paused. "I don't believe they did. Why would anyone from the government visit me?" A knowing look crossed her face. "Oh. Of course. Daniel. They only asked about Daniel. Well, I set them straight on that issue!"

Justin's expression grew intense. "I can't keep this a secret any longer, Nicole. I have to tell you what I discovered about Daniel. The news might not be what you want to hear, but just say the word and I'll stop talking, okay?" She gave a slight nod, so he continued. "Daniel killed Philip."

"How did you find out?"

"You already knew?"

"Yes. One of his guards, Switch, told me."

"Did he mention the reason?" She shook her head. Justin went on. "I pieced everything together after talking to Maureen. She said Daniel always phoned his coworkers before he came to your house to play poker. It suddenly dawned on me that Philip's poker buddies were actually Daniel's friends."

"So?"

"They were there on a mission, Nicole. Let's first discuss the afternoon of Philip's murder. Cristoff received a call from

Linda, one of the hookers at Carla's. She pleads with him to visit her and is so persuasive, Cristoff leaves."

"You think Daniel paid her," Nicole commented.

"Exactly. With Cristoff gone, he can do his dirty deed without any risk of being seen."

"But why did he do it, Justin?"

"Because Philip threatened to blow the cover on a secret government experiment... an experiment, Nicole, which used you as the guinea pig."

Nicole stared, dumbfounded.

"That's right," he continued. "There was no Dr. Bohman supplying Philip with drugs because Daniel was our Dr. Bohman." He studied her for a minute, unsure he should go on. She looked so distraught. "Are you okay?" he asked. She nodded and clutched his hand. "This drug, whatever it was, was to be used by the government on important foreign diplomats to alter their brain waves. I believe an agent could slip a pill into their drink, sit back, and in a few minutes, extract any information they wanted out of the foreigner. The medicine made them open to suggestions by melting their inhibitions, plus had the wonderful after-effect of loss of memory."

"Thus, they could even give this to a spy, gather knowledge from him, and he'd have no recall of it happening," Nicole remarked faintly.

"At least, this is what the Feds hoped. Daniel's coworkers needed to pay regular visits to your house to study the effects of the pills, so Daniel made an arrangement with Philip, convincing Philip that if he agreed to the experiment, Daniel's friends would feed his gambling streak. He told Philip they were lousy poker players and they were, on purpose. As long as they lost money to your husband, he'd consent to having them return. So the vicious cycle began. Enter Problem One: Cristoff comes knocking on the door during one of these episodes, asking to borrow record albums. He notices your abnormal behavior. Daniel plays the good guy and tells him, in private, that Philip is exploiting you. He paints Philip as the bad guy. Then, to look even more innocent, Daniel decides to join Cristoff in telling you the whole truth after your husband's death, which, in reality, was anything but the truth."

"That's when they told me about the drug," Nicole said.

"Yes, which brings me to Problem Two: I think your sterility is due to the drug."

"You're guessing," she pointed out.

"But it all fits together. You can't conceive. Philip is upset. He feels guilty when he begins to suspect it is because of the drug."

Nicole raised a brow, saying, "That's why he was so kind to me at that one time!"

"I'm afraid so. You were devastated. You left to visit your parents in Maryland. While you were gone, Philip probably phoned Daniel and vented his anger, threatening to go public about the entire project. Daniel is left with no other choice but to destroy him because he knows if Philip goes through with his threat, Daniel will either end up being prosecuted, or the Feds will come after him to shut him up. If the government agents had murdered Philip, they wouldn't have left his body in the living room, to be found by you. They wouldn't have left any trace of the murder. So, because of the manner in which the killing took place, I assumed Daniel must have pulled the trigger, himself. He could not bring himself to move the body, however. Maybe guilt had set in. Realizing this, he needed to get someone else to do it, someone whom he could trust to keep quiet. You arrived home before he could find someone to finish the dirty deed."

"Wasn't he taking a chance on Cristoff going to the house and seeing Philip?"

"Daniel had the prostitute detain Cristoff long enough that it was too close to the time he needed to leave to pick you up at the airport. Cristoff told me he didn't have time to stop back at the house. I didn't understand why Philip wasn't the one picking you up, but Cristoff said he was asked to do it because your husband had an important appointment to attend to around the time your flight was coming in."

Justin squeezed her hand, briefly pausing to make sure she

was still okay. "Enter Problem Three: They had administered the drug enough times to you, but now they had to keep tabs on your health for any side effects to be noted. So, Daniel makes regular visits to the ranch, always asking how you are, always asking Cristoff if you are well. The government may or may not, at this point, believe the drug made you sterile."

"Now comes Problem Four: Cristoff mentions you are having flashbacks. This is not a good sign. Daniel panics, fearing you might start to piece everything together. He tells the Feds. They want proof. Daniel tells you he is bringing a doctor to your house who will try to help you. Instead, he brings a Federal Agent in disguise to witness what occurs when you are given alcohol."

"And that is when they drew blood from me," she murmured, still incredulous.

"Yes. Now you know why Daniel bugged your house and office."

"But when I confronted him, he said it was to protect me from George Craiger, the poker player who had a grudge against Philip."

"Very easily staged," Justin commented. "When Cristoff got rid of the microphone in the vase, Daniel must have heard something. Not taking a chance, he called George and staged the phony grudge story. You played right into their hands."

Nicole's face suddenly paled. Justin ran his hand up to her shoulder, lightly stroking. "I just can't believe it," she said. "How could Philip have allowed this? I was his wife!" Anger, betrayal, hurt radiated in her eyes as she looked helplessly at Justin.

"Nicole," he softly said, pulling her into his arms.

She let him embrace her as tears spilled silently down her cheeks. "I shouldn't cry," she mumbled. "Not yet... not yet. I have to be strong. I have to see Daniel's lawyer in a few hours." Still leaning against him, she held back more tears and bit her lip. He brushed away the two wet streaks with his thumb. Then he held her face in his hands and gazed longingly into her eyes. She was vulnerable right now, easily influenced.

"Nicole," he said, whispering her name like a prayer while his mouth captured hers in a soft, sensuous kiss.

Then suddenly, it was over. Nicole pulled away. Her timing was uncanny, as a knock sounded at the door. It was as if Nicole had sensed it. Taking a deep breath to calm herself, she gracefully walked away from the flustered male. Justin marvelled at her remarkable transformation; all traces of passion had disappeared in the blink of an eye. Cristoff suspected nothing when he entered. He strode calmly into the living room.

Then he saw Justin and stopped in his tracks. The blond's face was crimson red, sparks of excitement still glittering in his cobalt blue eyes, clear evidence that Cristoff had definitely interrupted something.

"I forgot to mention an important matter to the two of you," Nicole quickly said, interrupting Cristoff's thoughts. "Take off your coat, Cristoff. Let's sit at the dining room table. I have to fetch some papers, first. I'll be down in a minute." She hurried upstairs while the two men casually strolled over to the table.

Cristoff pointed to his upper lip. "You have lipstick on you."

"Oh, do I?" Justin nervously said, swiftly wiping the area. He changed the subject. "I told her, Cristoff," he said, pulling out a chair.

"Told her what?"

"The whole story about Philip and Daniel."

"She seems to have taken it well."

"There were a few tears. She's trying to stay calm because of her appointment with Daniel's lawyer."

The sound of Nicole's footsteps ended their conversation. She opened a manila folder in her hands. "Now, Cristoff, I had the opportunity to review the finance books one night this past week. I noticed you took a cut in pay after my abduction." She handed him a check. "This is what I owe you." She halted his protest. "No arguments, please. What's fair is fair." Her large, chocolate eyes warmly gazed at both men. "I am overwhelmed by the loyalty of you two. I never expected the ranch to survive my kidnapping and it wouldn't have, if it hadn't been for both of you."

"It was mainly Justin's doing," Cristoff commended. "He used his money to pay Kevin and Billy's salary."

"Money is nothing without experience," Nicole pointed out. "You know my horses' personalities, Cristoff. You know which methods of teaching work best for each animal. Don't downplay your role in this ranch." Reaching into the folder, she pulled out another check and handed it to Justin. "This should cover the amount you spent on Kevin and Billy. Plus, I noticed you didn't pay yourself for the past months. I've added that on, too. Are there any other expenses you paid for?"

Justin shoved the colored paper back across the table. "I don't need your money, Nicole. Besides, you can't afford this."

"But I can and I have! I told you I had another bank account." She slid the check back towards him. "If you don't take it, I'll have to ask you to stop working for me."

He saw the determination in her eyes, and threw a skeptical look in Cristoff's direction, muttering, "I thought you said she only had a small bank account somewhere?", to which Cristoff merely shrugged.

Nicole smiled. "Now that that is settled..." She opened the folder again, glancing at two contracts. "Both of you are true friends in every sense of the word. I am so lucky to have you. You not only kept the ranch running—you kept my dream alive; and for this, I will always be indebted to you. I cannot thank you enough; however, I can offer you a partnership in Desert Wind Arabians." She handed out the contracts. "Twenty-five percent is not very much, but if I gave you anything higher, together you could override my decisions." A beautiful grin spread across her face at their stunned expressions.

"Are you sure you want to do this?" Cristoff quizzed.

"I've never been more sure of anything in my life," she firmly stated. "As a partner, you'll also receive a share of the profits." Silence fell about the room as the two men studied the typed pages. "Well?" Nicole chirped.

Justin glanced at Cristoff. "I'd say we'd be a fool to pass up the offer." Both men hastily signed the paper, handing two copies to Nicole while keeping one copy for themselves. To seal the deal, Nicole pushed back her chair, stood up and declared, "Gentlemen? Welcome to Desert Wind. I hope your stay is pleasant. It will be an honor to work with you."

They all shook hands, Nicole's excitement evident in her eyes. But that was not the only emotion conveyed; affection radiated in those depths, also. Justin felt positive now that she would recover from the recent trauma. She finally appeared to be her old self again. Taking advantage of her cheerful mood, he inquired, "Can we accompany you to the lawyer's office, Nicole?"

"I don't see why not," she agreed. "It never hurts to have someone else's point of view. My appointment, however, isn't for another hour."

"Why don't we go into town and grab a bite to eat, then? My treat."

"Count me in," Cristoff smiled.

"All right," Nicole said, heading to the closet to retrieve her coat. "I'll drive."

They took the cover off the Shelby, climbed in and drove to town, choosing a small diner for their meal. Conversation flowed easily, although internally, Nicole was a nervous wreck. She had a good idea why she was summoned to the lawyer's office and she dreaded the meeting. Her intuition right on target, Nicole's assumption proved true.

Daniel had named her as sole beneficiary of his entire estate. "Guilt money," she had called it when they drove back home. "I don't want any part of it!"

"Take it," Justin prompted. "You deserve it, Nicole. Look at what Daniel did to your life! We don't even have an antidote for the pill he gave you."

As if she hadn't heard a word he said, she ranted, "I wonder why he made me wait two weeks after his death?"

"The lawyer told you. Daniel put that clause in the will to

allow you time to grieve."

She swung around to face both men as they departed the car and entered her house. "Do I look like I'm grieving?" she challenged. "Well, do I?"

"Of course not; because you know he killed your husband. But Daniel didn't expect you to find that out. He also felt guilty when Philip gave him most of his wealth. He wants to pay you back. You deserve the money. Are you going to move into his mansion?"

"Heck, no," she replied. "I don't want any memories of him around. I'll sell it and send the money to Charlie King's wife for her to use on herself and her children. It's the least I can do."

Justin nodded his approval, amazed at her generosity.

Cristoff suddenly said, "Wasn't it odd that Daniel mentioned the Feds in his letter to Nicole?"

"At least we have a contact person's name now, if any agents should bother her." Justin glanced at the name scribbled on the piece of paper in his hand.

"But why would this person help me," Nicole pointed out, "when he didn't help Daniel? You said Daniel was probably running from the Feds."

"But I think they were after him because he murdered Philip. They thought he was losing his sanity. They felt he couldn't be trusted."

"Well, I'm not calling that, that..." she snatched the paper from Justin's hand, "Mr. Joe Williams."

The three of them started to sit down when the sound of an approaching vehicle reached their ears. "Who could that be?" mumbled Cristoff, peering out the window. "It looks like the sheriff!"

A cold shiver passed over Nicole as she walked towards the door. Opening it, she noticed the sheriff had his deputies with him. The expression on his face was grave, very grave.

"Nicole Tyler?" he asked, staring into her eyes. Nicole's heart began to flutter. He knew darn well who she was. "Nicole Tyler?" he repeated, growing uneasy in the presence of Justin and Cristoff.

"Yes," she finally answered.

"What is it, Jack?" Cristoff quizzed.

The sheriff nodded to the deputies, who now proceeded to cuff Nicole's hands. "I have a warrant for your arrest in the murder of Daniel Michael Tyler..."

His words faded in Nicole's mind as the obvious raced through her brain. How could this be? Downing told them Switch had killed Daniel! Why was she accused? Even the newspaper listed Switch as the alleged murderer.

"You have the right to remain silent..."

The sheriff's voice droned on and on. In a panic, Justin grabbed the telephone to call a lawyer. Cristoff, livid with rage, began arguing with the authorities, shouting and cursing until the men placed Nicole inside the squad car and drove away.

"What the hell is going on?" he screamed when Justin hung up the phone.

"This is why they kept the guns," the blond snapped. "Nicole's fingerprints are on Switch's gun."

"Only because she picked it up after she shot Switch," Cristoff countered.

"Apparently, the detective doesn't believe her. I'm going to meet the lawyer at the sheriff's office. You watch the ranch, Cristoff."

Justin grabbed his coat while Cristoff followed him to the door, the ranch hand's voice furious. "I bet the government's behind this! You wait and see! They want Nicole behind bars, where she can't be heard. They want to shut her up. They're afraid... yes, that's what it is... they're afraid she'll speak out. Perhaps if we can assure them she doesn't know anything—"

"We'll talk when I get back," promised Justin, sprinting to his car. He fought back his own feelings of despair as he drove towards town. None of this should have happened. Had Daniel cursed them all?

For Nicole, the nightmare was just beginning. She was not only charged with premeditated murder, but also conspiracy to murder; the second charge filed in regards to Philip. As her lawyer, Bill Bradley, explained it later, the prosecution had decided she had Daniel kill Philip, thinking she was his beneficiary. When she discovered Daniel inherited the money, she secretly became his lover, then suggested they run off together. Her abduction was staged, so no one would suspect they were lovers, for it might throw suspicion on Philip's murder case. Once Daniel took Nicole to West Virginia, she easily killed him to regain Philip's money. According to the prosecution, it was all neatly planned. Nicole's canvas painting proved it. Someone who was being held hostage would not paint such a cheerful painting. Obviously, the woman was not being held against her own will. They reasoned that she would have gotten away with the plan, had it not been for Cristoff, Justin and Aaron surprising her. Their sudden appearance caused her to change horses in midstream; she pretended to be on their side. The prosecution labeled her as dangerous.

Unless Justin could post bail, Nicole would be shipped to a jail in West Virginia, where she would spend the next several months waiting to stand trial for the first offense. In his heart, Justin knew she would not survive prison—not after just coming out of captivity two weeks ago. It would destroy her, if not physically, then mentally.

But Nicole assured him otherwise. She pleaded with him to leave her in prison. "I don't want bail posted with money designated for the ranch," she said. "And I certainly don't want you using money from your own account. In fact, I have a favor to ask."

"Anything," he had replied.

"Tell Bill Bradley to bring the necessary papers for me to sign in order to sell the ranch."

"What?!" screeched Justin, appalled.

"Look, Justin. Whether the court finds me innocent or not, the scandal has already begun. Maureen told the detective I've slept with Daniel. Now the prosecution is positive we were lovers. My name is mud. The ranch doesn't stand a chance of prospering if I'm still the owner. You know how fickle people are. I want to transfer ownership to you and Cristoff. Then, if

I'm released and the rumors die down, you can sell it back to me."

Justin was astounded. "You are more important than the ranch," he firmly stated. "I can't imagine anyone choosing jail over freedom."

"Desert Wind is my dream," she emphasized. "Without it, freedom means nothing."

"You can't be serious? What about your life, Nicole? Isn't that worth something? What kind of life will you have in prison?" What he wanted to say was, "What about me, Nicole? Don't I mean anything to you?", but he refrained, already hurt by her declaration. He realized then, how captivity had changed her. Apparently, she only cared about one thing—her precious ranch. "I won't allow you to remain behind bars," he announced in a stern voice. "I'm posting bail with my own money, whether you like it or not!"

Her response was quick and to the point. "You do, and I'll never speak to you again!"

"Why?!" he stormed. "Because you're too damn proud to accept my money?"

"It'll be a debt I'll never be able to repay."

"Then think of it as a gift."

"You know I won't."

Their visit ended with both parties furious. Justin climbed back into his car, spewing curses like a drunken sailor. "She's going to drive me crazy!" he fumed, heading towards the bank. The vehicle screeched to a halt in front of the building while he thought over his decision. If he did post bail, Nicole would probably play the role of the indentured servant for who knows how long. He'd never be able to ascertain what her true feelings were for him; she'd always be polite and yielding. She'd be more like a slave than her true self. This simply would not do. He desperately needed an alternate scheme for gaining her release from prison...

Thus, on a bright Tuesday morning, Justin put a new plan into motion for freeing Nicole. It took a lot of persuading, two weeks of waiting for an appointment, but finally he was ushered into Joe Williams' office and the door was firmly closed. Like a king on his throne, the large, overbearing man leaned back in his huge leather chair, staring at Justin with a critical eye. "You're wasting your time and mine, Mr. MacFierson," he bellowed. "But I said I'd give you five minutes," he glanced at his watch, "so start talking."

"I need to speak with you about Nicole Tyler. She's been falsely accused of murdering Daniel Tyler."

"So?"

"In his last will and testament, Daniel noted that she should contact you if she has any problems with government agents bothering her."

"Huh," grunted Williams, his interest piqued.

"I have reason to believe that certain agents put pressure on the authorities to arrest Nicole. You see, Nicole and I know about the government's experiment conducted at her house."

"I have no idea what you're talking about," huffed the large man. But Justin sensed differently by the manner in which his gaze now darted about the room. He was getting nervous.

"Mr. Williams," Justin drawled, stretching the syllables in a mocking tone. "Must I spell it out for you? You used Nicole Tyler as a guinea pig..." He relayed every last detail of the experimental research to the man, verifying his original statement. Joe Williams acted indifferent during the speech, but the muscles in his jaw tensed involuntarily. After calmly waiting for his visitor to finish, he said, "That's quite an imagination you have there, MacFierson. I still don't understand why you've come to me?"

Justin began to grow agitated. "Why would Daniel give us your name if you couldn't be of any help to Nicole? She's in prison, Mr. Williams! And she's innocent! It appears that your men would prefer she conveniently disappear from the face of the earth. But it isn't necessary. Nicole is not a 'kiss and tell' type of woman. She's very private. She doesn't want to stir up trouble. She wants to put this all behind her, including the experiment, even though any other normal citizen would take the federal government to court!"

At this point, Justin jumped up from his chair, placing both hands on the man's desk and, leaning forward, growled, "You've ruined her life. You've ruined her chances of bearing children. The least you can do is give her her dignity by clearing her of all charges! The very least, Mr. Williams! And if that doesn't move you to action, perhaps this will: When Nicole Tyler is on the witness stand and is questioned about her affair with Daniel Tyler, she will have to speak the truth. The truth, Mr. Williams. She will describe the circumstances leading up to her rendezvous with her brother-in-law, which included the inability for her to control her own actions, due to the pills administered to her."

"We don't have any records of such an experiment," Williams beamed with satisfaction.

"But we do live in a skeptical society," Justin countered. "The public enjoys juicy gossip, don't they, sir? Someone, some news journalist somewhere, to appease the demand, will begin investigating her story. I'm sure they'll find a willing informer who can be bought off. Think about that, Mr. Williams! But if you drop the charges against Nicole, she will keep quiet about the issue. It's your decision, sir." Justin donned his coat.

"She probably wouldn't have even had been kidnapped if government agents had not been following Daniel around."

"I can assure you nobody was following him around," refuted Joe. "We have better things to do with our time."

"Yes," mocked Justin, "like experimenting on defenseless women." His cold eyes pierced Joe's. "Good day." Justin managed a slight sarcastic smile. "I wish I could say it's been a pleasure."

Although he had no clue whether Joe Williams would take his advice, Justin had to hope for the best. He was emotionally worn out from the entire ordeal. He and Cristoff also had to handle the frantic phone calls from Nicole's parents during this time. It wasn't easy. Cristoff had telephoned them right after Nicole had been arrested to inform them of the turn of events so they wouldn't find out first from the news media. He assured them that he and Justin would do all they could to secure their daughter's freedom. A new problem arose when the Hendersons insisted on getting their own lawyer for Nicole. Justin and Cristoff bristled at the thought of someone else investigating the case and possibly discovering more information than Nicole would want them to have. So they told the parents that Nicole already selected a topnotch lawyer who was local and familiar with her. Luckily, this placated them. All they could do now was wait.

"One thing keeps bothering me, Cristoff," Justin began. "Joe Williams seemed very truthful when he said nobody was following Daniel around; and if that's so, then Daniel must have been imagining it."

"Scary thought," agreed Cristoff. "He was paranoid, probably. Bad enough for Nicole to have been kidnapped, but for her abductor to be insane... who knows what could have happened to her?"

"Did she ever talk about it with you, while I was still in West Virginia with Aaron?"

Cristoff shook his head. "Nope, not a word. She was fairly quiet until you came back to the ranch. Maybe nothing went on between her and Daniel while she was held hostage?"

"We can only hope," replied the blond as he gave a weary sigh.

CHAPTER TWENTY-THREE

Wednesday, a prison guard walked to Nicole's cell, placed a key in the lock and announced, "Nicole Tyler? You're free to go," much to her amazement. Even when she had finally returned home, she still could not believe the story Justin told her. "I don't know what to say," she quietly remarked. "This is the happiest day of my life!" She hugged him, tightly. Then she phoned her parents to give them the good news. When she finished her conversation with them, she turned her attention back to her friends.

"I suppose you're tired from the long trip," Cristoff commented, "But Justin and I were hoping you'd consider celebrating your new freedom with us at the Midnight Lounge?"

Nicole smiled. "I'd be delighted." And she meant it.

Thus, that evening, the three of them went to the nightclub with Jan, Aaron (who could now get around on his own), Shane, Kevin and Billy. The two women danced with each man at their table, happily chatting about various items. Since his back was still sore, Aaron refrained from the faster dances. The men, for the most part, were on their best behavior, politely exchanging insults while joking with one another. It was quite a merry atmosphere. Nicole sipped a slow gin fizz, feeling very exhilarated. The band struck up a slow song, prompting Justin to guide her out to the floor. After everything he had done for her, she could not decline, nor did she want to. She was so happy to be home! "Did I ever say thank you?" she whispered in his ear.

"Many times," he replied, charming her with a smile. "I've missed you."

"I've missed the ranch," she replied, aware she had not given the appropriate response. "That reminds me, I must get in touch with Bill Bradley so I can reclaim ownership of Desert Wind."

She had barely finished her sentence when, suddenly, she was surrounded by a horde of anxious reporters rapidly firing questions and snapping pictures. Sensing Nicole's confusion, Justin grabbed her hand. "Where's your purse?" he asked.

"At our table," she replied, shoving a microphone away from her face.

"Miss Tyler!" called a journalist. "How did you manage to get the prosecution to drop all the charges against you?"

Justin swiftly pulled Nicole through the crowd and towards their table, yelling to Aaron, "Pay our tab. I'll reimburse you, later. I have to get Nicole out of here!" Handing Nicole's purse to her, Aaron nodded in response, then watched the mob of reporters give chase to the fleeing couple as they headed out the front door.

"What a set-up," muttered the twin while he crushed his last cigarette against the bottom of the glass ashtray. Glittering blue eyes painstakingly searched the noisy room, darting from face to face until they came to rest upon one solitary man. "You, devil," he whispered.

"Hey! What happened to Nicole and Justin?" Jan called, racing to her brother. She was soon followed by Kevin, Billy, Cristoff and Shane.

Aaron placed a wad of bills upon the table, stood up and put on his jacket. "I guess someone got hold of the media and just couldn't keep their mouth shut."

"Even so," broke in Kevin, "I don't see how those reporters got through the front door?"

A lopsided grin tugged at Aaron's mouth. "Money, my friend. Money. They bought their way in. Now, if you'll excuse me, I have an errand to run. Do you need a ride home, sis?"

"I'm not ready to leave, yet," Jan said.

"I can drive you home when you're ready," piped Billy, to which the young girl smiled her approval.

"Don't be too late," Aaron cautioned.

"I think I'll be going, too," Cristoff suddenly said, paying his tab.

Unable to resist the urge to torment the ranch hand, Aaron jeered, "Better hurry, Cristoff. We wouldn't want to leave Justin alone with Nicole now, would we?"

"Shut up, you imbecile!" Hazel eyes flashed angrily at the blond, but Aaron simply laughed, then strolled slowly across the room to the door.

"He's an antagonizer," Shane grumbled. "I don't know how Justin can stand living with him."

"Aaron isn't all bad," Jan defended. "He has a kind side, too."

Her words rang true. It was the virtue of kindness which indeed prompted Aaron MacFierson to drive to Nicole's house in order to alert her to possible future problems with one of their companions.

"Hello, Nicole. Justin," he remarked when the front door opened to reveal the couple standing patiently before him.

"Aaron, is something wrong?" Nicole asked. "Is Jan all right?" She gestured for him to enter.

"Jan's fine," he said. "I thought I'd stop by to see if the two of you were okay."

"We are," Justin stated. "I was just mentioning to Nicole that I couldn't imagine how those reporters found out about her release, so quickly."

"Oh, I can hazard a pretty good guess," Aaron said, scratching his chin. "That's another reason I came over here. I wanted to tell you that I noticed a huge grin on Shane's face when those reporters swamped you. He stood out like a sore thumb. I think he rather enjoyed the whole episode."

Nicole looked perplexed. "But why?"

Aaron stared at his brother. "Are you going to tell her or shall I?"

"There's nothing to tell," Justin firmly stated.

"What?" begged Nicole, glancing from one twin to the other. "Tell me, Aaron!"

"Shane has a grudge against you."

"Ridiculous!" snorted Justin.

"He does," Aaron insisted to Nicole. "Big time. He was filling Justin's head with all kinds of morbid thoughts while you were gone. He definitely doesn't like you."

Nicole turned to Justin. "Is this true?"

"Shane's critical of everyone. You have to take what he says with a grain of salt."

"You underestimate him," Aaron warned. He fixed his gaze upon Nicole. "I wouldn't lie to you, Cat—not after you saved my life. Take my advice; watch your back when you're around Shane. He's sneaky."

"Considering you never did like the guy," Justin countered, but Aaron had already turned and was headed back to his car.

"Imagine that," Nicole remarked, quietly closing the front door. "Your evil twin traveled all the way to my house just to issue a warning."

"Yes, imagine that," Justin echoed before slipping his arms around her slender waist. "Perhaps, for safety's sake, I should spend the night here?" His teasing drew an unexpected response from Nicole.

"Maybe it isn't such a bad idea," she murmured. "You could sleep in the extra bedroom." A tormented look crossed her face; suddenly she was afraid to be alone. "Will you?" she quickly pleaded. "Will you stay? Just for tonight. Yes, one night, that's all." Gazing into his eyes, she looked like a frightened child.

He kissed her forehead. "All right, Nicole. I'd like to stop home first, though, and grab a shower, pick up another set of clothes. Do you want to come with me so you're not here by yourself?"

"No. I'll be okay. I'll take a nice relaxing bath while you're gone. You still have a key, don't you?" Upon seeing him nod, she inquired, "With the exception of you and Cristoff, no one else has a key, do they?"

"Of course not, Nicole. Did you think we gave out a copy to all the employees while you were away?"

"I just wanted to be sure Shane couldn't gain entry."

Justin kissed her goodbye. "Don't worry about Shane. He wouldn't harm a flea." The tall blond ventured out into the cool night air, pausing briefly at the bottom of the porch steps when a vehicle's headlights loomed into view. Nicole had already closed the front door and was walking upstairs when Cristoff's truck pulled up outside.

"Hello, Justin," called the ranch hand, shutting off the engine. "Is Nicole all right?"

The blond approached the driver side door. "She's fine. I was just heading home to get a shower. Nicole wants me to stay with her for a while."

"Oh." Cristoff's face fell. "Perhaps I'll just sit with her until you return, then."

"You can't. She's taking a bath. I'll tell her you offered, though." Turning to depart, he was halted by Cristoff's voice.

"Justin? Can I speak with you for a moment?"

"Sure." He pivoted back around. "What's on your mind?"

Cristoff hesitated. "You... you really love her, don't you?"

"I suppose I do. Why?"

"Have you told her yet?"

"No."

Cristoff grew silent. Justin studied his friend. "I'm sure this is no surprise to you, Cristoff?"

"It's just a shame it has to come to this."

"What?" Justin's brows drew together. "What the devil are you babbling about?"

"Nicole," came the reply. Hazel eyes zeroed in on the blond like a bullet searching for its target. "I'm in love with her, too, Justin."

A deafening silence ensued while each male assessed

the other. But, try as he might, Justin could not contain his rage. First, he paled. Then, a deep crimson red spread up his neck to his chin, flaming across the strong cheekbones before rapidly rising upward. "I knew it!" he thundered, banging his fist against the top of the truck door. "Damn it, Cristoff, why didn't you just come out and say this back when I found the two of you in the hayloft?!"

"I didn't know it, then," he defended.

"Well, what the hell do you expect me to do now? Graciously bow out? Not on your life!"

"Does Nicole love you?"

Justin's mouth promptly clamped shut.

"Well, does she?" Cristoff persisted.

"She hasn't admitted it, yet."

A slow smile lifted the corners of Cristoff's mouth. He cranked over the engine. "Well, my friend," he gently said, "she's fair game, then." He arrogantly raised his chin, just as Justin's hand reached in to grab his sleeve.

"Why don't you step out of your truck," the blond growled, "and we'll settle the issue, once and for all?"

"Right here?" mocked Cristoff. "Now, wouldn't that be a sight for poor Nicole to see—her two best friends duking it out on her front lawn?"

"Just name the place and I'll be there."

Cristoff's tone turned cynical. "I had no idea you were the violent type, Justin? Perhaps I should mention this to Nicole." Without waiting for a response, the ranch hand jammed the shifter into reverse, nearly taking Justin's arm with him as the vehicle jerked backwards. Upset, Justin loudly cursed, then jumped inside his own car. Perhaps Cristoff was bent on finding some way to get even, but Justin was the lucky guy who was spending the evening with the damsel in distress. He quickly drove to his own house, a satisfied smile on his lips.

The smile slowly faded, however, when Justin later returned to the ranch, only to find the object of his affection fast asleep beneath the covers of her own bed. It was all he could do to keep from waking her. "This is so unfair," he mumbled, studying the sleeping beauty with adoring eyes. He cautiously leaned forward. "Nicole?" he softly said, brushing the back of his hand along her prominent cheekbone. But no sound fell from the rose petal lips. "Nicole," he said again, bending low to gently kiss her forehead. This time, she stirred slightly beneath the sheets, a gentle sigh escaping her.

"I'm here now," he continued. His fingers combed through the luxuriously thick hair.

"Oh..." She suddenly breathed without opening her eyes. "... no Switch... no!"

Justin's large hand promptly fell away from the raven hair, an icy chill freezing him to the bone. He slowly retreated from the bed, his cold blue eyes narrowing in pain. Of course she had slept with her captors, he reminded himself. They probably gave her no choice. Yes, that was it. She had no choice in the matter—it was either yield or be killed.

He swiftly left the room to enter the adjacent one to undress, recklessly stripping the clothes from his body like someone half demented. Climbing under the covers of his bed, he lay wide awake, thinking, thinking… He kept turning over the same question in his mind—did she give herself willingly or not? "It no longer matters," he finally told himself. "It's all in the past." But what if the incident scarred her, emotionally? What if she truly despised intimacy? Justin had to know.

Thus, the very next morning, after breakfast, he broached the subject, carefully choosing his words. "You spoke in your sleep last night," he mentioned.

Nicole grabbed her coat to go out to the barn. "Is that so odd?"

"Normally, no. But you spoke about Switch." He noted the surprise in her eyes as he continued, "And you started talking about..." Unable to put it delicately, he faltered. "Um, uh... some sort of sleeping arrangement the two of you had."

"Oh," muttered Nicole, bowing her head to fasten her coat. She had cleverly avoided his gaze, but not for long. Justin lifted her chin with one strong finger, compassion in his voice.

"I know you slept with him, Nicole. It makes no difference

in how I feel for you. I just wanted you to be aware of the fact that I know. If you ever need to talk—"

"Talk?" she snapped. "Why, on earth, would I want to talk about it!? Ohh..." a sarcastic smile turned the corners of her mouth. "You think I willingly gave myself to him, is that it?" A low, throaty chuckle escaped her lips. "You men! Always thinking you have it all figured out... always jumping to conclusions." She shook her head from side to side in disbelief. "Tsk, tsk, Justin MacFierson! I really should let you keep believing your demented thoughts. However, I'm going to be a good girl today, and ease your conscience. I did NOT bed Switch. He tried to violate me, that much is true. He did not succeed. And for some odd reason, he left me alone after that. Feel better now?"

"I'm sorry, Nicole, if..." The words died on his lips as he watched her depart, the front door slamming with a bang. He stood alone in the middle of the living room floor, sighing with exasperation. Picking up his tan coat, he roughly threw it on and ventured out to the stable, where he found Nicole in the barn office, rummaging in her desk drawers. "I apologize," he began, ignoring her irritable glance, "if I upset you. Please don't hold it against me?"

"You're forgiven," she coolly said. "I'm going to Daniel's lawyer this morning, so tell Cristoff to stick around. Right now, however, I think I'll saddle The General."

"I'd rather you didn't," he cautioned. "Your muscles have weakened since you've been away from riding. Get your strength back before you risk breaking your neck. The General has been a bit wild lately."

The distinct thud of the desk drawer slamming shut resounded in the room. "Don't tell me which of my horses I can and cannot ride."

"It was only a suggestion, Nicole."

She was about to make an angry retort until she noticed the white flag of surrender waving in his eyes; he clearly had not wanted to cross her. "I'm sorry," she muttered, shuffling some papers.

He nodded before stepping towards the door. Still apprehensive about losing her, he kept a close eye on her the next few hours while she tended to the horses, until she drove off the property to meet with Daniel's attorney in regards to claiming her inheritance.

As Nicole spoke with the lawyer, she began to feel more relaxed. "I'm quite surprised," she mentioned, "that Daniel had such a significant sum of money left. I was sure my abductors had spent most of it?"

The young man smiled. "Daniel invested wisely, Mrs. Tyler. I'll give you the name of his accountant so you can inquire further of his stocks and bonds." With haste, he scribbled the name and number down, then handed it to her while she refastened her coat. She smiled, shook his hand, then bid him goodbye.

Driving back to the ranch, Nicole began to ponder Aaron's warning last night. Why was Shane so opposed to her? Could he be trusted with the horses? He did attend some of the shows with Kevin and Billy, bringing home ribbons, so his grudge must not be too serious. Still, she felt uneasy as she drove past the corral where the trainer was working a chestnut stallion. After exiting her vehicle, she headed towards Shane, determined to confront him. At worst, they would fight; and now that Nicole had acquired Daniel's wealth she need not worry about Shane quitting, she could hire a more expensive trainer. In fact, Kevin may have learned enough from watching Shane that he could actually replace him.

"I'd like a word with you, Shane," Nicole announced, advancing to the fence rail. She watched his eyes quickly scan the premises for the location of the other employees; Kevin and Billy were nowhere in sight, Cristoff was exercising a bay stallion off near the edge of the woods. Shane took his good old time untacking his horse before boldly striding towards the raven-haired beauty. Once he reached her, emerald eyes penetrated her own. "Well?" he prompted, folding his muscular arms.

Nicole matched his steady stare. "Rumor has it, you were

the one who tipped off the media last night at the club. Is this true?"

"Rumor has it, you're not the same since you came out of captivity," he shot back.

"Don't change the subject," Nicole persisted. "Is it true about last night?"

"What if it is?" he challenged, raising his chin.

"Then I demand an explanation, and don't use that cocky attitude with me."

"Actually, Nicole, I was trying to do you a favor. I thought if the press could see you enjoying yourself, it would dispel all those ugly rumors."

"Next time you get a bright idea, pass it by me first!" she exclaimed in anger.

He held up his hands. "Okay, okay. Sorry I ruined last night. Is that what you wanted to hear?"

"Yes!" Nicole swung around to head back to the barn.

"Oh, Nicole?" Shane called, causing her to stop, momentarily. "I've been itching to ask you a question." He patiently waited until the young woman returned to the fence rail. "When I heard the details of your episode with Daniel, Switch and the others, I began to wonder whatever became of the first three guards you got fired? You remember them, don't you?"

"Of course I remember them," she nervously hissed.

"Did the police hunt them down?" He smugly watched the traces of fear surface in her eyes. "Or... are they still loose?"

"I'm sure they're on the west coast by now, if they have a brain left in their heads."

"I sure hope so," he carefully said. "It makes you want to look over your shoulder every once in a while, doesn't it?"

She recognized his ploy and refused to give him the satisfaction of unnerving her. Fear vanished in the blink of an eye. Nicole squared her shoulders, drawing herself up like a soldier. He was begging for a fight, she was willing to comply, but Cristoff was riding toward them now, so she changed her strategy. Donning a slight smile, she leaned close to his ear and whispered, “I suggest you remain on my good side, Shane, unless you want me to tell Justin the real reason you don’t like him being close to me? You see, you may have fooled everyone else, but I’m very perceptive. I also know it would mean the end of your friendship with Justin, if he ever discovered your true feelings for him.” She watched the color drain from Shane’s face, and felt a smidgen of pity for him. It couldn’t be easy for him to have to wrestle with his emotions, day in and day out, poor guy. They locked eyes, briefly, a silent agreement finally reached.

Satisfied, Nicole turned her attention to her other ranch hand. Cristoff pulled up his mount.

“There’s something I picked up from the post office while you were out today I think you’ll want to see. It’s in your office.” Cristoff said.

“Thanks, Cristoff.” She hastened across the grass to enter the stable area. Inside, Kevin and Billy called a passing hello while they finished mucking stalls. Justin’s warm smile met her in the aisleway.

“You have a package,” he beamed, his happiness evident. Justin addressed his sister. “Why don’t you go get the package which came for Nicole?”

“Oh, yes!” Jan exclaimed. “I almost forgot.” She hurried down the aisle to the office, momentarily disappearing inside. When she reappeared, a square object wrapped in brown paper was firmly clutched under her arm. She handed it to Nicole, who glanced with curiosity at Justin before eagerly tearing at the paper.

“I can’t believe it!” she cried, overwhelmed with joy at the sight of her long lost picture. She thrust it towards Justin’s sister. “It’s for you! I painted it while I was in captivity. I call it ‘Jan’s First Day’. Remember when you told me how beautiful the world looked the first day after your headache?”

“Oh!” mouthed Jan, awestruck, her gaze fixated on the vivid colors. “It’s positively gorgeous, Nicole! B-But, I couldn’t take it...”

“Nonsense,” smiled Nicole. “I would be hurt if you didn’t

accept this gift."

"I don't know what to say." Jan gave her a quick hug. "Thank you! I'm going to put it in the office until I leave." She studied the art for another moment before rushing off down the aisle.

"Did you eat lunch?" Justin asked, turning to Nicole after his sister disappeared.

"No. I'm not hungry."

"You should eat. You need your strength. Let's go into the house and I'll fix you some soup." Upon his insistence, she reluctantly followed him out of the barn and across the lawn, suddenly feeling very tired as she climbed the few steps to her porch. They went inside, Nicole heading for the sink to wash up. She then sat on a kitchen chair, just as she was instructed, patiently waiting while Justin cooked her meal.

"You didn't have to do this," she said. "Thank you, Justin."

"My pleasure." Using a dipper, he transferred the food into a bowl, the strong aroma of chicken noodle soup enticing the young beauty. "I'm concerned about you, Nicole," he began, pulling out a chair for himself. Justin leaned forward, his ocean-blue eyes intense. "I won't risk losing you, again." By the firmness of his tone, she knew his words were final; and, somehow, she felt comforted by the protectiveness. A shaft of sunlight streaked through the kitchen window at that moment, outlining the handsome blond's profile in a stream of liquid gold, the sight so majestic it stole the breath from Nicole. Instantly, a deep peace filled her, the likes of which she had not felt in years. Whereas before, Justin's presence could cause a sense of conflict; now, his presence evoked tranquillity, security.

"Nicole," he said, leaving his chair to kneel before her. His blue eyes filled with adoration as he half smiled. He slowly reached up to brush back a stray wisp of her dark hair. Nicole noticed his hand was shaking, slight though it was. It was as if he were afraid to touch her, afraid she'd vanish like a dream. "Nicole," he whispered with emotion, his voice unsteady. "Nicole, there's something I've been longing to say." His fingers combed through the shiny strands of hair. "I love you. I've always loved you... from the moment I first saw you." His eyes grew misty. "I think of you day and night. All I want is you... all I ever wanted was you..." Gazing into her eyes, his heart hammered fast and hard.

But Nicole turned away.

Justin was devastated. She might as well have sunken a knife into his chest and slowly twisted it. "Look at me," he pleaded. "Don't shut me out. Please. I have to say what I feel. I can't hold it in, anymore." Desperation laced his words. Even so, Nicole could not face him. Instead, her defensive shield quickly put an end to any sign of emotion, causing the blond to remark, "Why do you keep building walls around you? Why the fortress, Nicole? Is it safer inside? Is it better to remain indifferent and alone, than to take a chance at love?" He shook his head. "I don't believe so. It's not you, Nicole." His fingertips softly brushed her cheek. "You're a strong, sensitive woman; a woman whose passion runs as deep as her loyalties. I've seen you stare at me, when you thought I wasn't looking. You're attracted to me—I know it. And yet, you fight the attraction. At first, I thought it was your fear of men. But when I saw you with Cristoff, embracing him, kissing him, I knew this couldn't be the reason. And it isn't, is it?"

"You don't know what you're talking about," she swiftly said.

"Yes," he whispered. "Yes, I do." He hesitated before continuing. "You gave away your heart to Philip and he broke it. You're not afraid to engage in a spurt of passion; you're afraid of commitment. You don't believe anyone is worth the high price you may have to pay. But, I'm telling you, I'm not like Philip. I can give you a good life, security, love, everything you ever dreamed of. I won't betray you. I won't belittle you." He gently squeezed her hand. "Please... please marry me, Nicole?"

Her reply was quick and to the point. "I'm not ready to settle down, Justin. So much has occurred the past couple of months. I feel out of touch with reality." Chocolate brown eyes searched his. "Don't you understand? It wouldn't be fair to either one of us. I need time."

"How much time?"

"I'm not sure."

"A day? A week?" He paused. "A year?"

Nicole shifted uncomfortably in her seat. Then the question she dreaded most, tumbled from his mouth.

"Do you love me, Nicole?"

He penetrated her eyes, searching for the answer he longed to know, watching as her body stilled. He moved closer, raising her hand to his lips where he softly kissed the velvet skin. "Do you love me?" he asked again, straining his ears to catch the faintest word, the tiniest sound. "If you don't, I'll understand. I still want you for my wife."

Nicole now realized Aaron had never told Justin about the time during her rescue, when she mistakenly thought he was Justin and blurted out that she loved him. Nicole raised a sable brow. "You'd spend the rest of your life with a woman who didn't love you?"

"Only you," he whispered. "Only you, Nicole... because I love you that much. Now, tell me... don't make me wait any longer... Do you love me?"

She held his gaze for what felt like eternity while she turned the question over and over in her mind. After living through one hellish marriage, she was not so sure she knew the meaning of the word "love". "Justin," she began, staring down at their entwined fingers, "I believed I was in love when I wed Philip; and, like a wounded puppy, I kept returning to his side, begging for the affection which I intuitively knew I'd never receive." Her eyes swept up to meet his. "I know you are not Philip. Neither am I that innocent girl. I'm wiser now. But, somehow... in the transition..." She hesitated to bare such personal feelings. "I've lost the ability to trust. I've grown cold inside. Sometimes, I actually feel numb." The lovely face twisted in anguish. Her voice fell to a whisper. "I'm sorry, Justin. I'm so, so sorry. I don't think I could be the kind of wife you need." She buried her head in her hands, but he gently cupped her face, forcing her to meet his gaze.

"Then tell me this," he begged, undaunted. "How do you feel when we are together?"

She weighed the question carefully. "Today, I experienced a serenity I haven't felt in years. It was as if just the sight of you calmed my very soul. It was quite wonderful, actually." Her expression slowly brightened. "And I thought to myself—this must be what it's like to have a best friend. Yes, yes, of course. What a nice feeling. And then I looked at you again." The corners of her mouth lifted ever so slightly. "And I surprised myself by wondering what it would be like to be Mrs. Justin MacFierson."

Her words made his heart skip. "Then do it, Nicole! Become Mrs. Justin MacFierson. Step inside my world and I promise you you'll never look back."

The mere thought of it put butterflies in her stomach. Sincerity shone from those gorgeous blue depths, that adoring gaze. Nicole began to feel the first twinges of excitement. Could this possibly be the man she was destined to spend the rest of her life with? The emptiness inside her mysteriously vanished, replaced by a mixture of hope and profound peace. "I have a confession, Justin. I do love you. I've just been afraid to admit it," she finally conceded, bestowing a generous smile upon the object of her affection.

Tremendous joy exploded inside the surprised male as he let out a deafening whoop. He yanked the unsuspecting woman to her feet, hugging her with a fierceness that forced out a shriek of protest. "I didn't say I'd marry you," she shouted above his gleeful outburst.

"But you love me!" he repeated. "You said you love me!" He scooped her up in his arms and kissed her, then spun around as he held her until they both became dizzy.

"You're going to drop me," she warned, giggling at the silliness. He promptly set her feet back on the floor.

"What kind of wedding do you want? Big? Small?"

"You're jumping the gun," she reminded him. "I'm not getting married yet."

"Of course you are! You love me." His dazzling smile made her feel guilty. Nicole began to wring her hands.

"I need time, Justin."

"Oh, no," he waved a finger in her face. "If I let you think about all this, you'll talk yourself out of marrying me. Uh-uh. No way. I can't allow that to happen. I have to keep you in your present state of mind. Hmmm... How can I do that?" He suddenly grabbed her and kissed her, long and deep, the heady sensation sending him reeling. Then just as suddenly, he stopped. "Oh, I almost forgot. Wait here. Don't move. Don't go anywhere. I'll be right back." He sailed out the door before Nicole could utter a word, the front door slamming in his haste.

"I've created a monster," she mumbled to herself, quite flabbergasted by the whirlwind of what had just occurred. But, in her heart, she knew she did love the man. It actually felt good to say so. She had never thought there could be the possibility of a bright, cheerful future with someone who truly cared for her. Nicole suddenly realized that Philip had made her feel so unloved, she had not been able to accept the fact that Justin loved her—at least not until now. No matter how many times Jan had told her that he loved her, she couldn't believe it. And that was why she fought so hard to place limits on their friendship. But things were different now... yes, very different. As she watched the handsome blond jump the steps up to her porch, Nicole suddenly could not imagine her life without him.

"This is for you," he gasped, out of breath. A small jewelry box was shoved into her hands. "No. Wait. This isn't the way you'd want it to happen." Taking it back, he opened the lid, then knelt before her while placing the large diamond ring on her finger. "Nicole, my love, will you please marry me?" She stared at the huge rock sparkling like a hundred stars. It was the ring they had used when they had pretended to be engaged. Cristoff had been right—Justin had planned this all along.

"Will you marry me?" Justin asked again, a bit perturbed now that she had hesitated.

Nicole carefully chose her word. "Eventually," she said.

Justin frowned. "What kind of answer is that? It's a 'yes' or 'no' question. No one says, 'eventually'."

Nicole could not help but grin. "Yes," she finally said. "Did you have this ring in your car?"

"Yeah," he chuckled. "I wanted it nearby for the big occasion."

"So you knew that one day you would propose?"

He nodded, then hugged her. "I'm so happy, Nicole! You have no idea how happy I am. I can't wait to tell the others."

"Cristoff," Nicole whispered with concern.

"What about Cristoff?"

"I think this would sound better coming from me, Justin."

He shrugged. "It doesn't matter to me." He suddenly jumped up, his Cheshire cat smile racing up his cheeks. "You sit there and finish your soup, sweetheart. I've got an errand to run."

"Where?"

"The florist shop." He leaned down to steal another kiss. "I'm going to buy you the biggest bouquet you've ever laid eyes on!"

"That's really unnecessary, Justin."

"Don't spoil my fun. I'll be back in a jiffy." He flew out of the kitchen before she could say goodbye, his recklessness evident by the loud slamming of the front door, which she easily forgave.

Nicole reheated her meal and ate, basking in the glow of her newly discovered love. Ten minutes later, she ventured into the barn, found Jan, and sprung the good news. Justin's sister was elated. She squealed with delight, hugging Nicole before launching into a series of talks about how to handle her brother's different moods. Like a good friend, Nicole politely listened, until she saw Cristoff heading their way. "Shhh," Nicole motioned to Jan.

"Cristoff," called Nicole. "May I see you inside my house for a moment, please?" The ranch hand nodded, smiled, then followed her over to her home. "Have a seat," she said, motioning for him to sit beside her on the sofa.

He had no sooner sat down when Cristoff's eyes suddenly caught sight of the sparkling object on her finger.

His next sentence died on his lips. His mouth went dry, his heart leapt into his throat, and the rush of blood to his face made him feel as if his head would explode. He wanted to yell his denial, to shake Nicole until her head rattled. No. He wanted to yank the offensive object off her hand and flush it down the toilet. Then he wanted to find Justin and beat him senseless. But he chose to control his rage, cleverly hiding it beneath a forced smile.

"What's this?" he pretended, holding up her left hand.

"Well, that's what I wanted to speak to you about," she slowly said. "Justin proposed to me."

"Are you two playing games, again?" he taunted, giving her a playful shove.

"No. I've accepted, although... I'm not quite sure when I'll be ready to marry."

"You've just got out of prison," Cristoff quietly said, his voice so soft-spoken, she would have thought he was speaking to a child. "You're vulnerable right now, Nicole. I think it is terrible that Justin took advantage of you during such a turbulent time in your life. Someone compassionate would never do such a thing." He tsk, tsked, shaking his head. "It's just awful, trying to force you into commitment so soon."

"Well," she shrugged, "I really didn't want to be pushed into a decision, but..."

"But what?" he prodded, encircling her with his arm.

"Justin was so intense, so emotional... proclaiming his love for me." She looked again at the hazel eyes which were now twinkling with mischief. She thought it rather strange, but was too stunned by the day's events to attempt fathoming the meaning.

"Do you love him, Nicole?"

"Yes. Yes, I do."

Cristoff glanced away, his heart dropping like a lead weight. "Are you sure?" he persisted.

"Yes, although it was quite a shock to realize it."

"Then, maybe it's not the real thing. Besides, it was only this morning that you two were fighting."

"Lovers quarrel."

"Not as often as both of you," he remarked. "Tell me, do you feel as comfortable with him as you do me? Think of the trail ride we took. Think of the time you fell asleep in my arms up in the hayloft. Think of our painting sessions in my studio. We have so much in common, Nicole. Is that how it is with you and Justin?"

She considered the question. "Not exactly. But I love him. I don't want to discuss this anymore," she gently stated.

"Then please don't rush into marriage. The commitment is forever, remember? Make Justin wait until you are absolutely positive this is the route you want to take."

He stood to leave. "Think about it, Nicole."

"I will, Cristoff," she agreed, seeing him to the door. As Nicole watched the handsome ranch hand slowly make his way across the lawn, she had the distinct feeling her news had upset him a great deal more than he had let on. It brought a touch of sadness to her eyes, and a prayer to her lips that Cristoff would take this like a man and not seek solace in a bottle of his favorite scotch.

CHAPTER TWENTY-FOUR

Upon seeing Justin's car come down the driveway, Nicole ran out to meet him with a warm hug and a kiss. He promptly presented her with a huge flower arrangement of stunning variety. "Oh, how lovely!" she exclaimed, as he carried them inside her house. "They can go on the table there. Thank you so much, Justin!" He noticed she seemed a bit nervous. "By the way, I just informed Cristoff of our engagement. Hard to tell how he took it."

Justin frowned. "I saw him staring at me from the barn. He looked pretty mad."

"We need to give him some time to adjust."

"Yes. I agree. I need to discuss some things with Kevin, so if you don't mind?"

"Sure, I understand," Nicole replied. "Are we having dinner together tonight?"

"I'd love to," he grinned, giving her a quick kiss. "I'll pick you up at six o'clock, if that's okay?"

She nodded her approval before he walked out the door. She watched him disappear around the corner before heading upstairs to get her laundry. She needed to catch up on some chores. But it wasn't long before her conscience began to nag her.

Nicole donned her coat, silently slipping past the back door to enter the corridor leading to the rear end of the stable. Once there, she tiptoed up the long aisle, scarcely making a sound until she reached the ladder to the hayloft. As she ascended the wooden steps, she could hear Kevin's voice in the office, apparently on the telephone. Nicole was glad no one else was around; apparently Justin must have left to do other things. She needed to be alone with Cristoff right now, and she was correct in assuming he had come to the loft to do his brooding.

"Cristoff," she softly said, noticing his back was to her as he sat perched on a bale of straw. The ranch hand twisted around in surprise, then faked indifference.

"It took you long enough," was all he said, conveying his anger by refusing to grant her enough room to sit beside him. Nicole plopped down, anyway, forcing him to scoot over.

"I know you're hurt, Cristoff. I'm sorry. I had no idea you'd take the news so hard. I believe, though, if you think about it, you'll realize this engagement doesn't mean you'll be losing me—you'll just be gaining Justin's loyalty. The two of you won't have to compete, anymore."

"Compete?" Cristoff scoffed, his eyes ablaze. "By the devil, girl! Justin never gave me a chance to compete. It wasn't very long ago that I told him..." Cristoff suddenly stopped, turning his face away.

"You told him what?" Nicole quizzed.

Cristoff frowned. "Never mind." He wagged his head from side to side in complete frustration. "Go away! Leave me alone."

The young beauty's eyes suddenly widened. "Cristoff!" she whispered. "Tell me it isn't true." She firmly took hold of his shoulders, forcing him to meet her gaze. It only took one look at his pained expression to confirm her suspicion. Nicole gave an exasperated groan. Pressing the palm of her hand against her forehead, she slowly rocked back and forth, muttering, "How could I have been so blind..."

"So it's in the open now," Cristoff coldly announced. "Well, so be it." He stood up and shoved his hands inside his pockets. "I believe I have some work to do downstairs."

Nicole went after him. "Cristoff, wait. I feel terrible about this."

"Why should you?" he snapped. "It was my own cowardice that kept me from telling you I love you. Now, it's too late." He stared at the floor. "It's too... damn... late..." He suddenly sported a wicked grin. "Of course, you could always ditch Justin and marry me, instead?"

"It would break his heart."

"It would serve him right! He knew I was in love with you. I even told him of my intention to pursue you, and what did he do? He suddenly proposes to you, out of the blue! If that doesn't sound like someone who is insecure, I don't know what does!"

"Are you insinuating that the only reason he proposed to me was to win a competition?"

"Well, it was awful sudden, wasn't it?" he countered.

Nicole's eyes glittered gold like a tigress. Cristoff expected her back to arch, ready for combat, but she kept her cool, her fury clearly contained in those fiery, feline eyes. "Why are you doing this to me?" she slowly asked. "I'm your friend."

"Are you still going to marry Justin?"

"Yes."

"Then I owe it to you to be honest with my feelings about this engagement."

"You weren't there when he proposed," she argued. "You didn't see the ecstatic joy on his face, the relief in his eyes when I gave my approval."

"No, I didn't see it. But answer me one question, Nicole? Has he given you the ranch back yet?"

"What difference does that make?"

"Seems to me," Cristoff wryly replied, "if he weds you, he stands a better chance of retaining ownership. After all, it would look a bit distrustful if you demanded to resume ownership after you were married. How could you explain such a demand to your new husband?"

"Be serious, Cristoff! Justin is wealthy enough to start his own horse farm, if he so desires it. He has no need to hang on to Desert Wind."

Like a man with a well kept secret, Cristoff's eyes began to twinkle. "But you haven't been around lately, my dear. You haven't seen the way Justin flaunts his authority. You should have heard him issuing orders the past few months. Even Billy complained that he felt like he was in boot camp."

"One thing is for certain, Cristoff, your theory can easily be proven wrong. I'll simply have the papers drawn up to transfer ownership before we get married. Will that satisfy you?"

"It will ease my mind," he agreed.

"But that reminds me," she cocked her head to one side. "You still owe me your share in the ranch, dear Cristoff. I split the ownership between you and Justin."

"And I will gladly return my share to you," he stated. "Just send me the papers to sign." He turned then to leave, but his stride was stiff and hurried, as if he couldn't wait to get away from her.

It occupied her thoughts, even during her quiet dinner with Justin. When Justin decided to retire for the evening, assuming Nicole's silence was due to fatigue, Nicole almost sighed with relief. She couldn't wait to crawl into her own bed. Nicole's sleep, however, was anything but peaceful. Several times during the night she bolted upright in bed, seized with fear that someone was watching her—someone evil. Of course, she knew no one was actually in the room. Still, she could not shake the slow panic building inside. Her palms broke out in a sweat and she mumbled a faint prayer, determined not to run to Justin for security. Turning on the lamp next to the bed, she nervously glanced about the room, waiting patiently for the eerie sensation to subside. When it finally did, she switched off the light, pulled up the covers, and tightly shut her eyes. But sleep never came...

When morning arrived, it was evident to Justin that Nicole was definitely not herself. Yet when he questioned her, she merely claimed to have been uncomfortable in her bed the previous night and hadn't slept very well. He let the excuse slide by, but kept a watchful eye on her the remainder of the day. She perked up considerably by suppertime, leading him to believe she had somehow stolen a quick nap in her office. A sunny smile replaced the worried expression she had worn earlier.

Aaron came by, asking if they'd like to go out to dinner, along with the rest of the ranch hands. Nicole eagerly accepted. "Hey, congratulations on the engagement!" he added, giving her a big hug. "When's the big day?"

"Uh..." Nicole faltered, looking sheepishly back to Justin. "Haven't chosen the day yet. But I'll let you know when we do." She graced him with a smile. An odd look passed between the twins before Aaron left them so he could get changed for dinner. Justin went home to do likewise.

A while later, they all headed to the local steakhouse, with the exception of Shane, who had an excuse for not joining them. Conversation mixed with occasional laughter as Kevin relayed some humorous tales he experienced in the horse industry. Nicole relaxed, enjoying the company as she ate her meal. Cristoff even seemed to be his old self, joining in the banter. The atmosphere was friendly, full of good cheer.

"I see Shane's parents," Justin remarked when they had finished eating. The couple waved to him, so he waved back. Taking Nicole's hand, he said, "Let me introduce you to them, honey." Thus, the two headed over to the Anderson's table.

Before reaching their destination, however, a stylishly dressed young woman who sported a young stud on her arm stopped them in midstride. As she made a direct beeline to Justin, Nicole felt her heart begin to race. "Why is she here?" she whispered with alarm, sensing Maureen was a desperate woman on a mission.

"Hello, Justin," came the cool greeting. Maureen moved her hand up to her beautiful auburn hair, making sure each strand was in its rightful place.

"Hello, Maureen," the blond casually replied.

She threw Nicole a hostile glare, green eyes shooting daggers. At this point, the fashionable woman detached herself from her male escort and approached the raven-haired beauty, eyeing her up and down. "So," she began in a snide manner, "you not only stole my former husband, but now you are after Justin, too! Are you that envious of me, dear girl?"

"Envious?" sputtered Nicole, suppressing a laugh. "Not at all, Maureen. For your information, I did not steal Daniel. Daniel came to me after you asked for a divorce, not before. As for Justin, he never was yours, Maureen."

"Oh, that's right," scoffed the jealous female. "I keep forgetting that Justin simply used me to obtain facts about Daniel and his buddies."

"What's done is done," Nicole remarked, attempting to end the discussion. "This isn't the proper place for a confrontation, in case you haven't noticed."

"It certainly isn't," Maureen quickly agreed, turning away. She slinked off to a neutral corner to lick her wounds, quite content to stand and observe the newly engaged couple as they made small talk with Shane's parents.

Nicole felt those green eyes burning holes in her back. "Can we leave?" she quietly asked Justin.

"I suppose so," he agreed.

"Let me use the ladies' room first," she said. "I'll only be a minute." Nicole briskly walked the length of the room towards the restroom, but was halted at the door by claw-like fingers wrapping around her arm.

"I'm not finished with you, yet, Missy!" Maureen hissed between clenched teeth, a malicious gleam in her eyes.

"Please, Maureen!" Nicole whispered, jerking free. "What on earth is your problem?"

"You! You little tramp! You have everything now, don't you? A new boyfriend, Daniel's money..."

"Is that what this is all about? Daniel's will? I was just as surprised as you that he named me as his heir. If you're so upset about it, why haven't you contested the will?"

"Don't you think I would if I could?" Maureen spat. "But my lawyer advised against it because Daniel specifically mentioned in the document that he did not want any of his wealth to go to me. Oh, you had him wrapped around your little finger, didn't you? You couldn't wait to get your greedy hands on his money. I knew the moment I heard of his death that you were the one who pulled the trigger!"

At the mention of the horrible incident, Nicole's blood pressure skyrocketed. "How dare you insinuate such a thing! No wonder Daniel divorced you—you're so cold, I'm getting frostbite just looking at you!"

Maureen's mouth flew open in surprise. Without thinking, she slapped Nicole across the cheek, her green eyes blazing with indignation. Not to be outdone, Nicole returned the gesture, smiling triumphantly as the older woman momentarily lost her balance. "Oh!" cried Maureen, huffing and puffing like the big, bad wolf. She grabbed hold of Nicole's long hair, twisting the strands tightly around her fist until Nicole yelped in pain. It was then Justin swung around, as did everyone else in the room, to locate the persons responsible for the sudden raucous. What he saw, however, sent his head spinning. His beloved fiancée, the woman he was to marry, was now thrusting her previously coiled arm towards her attacker, Nicole's fist swiftly making contact with Maureen's perfectly sculpted jaw. Justin simultaneously groaned upon impact, anger surging through his veins as he watched Maureen do a half spin, then fall silently to the floor.

Too caught up in the moment to notice her stunned audience, Nicole shook her hand to ease the stinging, then studied her nails to make sure none had broken. She didn't see the ball of fire headed her way—not until a massive hand encircled her upper arm in a painful, steely grip. She was too shocked to fight the domineering man who now yanked her towards the exit, amidst a whispering crowd. Suddenly her coat was thrown at her, an order was barked, and she was pulled outside into the cold night air. After being shoved inside the Ferrari like a common criminal, Nicole finally became angry. Fortunately, she looked over at Justin before uttering a word, and realized he was much, much more furious than she. He was gritting his teeth, his jaw was clenched, and those funny little veins were popping out again on his face. She decided it would be in her own best interest to refrain from speaking of the incident until he appeared a bit calmer.

"What the hell did you think you were doing, causing a scene like that?" he growled.

Nicole's chin went up. "Maureen started it."

"I don't care who started it!" he bellowed. "Why can't you act like a lady and show some self-restraint? You humiliated me in front of Shane's parents! Now I have to go back there and apologize for the atrocious behavior of my fiancée!" He practically spat the word at her.

"Well, if I'm such an embarrassment to you, then perhaps you should pick someone else to marry!" She tore the ring from her finger and slammed it upon the top dashboard. The Ferrari came to a screeching halt.

Justin was now growling through clenched teeth. "Put... the ring... back on!" There was no mistaking the warning in his tone.

The raven-haired beauty calmly folded her arms and looked out the window. "No," she murmured, bracing herself for the worst. The car grew silent. Seconds ticked by. Justin's breath deepened as he fought to control his rage. He was not in the mood for Nicole's games and he would show her so. Like a snake striking its prey, he snatched her hand, then the ring, and shoved it onto its rightful place before she realized it.

"Don't take it off," came the harsh command as the car engine was started. They zoomed down the road, traveling the rest of the way without speaking. It was after they had pulled up to the house and Nicole had two legs safely out of the car that she decided to comment, "I suppose you would have preferred I let Maureen slap me senseless."

"For someone who deplores violence, you sure make use of it enough," he curtly replied. She slammed the car door. Justin rolled down his window. "I'll be back, shortly."

"Don't bother!" Nicole snapped, hurrying up the porch steps. Stepping inside her house, she firmly closed the door and locked it. Throwing her coat over a chair, she kicked off her shoes, made some hot tea and turned on the radio, increasing the volume until bass notes vibrated off the walls. Ten minutes later, she barely heard the loud knocking on the front door. "Who is it?" she shouted before turning down the noise.

"Aaron!" came the answering yell.

Having nothing to fear from Justin's brother, Nicole allowed him entry. Jan followed behind him.

"Thanks for letting me in," Aaron remarked. "I wanted to make sure you were all right. Are you?"

"You were concerned?" she asked, a bit surprised.

"Naturally. You were struck pretty hard; although, I must add, Maureen got the worst of it." He flashed a wicked grin, prodding a smile from Nicole.

"It seems you're the only one who finds humor in the situation. Justin was furious. We had a fight."

"I thought so," Jan quietly said. "He'll get over it. He's just upset."

"I never knew he could be such a bully. He wasn't even interested in my side of the story." She sighed. "I can't dwell on it. I'm depressed enough. Would you like a drink?"

"No." Aaron studied her with a twinge of pity. Another knock sounded at the door.

"Now, who could that be?" she muttered, briskly walking across the room.

"Hi, Nicole," Cristoff greeted, stepping inside. It was the nicest he had been to her all day. "I was wondering if you were okay?"

"At least I have three friends who care more about my welfare than they do about whether I humiliated them tonight."

Cristoff caught sight of Aaron and nodded before turning back towards Nicole. "You didn't embarrass me. Maureen deserved a good whack. I take it from your tone, though, that Justin wasn't too pleased."

"Didn't you see the way he practically dragged me out of the room?"

"I missed that part. I did hear about it. Everyone was

buzzing after you left."

Nicole began to wring her hands. Upon seeing this, Aaron suddenly said, "Hey. I know exactly what you need, Nicole. You need a night out on the town. Don't you agree, Cristoff?" The blond nudged him in the side.

"Sure," Cristoff chirped. "Something to take your mind off of things."

Nicole shook her head and held up her hand. "Have you forgotten this ring, guys? Justin is coming back here later tonight. He'd be angry if I wasn't here when he arrived."

"Leave him a note," Aaron suggested. "You deserve a little fun. You've been through hell, Nicole." He gave her a friendly wink. "Come on. This isn't a date. It'll be the four of us."

"We could teach you how to shoot pool," Cristoff added, remembering Nicole had mentioned once that she had wanted to learn. "Afterwards, we could listen to a band."

"Great idea," Aaron smiled. "What do you say, Cat?"

The young beauty sported a slow smile. "Sounds better than sitting here, sulking."

"Good!" Cristoff said.

Nicole quickly wrote a note for Justin, in case he followed through with his plan to stop by. She knew he'd let himself in with his own key when she didn't answer the door. Grabbing her coat and purse, Nicole followed Cristoff out the door and into Aaron's Road Runner.

"I hope you don't mind my tagging along," Jan said, glancing over her shoulder at Nicole. "I had just returned home when Aaron came in. I was going to phone you to ask if you were okay."

"I'm glad you're here," Nicole smiled. "I'm just fine now that we're heading out for the evening. Is Justin still at the restaurant?"

"Yeah. I thought he'd leave with us, but last time I saw him he was engrossed in a lively discussion with Mr. Anderson.

"Well, he seems to have recovered from our fight," Nicole remarked. "I'm still trying to forget about it."

"And you will," Aaron grinned from behind the wheel. "I

promise."

He spoke the truth. They had only been at the pool hall for twenty minutes when Nicole completely forgot about Justin. She was too involved in mastering the game, her concentration centering on angling her cue stick. The clacking of numbered balls slamming into each other produced another groan from Cristoff. "I told you," he said to Aaron, "Nicole is a quick learner." Her perfectly executed shot sent the rotating circles spinning into corner and side pockets, much to Aaron's amazement.

"Damn!" he swore. "You keep playing like that and I'll have to throw some money on you and set you up in a real game!"

"Beginner's luck," Jan teased, elbowing her friend. Nicole coyly smiled.

They played for an hour and a half before finally calling it quits. Piling back into Aaron's car, they took off for the Midnight Lounge, where a round of drinks were ordered. Nicole stuck to club soda, although she would have preferred her usual slow gin fizz.

"Aren't you drinking?" Jan asked. "Everyone else is."

"Not tonight," Nicole replied, her attention drawn to Cristoff. He was seated directly across from her, his fingers encircling a glass of scotch. When Nicole raised her brows questioningly, he gave her a dead stare. "Cristoff," she quietly said. "Please don't." Cristoff raised the glass to his lips, his eyes mocking her. "Please," she begged again. His hand halted, but only briefly as he replied, "I stopped drinking when you needed me. You don't need me anymore, Nicole. You have Justin." That said, he eagerly swallowed the strong liquid. Jan and Aaron exchanged glances.

"Waitress!" Cristoff called. "A double, please."

In desperation, Nicole leaned forward. "Don't do this, Cristoff! You were happy being sober. You were proud, full of confidence. I can't sit here and watch you drag yourself down. I won't do it!" She pushed back her chair.

"I'm just having a good time, girlie," he grinned. "And you should, too. That's why we came here tonight, isn't it?"

"Well, I'm not having a good time now, in case you haven't noticed!" She turned to Jan and Aaron. "Excuse me, but I think I'll call a cab and head home."

"No, no. Don't leave on my account," Cristoff remarked, standing up. "If my drinking bothers you, I'll just sit at another table."

The palm of Aaron's hand slapped the wood surface, making them both jump. "Sit down! Both of you!" he barked, clearly agitated. His outburst caused several people to curiously turn their heads. Embarrassed, Nicole slid quietly onto her chair, as did Cristoff. Glittering blue eyes focused upon the raven-haired beauty. "This is a nightclub, Nicole, and if Cristoff wants to drink, that's his prerogative. What difference does it make if he does it here, or waits until he gets home? Either way, he isn't sober anymore, so just accept it." His gaze switched to Cristoff. "And you! Your timing stinks! Did you have to go back to the bottle tonight? Weren't we supposed to cheer up Nicole—-not drive her into another depression?"

Cristoff looked down at his hands, a permanent frown etched on his face. "All right," he muttered. "I'll have soda for the rest of the evening." He raised his lids just high enough to see Nicole's expression. She appeared placated for the moment as she toyed with a napkin. Across the room, the musicians returned from their break and began playing their instruments. "You, two," Aaron shouted above the blaring music, pointing to Cristoff and Nicole. "Get up and dance. That's an order."

As if on cue, both Nicole and Cristoff grimaced. Like punished children being forced to make up, they slowly pushed back their chairs and obeyed. Jan cracked a smile after the two departed. "You handled that real well! I'm surprised they listened to you."

"Neither one truly wanted to fight," Aaron replied. He studied the two on the dance floor, suddenly feeling envious. "I only wish I was able to fast dance."

"Will you ever recover to the point where you can?"

"Sure. It'll take a while, though." His gaze fell to a

handsome young man seated at another table. "Hey, sis. I think someone over there likes you." He nodded in the appropriate direction, smiling when the stranger winked at Jan. "Here he comes. Be nice, now." Jan blushed, smacking her brother on the arm for teasing her. The newcomer introduced himself, then politely invited her to dance, which she eagerly accepted, leaving Aaron alone and edgy. He played with his glass for a few seconds before emitting a small groan of boredom. Then suddenly, he had the queerest sensation someone was watching him. He slowly rotated his head to peer over his shoulder.

Identical blue eyes met his.

Aaron scowled, then cursed. "Here comes trouble."

Justin MacFierson marched across the room, his long-legged stride swiftly carrying him to where his brother sat, guzzling beer. "Hello, Justin," Aaron muttered with a frown. "You just couldn't sit at home, could you?"

The twin pulled out an adjacent chair and seated himself. "Did you really think I would?"

Aaron scoffed. "I had high hopes. We're trying to show Nicole a good time; no brooding allowed."

Justin's eyes narrowed. "I didn't come here to brood."

"Bravo. Then put a damn smile on your face. The song's almost over." He slid his half empty beer bottle to his brother. "Have a drink."

"I'll get my own, thanks."

"Suit yourself."

Aaron snorted and focused his attention on Nicole and Cristoff, who finally appeared to be enjoying themselves. Too much, thought Justin when his gaze settled upon the couple. He didn't care for the way Cristoff was lusting after his fiancée. He would tell him so, too—-after the dance had ended. For now, all he could do was watch. Unless...

Just as the agitated blond stood up, Aaron's hand gripped his wrist to yank him back in his seat. "Don't even think it!" he growled to the twin. "If you cut in on Cristoff, Nicole will know you are jealous. Let her have this one dance. It won't kill you. See how happy she is?" Justin grunted his annoyance but could not deny the smile which lit up Nicole's face.

The song soon ended, but upon hearing the band strike up a slower tune, Aaron quickly rose from the table and approached the dark-haired beauty as she was headed back towards them, politely asking her, "Come dance with me, Cat? It will take your mind off of things."

"If anyone is going to dance with her, it's me," Justin objected. But his anger had little effect on the twin who now placed a protective arm around the flustered female.

"You'll have the rest of your life to dance with her," Aaron argued. "I've sat here a long time, hoping for a slow song." Without waiting for a response, he guided Nicole onto the dance floor.

"I'm surprised Justin came here tonight," she remarked to Aaron when they were a safe distance away. "He doesn't look too happy."

Her partner grinned. "Well, that must have something to do with Justin discovering Cristoff stepping in for him. I think if Justin could lock you in a tower, he would."

"Shame on you." Her laughing eyes met his. "By the way, thank you for not telling Justin I love him, and allowing me to do it, myself. I felt like an idiot when I blurted that out to you back in West Virginia."

Aaron's voice deepened. "You're beautiful when you smile. Has anyone ever told you? I could watch that smile all evening." Upon seeing her blush, he grinned again, pulling her closer. He was lost in his own thoughts, unaware she had uttered, "Did you hear something?"

Nicole turned her head to the side, her eyes scanning the room. The sound of escalating male voices drew her attention back to their table. Her swaying body froze in motion when she suddenly caught sight of Cristoff and Justin engaged in a heated argument. "Oh, no!" she cried. Aaron swiftly followed her gaze, a look of mild surprise crossing his face.

"What on earth do they think they are doing?" he muttered. "They'll get us thrown out of here." He felt Nicole quickly let go of his hand to hurry towards them, but he seized her by the arm.

"Let them be," he said, pulling her away from the now ensuing brawl.

Nicole fought to free herself. "No! I have to stop them!"

"You can't stop them. You'll get hurt. Let's take off before someone calls the cops. We don't need your name in the papers again, darling." Despite her protests, he ushered her to the cloakroom and retrieved their coats. Nicole stood helplessly near the door, despair in her eyes. Aaron was right—-the scene had definitely turned ugly; there was nothing she could do.

"My purse," she remembered. "It's at the table."

"You stay here. I'll get it."

She began to follow, but Aaron was adamant. "Stay here! You can't stop the fight, Nicole. It was bound to happen sooner or later. They have to get this out of their systems."

"You sound as if you know what they're fighting about?"

"I do. There's only one reason a man would risk being thrown out of a nightclub... that reason is a woman." Without waiting for a response, the blond weaved through the gathering crowd. Justin and Cristoff had bumped into several other couples, provoking a major outbreak of flying fists. The private fight had turned into a massive brawl, with women now partaking in the feud. Nicole searched their faces for Jan, but to no avail. She was still glancing around when Aaron grabbed her hand and led her away from the chaos. Just in time, too. Several police cars were entering the parking lot.

The couple jumped inside of the Road Runner and sped off towards the main road. "I couldn't find your sister," Nicole said. "I hope she's okay."

"Justin will find her," Aaron replied, turning down a narrow country road.

"Do you think he'll get arrested?"

"I'm sure he'll duck out in the nick of time. He has a knack for doing those kinds of things." He took his eyes off the road to throw her a quick look. "Are you hungry?"

"I'm too nervous to eat." There was a tremor in her voice. "I just can't believe he'd do this."

"Fight? Are you kidding? Justin loves a good rumble."

"Not in a public place," she shot back. "He knows better. And he was going to give ME a lecture on how to act out in public? Ha! What the devil has got into him?"

Aaron shrugged. "My best guess is that Cristoff antagonized him. Justin wasn't in the best of moods tonight, you know?"

"Don't remind me," she said with a note of sarcasm.

Aaron slowed the vehicle, gradually pulling off the street.

Nicole frowned. "What's wrong?"

"Nothing," he calmly said, shutting off the engine. "Let's just sit here for a few minutes and relax." He turned the key slightly so he could play the radio, choosing a station with easy listening music instead of hard rock 'n roll.

"I'd really like to go home," Nicole commented.

"It won't kill you to sit here a while."

"But I'm getting cold."

Aaron slid across the seat, wrapping one arm around the shivering female. "Just relax, Cat. You'll feel better soon, I promise."

It seemed odd to be in her future brother-in-law's arms, on a lonely country road, but Nicole wasn't afraid of Aaron or his motive. It was comforting to be protectively embraced when her world seemed so topsy-turvy. She listened quietly to the soft music, allowing it to dissolve every worry, every care. Little by little, she grew tired, her head finally resting against the top of Aaron's shoulder. His leather jacket, although it was only lukewarm from his body heat, provided a cozy cushion, prompting her eyelids to soon close.

Noticing the shift in her weight, Aaron gathered she had dozed off, so he turned the key in the ignition to shut off the radio. "Poor Cat," he whispered, touching his lips to the crown of her head. As the flowery scent of her hair filled his nostrils, he had the sudden urge to kiss her, but resisted. His own fascination with the young beauty was bewildering. She wasn't his type at all; he liked liberal minded, empty-headed females, the kind he could easily manipulate. He was a true rogue—-

always had been. But the more time he spent with Nicole, the more he surprised himself by playing the role of a gentleman. If he wasn't careful, he might actually become one.

That was a scary thought. He unconsciously shivered and forced the notion out of his head. Closing his eyes, he allowed himself to drift into a light slumber until several vehicles whizzed by, producing a small volume of wind to gently rock the fancy Plymouth. He reawakened, then promptly lit a joint. Nicole, who was currently dreaming of a utopian world where worry did not exist, suddenly had the distinct feeling she was slowly being choked to death. Yes, she was positive every ounce of breath had been sucked from her lungs as she began to suffocate. She coughed and sputtered. Her eyes flew open, only to rapidly blink amidst the haze that engulfed her. Gasping for air, she leaned across the seat and wound down the passenger window.

"Problem?" spoke Aaron, oh so coolly, a lazy smile on his lips.

Nicole wanted to kill him. "Are you crazy?!" She snatched the marijuana cigarette and flung it out the window, ignoring his loud protest. "What are you trying to do?!" she snapped. "Get me thrown back in jail?"

Aaron glanced over his shoulder. "Relax, Cat! There isn't a cop around for miles; although, I do understand your paranoia. It isn't much fun feeling like hunted prey, is it?"

"What are you babbling about?"

He gazed at her through half-closed lids. "You know... those men who might be after you."

"What men?"

"The guards." Upon seeing her face scrunch up like an accordion, he gave a weary sigh and explained. "I'm talking about the couple of guards Daniel fired when you were held hostage."

"I knew I should have never told you about them."

She angrily folded her arms. "For your information, I am not paranoid about those guys! Justin said they probably took off to another state when they heard about Daniel's murder.

They are not going to risk their necks coming back here to look for me. You're the second person now who has brought this up to me."

"You're the only one left who can identify them," Aaron pointed out.

"Oh, I feel so much calmer after hearing that!" Furious, Nicole threw open the car door, stepped out, slammed the door shut and marched around to the driver's side, where she commanded, "Scoot over! You're in no condition to drive!" Just then, a car whizzed past, threw on its brake lights, and spun around. "Oh, great!" Nicole fumed, still standing outside the vehicle. "I bet it's an unmarked police car."

"I don't think so," muttered Aaron while he watched the vehicle zoom towards them. Through the darkness, he finally recognized the sporty headlights. "Oh, sh—." The words died on his lips as he threw his head back against the headrest. Outside, the familiar vehicle screeched to a halt. Nicole nervously waited while Justin leapt from the driver's seat, his quickening stride swiftly carrying him across the road.

"What happened?" he snapped. "Did the car break down?"

"Not exactly," Nicole said, desperately wishing there was some place she could hide. It took her a moment to regain her senses. Why should she feel guilty? After all, it was Justin's fault she had to leave the nightclub with Aaron. She straightened her posture with new confidence, preparing to demand an explanation for the adolescent brawl with Cristoff, when Justin drew near and suddenly grabbed her arm.

"What the hell have you been up to?" he barked, taking a long whiff of the smell in her hair. Nicole never had the chance to reply. She was flung to the side in Justin's haste to get to his brother.

Aaron's life flashed before his eyes. "Now, wait just a minute, bro! Nicole and I did nothing wrong."

"Oh, yeah?" came the resounding growl as strong hands grabbed Aaron's collar.

"He's telling the truth," Nicole echoed. "I fell asleep in the car and he smoked a joint, that's all."

“Do you expect me to believe this?” Justin bellowed, releasing his hold to confront Nicole.

“I told you it’s the truth!” Sensing she had the advantage now, she boldly added, “What happened between you and Cristoff?”

“That’s none of your concern.”

“Oh, no? If I had become drawn into it, I could very well be visiting the police station. Did that thought ever enter your tiny mind, Mr. Macho?”

Justin shook his finger at her. “Don’t you get me any more riled up than I am right now, do you hear me?”

“Or what?” she taunted with a sneer.

He began to promise something, but Nicole stuck her fingers in her ears and hummed a little tune. Justin took a firm hold of her arm and proceeded to pull her towards his car. “No, thanks,” she said, yanking free. “I’m not about to drive home with you.”

“Fine,” he tersely replied. “I’ll see you when you get home.”

Standing defiantly near the Plymouth, Nicole reiterated his words. From inside the vehicle, Aaron began to laugh. He couldn’t help it. The whole scene seemed so ridiculous, it struck his funnybone.

“What are you laughing at?” Nicole frowned, seating herself behind the steering wheel. She turned on the ignition.

“Both of you,” he snickered, shaking his head. “By the devil, you two are a perfect match!” Nicole began to drive. Aaron gazed at her with new respect. “Did you hear the exasperation in his voice? It was great!” he continued. “I’ve never heard my brother sound so flustered before.” He laughed, coughed, then laughed again. “He doesn’t know how to handle you.”

“Good!” Nicole smugly said. “I intend to keep it that way.”

“Oh, no, darling. Mark my words, when you get home, he’ll have already figured out a solution to his problem. Justin isn’t the type to let you trample his pride.”

“We’ll see,” was all she said, keeping her eyes on the road. They traveled the rest of the way in silence until Nicole turned onto her driveway. “You’re welcome to spend the night, Aaron. I’d rather you didn’t try to drive yourself home.” She parked the car.

“I only had one joint,” he countered. “You make it sound as if I’m completely dysfunctional.”

“You were drinking tonight, remember?” She got out of the car.

“There’s no way in hell I’m gonna come in there and listen to my brother rant and rave. See ya later, Cat!” He slid over to the driver’s seat, calling from the window, “Thanks for the exciting evening!” Then he sped off, leaving the young female in a perpetual state of apprehension as her gaze focused upon her front door. Did she really want to step through that doorway? Did she truly want to see what was on the other side?

“Naa.” Nicole peered through the darkness towards the tenant house. No lights were on inside. She could stay there until Justin cooled off. Good idea. She gingerly stepped onto the lawn and heard the front door suddenly open.

“Going somewhere?” spoke a deep, masculine voice.

“Not anymore,” she reluctantly groaned, pivoting around. Justin watched her slowly ascend the porch steps. She had barely set foot in the living room when he quickly blurted, “Did my brother lay a hand on you?”

“No, Justin. Is that what you were worried about?”

He let out a long exhale. “I don’t trust Aaron. I was afraid he may have enticed you to smoke a joint with him.”

“I’d never consent. I’m not into drugs. Why didn’t you warn me that he was a user?”

“Slipped my mind.” The tall blond plopped down on a chair. “I probably should have never allowed him to move in with me, but I was hoping to be a good influence on him.” He stared at the floor.

Nicole knelt beside him, her voice softer now. “Tell me what happened at the nightclub? Why were you fighting?”

He openly grimaced, hesitating. “I didn’t like the way Cristoff leered at you.”

“Leered? I don’t recall Cristoff leering.”

He looked at her through tired eyes. "I'm not about to begin another argument, Nicole. What's done is done. Funny thing is, when other people began throwing punches, Cristoff and I became a team again and fought against them. It was like old times, when we were teenagers. And it suddenly occurred to me, how stupid I've been acting, how dumb to be jealous. He's a good friend. He couldn't help falling in love with you. I trust you. I think I can trust him, too. I guess my bad behavior was mostly due to my fear of losing you, again. All those months you were held hostage, I just agonized over not being able to locate you. Seems like I haven't come to terms with my own insecurities." Nicole reached for his hand and held it, tenderly. He saw understanding in her eyes.

"Nicole," he quietly said. "I'm really sorry for all the upset I've caused you. I feel calmer now, knowing what was driving me to act in that manner. I'll be more peaceful, I promise."

"We'll both be fine," Nicole assured him, beginning to softly smile. "I haven't been on my best behavior, either, in case you haven't noticed." They both laughed.

"You know," Justin admitted, "when you weren't around, I used to refer to you as 'the little hellion'. But I've seen the softer side of you, the side you like to keep hidden."

"Ahh," murmured Nicole. "So what am I now?"

"I guess you're a velvet hellion now," he chuckled, watching as Nicole, too, broke into a laugh.

"But I'm only your velvet hellion, darling," she beamed. Reaching up to him, she placed her arms around his shoulders to give him an affectionate hug.

Justin stood up, pulling her with him so he could bestow a soft kiss on her pouting lips. "If you don't mind, I think I'll head home now? Unless you want me to stay?"

"That would be too tempting," she smiled.

He fastened his coat and walked to the door, but was stopped by Nicole.

"Justin? Did you see Jan at the club? Do you know if she got out all right?"

"She's fine. I took her and Cristoff to my house before I

went looking for you. Apparently the two of them wanted to talk. Everything's okay between us."

"That's good to know," she agreed.

With that, the blond giant said his goodbyes and reluctantly disappeared into the darkness.

CHAPTER TWENTY-FIVE

On Saturday morning, Nicole bumped into Cristoff in the stables, getting the horses' food ready. "Hey," she quietly said, "you okay?"

"Of course I am, girlie. Why wouldn't I be?" chirped the ranch hand. The sweet smell of fresh oats filled the air as Nicole carefully studied his expression. He did seem okay, even happy. Guessing what was on her mind, he put down the food scoop and turned to her, saying, "Look, Nicole, I realized when Justin and I were fighting, that our friendship is too important to allow it to dissolve over you. And I feel the same way about your friendship with me, I don't want it being ruined just because Justin is marrying you. Obviously, you care deeply about him. I think we can all handle this like mature adults, don't you?"

"I'd like to think so," she replied, a bit of relief in her eyes.

"I won't expect Justin to make me Best Man at the wedding, though." He burst out laughing, with Nicole soon joining him. They finished their chores amidst humorous banter, all the former problems forgotten.

The next few weeks passed swiftly by. The ownership of Desert Wind Arabians was legally changed back to Nicole, while Cristoff and Justin remained partners. Cristoff began to enter into a new special friendship with Justin's sister. Nicole and Justin spent the weekends going on trail rides, picnics, or visiting local events with them. The four seemed inseparable. Justin still made time to see Shane, although their friendship was slowly losing its closeness. The rest of the ranch hands continued joining them for occasional evenings out, which often included Aaron. It was after one of these evenings, that the group decided to grab some takeaway food and head over to Justin's house to play music and dance the night away. But upon walking through the doorway, Justin's phone was ringing. He promptly picked up the receiver while Nicole and Jan went into the kitchen to gather plates and utensils for the food. After a few minutes, Justin placed the phone down and excitedly called to Nicole.

"They found him!" he joyfully shouted. "Nicole! They found Charlie King! He's alive!"

Nicole bounded from the kitchen in haste. "Tell me everything!" she begged. "Where? When? How?"

The room grew quiet as everyone turned to the blond. "It's strange," he admitted. "They found Charlie wandering down a dirt road. He was confused. At first, they thought he had amnesia, but he recognized his wife and children. The police are trying to discern what happened to him, but he claims he can't remember."

"Wow," gasped Jan. "How weird!" The rest of the men chimed in, agreeing. Justin, Cristoff, and Nicole exchanged knowing looks. Chances were, he had been given the same drug that Nicole had experienced, which meant that federal agents probably played a role. But Nicole wasn't going to try and solve this mystery, she was just thankful Charlie was reunited with his family again, and not six feet under the ground.

"A celebration!" she beamed. "C'mon now, Charlie's alive and home, and I can't wait to visit him and his wife."

"Here! Here!" exclaimed Cristoff and Justin in unison. The rest agreed, gathering around while the beverages were poured out. They ate with good cheer, playing music afterwards and dancing until weariness overcame them; and so ended a night of much camaraderie.

It was only a few months later when Nicole and Justin decided to wed. It was a small but beautiful wedding, with Nicole's parents beaming from ear to ear as they watched their ecstatically happy daughter join her heart with Justin in a new chapter of her life. If Justin had experienced any doubts about his wife's ability to be intimate, they were quickly dissolved on their wedding night in a luxurious hotel by the seaside. The marriage not only began on a happy note, it continued to be filled with much merriment and affection. The ranch hands, along with Cristoff, Shane, Aaron and Jan, continued to socialize together, and always looked forward to the times when Justin and Nicole joined them. They seemed to radiate the type of love that extended outwards to touch all who came in contact with them. But one single event triumphed over all this. Seven months after the wedding, Nicole joyfully announced she was pregnant. Justin was too shocked for words. He couldn't believe it. As he embraced his lovely wife, tears of happiness spilled down his face to mingle with hers. They then knew that whatever drug had been used on her in the past, it had lost its effect.

"A winter baby?" quizzed Justin, still in disbelief.

"Yes," laughed Nicole. "I'm a winter baby, too. So you never know, darling, you may end up with another little velvet hellion." Her laughter bounced off the walls as she threw him a mischievous glance, but Justin was laughing, too.

The End

33990088R10288

Made in the USA
Charleston, SC
28 September 2014